THE WORST GUY

KATE CANTERBARY

VESPER PRESS

Editing provided by Julia Ganis of Julia Edits.
Editing provided by Erica Russikoff of Erica Edits.
Proofreading provided by Jodi Duggan.
Ebook cover photography provided by Wander Aguiar
Ebook cover design provided by Sarah Hansen of Okay Creations.
Paperback cover design by Murphy Rae Designs.

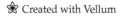 Created with Vellum

ABOUT THE WORST GUY

Eight weeks of forced proximity is a long time to hate someone you're trying not to love.

Sebastian Stremmel doesn't need another headache. He has enough of his own without Sara Shapiro, the noisy new reconstructive surgeon, stomping all around his surgical wing with her chippy, chirpy cheerfulness.

But Sebastian doesn't usually get what he wants.

No one gets under his skin like Sara - so much so a heated "debate" and an exam room left in shambles later, they land themselves in eight weeks of hospital-mandated conflict resolution counseling. Now they're forced to fight fair… which quickly leads them to playing dirty when no one's looking.

They know it's a mistake.

They promise themselves it will never happen again.

They swear they got it out of their systems.

They didn't.

Author's Note: *Grumpy/recovering people-pleaser sunshine. Introverts attract. Enemies-to-lovers in the workplace. Banter,* bicker, and button-pushing foreplay. Don't tell the friend group, get jealous when the friend group tries to fix her up.

Heat: *rip her clothes off before you get the front door open.*

CW/TW: *chronic illness, absent/negligent parents, history of disordered eating.*

for the messiest girls

CHAPTER 1

SEBASTIAN

My dick was languishing.

I'd learned that word recently. Languishing. Not depressed but not thriving. Just drifting along, one unsatisfied day melting into another.

And—before you get the wrong idea—this wasn't a performance issue. I performed *beautifully*. I always rose to the occasion and I stayed standing until everyone was satisfied. Most mornings I awoke to find myself at full salute, wrenched out the quickest flash of gratification, and then went back to feeling nothing.

With the bitter aftertaste of that thought in my mouth, I kicked the bedsheets away and rolled my head to the side. Glaring out the window felt right, seeing as my view consisted of a brick wall and a hazy slice of early morning sunlight. I understood everything about that wall. Hard as fuck and not a damn good thing to be done about it.

Languishing, to be sure.

None of my usual vices did the trick. There used to be a time when the mere mention of college cheerleaders was enough to get me off. God, I missed being twenty-four.

Most people assumed my fascination with hardcore competitive cheerleading was about the skirts. It wasn't. Those competitions—the ones where they tossed small, weigh-nothing women into the air like permanent neurological damage was no big deal—chilled me the fuck out. Cheerleading was to me what true crime podcasts were to women with attachment issues. Also, I couldn't tear my eyes off the bases. There was something about their thick, powerful thighs. They all had them. Of course they did. You couldn't launch a lady into space without some rock-solid quads and they had them. Fuck, did they have them.

I wanted to live in a world of pear-shaped women and wear those thighs as earmuffs every night. Every damn night.

Wanting it didn't mean it would ever happen.

The primary reason for that was the gaping hole where my interpersonal skills should've been, the hole I was certain I'd had from the early days and which had widened over the years. I lived a solitary life and I liked it that way for reasons I was too hard and miserable to enumerate this morning. The fact I had a group of friends at all and they continued to request my presence was a curiosity I still did not understand. I assumed they'd adopted me as some sort of wonky mascot.

The secondary reason—not far disconnected from the first—was I didn't enjoy people and I really didn't like them in my space. If there were to be earmuffs in my life, I'd have to haul myself to the earmuff's apartment. That sounded great at first but I knew it would become a hassle. My work hours tended toward unpredictable—trauma surgery was a pain in the ass like that—and there were many days when I came home too fried to form words. As much as I liked the

idea of a sexual relationship conceived without the requirement of speaking, I knew that wouldn't last. It couldn't. The
day would come when I'd hear—barely, since her thick,
glorious thighs would cancel out most sound—her ask about
my day. Or, god forbid, she'd want to talk about feelings or
the unholy curse of *where is this going*.

That led quite naturally to the final reason that nothing
so miraculous would ever happen to me: I didn't know how
to keep people in my life. I could give all the beard rides in
this time zone but that didn't change the fact I was forty-two
years old and didn't know how to make anyone stay. My
mother was the only person who'd ever stuck around. My
little sister Vivi too, but it wasn't as though she'd had much
of a choice in the matter.

So, here I was, with my languishing dick and sudden
apathy for collegiate cheerleaders with thunder thighs.

Not that my dick ruled my life. It did not. Hell, I didn't
know who had the time to live that way. Maybe when I was
in my twenties, grossly self-involved and capable of
engaging in social activities after work, but I couldn't do that
anymore. These days, my life went to hell if I didn't get at
least seven solid hours of sleep a night.

Maybe it was wrong but I was more interested in chasing
a good night's sleep than a partner for some earmuff action.
Just didn't seem like there was any point, and I knew that
didn't make sense. Not that any of this made sense. A lot of
things were going right in my life these days. I didn't have
any reason to be so...bored.

Things were finally, strangely good for me and I was
more unsettled than ever. I hated that feeling. It was like my
skin was too tight and the sun too dim and every passing
minute a second too long.

Everything was off, and my dick, the original canary in this coal mine, had figured it out before I could.

Rude.

What the fuck did I have to be unhappy about? Why couldn't I be content with the handful of decent, functional things I had in this miserable, broken world? Why couldn't any of this be enough for me?

I shifted away from the window with a long, obnoxious sigh. Enough of that whining. I had to get ready for work. I didn't have time for this. Emergency surgery didn't care whether my dick was in high spirits or not—and that was why this was the gig for me. I didn't have to think about myself at all.

———

MY LIFE LOOKED a little something like this: surgical on-calls, sleep, research, complaining about the weather in this dark, frigid marshland of Massachusetts, hunting for good avocados, college cheerleading, clinical care, death march running sessions with my part-time sadist friend Nick, hating everything, third-wheeling it with Nick and his wife because they were the only people who tolerated me on account of me vocally hating everything, migraines, and covering for other surgeons in my practice who, unlike me, went places, did things, and enjoyed the company of others.

And that was how I found myself working a twenty-four-hour surgical on-call shift because someone else in the practice was going to a wedding or vacationing or some other nonsense. When these storms of my own stupidity arose, I always swore up and down I wouldn't cover for anyone ever again, and then I prayed the last few hours wouldn't blow up into a massive shitshow.

Today was one of those shitshows but instead of waiting until the last hours of my shift to blow up, it started the minute I arrived. I was too busy to notice hunger, exhaustion, anything. Surgery had a way of putting those basic needs on the back burner.

All the same, the last hours were a damn mess. All of my residents and their interns were slammed, I couldn't find my fellow anywhere, and every time I cleared one surgery consult, another two sailed in. It was two hours past the end of my never-helping-another-colleague-again marathon shift and I was jamming through the last of my charts when I heard, "Stremmel? Is Stremmel down here?"

There were several reasons I hung out in the emergency department, but chief among them was I could always find a quiet corner where I wouldn't be disturbed. It was the noisiest, most hectic spot in the entire hospital complex but calm could always be found in chaos.

Except right now.

I knew that voice. It had been burned into my brain on a daily basis with all of her perky, peppy screeches of "Hello there!" and "Good morning!" and "Have a good one!"

My god. The last thing in the world I needed was a conversation with Sara Shapiro. I'd sooner fling my body into the Charles River and wait for nature to do its worst than willingly submit to a conversation with the reconstructive surgeon who lived in my apartment building while I was operating on zero minutes of sleep in a whole fucking day.

Maybe I was fragile as fuck but I required a full night of

sleep and a protein-packed breakfast before daring to look her in the eye. I had to be *prepared* for her.

The exam room curtain clattered along its rod as Shapiro whipped it back. "Dr. Stremmel. I'd like a word with you."

With a quick glance starting at the floor, I took in her yellow sneakers, navy scrub pants, and t-shirt announcing *Vaccines Cause Adults*.

That much we could agree on.

I returned to my charting. "By all means."

"Did you *staple* a facial laceration?"

"I've been here since eight yesterday morning. I've stapled a lot of skin in that time. I'm going to need you to be a hell of a lot more specific."

She let out a huff, like the aggravated little noise that puppies made when you didn't give them the precise form of attention they wanted. "Female, age twenty-eight, orbital fracture and—"

"—a perforated bladder and internal bleeding from an MVA. Yeah." I'd worked on her and another case from that motor vehicle accident twelve hours ago. It felt like it'd been twelve days. "What about her?"

Sara's grip on the curtain tightened. "You *stapled* her face."

I pecked at the keyboard for a moment. I was shit at dictation and I didn't believe in using interns as scribes so that left me to write up my cases, which I did with the most specific, detailed notes to minimize the risk of a resident calling me in the middle of the night with a question. When I walked out the door, I was gone, and I wasn't letting anyone pull me back in until it was my time. "Sure did. She wasn't in a position to lose any more volume and it was my call to address the lac pre-operatively."

Sara huffed again, and though I didn't see it, it certainly sounded like she'd stomped her foot. I watched her push her black-rimmed glasses up her nose. She didn't wear the glasses too often which was for the best, it really was. They made her look like she was inspecting something and never pleased with her findings. Her blonde hair was up in a ponytail with a few loose tendrils trapped behind the arm of her glasses. Those wisps were darker than the hair swept up into the ponytail, almost brown. And curly. I went back to the keyboard.

"Do you have other questions or is this it?"

"You *stapled* her *face*," she repeated.

This time, a metallic whine sounded from the curtain rod. She was still yanking the damn thing, her knuckles shining back at me, bony and white, as her fist tightened on the fabric. Her hands were petite, her fingers slim. Perfect for plastic surgery, I was sure. She was the substantial, sturdy kind of small—short, compact, could probably beat the shit out of a punching bag—and she needed a step stool to reach the table in the OR.

I'd never noticed her hands before. We saw each other in passing all the time though it was usually her big, messy, blonde bun that caught my attention. Couldn't miss it. We moved in the same group of friends too though we rarely talked. I could tell she was a bruiser behind all that outward sunshine. She'd be nice as hell but she'd cut you if you crossed her.

Not that I cared.

I spared her a glance as I returned to my notes. One last case and this annoying conversation to get through before I was done with this place for three whole days. "I suppose this is an inefficient way of telling me that—as far as plastics is concerned—staples are not the standard of care for such a case."

"I'm telling you that your staples were clumsy and careless."

I jerked my head up. I wasn't annoyed anymore. Now I was pissed. "I doubt that."

"You doubt—" She stopped herself, her lips pressed tight together and her shoulders sharp like she wouldn't tolerate my response. She stood tall—or as tall as a little bit like her could—her feet anchored a shoulder's width apart in a stance that said *fuck around and find out.*

I gave her a solid minute to finish that sentence. When she didn't, I said, "I staple lacerations all the time. If we're able to clean it up, we do, but we're also aware they can wait until we've saved the patient from dying on the table to make their superficial injuries look nice. I'm sure you can agree it's more important to stop a hemorrhage or preserve organ systems than wait for plastics to put a face back together."

Her eyes flashed as she drew in a breath. "Do you know *anything* about skin? Or suturing? Or healing? Because—"

"Especially when there's an orbital fracture involved," I continued. "Isn't that the entire reason for plastics and reconstructive surgery? To put things back together after the life-threatening priorities have been sorted?"

"What the hell is wrong with you?"

"Many things, but my treatment prioritization has never been one of them."

She would've continued her tirade, of this I was certain, if she hadn't delivered another feral yank to the curtain. Instead of further debate as to the hierarchy of interventions with trauma cases—and whether I knew my shit—she tore the curtain from its clips and dislodged the rod from the ceiling in the process.

What came next was pure instinct. I didn't think about my actions at all. Maybe I should have, but if stopping and deliberating over split-second decisions was part of my brain's wiring, I wouldn't be a trauma surgeon. If I wasn't a trauma surgeon, I wouldn't be hiding out in this exam room, arguing about treatment plans with this screech owl of a plastic surgeon.

I wouldn't have sprung off the gurney and pushed her out of the way as the rod fell, along with two ceiling tiles.

I wouldn't have flattened her to the floor when the rod hit a metal procedure tray and sent it cartwheeling into an interior window, wheels first, while the supplies stationed on that tray rained down over us and the unmistakable sound of slowly shattering glass filled the room.

I wouldn't have stayed there, in that small, half-hidden exam room, with my body curled over Sara Shapiro's and a hand holding her head to my chest while the glass crumbled from the window casing.

And I definitely wouldn't have yelled, "What the hell is wrong with *you*?" while a half dozen emergency department employees rushed into what was left of the exam room.

CHAPTER 2

SARA

NO ONE COULD KEEP A GOOD BITCH DOWN...BUT THAT DIDN'T mean she wouldn't end up on the floor.

The two-hundred-odd pounds of man on top of her, well, that was not part of the plan.

The code green lockdown of the emergency department wasn't on the list for today either.

Neither was the formal reprimand from the Chief of Surgery or the oversized, unnecessary consequence he dished out.

Sometimes, bitches overshot the mark. Sometimes, they made a mess.

The problem with being a savage-hearted bitch who was also a recovering people-pleaser was that I still had the "pleasure to have in class" good girl wandering around inside my head. On days like today when she couldn't decide whether to sit in the corner and panic or drown me in a highlight reel of my all-time worst moments until I was forced to admit I was a giant fucking fuckup, it was tough to find the truth.

Reprimands and consequences, those things didn't

happen to me. No truly compulsive people-pleasing perfectionist ever found herself in the kind of trouble that came with finger wagging and deeply disappointed frowning. People like me, we'd sooner condense ourselves down into smaller and smaller particles and disappear altogether than land in a situation where we were straight up told to our fragile little faces we weren't good or right or enough.

And yet I was furious. I was *break shit and scream* furious.

"It would be great if you could sit down for a second," Alex Emmerling said, holding up her surgical-glove-clad hands to stop my pacing. The women's changing room inside the attending surgeon's lounge wasn't big enough for any real pacing, though it was adequate for some abrupt marching. "Just sit down, babe, and we'll clean up those cuts and make sure you don't have any chunks of glass in your arm. I think it would also help"—she motioned up and down her chest—"to breathe a little."

The general surgeon—and my upstairs neighbor—gestured to the sofa beside her. I didn't want to, but I sat. It was that or pace my way into a panic attack and I really didn't need to call more attention to myself today.

"I'm fine," I said to her as she lifted my arm for inspection. "It's nothing. All superficial. Nothing worth noticing." I winced at the dried blood streaked from my bicep to my wrist. "It looks worse than it is. You should see the other guy."

She brought a gauze pad to my upper arm. It was the one spot that hadn't been covered by Sebastian's considerable mass. He was obviously a big guy—tall, broad, all those fun things—but he'd felt like a slab of solid muscle over me. It was excessive, really. He had enough. A full head of dark, thick hair—no receding hairline, no dignified dusting of grays. A deep, dusky olive complexion that seemed impossible considering he spent most of his waking hours in cold, windowless rooms. A jaw that managed to be both scruffy and sharp. Worst of all, he'd been gifted an outrageous set of eyelashes, the kind that didn't look real but when you saw him up close, you knew they were absolutely real and he was merely the recipient of heaps upon heaps of physical gifts. It was *excessive* and I knew what excessive looked like. My father was the top plastic surgeon in Southern California. Excess put me through medical school.

"I did see the other guy," Alex said. "He's the one who sent me up here."

"Why?" I wailed, so much louder than necessary.

"Because he's busy digging glass out of his own arm," she replied.

"But I need help doing it?" I blew out an aggravated breath and frowned down at my t-shirt. It was ripped in a few places, bloodied in others. I wouldn't be able to wear it again. Not to work. "Sorry. Ignore me."

Alex was the last person I needed to yell at today. I didn't need to yell at her at all—we were friends. We weren't besties who lived in each other's back pockets, although not for any lack of pocketing attempts on Alex's part. I was excellent when it came to having a small crew of close friends who I knew well enough to be selected as a bridesmaid in their weddings though never close enough to be the maid of honor. I was terrible at the bestie thing. I just didn't understand how to let anyone into that much of my life.

"Believe me, I am," she said. "I have some residents who want to learn compassionate holds. I'll page them up here if I need to restrain you."

See? This was why we were friends. She could joke about

these things and I could laugh in response because we shared a humor that was as dark as dirt.

I watched as she discarded another gauze pad into a metal basin. It sparkled with tiny, tiny flecks of glass. "I still don't understand why Stremmel tackled me like that back in the exam room."

"Because that's what he does," she said with a laugh.

I glanced at her. "Throw people across rooms? The bruise forming on my ass is no joke."

"He takes care of people." She said this as if I was extremely dense. "He's probably furious he missed this spot on your arm."

"We're talking about Sebastian Stremmel? The one who lives in the apartment above you?"

"One and the same," she murmured. "You'd have a better feel for him if you spent more time with the group."

Another reason we weren't on the best friend tier: Alex's social batteries far outlasted mine. She loved meeting up for drinks after work, parties, brunches, dinners, farmers market visits, all of it. She wanted to go places and see people, and I needed a week to recover from a single outing.

Most days, she ate lunch with Stremmel, Cal Hartshorn, the cardiothoracic surgeon who lived in my apartment before I did, and Nick Acevedo, the neurosurgeon who'd lived in the building a few years ago. If I did that much peopling *every day*, I'd be catatonic within two weeks. It wasn't an exaggeration, it was my nervous system.

"I don't make a habit of hanging out with people who condescend all over my specialty," I said.

"Sorry, honey, but you do now." She dropped a shard of glass into the basin. "At least for the next eight weeks."

———

Sebastian

I PRESSED the heels of my palms to my eyes. "This isn't even my fault."

"Are you sure about that?" Nick Acevedo asked as he distributed sandwiches from the delivery bag. After the shit-show in emergency—and the fallout in the Chief's office—he'd dragged me to the park across from the hospital complex with the promise of lunch.

"On this specific occasion, I am one hundred percent positive I didn't create this problem," I said. "I'm just picking up the tab for it."

"What did the Chief say?" Cal Hartshorn asked.

"Yeah," Nick said. "I can't imagine he came down on you at all in this situation. Accidents happen. You got into it with Shapiro but you're his boy, so—"

"I am no one's boy, Acevedo," I snapped from behind my hands. "I'm an accomplice in trashing an exam room; I get the same slap on the wrist as anyone else who's too stupid to get out before the ceiling comes down."

"Yeah, except you *don't* get the same slap," Nick said with a laugh. "I realize you're unaware of the privilege afforded to you from being the guy the Chief of Surgery trusts to save the day—"

I reached over and stole his apple. "Shut your mouth with that nonsense."

"—but you are still the guy who coordinated the largest and longest all-hands response to a crisis situation this hospital has ever experienced." Nick flattened his hands on the picnic table. "You are the guy who stepped out of his practice to lead pandemic operations for six months and—"

"It wasn't like I had anyone getting hit by cars or fucking themselves up on trampolines and ladders when the world shut down."

And if I hadn't done it, I would've lost my mind from standing by and doing nothing.

Cal shook his head. "Hate to break it to you, Stremmel, but you're the guy. You're definitely the Chief's guy. You're also our guy because you got all of us through it too. So, you need to deal with the fact that you play on a different level now. You're on the soon-to-be Chief of Emergency Surgery level. You're not on the level where you get penalized for a loud disagreement with a colleague."

"Funny you mention that," I said with a bitter approximation of a laugh. "Seems I won't be chief of anything until I can make it through a conflict resolution course with Shapiro."

Nick shrugged. "No sweat. That should be easy."

At the same time, Cal hissed out a heavy "*Fuuuuuck.*"

"Yeah. There it is. Somewhere between *no sweat* and *fuuu-uuck.*" Another bitter laugh broke free from my chest. "It would be one thing if I had to do a program on my own. But with Shapiro? Kill me."

"Wait a second with that," Nick argued. "She flies way under the radar but she's the best reconstructive person we have. I go to her skills lab sessions whenever I can and learn something new every time. Same with Hartshorn. He sends all his residents to those sessions too."

I glared at him as hard as my exhausted eyes could. "She's a little high octane, wouldn't you say? Pulled down half the ceiling with one hand."

"You are literally the only person who doesn't like her," Cal said. "Something to think about."

"It's handy that I have eight weeks of therapy with her to think about it, then," I grumbled.

The memory of Shapiro's clenched knuckles and the curtain balled in her fist pushed itself forward. She must have yanked the hell out of that thing. Nothing else could've set off that chain of events. It was impressive in an alarming, *give the lady a wide berth* sort of way.

Beside me, Cal crumpled the butcher paper from his sandwich and held the ball between his hands. "If I had to guess, I'd say this conflict res thing is some kind of human resources requirement following any incident between staff, but you have to know this is a mild response. No administrative leave, no suspension of privileges. All that said, Sebastian, I want to make it clear to you that she's the one taking the penalty here."

"And yet I'm still the one in therapy with her," I argued. "For two fucking months."

"You remember what it was like to be the problem-child surgeon," Cal said.

I shook my head as a gust of bone-chilling air cut across the park. "Please don't remind me of my fool-ass days. You know I'm sensitive about that, Hartshorn."

"I'm just saying," he continued, "Shapiro is probably feeling like a problem child right now. You have nothing to worry about. Your contract will get renewed. You'll sail through this and get the chief gig. You'll have your pick of the best candidates for fellowships. You'll get to research whatever the hell you want. You'll get to take sabbaticals whenever you feel like it. Nothing on the road ahead of you will be altered by this incident. Shapiro, on the other hand, will have to work this out of her reputation. She hasn't even been on staff that long, right? I lose track of time these days."

"About two years," Nick said.

"She has a lot more to lose than you do," Cal said.

Not wanting to concede this point, I yanked up the collar of my jacket against the wind. "Just so you know, it's too damn cold to be out here."

"It's fifty-one degrees and sunny, Stremmel," Cal said. "This isn't cold."

O'Rourke, the trauma fellow I'd lost earlier in the day, jogged toward the table. "If you want to talk about cold, let me tell you about Minnesota and—"

"Does it look to you like I need another Minnesota story right now?" I asked him. "And why the fuck haven't you answered a page in the past six hours?"

"I don't enjoy it," he said simply. "I really don't."

I pointed toward the hospital. "Go away. Go ignore pages to the nurses' faces and see how well that turns out for you."

"But food. Lunch," he complained.

Cal bobbed his head, saying to O'Rourke, "You have your orders."

"Boy has a death wish," Nick murmured.

"There are days when he's less mature than some of the worst first-year residents I've met," I said. "Then there are days when he's, like, fucking gifted."

"I don't even know how to teach to that," Nick replied.

"Me neither." Cal gestured to my forehead, asking, "Is that *your* blood?"

"Probably," I replied, reaching for the other half of Nick's sandwich. I didn't care what it was, I just needed to eat some more before I fell over and died from the horror show of this day. "Between physically shielding Shapiro from the conse-

quences of her actions and getting an earful about professional conduct from the Chief, I haven't really had time to
deal with my own problems."

"Why are you sitting here feeling sorry for yourself?" Cal
asked. "It's just couples therapy. It's not the end of the
world."

"He always feels sorry for himself," Nick said under his
breath.

"You did *not* just call it couples therapy," I groaned. "And
I don't feel sorry for myself. I just hate the idea of an hour a
week spent with Shapiro and a PsychD talking about feelings and shit. I have other things to do. *She* has other things
to do. And it's not like anything is going to come of it. Nothing's going to change. She's still going to screech at people
about staples and I'm—"

"Stop whining," Cal said. "And if you think you're getting
assigned a psychology doctoral student for these sessions,
you're forgetting, once again, that you're the guy. You're
getting top brass for your couples counseling."

I stole his apple too. "Fuck my life."

———

Sara

"I'M SHOCKED that Stremmel hasn't glared his way out of
this," Alex said. "He's so good at it. He just beams that hairy
eyeball at people and they fall in line real quick. I do it and I
look like I'm having a stroke."

"Mmhmm." If Stremmel did anything with precision, it
was glaring. The man did not smile. He was a human storm

system. His shoulders were a mountain range that could block out the sun, and his short, scruffy beard functioned as an added layer of moody darkness, slashing across his face and turning his scowls into a full-body statement.

"I bet there are a ton of politics at play," Alex continued.

I studied her as she opened another packet of gauze. I *hated* the politics game. I sucked up to no one, kissed zero asses. That worked for me because I was in the beautifully fortunate position of being only one of a few surgeons at this hospital specializing in reconstructive surgery for burns and other complex wounds, and that position came with enough built-in authority to save me from needing to get down in the trenches of any political.

"What do you mean?"

"Well, you know," she started, "Stremmel's in line for a chief job. That might be unofficial information. You didn't hear it from me."

I gave her a quick smile. "Of course not."

"Anyway, it's not like a formal reprimand is that bad," she said.

She was lying and I could tell but it was kind of her to try. "I'd like to believe that."

"I'm sure everyone gets a note in their file at one point or another," she went on. "Trust me, it won't matter in a year. You'll forget about this and it will drop from the collective memory soon enough. I went through some hell when I was a resident. I had a relationship with another surgeon, it went bad, I was branded with the scarlet letter. Everyone said all the worst things about me. All in the past and I hardly ever think about it, but believe me when I say I've ridden that roller coaster and puked when I got off. It's going to be okay. We're getting through this, babe."

Since I had nothing left to lose today, I said, "The Chief knows my father. Same intern class, or something."

"Oh, *shit*."

Alex knew enough about my father to understand the significance. Nearly everyone in surgery knew of him but Alex was one of the few who knew it was an emotional sink-hole for me. "Thought I'd cleared all the possible connections here but I missed that one."

She packed up the used gauze, shooting me a concerned glance. "How did this come up for the first time *today*? That sounds like some first-rate horseshit to not mention it until now and—"

"Doesn't matter," I said with a resigned shrug. "He expected me to be a carbon copy of my father and was disappointed to discover I am nothing of the sort and, well"—I sucked in a breath because I was *not* going to cry or break things—"he doesn't want me making a habit of destructive tantrums."

Alex whipped off her gloves. "What the *fuck*?"

"It was so wonderful to be lectured about my conduct and sentenced to eight weeks of counseling *and* reminded to be a good little girl all in one afternoon. It's really fun to get the disappointed daddy treatment when you're thirty-nine years old. And it's coming from your boss, who thinks it's okay to invoke your father in conversation. Kinda thought I'd passed that phase of my life but nope. Here the fuck I am."

She stared at me, nodding slowly. "That really sucks. I'm sorry."

"Thanks."

"What did you say? Please tell me you told him where to shove that."

"I didn't. I just kind of shut down." That was the most mortifying part. The shame of failing to stand up for myself when it was most essential slapped hard. I'd love to say this was unusual for me, yet this messy little pattern was uncomfortably familiar.

"I'm sorry that happened," Alex said. "But eight weeks isn't that long. And it's with Stremmel. You'll have fun."

I stared at her, unamused. "Hardly. He's the *worst*. He's the most arrogant surgeon in the hospital. No, wait. He's one of the most arrogant surgeons I've ever met, and that is an accomplishment considering my dad's ego needs its own area code."

Alex gave an impatient sniff that said she very much disagreed with me. I allowed her to sniff at me because she was the absolute best at letting people vent and then giving top-notch advice. She didn't take any of her own advice but that was an issue for a different day. "He isn't that bad. He likes to pretend he is but he's not."

I was treated to this man-sized cloud of arrogance at least twice a day as our schedules often aligned to guarantee we'd leave both the Beacon Hill brownstone we called home and the attending surgeons' lounge at the same times.

It would be tolerable if he wasn't so busy being drunk on his own exaggerated sense of self-importance that he fully ignored my attempts at polite conversation. I didn't understand why everyone liked him so much and willingly spent time with him outside work. I had to constantly remind myself that figuring him out wasn't worth my energy or attention, and I didn't have to keep going out of my way to connect with him as a colleague or neighbor when he couldn't manage complete sentences for me.

I reminded myself, but I hadn't broken the habit of doing it yet.

"Alex, the guy *growls* at people. We see each other almost every day and the only form of greeting he can manage is an irritable-looking jerk of his chin or a grumble of word-shaped sounds."

"Yeah, he's a little rough around the edges," she conceded. "But it's all bark, no bite."

"Maybe he shouldn't bark! Why can't we ask that of people? Don't bark. Don't treat female staff like children. Don't slut-shame anyone." I sent her an apologetic frown. "I'm not calling you a slut."

"Yeah, I know, I know," she muttered. "You psychotic bitch."

We shared a bitter laugh, the kind that cleansed wounds and taught scars how to stretch beyond their limits. We had it good but that didn't mean the good was easy.

"I should've ignored the whole thing," I said, mostly to myself. "Should've let it go and spared myself all of"—I gestured to the barely there cuts on my arm—"these brand-new problems."

"Would you have actually let it go?" Alex shrugged. "Or would you have resented the decision to make your professional expertise less important than avoiding a difficult conversation?"

"I would've moved on," I said, and that was at least forty percent true. "Eventually."

"But what does that really mean?" she asked. "Would you have written off the stapling issue as 'trauma surgeons gonna trauma surgeon'? Or would you have planted that seed in your field of fucks and let it grow?"

"Field of fucks. For sure. I'd bring up that issue to

Stremmel every time I saw him and I'd drive him insane with it, nice and slow. Only way to farm a field of fucks, Alex. You gotta long-game that shit."

Alex hummed as she pushed to her feet. "Eight weeks of counseling will be fun for you two," she drawled.

"Don't remind me," I said with a groan.

CHAPTER 3

SARA

MY SNEAKERS SQUEALED AGAINST THE LAMINATE FLOOR AS I rounded the corner to Dr. Milana Cuello's office. I would've preferred to slip into the restroom to check my hair and straighten myself before the first conflict resolution session with Stremmel but I was already running late. Just a few minutes, but I hated being late. It always filled me with the most pointless panic. I told myself it was pointless and that worrying in this way was a waste of energy but I was already wasting a ton of pointless energy so there was no stopping this mess now.

The truth was, I didn't choose the messy life.

All this messy chose me—and I was okay with that. I mean, I had to be. I was a perfectionist good girl with the heart of a raging bitch. Messy was the only way to rock this bun.

I was *really* good at my job, yet stupid old imposter syndrome kicked my ass on the daily.

I was scrappy as fuck and more delicate than anyone had the right to be.

I was vain as hell yet bristled at being judged on my appearance first, my surgical pedigree second.

I swore fluently and often.

I came across as inconsistent and moody. Hot and cold.

I was thirty-nine years old and a pickier eater than most toddlers. That, plus an endless list of chronic digestive issues meant no one could take me anywhere—but don't even think about not inviting me.

Even my hair got in on the action. Some of it curled, some of it fell stick straight, and the rest existed on a spectrum of wavy to frizzy.

I came by the mess honestly—as honestly as anyone could when growing up with drama-addicted parents who would've been better off divorced but elected to cheat on each other and complain about their unfavorable prenup to anyone who would listen, me and my siblings the most frequent audience. Despite living through this marital master class, I still found myself wanting to settle down with someone. Just as soon as I met them and learned how to be vulnerable. Easy peasy, lemon squeezy.

All of that left me holding the bill of sale for a whole lot of emotional garbage, most of which I'd processed and recycled into the kind of high-value skills that made me look like a well-adjusted, functional adult until I destroyed an exam room. Appearances, those funny little liars.

I stepped inside Dr. Cuello's office, surprised to find it filled with warm sunlight and green plants, a large Dominican Republic flag and crammed bookshelves—and Sebastian perched on the arm of the sofa, the hint of a smile lingering on his lips.

The man smiled? Since when?

Out of pure reflex I smiled back, but he was quick to

destroy the moment with a pointed glance at his smartwatch followed by a bent-eyebrowed stare. He raked that stare through my probably wild hair, over my white coat, and down to my lemon-lime sneakers.

What an asshole.

Just for that, I abandoned all discomfort over my late arrival and the state of my hair.

"Dr. Shapiro, you've found us," Dr. Cuello said, gesturing to the sofa. She was the kind of sixties-ish woman who could wear a poncho and make it look good, which was a true accomplishment in my book. Essentially, I wanted to be able to wear a blanket and call it fashion. Was that too much to ask? "Please make yourself comfortable. Dr. Stremmel and I were just trading Puerto Rican restaurant recommendations since we've made a habit of bumping into each other in line for the new Caribbean food truck. I miss the flavors of home even more when winter starts creeping in. Perhaps we could conduct one of our sessions over lunch?"

Oh, I hated that idea and I'd find a way to wiggle out of lunch without insulting Dr. Cuello and her food in the process, but those priorities were secondary to glaring at Sebastian as he pushed off the sofa's arm and stalked to the bookshelves.

I settled into the corner of the sofa closest to the door. "I was late finishing with the residents in my skills lab. Thank you for waiting."

It felt as strange to say that as it sounded. It would've been so much simpler to apologize for running late and it would've felt better too—until all the little concessions and apologies tightened and calcified inside me, a brittle organ that functioned only when fed a steady diet of shame.

I hadn't learned it was shame until the past few years.

Before, I'd thought this was perfectionism, type A personality, oldest sister syndrome. What harm could come from always wanting to be the top of my class, look polished and put-together all the time, solve problems before they materialized? What was wrong with controlling *everything*?

The organ still ticked inside me. It sputtered in innocuous moments like these when I said *thank you for waiting* instead of *I'm sorry*, and it panged with hunger when I stood up to badass bully surgeons like Stremmel because it would be so, so much easier to stay quiet.

Dr. Cuello was asking him something about a restaurant and scribbling a note on the pad perched on her knee. "I love a good rice and pernil lunch plate too," she said. "Especially when it's made right."

He nodded in agreement. He wasn't smiling anymore. No, the relaxed, amenable version of him I'd found when stepping into this office was long gone, and since I was the only change in this dynamic, I earned the prize of being the stick up his ass today.

Awesome.

"If not all of us together, then you two should visit the food trucks. It would be a fine opportunity to learn something about each other outside your hospital roles," she said.

I gave a slow nod and lukewarm smile but there was absolutely no way that was happening. Lunch with Sebastian was out of the question, but also, I couldn't even walk past the area where food trucks regularly parked in this neighborhood without my stomach turning. It drove me crazy that so much of everyday adult life revolved around eating *with* people. This setup wasn't designed for those of us with confrontational digestive systems.

Dr. Cuello shifted in her modern-style red wingback

chair to glance at Stremmel, her long silver hair gleaming in the sun as a smile tugged at her lips. "That's a defensive posture if I've ever seen one, Dr. Stremmel."

He stood with his shoulders against the shelf and his arms crossed over his chest. His scrubs were the darkest, most saturated navy blue I'd ever seen, the color one would receive if they asked for black with the barest pulse of life beating inside it.

When Sebastian replied with nothing more than a slow blink, Dr. Cuello continued, "Ah. Well. It is time for us to begin."

I reached into my coat pockets to check that all my devices were set to vibrate. From the corner of my eye, I watched Sebastian inspect the device clipped to his hip and the phone in his pocket.

"How's this going to go?" he asked. "Are we supposed to prove that we're not a danger to each other or hospital property? If that's the case, I can probably leave now, seeing as Shapiro is the one who likes to live dangerously."

"In this space, I'll encourage you to speak to each other using first names—"

"Shapiro is fine," I said. My whole life, I'd been Sara Shap, Shap, Shappie. No one ever called me Sara. I doubted I'd even respond to it.

"Or is this going to be naming feelings and exploring trauma and that whole dumpster fire? Because if so, can we just raw dog this thing and move it all along? My father hasn't been in my life on a consistent basis, my parents divorced when I was four, and I haven't felt anything since then. Shap, you're on deck."

I deposited my devices back into one pocket beside the color-coded notecards I used to prepare for my cases, and grabbed this afternoon's snack from the other. "I feel plenty of things but I'd rather intellectualize those feelings and bottle them up until they explode."

"See Exhibit A, the exam room I like for charting," he said.

Dr. Cuello hummed to herself as she steepled her fingertips under her chin. "I understand now."

"What?" Sebastian asked. "Why you, as the Associate Director of Behavioral Health, got stuck with us instead of shipping us off to a doctoral student?"

She inclined her head toward him with a generous smile. "Yes, and why I was promised I'd enjoy it so much."

I pinched my lips together to keep myself from shouting that this wasn't a game to me. That I'd been *chastised for my behavior by my boss*—which was the worst punishment in the world for any perfectionist, but especially this perfectionist, since it came coupled with a reminder that my fucking father would've been disappointed.

My entire professional life was spent defining myself as separate and distinct from my father and now...well, this wasn't a game to me. I wasn't going to let it be a game.

"I commend you both for being able to distill yourself down to, ahem, raw dog terms, as you say, though that's not how this is going to go, Sebastian," Dr. Cuello said. "If you're comfortable with it, you're welcome to call me Milana."

She glanced in my direction but I was too busy eating and organizing my pockets. Not for the first time, I observed that I could hide an entire kitten in one of these pockets.

"Our time together will be spent practicing de-escalation, social perspective-taking, and communication in high stress yet professional settings. I hope you'll view this as an opportunity rather than a punishment."

"It *is* a punishment," I said, mostly to myself.

"What—what the hell are you eating?" Sebastian asked.

I replied with the same amount of exasperation with which he'd asked the question. "Croutons."

"Why?"

"Why," I repeated. "What kind of question is that? Do you go up to people in the cafeteria and ask them why they chose that sandwich?"

"No, because it's a fucking sandwich, not a bag of croutons that belong on top of a salad. That's weird." He looked to Milana. "That's weird."

She held up her hands and let them fall, silently choosing neutrality in this battle.

"My croutons are not subject to your approval."

He cocked his head to the side. "And yet my treatment plans are subject to *your* approval?"

"Yeah, when the plan is lazy. There are better options than sloppy staples, especially when we're talking about faces, especially when we're talking about younger patients who—"

"Then your primary concern is aesthetics," he interrupted, nodding to himself like this confirmed all his worst suspicions. "Should've guessed that. Plastics and all." He lifted his shoulders and I could hear the smugness vibrating off him. "My primary concern is saving lives."

I bit into another crouton, staring at him all the while. I made him wait for my response, and I could tell from every tic of his scruffy jaw that he hated it. When I was good and ready, I said, "You're not accomplishing what you think you're accomplishing by drowning me in condescension. Instead of validating your expertise, you're undercutting yourself and showing your whole ass in the process by telling us"—I gestured toward Milana—"that the only expertise you value is your own. That doesn't speak fondly to your growth mindset, now does it, Dr. Stremmel?"

He didn't respond. I had to work at swallowing my smile. I wasn't positive but it seemed like he was grinding his teeth. He went on staring at me, his dark eyes hard and his arms locked tight across his chest. It was audacious of him to walk around with those bare arms, not a thermal shirt or fleece jacket to protect us from all that tanned, muscular obscenity. And that was no exaggeration. Stremmel was quite obscene and he deserved none of it. He had no more use for that crisp jawline than he did those broad, powerful shoulders.

Milana glanced between us several times as the silence thickened. Well, it wasn't entirely silent. These croutons were as good as pins loudly stabbing my Sebastian Stremmel voodoo doll.

Eventually, she broke the tension, saying, "You might not recognize it, but we've made progress today."

"Because there's no broken glass on the floor?" he asked.

I crunched down on a pumpernickel crouton as hard as I could manage. When I glanced at him, I found his gaze locked on me. Not exactly on me, but the hot pink t-shirt tucked into my green scrub bottoms. It read *Scrubs and Scalpels*, with an anatomically correct heart and a pair of surgical blades crossed like a pirate's skull and bones. His brows lifted and he laughed, a single *ha* that barely registered as a sound.

Then he met my eyes, his permanent scowl shifting into the finest fragment of a smile. I arched a brow in challenge and he responded with an eye roll so epic he probably gave himself a tension headache.

Ignoring all of this, Milana continued, "Progress doesn't stick unless you practice it. For this week's practice, I'd like you to share a meal—"

"No." I shook my head. The pumpernickel turned to bile, sharp and bitter and miserable in my throat.

"Go ahead and put me down for no as well," Sebastian said.

Because this kind woman with her gleaming hair and potted plants had an evil side, Milana repeated, "I'd like you to share a meal. Here are the requirements. You must convene outside the hospital complex. You must sit down at a table to eat. I might be old-school but I'm telling you coffee is not a meal. Not in my book. Finally, you must learn five new, non-professional things about each other."

Sebastian unfolded his arms and shoved his hands into his pockets, his scowl deep enough to stir up a thunderstorm of its own. "Here's my requirement. That hour of extracurricular work counts as one of the eight sessions."

I would've thrown my support behind this proposal if I wasn't busy cataloging ways to dodge the assignment entirely. If I asked around, I could probably find someone who needed a kidney. Donating a kidney would excuse me, right? It would. It would destroy my schedule but it was all about bargaining away the bad.

"This won't be the last assignment," Milana said. "But I'll consider your suggestion if this assignment is completed to my satisfaction by next week's session."

I closed my reusable snack bag and shoved it in a coat pocket. I couldn't think about next week's session yet, not when this one needed to end. I'd prepared myself for these visits but not activities outside the hospital. I really hated group projects. They always had a way of growing legs and ruining my life.

"I'd like you to make that allowance," Sebastian pressed.

"Dr. Stremmel, I'm aware that you are accustomed to getting your way. You've earned it. But you get your way on the surgical wing. Not in this office, not unless you earn it here."

I pushed to my feet. I didn't know if we were finished or not but I didn't have another minute in me. "Thank you for your time," I said to Milana. "Excuse me."

Before she could respond, I was out the door.

———

MAYBE IT WAS JUST me but being a people-pleaser had never been about making anyone happy. We called it people-pleasing but what we meant was we did whatever it took to keep from altering the status quo. Working extremely hard in school had been one of my most socially acceptable forms of maintaining the status quo and getting a dash of validation in the process. There was nothing to see here so long as I was earning good grades and engaged in the right after-school activities. Being obsessively obedient and helpful was another. Everyone loved the kid who was so damn mature for her age. They never saw it as the outward manifestation of inner stress. They never stopped to ask how that kid got to be so mature. They never asked why she couldn't just be a kid. They only reaped the benefits.

I didn't give a damn about *pleasing* people but I knew everything about playing the right part.

I knew better now. I knew I didn't have to do any of those things anymore but I still felt the twinges of guilt when it came to asserting my needs—or walking out of a counseling session when I'd had enough.

That same guilt ate at me now, hours after the session. We had homework to do and I always did my homework, even if it was homework that forced me out of my comfort zone.

After a bit of research, I drafted a text to Stremmel.

Sara: Here's a screenshot of my schedule for the week.

Sara: Here's a list of restaurants that work for me.

Sebastian: I thought you'd fight this to the death. I'm disappointed you caved so quick.

Sara: Shut up and choose a place.

Sebastian: I've been to Pastoral. Acevedo's brother-in-law lives near there. That works.

Sara: Date?

Sebastian: Yeah, I guess it's a date if that's what you want to call it…

Sara: No. It is NOT a date. You need to tell me when you're available, as in day and time. Which date?

Sebastian: Ah. Okay. Monday? 7 or 8?

Sara: 7 will be fine.

Sebastian: It's a date, right?

Sara: For fuck's sake, no!

Sebastian: Did I just hear you screech from three floors away?

I TOSSED my phone aside and groaned up at the ceiling. I'd distracted myself reading menus and forgotten for a few beautiful minutes that Sebastian was *upstairs*. By virtue of sturdy yet randomly flimsy brownstones, everyone in the building's three apartments knew when the others were showering, climbing the stairs, or loudly breathing. Forget about watching TV or having sex.

Not that I'd had a lot of sex since moving here from New York but Alex and her husband Riley had *a lot* of sex. I owned several different types of noise-canceling headphones and white noise machines, and scrolled the local real estate listings every day.

I'd never had a conversation with Alex about the sex noises. I didn't even allude to hearing them—and that was another difference between friends and best friends. One of them could say, "Look, sweetie, it's so nice that your husband's cock can make you see stars. Maybe now is a good time to invite some new toys into your play and try out a gag? Perhaps some light choking?"

Sara: I do not screech.
Sebastian: You do.
Sara: Monday. 7. I will meet you there. Please figure out your five things in advance.

CHAPTER 4

SEBASTIAN

"WHAT ELSE?" I ASKED O'ROURKE.

I paced the sidewalk across the street from Pastoral in the Fort Point neighborhood while my trauma fellow murmured a few lines from an old Snoop Dogg song through my earbuds. It was fucking freezing out here but I was a minute early, and I'd take all manner of damp, bone-chilling wind if it saved me from dealing with Shapiro. At least for one more minute.

"I think that's the last update I have for you," he said. I could hear him flipping through his notebook and the ambient noise of the hospital around him. "For now, that is. I will come up with something soon enough."

"Please don't complain to me about the general surgery fellow grabbing another case out from underneath you again," I said, giving the restaurant a resentful glance.

"Did you hear me complain? Because I didn't. You extrapolated a complaint about that case-thieving sneak from my overall report. The last time I complained out loud was when I was an intern and had so many pagers, my scrubs kept falling down."

That was fully inaccurate but I wasn't interested in debating that with him now. "And how many pagers does it take to drop your pants, O'Rourke?"

"Yeah, this sounds like a fully appropriate question," he snarked. "And for your information, it was nine. Nine pagers. Urology, trauma, ENT, cardio, surgical oncology, colorectal, vascular, limb salvage, plastics. What a fucking nightmare."

I stifled a groan at the mention of plastics and frowned at my watch. I was going to have to go in there and get this over with soon. I wouldn't put it past Sara to break a chair over my head if I rolled in ten minutes late.

I shoved my hands into my pockets as another gust of cold, raw air blew in off the water. I hated the way summer bumped and stumbled into autumn here, starting and stopping like there was some serious question over whether seasons were supposed to keep on changing. And then, after cold snaps and heat waves and hurricanes, there was always one day in October, just like today, when it all collapsed and the debate was over. Summer was finished, autumn was here to stay, and I fucking hated it.

I hated wintry weather and all the nonsense that went with it. Snow, ice, everything. Goddamn, it was awful.

"Anyway, that was a night I wouldn't wish on anyone," O'Rourke said.

"What?"

"Did you dip out on me there? You do that a lot, Stremmel. I have to check the paperwork but I think you're supposed to pay attention to me. You're also supposed to be teaching me, not flaking out in the middle of my twenty-car pileup story, but that's a neglect I've come to accept from you."

It had taken me a bit to get my arms around it but I now understood this was O'Rourke's personality. He was obnoxious in a jaded, cynical way, though he never pretended he was in this business for any altruistic purpose. He thrived on ego and half-baked contempt for everyone. I understood it too, even if I didn't function the same way he did. But the guy had a dry, silly side too and it often came out in stories about his intern years in Minnesota, his assertion that I didn't teach him enough, or riding the line between delinquent and savant.

O'Rourke was a brilliant surgeon but not a single day went by without me wishing I'd known all these quirks of his *before* selecting him for a two-year fellowship.

"What would you like me to teach you while you're recapping the greatest hits of your intern year?"

"You could start by explaining how you organize your shit. I bent down to tie my shoes and it took me twenty-five minutes to clean up the mess from my pockets projectile vomiting all over the place. It was a fucking yard sale, man."

"Sounds like a personal problem." I glanced at the restaurant again. I was notably late now. "Could you…uh, do me a favor? Could you give me a call in forty-five minutes?"

"Is that when you slip into a bath? Glass of pinot, chocolates, fizzy bath bomb? Get your me time?"

"What? No. I might need a reason to—" I stopped, neither wanting to nor knowing how to explain this. "Forty-five minutes. I might teach you something interesting tomorrow if you can save me tonight."

"Sold. Setting a timer now."

With that, O'Rourke ended the call. I popped my earbuds back into their case and accepted the fact I had to go inside, sit down with Sara for significantly longer than I could bear, and talk to her without rolling my eyes out loud.

I was going to fail my ass off.

It was warm inside the restaurant and I spotted her immediately. She was frowning at her phone while typing, pausing, deleting, and typing again.

"Excuse me, sir? Are you meeting someone?"

I glanced around to find the hostess with a stack of menus cradled in her arm. "Uh. Yeah, but—"

"Would you happen to be the most insufferable, arrogant surgeon in the entire city? If so, I can show you to your party."

I shifted to face the hostess fully. "How much did she pay you for that?" I reached for my wallet. "Whatever it was, I'll double it if you—"

She held up a hand and shook her head with a grin. "No, I'm pretty sure I'm on her side."

I shoved my wallet back in my pocket. "How righteous of you." I jerked my chin in Sara's direction. "My insufferable arrogance will lead the way. Thanks."

I reached the table in a few long strides, yanked back the empty chair, forcing a rough squeal of wood scraping over the stone floor. Sara startled, her phone dropping to the table and a little gasp slipping past her lips.

"Arrogant, huh?" I asked, dropping into the chair. "Insufferable too? How long did it take you to come up with that scheme? Did it take all week? Or did lightning strike while you were waiting?"

She leaned back, folded her arms across her torso. That move had the unfortunate effect of reminding me that she was a pointlessly beautiful woman who could wear the shit out of a turtleneck sweater. But I didn't care. Really, I did not.

She could wear all the sweaters she wanted and have all that long, blonde hair and be annoyingly, disturbingly beautiful and I didn't have to care. Not my problem.

"You're late," she snapped.

"You were late on Thursday." I reached for the menu waiting at my place setting and gave it a quick glance. "Seemed only appropriate to return the favor."

With a glare that could dilate blood vessels, Sara collected her phone and tapped the screen. She set it in the center of the table with a pointed nod.

After holding her glare through several blinks, I glanced at the screen. "What's that supposed to be?"

"It would help if you could make an attempt at critical thinking," she replied. "It's a timer. There's no reason this should exceed thirty minutes."

Still staring at her, I raised my hand into the air. Soon, a server appeared at my side.

"Hey there, folks. Can I interest you in—"

"A beer, please," I interrupted. "A wheat, nothing pumpkin." I blinked at Sara. "The margherita pizza."

She arched a brow up as she said, "The bucatini, please. No arugula."

"Anything to drink?" the server asked.

"Water is fine, thanks," Sara replied.

"And what about nibbles for the table? Calamari, eggplant frites, burrata—"

"No," we said in unison.

"Okay, then," the server murmured. "I'll get that right in for you."

Once we were alone, Sara slid an index card across the table. "Five things about me. There you go."

I peered at the card. "Did you buy a package of index

cards just for this purpose? Or do you have index cards lying around? Like you're an intern presenting at rounds for the first time? Do you still make notes for rounds? Please tell me you're past the index card phase, Shap. I couldn't stand it if I knew you were walking around with little color-coded notes every day."

She regarded me with a smug grin that made it pretty clear she'd rip my face off if I took my eyes from her for a second. "You're the kind of teacher who abuses interns and residents, then? Do you throw things too or is it just shaming and torment?"

"You are the one with the track record with projectiles." I plucked the beer from the server's tray and drained half of it before continuing. "And I'll have you know I'm a great teacher—"

"I'm sure you think so," she interrupted. "And that's fantastic for you. Really, it is. But I don't have a single fuck to give about any of that because I'm walking out of here in twenty-three minutes. Fork over your five things, Stremmel."

A snarl sounded in my throat as I studied Sara. I couldn't stop staring at her. It was mostly self-preservation but a shred of confusion lingered there too. I had so many questions right now but the first and most essential among them was: Who the hell was this woman and why did she kill for sport?

I set the beer down, folded my arms on the table, and leaned in close. "I don't think this is what Milana had in mind when she said we were supposed to get to know each other," I whisper-growled. "If you could just be nice—"

"You want me to be *nice*?" she whisper-screeched right back. "Nice? That's what you want?"

"It wouldn't kill you."

"But clearly it will kill you," she said. "Seeing as I've made a point of being nice to you since moving into the building and you've—hmm." She tapped a finger to her chin. "Right, yes, you ignored my pleasantries. And now you'd like me to be all sugar plums and lemon drops because it suits your purposes?" She shook her head, that maniacal grin still pulling up her pale pink lips. "I don't think so. No, I don't think so."

I took my time responding to that attack and finished off my beer. I was drinking too fast and practically inviting a migraine into my day tomorrow but I could barely think about anything other than the blonde ball of fury seated across from me.

"What the hell are you talking about?" I set the empty glass on the table and ignored a sudden, perverse interest in what she was wearing with that turtleneck. She'd been seated when I arrived and she hadn't yet leapt up to bludgeon me with a saltshaker so I was clueless as to whether she wore jeans or a skirt or—fuck, I didn't even know. And I didn't care. Not at all. Which was why I ignored that thought entirely.

"I am talking about saying hello to you in the hallway," she replied.

"Right. Let me see if I understand this." I reached for her glass of water and drained it while she gaped at me. "I didn't give enough attention to your chirpy little greetings so you went all tiny tornado on an exam room, and you're going to hold it against me until you can find a way to be rid of me, even if that involves strangling the life out of me with your precious plastic surgeon hands. Do I have that right?"

Okay, so I knew I was an asshole. I *knew* this.

And now Sara did too.

She gave her empty glass a mortified stare before meeting my gaze. "We both know the exam room was an accident and fully unrelated to our prior interactions outside the hospital. I am not going to revise history with you. I am not going to be *nice* simply because it makes you comfortable."

"I don't remember the last time I was anything close to comfortable. Okay? Whether you screech at me or not won't change that." Drumming my finger on the table, I continued, "I'm just saying we have to get through this thing. We shouldn't kill each other in the process."

The server arrived with our meals and another round of drinks, which was a huge fucking relief because I urgently needed something to do with both my hands and my mouth. But I made the fatal error of glancing across the table as the server set Sara's dish down—a dish topped with a whole damn field of arugula. Not only did they not hold the greens, they seemed to treat her to an extra helping because there was no way that was the standard quantity.

I watched Sara purse her lips together and I figured we were in for another explosion now. She'd send that dish back so hard, the chef would set fields of arugula on fire.

But she said nothing when the server asked if there was anything else we needed. And she blinked down at the heap of curly greens, fork in hand, like it was a project she'd inherited and didn't have the heart to abandon.

I sat there, my fingers curled around the fresh glass of beer, and stared while Sara excavated a strand of pasta from beneath the arugula.

What the fuck was I watching?

Where was the tiny tornado? Or the screech owl? Or even the hunter who'd happily mount my head on her wall?

And who the hell was this?

We ate in silence for several minutes. It wasn't until the server arrived at the table to top off Sara's water that we shared a momentary glance at the woman's veiny hands. Those were legend-status veins.

Once we were alone again, I said, "I could get a gray cannula in on the first shot and she wouldn't even feel it."

Sara gave a dry laugh. "When was the last time you started an IV?"

"Not recently," I admitted. "I usually practice on my residents at the start of their trauma rotation. Gets us off on a good, abusive foot and it helps me rank them by vascularity. Least being best, of course, since they'd never get pulled off the floor to donate blood. It comes back to haunt them when they're inevitably enrolled in a clinical trial."

"You're such an asshole," she said, but there was no heat behind it. She almost sounded amused.

"And what about you? When was the last time you started a line?"

She set her fork down and busied herself with the napkin on her lap. "You have no idea what I do, do you?"

I dropped a piece of crust to my plate. "Plastics. You make people look pretty after I put them back together."

She dabbed her lips—they were so pale, barely even pink —and set the napkin beside her mostly untouched pasta. She'd moved it around plenty but she'd hardly made a dent.

And then she held up her phone to me as the timer counted down the final five seconds she'd set for us. After swiping away the alarm, she slipped the index card off the table. "I didn't get yours, so you're not getting mine."

Sara pushed away from the table and I had no choice but to watch her cross the restaurant. She didn't bother with backward glances, not when she was busy walking like the floor owed her money.

I returned to my beer and pizza, and attempted to figure out what the ever-loving fuck happened here tonight. I was halfway through the last slice of pizza when my phone buzzed in my pocket. I assumed it was Sara texting me a thesis on my arrogance though I was wrong. When I saw O'Rourke was calling, I tucked the phone against my shoulder, saying, "What's up?"

The blaring roar of the emergency room came through the line before he said, "I'm early but I gotta deal with an issue. Consider this your fake crisis call so you can get the hell out of whatever you've gotten yourself into now."

"I don't get myself into things," I said, dropping the last of the crust to my plate. "I actively avoid getting into things. I hate things."

"Yeah, yeah. I don't have time to unpack any of that tonight but maybe tomorrow if you buy me lunch."

"I'm not buying you lunch."

"That's cool. I'll get Acevedo to pick up the tab. He'll want to hear about this. He pays for updates on your misery." A siren wailed nearby and O'Rourke groaned. "Really gotta go now. Be good."

He hung up as the server came to gather our plates. I pointed at Shapiro's pasta. "She said no arugula. What does this look like to you?"

The server frowned at the dish. "Why didn't she say anything?"

I motioned to the empty seat. "And you think I have any idea?"

CHAPTER 5

SARA

MY GOOD GIRL ALWAYS DID HER HOMEWORK. SHE COULDN'T LIVE in a world where she didn't comply fully and confirm to everyone that she was perfect and worthy of the little slice of space she occupied.

That good girl was shaking in her boots as I jogged up the stairs to Milana Cuello's office, right on time for this week's session. The other side of me welcomed the opportunity to show off Stremmel's epic inflexibility. Milana was sure to see how that man was *impossible*. She'd sympathize with me. She had to.

As I exited the stairwell and approached her office, I found Stremmel leaning against the wall, his gaze fixed on Milana's door as if he could force it open by will alone. He wore the same dark blue scrubs as last week and hadn't yet realized his forearms were too profane to flash around these halls. Unfortunate. Someone really needed to talk to him about modesty.

I stopped several feet from him and grabbed my phone. I had no intention of speaking until the session started and I'd divert myself by any means necessary. Even when the session did get underway, I intended to let Sebastian implode and prove my points.

However.

"Last chance," he said.

"Excuse you?"

"Last chance, " he repeated with a scowly side-eye. "Still have that index card?"

"You had plenty of opportunities to take advantage of my index card. You chose not to and that was all your decision."

"Hmmm." He crossed his arms over his chest and went on staring at the door. Then, "Hmmm."

"What?" I snapped.

"Oh, nothing. I was just thinking about how we're going to end up with another homework assignment because we didn't complete this one."

"I completed my part of this," I argued. "You're the one who couldn't be bothered to write down five little things."

He turned his head and proceeded to drag his stare from my sneakers to my (again, still, always) untamed hair. "And you think that actually matters?"

I shoved my fists into my pockets. "You should've done your part last week. Or at any time prior to this exact moment."

"I'm ready now. Got an index card I can borrow?"

Before I could tell him what I thought about lending him anything, Milana swept into the hall, all smiles and silver hair. "Ah, my friends! You're back for another visit. Come. Inside now, inside."

Sebastian resumed his spot at the bookshelf and I sat on the sofa, my hands clasped in my lap. Battle stations ready.

"Don't get too comfortable," Milana called from behind her desk. "We won't be sitting today." She hefted an old milk crate onto her desk. "Playing is much more fun. We don't play enough as grown-ups, do we? It's like we forget how to do it."

"Or, after four years of undergrad, four years of medical school, another four or so years of residency, and then a year or two of fellowship, you have a bunch of socially stunted, sleep-deprived teenagers who know how to cut people open but not how to take a day off," Sebastian said. "Comes with the territory, wouldn't you agree?"

She chuckled at him. "I call it job security." With a fond smile for each of us, Milana carried the crate to the coffee table. "As I said, we'll be playing today." She beckoned to us, adding, "Up. On your feet."

I stood, shrugged out of my white coat, and draped it over the arm of the sofa. When I turned back toward Sebastian and Milana, I was greeted with a decidedly masculine snort.

I threw *what the fuck?* hands at him but he shook his head with a slight laugh. I went on glaring until he said, "It's nothing. Just"—he glanced down at my t-shirt, the one that read *Running On* and the chemical structure of ATP, the stuff that carried energy in cells—"nothing. Forget it."

"And forget we shall," Milana said as she plucked a squishy ball emblazoned with a pharmaceutical company's logo from the crate. "Since this is not my first visit to the circus, I am not going to ask you about the homework from our last session. We'll play our game and have fun instead. All right?"

"This is obviously a trap," Stremmel said.

I ran my palms over my thighs, knowing he was right about that yet completely unwilling to tell him as much.

"Trap? From me? No," Milana drawled. "I'd never." She

tossed the ball from hand to hand. "All I want you to do is play a game of catch but do have a care for my plants. The string of pearls needs only a slight invitation to fall apart, and while the pothos looks hardy, it offends easily." She lobbed the ball to me. "Sara. Start us off. My one rule is we don't let the ball hit the floor."

"And if we do?" Stremmel asked.

"You won't," she said.

"If we do?" he repeated.

With a deep grin, she said, "Embrace the challenge, Sebastian, even if you don't know what might come of it."

It started out simple, just me and Sebastian throwing pharma swag back and forth across Milana's office. But then she reached into the crate and retrieved a plush pineapple. "Let's add this one," she said. "Sebastian, you're up."

He caught the pineapple after sending the ball to me. It took us a few tries to get the rhythm right but we got there while Milana slathered on the praise. Sebastian wanted no part of that. He narrowed his eyes or locked his jaw every time she acknowledged us for playing along. All of that was annoying enough but he did it while flaunting those damn arms at me too. Terribly rude of him.

Then, she said, "It's too quiet in here. Let's have a little chat."

"And there's the trap," he muttered.

"Now, Sebastian," she started, clearly enjoying his misery, "where is Sara from?"

"I don't know," he replied. "Hell, probably."

I winged the pineapple at him hard. He had to stumble backward to catch it.

"And Sara," Milana said, "where is Sebastian from?"

"If I had to guess, I'd say a defective condom."

The pineapple struck my shoulder and I had to flail a bit to grab it before it hit the floor. I glared at him with as much heat and violence as I could summon. He rotated the squishy ball in his palm as if he was finding the right grip just as I shot the pineapple back at him. The ball landed square on my chest.

"Lovely, lovely," Milana sang. "Sebastian, what is Sara's favorite color?"

"Necrotic kidney," he said, spiking the pineapple high over my head. I barely caught it, and ended up with my t-shirt half untucked.

"Sara, your turn—"

"Anything infected with C. diff," I replied, putting all my weight behind sending that stupid pineapple to his scowly face.

"Oh, god," he groaned, catching the toy as it bounced off him. "Not fair, Shap. Intestinal bacterium is out of bounds. Don't make me think about that. I'm gonna gag."

"Next question," Milana called. "Sara, did Sebastian have any pets as a child?"

The ball connected with my thigh as I said, "They all ran away."

Before he was prompted, Sebastian said, "You're the one who can summon monsters with your screeching. It must be difficult with yetis and the Chupacabra and the Loch Ness monster showing up all the time. Do they stay for dinner?"

The pineapple hit my other leg as I scrambled to catch it and throw back the ball without either touching the floor. The ball connected low on his torso and his eyes flared as he caught hold of it. These toys were small and light but I was breathing hard and sweating from this activity, and so was Sebastian.

"Let's move on to siblings," Milana said.

"You can find Stremmel's on a true crime podcast," I said, aiming the pineapple at his jaw.

"As victims?" he asked. "Or killers?"

The squishy ball connected with my loose bun and half my hair slipped free from the tie but there was no time to stop and fix it. "Does it matter?"

"A bit," he yelled. "Am I the murderer? Are they? Come on! Get your game right, Shap. Don't fall apart on me now. If you're taking these shots, you better shoot to kill."

"Then, yeah. You're the serial killer here."

"Thank you," he shouted.

"Sebastian," Milana started, "tell us about Sara's—"

"You mean the Children of the Corn?"

"*Very* inventive," I said, sending the ball to his jaw again.

"Better than serial killer," he replied, nailing my thigh with the pineapple.

"Really, though?" I argued. "I don't see how corn-harvest murderers are any different. Do better."

With an eye roll, he turned to Milana. "Do you have anything harder?"

I took that opportunity to fire the pineapple right at his chiseled cheek. His head snapped back and the pineapple rolled under the coffee table. There was a full second where he was stunned silent.

But then he rounded on me, his signature scowl replaced with a flat, open-mouthed stare that was many, many times more dangerous than any other look he'd ever sent my way. At the exact same second, we dived for the crate and grabbed all the ammunition we could carry and let loose on each other. Plush toys, bouncy balls, stress balls, tennis balls, every variety of pharma swag—it was a wild, hiccuping blur of hits and throws.

"You just don't know when to stop," Sebastian shouted, an eggplant stress toy with the brand name of an erectile dysfunction drug printed on it flying from his hand.

"And you do?" I cried, throwing two miniature frisbees. "You could've stopped this shit last week but you didn't!"

"Oh, because I wouldn't fall in line with your precious little terms?" A series of three hard bouncy balls ricocheted off my thigh. They were going to leave a mark. "You have got to be fucking kidding me."

"I was trying to make this easier on everyone," I yelled.

"And who the fuck asked you to do that?" he countered, whipping a small cactus plush at my face. "I don't need you looking after me. If I need to staple a fucking laceration, I'll staple it—and just so you know, I'm fully aware that staples aren't right in every case. I fucking agree with you but you're too busy force-feeding me to even hear that and—"

"You're too condescending to force-feed," I said.

"You are relentless," he panted, his eyes flashing with heat and his jaw locked in the most stern, severe line.

Before I could reply, Milana placed herself in the middle of our skirmish, her hands out. "You're both relentless—or do you not notice it in yourselves the way you see it in each other? That happens more than you think. It's similar to the way our eyes can see our nose but our brain instructs us to ignore it." She gathered the toys where they'd landed all around us. "Thank god my string of pearls was spared in this skirmish. Small mercies," she said under her breath. "For your homework this week, I'd like you to think about that. Your commonalities—and why they trouble you so much."

She dumped the toys into the crate as Sebastian and I

looked on. We were still breathing heavily, our clothes disheveled and my hair wilder than ever as we glowered at each other. I wasn't going to say he'd started it—though he did—or pretend he'd been the only one to deliver snarky, juvenile comments. But the way he'd looked at me as he'd said I was relentless, the way he'd stared me down as if he was the only one who could call the terms of this war—it made me crazy enough to want to grab that pineapple and the eggplant and pelt him with them until he begged me for mercy.

Milana glanced between us. "That will be all for today."

With that, I grabbed my white coat and bolted out of there. I didn't need to be asked twice and I didn't need another minute with that man trying to stare my skin off.

CHAPTER 6

SEBASTIAN

THERE WERE ONLY THREE THINGS I NEEDED RIGHT NOW.

1. Get the hell out of this hospital.
2. Watch the latest collegiate cheer competition in Orlando while shoveling a burrito bowl into my mouth.
3. Sleep off the shitshow that was this day.

It was a really good plan, and if I could accomplish the first item, the last two were bound to fall in line for me.

But that wasn't happening. No, ma'am. Not today. Not when I walked into the attending's lounge an hour after the juggle fight from hell only to have Shapiro plow right into me.

"Oh, sorry," she said. But then, "Um, hello? You just walk into people and—"

"I did nothing of the sort, you blind little bat," I argued. "You head-planted yourself into my chest because you weren't paying attention."

"I was fixing my hair," she fired back.

"You weren't looking where you were going."

"You could apologize."

"You could get out of my way."

Once again, we stared at each other, neither willing to back down. For fuck's sake, this lady was going to send me to my grave. She was a ninety mile an hour downward spiral if I'd ever seen one and I could not stop seeing her. She was everywhere. I couldn't go a day without spotting her bright yellow sneakers or all of that hair, and her voice wouldn't leave me alone. She was here at the hospital, she was in my apartment building, she was even yammering at me in my dreams. And today—my god, today—was just a hot, horrible journey to the center of the earth with her.

There was no exiting this hostage situation.

I rubbed the spot where her head had connected with my chest. She wasn't especially tall so she'd nailed me right on the midline of my pecs.

"Shut up, it doesn't hurt," she said.

She'd changed out of that chemistry t-shirt, the one I'd grudgingly found amusing, and into a pale sweater and trousers the color of spilled red wine. She looked expensive. Really fucking expensive. Like it would cost me to touch her. "Your skull is made of stone."

"Do we actually have to do this again? We've spent enough time yelling at each other for no reason today, don't you think?"

The door opened again, this time admitting Cal Hartshorn and Nick Acevedo into the room. I dropped my head back and I rolled my eyes at the ceiling. They were the last people we needed to see.

"Shap! Stremmel!" Hartshorn boomed. "Can we interest either of you in—"

"I'm gonna stop you right there," I said. "Whatever it is, no. Don't want it, don't need it. Sell it elsewhere. Thank you. Goodbye and good night."

Acevedo approached us, his gaze on Shapiro. "Is he bothering you?" Acevedo asked, a finger pointed in my direction. "We run together and I like making him suffer so please tell me the truth or lie flagrantly, whichever gives me more to work with."

She glanced up at me, a brow arched high and a vicious glint in her eyes. She was going to tattle her ass off and I was going to—

"Hardly," she said. With a wave for Acevedo and Hartshorn, she added, "Good evening" and slipped past me into the hall.

What the actual fuck was that?

I turned and stared at the door as if that could explain why Sara skipped out on a perfectly good opportunity to put my jackassery on display for these guys to see. When the door failed to explain a goddamn thing to me, I retreated to my locker to get out of these scrubs.

"I'd love it if you didn't run Shapiro out of here," Hartshorn said as he strolled to his locker. "As far as gifts go for me this holiday season, that would be at the top of my list."

"I am not running anyone out of anywhere. We were just having a"—well, it had been another ridiculous fight about nothing but I wasn't going to tell these guys any of that —"conversation."

"You could try being pleasant to her. Wouldn't hurt," Acevedo said.

"It would. Not my blood type," I replied.

"We're getting a beer since our wives are traveling for work," Hartshorn said. "Come with?"

"No." I zipped up my coat and headed for the door. I really needed some cheerleading tonight. I didn't know what it was about all the glitter and high ponytails but it always chilled me out. Some people watched sitcom reruns or listened to podcasts. Others preferred wine and weed. I watched competitive cheerleading while sprawled on the sofa.

I took a shortcut through the hospital complex that let out a few blocks from my building, effectively avoiding the clusterfuck of traffic at the hospital's main exit. I toggled between texting O'Rourke and placing an order for that burrito bowl as I headed home. Every step was one closer to putting this fucking day to bed.

I was almost there. All I had to do was get in the building and up three flights of stairs, and I'd have all the solitude I wanted.

Except Sara was cursing at the door and I was presently unable to walk through walls without injuring myself. Oh, my fucking life.

"What," I called, stomping up the stone steps, "the fuck."

She sighed for ten minutes before saying, "My key is stuck."

"Move." When she went on screwing with the door, I tapped her upper arm, saying, "*Move.*"

"I have it," she snapped.

"Obviously, you don't."

"If you'd just give me a minute—"

"You've had a minute," I said.

"Your reaction is excessive relative to this situation."

I shook my head and hoped some lightning would strike

and put me out of my misery. "My reaction is not the problem."

"Your reaction is always the problem," she cried, abandoning the door to whirl around and step into my space. "Why do you always have to be right? Even when it doesn't matter?"

I'd assumed her eyes were brown but I was wrong about that. They were hazel—mostly golden amber with flecks of brown and green. They were lighter up close than they seemed at a polite distance. I wasn't polite.

"I don't give a good fuck about right. I just want to get upstairs and change into soft pants before my burrito bowl arrives."

She narrowed her hazel eyes at me and I could tell by the way her lips curled that she was about to gut me here on the stoop. "You are such a—"

"Oh hey, guys."

We turned at once to find Riley Walsh coming through the door. He spied Sara's keys hanging from the lock and freed them with one deft turn of the handle. Riley lived on the second floor with his wife Alex. He hated me on account of me attempting to flirt with Alex in front of him on several occasions before they were engaged. I hadn't in years but that didn't deter him from giving me death glares every time we crossed paths.

So, daily. Daily death glares. For years. Fun times for me here in the doctor dorm.

"Was this thing sticking again? It's the weather. Whenever it's damp like this, old hardware gets wonky." He pointed to the hinges and panel. "The wood swells too."

Sara grabbed her keys from him, saying, "Thanks. Maybe

it's time to replace this door so it can function in all weather conditions."

"I'm going to pretend you didn't suggest we ditch a door from 1880 simply because it reacts to the weather," he replied as he jogged down the steps. "You're hurting my preservationist heart."

Sara pushed her way inside and made a notable effort at slamming the outer door on my face but I was right behind her and caught it as she threw open the next door into the foyer. I didn't understand why this place had so many doors that all led from one little room into another—vestibule, foyer, entry hall—but it meant I got to repeatedly thwart Sara's attempts at making a fuck-ton of noise.

"You're the one who can't stand to be wrong," I said to her back.

"That's rich coming from you."

She went to her door, shaking her head and murmuring to herself as she fumbled with her keys. Her door stood to the left of the steep, winding staircase, and since I didn't have to look at her eyes anymore, I should've been on my way and out of this mess. I wanted to leave. I gripped the banister, stepped onto the first stair.

But— "Could you press pause on all your slamming and screeching, and explain to me what you're so pissed off about? Because I'd really like to know."

She gave a dark, brittle laugh. "I doubt that."

"Okay. You're right. I don't really care why you're so pissed off. I just want it to stop."

She turned slowly. "What you want is to avoid all consequences of your actions."

I abandoned the stairs because this shit could not go

unaddressed. "My actions? And who is holding *you* accountable for *your* actions?"

She brought her hands to her temples, shaking her head. "You have all the power here and it's a fucking game to you."

"It's not," I said. I didn't know when I'd crossed the foyer but I was close enough to find the green in her eyes again. "It's not a fucking game, Shap. It never was."

She flung her arms out wide and I caught her wrist before it smashed into the banister's thick, round newel post. "You need to be more careful."

Her pulse thrummed under my thumb as she blinked up at me. I watched her, waiting for the next biting comment from that wicked tongue of hers, another blistering glare, anything. Whatever she had to give, I was ready for it. I *wanted* it.

But then she parted her lips and looked at me with those big golden-green eyes and I lost my fucking mind.

I advanced into her space and shoved a hand into all that wavy blonde hair and I stole her lips, taking everything I wanted, just fucking taking it all. There was a split second when the only response was a squeak in her throat but then—*then*— she softened and sighed and everything that once was ceased to exist because there was no going back. Not for either of us.

I roped an arm around her waist and backed her up against the door as she fisted her hand in my shirt and sank her teeth into my bottom lip. It hurt like hell and I responded by pinning her hips to the door. She purred, though it was a purr in the way a cheetah purred before ripping your throat out.

I entertained no thought as to whether this was right, wrong, or fucking suicidal. She was as perfectly vicious as she looked and I couldn't get enough, and none of those thoughts would've trumped that truth. I could not stop kissing her, touching her, just fucking inhaling her as she fought me for control because of course we fought. *Of course* we did.

She tore her lips away only to drag them down my neck and light my skin on fire. "What do you think you're doing?"

"This is another one of those moments when you should shut up." I ran my hand over her ass, exploring all that lush, glorious skin through her trousers. The more appropriate description would've been fondling or manhandling as there was nothing polite happening here. Nothing gentle or tentative. This wasn't even decent. No, *fuck* no. It was as irreverent as everything was with us.

I dragged my hand to her thigh, down to the back of her leg. I brought her knee to my waist and notched myself between her legs, and if I'd thought I'd crossed a line a few minutes ago, I dropped a bomb on those lines by grinding my cock where she wanted it. She purred again and there was plenty of murder in that sound but now pure need was woven into it too.

"You like that, don't you?" I asked. "Is there something you want to ask me?"

She yanked my shirt from my trousers and ran her hand over my torso, rude and possessive and perfect with her fingers clawing, digging, clinging. "You're such an asshole."

I slipped my fingers free of her hair to curl them around the back of her neck. "You're nothing if not consistent."

She reached for my belt and it seemed entirely possible she'd whip me with it if I didn't tie it around her wrists first. "There's nothing in this world I'd ask you for."

I pried her hand off my belt before things got fully out of

control and I spun her around to face the door. Her hands landed flat on the panel, her cheek too. I leaned into her, my lips coasting over her neck, her earlobe. Her skin was magic. Demonic magic but wasn't that the best kind of magic? It was the best for me.

Give me all your hellfire, honey. Give me your worst.

And she smelled amazing. There was no singular scent I could identify but every breath of her was maddeningly lovely and precious. Maddening. Having her like this left me furious yet somehow desperate for more. Like I didn't have enough problems.

"Then don't ask," I said. She shuddered as I passed a hand between her breasts and down her belly. I slipped my palm between her thighs, cupping the heat of her for a moment before giving her a hard, profane squeeze. It was wrong. So wrong. "Don't ask. Tell me what you want and I'll give it to you."

I kept my face buried against her neck and my palm on the most dangerous cat in the known world. It was all I could do.

Then a jingle sounded, followed by the metallic zip of a key into a lock. She heaved out a halting breath. "Don't think for a minute that I'm finished despising you."

I pressed my teeth to her neck, holding her steady with an arm around her waist. "Couldn't even if I tried."

She opened the door and—to be completely honest, I had no idea how we got into the bedroom. There were walls and corners and doors but my only priority was keeping my hands and mouth on her body at all costs. I'd succeeded at that, seeing as I had her flat on her back and her pants flying over my shoulder.

"Get that sweater off," I barked. "Show me those pretty

tits."

The sweater sailed over my head. "I'm going to pretend you didn't say that."

"What would you prefer I say?"

I kept both hands on her thighs as I dropped my knees to the floor. I just wanted to feel that satin skin against my cheek. That was all I needed. After that, I'd give her anything she wanted before I woke up from this sex nightmare. Was that a real thing, a sex nightmare? And was that what was happening now? Because it wasn't a dream. Perhaps a hiccup in my consciousness or a snag in the space-time continuum but definitely not a dream—aside from the fact I was about to rub my face all over her and lick her until she cried. Aside from that, not a dream.

"I'd prefer you not pretend my tits are anything worth talking about," she said, whipping her bra at my head.

"You're telling me I have to deal with your insecurities too? Jesus Christ." I pressed one hand to her panty-covered pussy, tapped a finger against the wet spot waiting for me, and then dragged the other hand up over the soft rise of her belly to the small but definitely pretty tits. Her nipples were large and pale, dusky pink, and gathered in tight pebbles. I wanted to bite them more than anything else in the world. "It's amusing that you think I'd bullshit my way through this with empty compliments but I'm gonna have to disappoint you. I don't know how to give empty compliments, certainly not to you. Your tits are pretty. Deal with it."

"You are—"

"Whatever you're going to say, don't. Just don't. I'm getting rid of these panties and then I'm gonna spend a lot of time licking your clit. *A lot* of time. Probably too much but the idea of torturing you does real good things to me. The conversation ends now. Understood?"

She blinked at me down the soft, curved line of her body. My eyes couldn't stop eating her up. Her insecurities could fuck right off because there was nothing but plush, *annoying* perfection in front of me. That I was turned on enough *by this woman* to be dizzy was highly inconvenient.

"I'm going to pull your hair," she said.

That seemed like enough of an invitation to get rid of the panties. "Go for it," I replied, pushing her thighs apart and running my knuckles down the center of her. I already knew she was going to taste like heaven. The scent of her alone had me growling into the silky smooth of her leg, teeth bared. "Strangle me for all I care. If I die, I die."

A laugh rolled out of her, a sound I couldn't remember ever hearing before. I found myself smiling up at her while I sucked on her thigh and pet her pussy. It wasn't supposed to be like this. We weren't supposed to stop and grin at each other. We were supposed to hate each other, to resent each other, to cut each other down at every turn—and that was all the reminder I needed that no one was thinking right now. There was no way in hell we'd come out of this any better than we went in. Odds were high it would be much, much worse but I really needed to feel her clit on my tongue so I didn't care about the impending misery. I did not care.

I shoved both hands under her ass and dragged her to the edge of the bed, just where I wanted her. She yelped and flailed a bit, but it wasn't like I was going to let her fall off the bed so I bit the inside of her thigh to quiet her down. It was a logical solution to me although—

"Did you just *bite* me?"

I swept my tongue over her clit because I meant what I

said about the conversation being finished. My cock didn't have the patience for this and frankly, neither did I. "Yes. Enough talking from you. Can't you see I'm busy?"

I hooked her knee over my shoulder and pushed two fingers inside her. She was wet like I couldn't believe and I didn't want to love how incredible she felt. Her clit throbbed against my tongue and that almost did me in. I wasn't above admitting it. I mean, I didn't have to like her to nearly blow it because I made her clit happy.

There was a minute where all I did was lick that sweet pearl and rub her pussy while Sara shook and groaned against me. She had her bottom lip snared between her teeth, her hands busy balling the bed linens. But then she sat up, half her hair falling from its tie and her lips pink and swollen, and she said, "I can't take this anymore."

In the time it took me to peel my mouth off her body, she reached for my shirt, slipped her fingers between the placket, and tore it the fuck open. Buttons pinged off the walls, the furniture. I didn't know what was going on until she fisted her hands around the remains of my shirt and jerked me up to her mouth. She kissed me like she was drowning and needed the air.

"I can't, I can't," she whispered against my lips. "I can't wait."

"Why didn't you say so?"

"Because you had this whole speech about licking my clit and it sounded really great—damn you for that, by the way —but I can only come once and it's never very good when it's oral and—"

"That's enough." I pushed her back down to the bed. I shrugged out of the shirt, brought my hands to my belt. Had to focus on one thing at a time or else I'd jog back to the whole *it's never very good when it's oral* and *I can only come once* business and disprove some hypotheses. No need to threaten me with all these good times. "Where do screech owls keep their condoms?"

She pointed to the blue bureau beside her bed. I flung it open, sifted through the nonsense there. Prescription bottles, lotion bottles, a million hair scrunchies. Then, way in the back, an unopened box of condoms.

My cold, shriveled heart gave a stupid kick at that. Goddamn caveman brain.

I dropped my pants, brought a knee to the mattress, rolled down the condom.

"That's just unfair," she whined with a dismissive wave to my cock. "You don't deserve all that."

"Maybe I don't but you get to use it, so we're even." That I was standing here and staring down at her while I stroked my cock rather than blacked out and balls deep was remarkable. I didn't know who I was right now or how I got so fucking smooth but here we were. "Let's get you where you need to go before you rip my spine out, shall we?"

"Assuming you know how to use that thing, yeah." Her hair was a god-awful mess and I kinda loved it. Wanted to pull it just to see if she'd scream. Wanted to scoop it all up and hold it back while she swallowed my cock. I wanted everything, which seemed like a terrible idea. "I still hate you."

"Trust me, I know." I settled between her thighs. She was so pale next to me that I had to press a hand to her leg just to admire the difference. She was raw silk to my sunbaked leather. "You're the fucking worst."

She reached for me as I notched myself at her opening, ran her hand down my chest and slipped her fingers through the dark trail there. I almost died from that whispered exploration. I was prepared for her to rip my hair out and keep it as a trophy but I wasn't prepared for her to be gentle. "You should know this is completely insane. You're not allowed to look like this."

"Why not?"

I didn't have it in me to take it any slower even though slow was the only way to go for several reasons. First, I intended to work my ass off at getting her there twice because I didn't walk away from challenges. Second, and most importantly, this had to blow her mind. She could holler at me about staples and whatever the fuck else she wanted but she wasn't going to holler at me about lasting for two minutes and passing out on top of her, even if her pussy was forged from demon magic.

We groaned together as I pushed inside her. There was nothing better, not a goddamn thing better than that first clasp. I dropped a hand beside her shoulder, settled the other on her hip. I leaned down, brushed a kiss over her lips once I was fully seated between her thighs. "Why not?" I repeated.

She shifted beneath me, brought her knees up to my waist as she linked her arms around my neck. I didn't think I could get any deeper but her pussy proved me wrong. "Because you're supposed to be hideous under your clothes, not some slab of carved freaking granite. And you're tan and golden everywhere. It's obnoxious. No one with your personality should be this hot and endowed. Shouldn't be allowed."

My hips started rolling, bucking against her, and it took me a few seconds but I quickly realized we fit each other in the *best* ways. Sara was petite but she had these wide, gorgeous hips that held me tight and close. She was soft like

I couldn't believe, like she was made for all the hard I had to give. Her waist was nipped just enough for my hands to span the distance between the flare of her hips and the underside of her breasts. Her tits filled the cup of my palm. And her cunt...well, that would be the end of me. "Fuck, *you're* not allowed to feel like this. Jesus, why? Why can't you be cold and toothy?"

"Toothy?"

She arched back, her chin pointed at the ceiling, lips parted. I wanted to lick her neck and I didn't even know what that was about. Nothing made sense anymore. All that existed was the rock of her body against mine and the hot, dizzy gathering of sensation down my spine. It started at the place where her fingers pressed into the nape of my neck and ended where I pressed into her. That was it. That was everything.

"Yeah, you seem like the kind of woman who'd own a pussy that would just bite a dick clear off," I said. She pushed a hand through my hair. My eyes rolled back in my head. I felt that hand everywhere. "Apparently, you're not the hunter I'd expected."

"I can be a hunter. Let me give it a try." She clenched around me, her muscles kicking and fluttering and sucking the marrow right out of me. I made a slurring attempt at speech and then hid that disaster with an open-mouthed kiss to her neck. I could live in this spot forever. "Is that the kind of hunting you had in mind?"

"You're wicked," I growled.

"You're an asshole."

"So you've said." I ducked away from her neck as I grabbed her waist with both hands. It took a lot of concentration to fuck her and fight her at the same time but I also wanted to keep every ounce of it, every minute. I wanted to shove these insults into my pockets and swallow up every little touch and groan she gave me. "I think you like it."

She twisted her fingers around my hair and pulled as she'd promised. I leaned into her hand, wanting more of that glorious torment. I'd die from it if she let me. "I don't like anything about you."

I pulled all the way back, my cock barely brushing her folds. "Nothing?"

She hooked a leg around my waist, urged me closer. "Whose insecurities require tending now?"

I didn't respond, instead turning my attention to her nipples while I worked her over my cock. There was something magical in that combination from the way her lips parted and her eyes glazed over, and I rode it all the way through the quietest screech I'd ever heard from her. I'd expected a loud thrash, maybe some scratching. I got none of it. Just an exquisite little sigh and a full-body shudder that tested the limits of my control.

"Oh, wow," she whispered, blinking up at me with a startled smile. "That—"

"Nope. Not happening." I pulled out, shifted to the side, and flipped her on her belly. "Here's what we're doing now. Come here. Scoot back unless you want me dragging you and you know I will. Give me that ass. That's my dick hunter, right here, *good girl*." I pressed a hand between her shoulder blades as I stationed myself at her entrance. She was still throbbing and wet like a waterfall. "I really don't want to like your pussy as much as I do but it's made out of demonic magic so I'm helpless here."

Instead of waiting for Sara to respond, I took hold of her hips and thrust inside her. Heat spiraled through me and all the bickering and bullshit between us took a back seat to instinct. There was nothing left but two bodies that fit together in intolerably good ways, and these bodies knew exactly what to do to each other, even when we could barely function beyond our mutual hostility.

I had to be honest, things took a wild turn at that point. More wild than all the previous turns in this square dance. The pillows—and there were a number of them—went flying. I grabbed her hair, gave it a rough twist. The blankets were fully fucked. Something fell off her bureau and landed with a clatter. I ran my knuckles down the seam of her ass, did it harder when she cried and bucked against me. Then I said some mortifying things about how she made me feel. She said some equally mortifying things about my cock.

I didn't even know how I'd lasted this long but the shiver-pulse low in my belly said I didn't have much longer.

"Be a good girl and give it to me now," I barked. "Your pussy can buy and sell my soul for all I care but you won't be able to get rid of me until you come on my cock one more time."

"I *can't*," she yelled into the blankets.

"This is not the time for your insecurities to pay us a visit," I said. "You can and you will. I can feel it. Stop trying to be right all the time and let it happen. Let go."

That was probably the sex equivalent of telling someone to calm down but I didn't care. I didn't have time to care and I just didn't want to. I wanted her to do as I fucking said the first time and let me give her what she wanted, but since that wasn't an option, I pressed hard below her belly button. It was enough pressure to make all of this *much more* intense which she confirmed by screaming "I hate you" into the mattress.

She could hate me all she wanted because I was very busy keeping myself on the right side of consciousness. So busy that I nearly missed the first flutters and shudders of her body joining the two-timers club.

"There it is," I growled. "That's a good girl for me."

They said pleasure was a product of the mind and I had problems with that assertion but this time it was true. Whether it was the satisfaction of proving her wrong for once or the joy of commanding her body to meet my demands, I needed no other invitation to curl myself around her and fill the condom in a series of jerks and spasms so violent I was concerned I'd cracked a rib.

We stayed frozen in that awkward, sweat-soaked position for a few minutes while we tried to catch our breath. A peculiar little voice in my head wanted me to brush her hair away from her face and tuck the blankets up to her shoulders but I wasn't doing that. Peculiar voices got me in trouble. They were probably the reason I was here in the first place.

An elbow connected with my flank and Sara said, "Kindly get your slab of granite ass off me."

I rolled to the side with a grunt. I blindly patted the bedside table, thrilled when my hand connected with a box of tissues. This condom required attention but these legs weren't ready for standing of any sort. Not unless I wanted to turn this into a slapstick comedy routine, and I was too old for that.

A couple more minutes passed with only our ragged breathing and the creaks of an old home to set the soundtrack.

Where it came to fucking the words out of a woman who voraciously hated me, I was unclear on the appropriate after-care. Was I supposed to hang out? That couldn't be right. Was she expecting another round? I could be talked into that but it was going to be a hell of a lot less athletic and it wouldn't be without some fluids first. Or was I supposed to leave? Just walk out and…what? This couldn't be the end.

And what fresh hell was that fucking thought? No, this was *over*. I was a hundred percent certain of that. It was a fucking mistake if I'd ever seen one and now it was over. Done, finished, soul sold to the sharp-toothed cunt in the first row.

I tossed the balled-up tissue into the wastebasket beside the bed. "What was that you'd said about only coming once?"

She reached out to swat me for that but caught a stray pillow instead. "Shut up, Stremmel."

"That *is* what you said though. That you can only get there once." I was being a dickhead. I knew that. It never escaped my notice when I was behaving like a complete and total miscreant. Stopping myself when I'd stumbled down this path was often the issue. It was easier to drop dead than it was to shut myself up once I'd started. "It seems I proved you wrong."

"I think you should leave," she mumbled into the pillow.

I turned my head in her direction. I couldn't see her face but fuck, her body really was amazing. I reached down, grabbed her ass. "That's probably a good idea."

"Then what are you doing?"

"Don't know," I murmured. "I guess I just like making the most of my bad decisions."

Sara pushed up from the mattress, shaking off my hand. Her back to me, she tossed her hair, saying, "Don't be here when I get back."

I watched her walk to the adjoining bathroom on legs she was pretending weren't shaking. The lock clicked behind her then the faucet turned on. The walls were thin enough for me to hear her slap her hands against the sink and blow out a breath.

After a minute of willing my limbs to work, I started hunting for my clothes. I had to perch on the corner of her bed to step into my boxers and trousers to save myself from wobbling straight into a wall. My shirt was wrecked though I couldn't help admiring the wreck. Tiny tornado struck again.

I located one shoe, then the other, and took a moment to study Sara's apartment as I stepped into them. It was different than when Hartshorn lived here. The walls were a fresh new color, the kitchen cabinets spruced up, the furniture in pale pinks, yellows, and blues with lots of deep teal velvet. A woman lived here now and it showed.

I patted my pockets to confirm I had all the devices I'd entered with—god help me if I had to come back here tonight for my phone—and noticed an open shelf lined with glasses beside the kitchen sink. There was nothing special about these glasses. They matched the rest of Sara's pastel-y stuff—all rose quartz pink, watery blue, sunny yellow, mint green—and I wouldn't have cared but I couldn't reconcile that badass bulldozer of a woman drinking out of a princess pink glass.

For no good reason at all, I shuffled into the kitchen and picked up one of those glasses. It was adorable. It really was. But Sara wasn't adorable. She was…fuck, she was a cutthroat queen. She'd kill me and anyone else standing in her way, and, in a very sex-fogged way, I appreciated that about her. Even if it was a giant pain in my ass.

Since I was already holding it, I held the glass under the tap and filled it. It only took a moment to return to Sara's room and set it on the bedside table. I paused near the bathroom door. There were no appropriate parting words for this situation—the *oops I just fucked the woman I hate and yes, I do have to slog through two months of conflict resolution sessions with her* situation—but I couldn't get out of the gravitational pull of this moment until I forced myself out of it.

"Lock the door, okay?"

She gave one of those short, huffy sighs, the ones smothered in annoyance and eye rolls. Then, "Shut up."

I was an expert in nothing but that sounded to me like "Yeah, babe, it was great for me too."

I stumbled out into the foyer, my shirt hanging open and my jacket in a ball under my arm. This place looked different. Also, my legs felt about as solid as gravy. Walking more than a few steps at a time was rough. Also, concerning. It wasn't like this the last time I'd had sex. It was never like this. What kind of sorcery was she keeping in that cunt?

I started for the stairs but the front door buzzer stopped me. Also, my brain was gravy. It was safe to say that gravy had replaced the internal contents of my body.

I crossed to the door, realizing as I turned the bolt that it was the delivery person with the burrito bowl I'd ordered in a previous life, one where I hadn't fucked a woman I wanted as much as I wanted to strangle her.

And it went both ways because she'd taken my cock like she owned it, but there'd been more than a few moments when she'd looked at me like she was debating whether it would be difficult to dispose of my body. She hated me more than anyone else had ever hated me and I had a bit of experience with being everyone's least favorite person.

I accepted my order and waved to the delivery person as I retreated into the scene of the crime. I couldn't see this space without remembering everything, but the one thing that elbowed out the rest was the beat of her pulse against my thumb.

I stared at her door for a minute or two. I wasn't sure how long it was, on account of the gravy and all.

What the fuck had happened here tonight? And what the fuck happened now?

CHAPTER 7

SARA

Alex: My sister-in-law and I are going out for pedicures tonight. Want to come along?

Alex: I know you don't love the huge group outing thing but it's just me and Andy this time. I'm sure you remember her. I brought you to her holiday party. We also went to the farmers market with her in the summer. She's your vibe, you like her.

Alex: I just checked the board and I'm not seeing you scheduled for any ORs...

Alex: Okay, well, I'm just going to assume you're at yoga or out somewhere, or something. If you see this later and decide you want to meet up, shoot me a text. We're probably going to stop at a new spot Andy's been telling me about in the Seaport for some drinks and nibbles after.

Alex: Oh, shit, I forgot this is the day you have your meetings with Stremmel for the conflict stuff. That's why you're not on the board and not responding to texts. Sorry! My bad.

Alex: If you need to decompress from that, here's the address of the restaurant. Just so you know, it's not super busy here. Not loud at all. And we ordered the entire appetizer menu, so there's food for 8 regular people or 2-3 hungry girls.

Alex: Just give me some sign of life, okay? Or proof you and Stremmel haven't been arrested. Either one.

Sara: Sorry! I'm so sorry! I'm alive and not under arrest.

Alex: Phew. I was getting ready to call Hartshorn for bail money.

Sara: Why Hartshorn?

Alex: Why not? He can afford it.

Sara: You're probably right.

Alex: I know I'm right. Now that you're alive, do you want to join us? I would love a dramatic reenactment of today's events.

Sara: I don't know if today's events are fit for a drinks-and-apps discussion.

Alex: There's nothing you can't say over drinks and apps. I swear it.

Sara: While that may be true…

Alex: You're right. It's not cool. You're also a million times more mature than me so congratulations on that.

Sara: Not sure about that, my friend.

Alex: Believe me, you are the mature, sophisticated one here. I'm the one who crammed half a room-temp barbecue ranch pizza into her mouth before surgery at 5 a.m., is going to dry shampoo herself bald sooner or later, and wants to cackle with you over the stupid punishment you're enduring with Stremmel.

Sara: Well…I have a few questionable decisions of my own.

Alex: Name one.

Sara: Sebastian Stremmel.

Alex: I snorted. I actually snorted.

Sara: I bet.

Alex: There's liquor in my nose. Thanks.

Sara: Enjoy your drinks and apps. Say hi to Andy for me. I have to put myself back together now.

Alex: You're funny. You know that? You're really fucking funny, Shap.

Sara: That's a strange way of pronouncing self-destructive.

Alex: You are not self-destructive! You are fierce! You are a fucking badass surgeon and you take zero shit from the shit sellers!

Sara: Except on the occasions when I take all their shit and can't even stop myself from enjoying it.

Alex: I know you and I know you don't do that! What are you even talking about? Heresy, that's what this is.

Sara: Honey, are you in the OR tomorrow? Because this might be the time to switch over to water if you are.

Alex: Nope!

Sara: Carry on, then.

CHAPTER 8

SARA

I WAS AN EXPERT AT PRETENDING NOTHING WAS WRONG. IT WAS my oldest and most convincing trick. Nothing out of the ordinary, nothing to see here. Definitely no catastrophic sex mistakes.

Nope. None of that.

After a full—and blessedly distracting—morning of surgery, I finally had a break and wanted to use this time to walk the Thoreau Path in the West End neighborhood that bracketed the hospital complex. I felt better when I went outside and put my face in front of the sun every day. Even better if I burned off some nervous energy in the process. It wouldn't erase any of yesterday's catastrophes but it would help chase away the worst-case scenarios chilling out in the forefront of my mind.

I headed for the stairwell at the far end of the wing, the one no one else used because it dead-ended on the second floor and required a journey past a bunch of offices to reach an actual exit.

Glancing at the notifications on my phone as I descended the stairs, I didn't realize until too late that I wasn't alone.

Sebastian didn't notice me right away, and it was a good thing because I needed a second to fortify myself. He was wearing another set of near-death scrubs and that annoyed me for no good reason. I mean, did he have to be a rain cloud all the time? And again with the forearms. Really. This was becoming flagrant. It was like he wanted me staring.

He probably relished the attention. *Look, ladies and gentlemen, look at these arms! They can flip you on your belly and fuck you from behind before you can say yes, please.*

We reached the landing at almost the same time and it was hilarious to watch as recognition slackened the permafrost of his scowl.

I had no intention of stopping to chat with him—as if there was anything to chat about. *Oh, yes, you're right, you are the* only *person to give me an orgasm without prolonged and significant attention to my clit. And two of them! So good of you to remind me.*

As if Sebastian had exactly that discussion in mind, he reached for the railings on either side of the stairs and trapped me on the landing. I could've retreated up the stairs so I wasn't truly trapped but the gesture made his prerogative plain.

"There you are." He managed to sound exasperated as he said this, as if I'd been avoiding him.

Obviously, that was not the case. I merely left my apartment two hours earlier than usual to take a yoga class in the Back Bay before work and bypassed the attending surgeons' lounge entirely when I arrived at the hospital. No avoidance to be found.

"Here I am." I gestured down the stairs. "There, I am going."

"Wait just a minute." He winced before dragging a glance

up from my sneakers to settle on my plain hospital-issued scrub v-neck. "No wordy t-shirt today?"

I shook my head. No t-shirt today because I never went to yoga before work, and I failed to bring the right clothes in my haste to get out the door. "Evidently."

The frown dissolved into his usual scowl, and there was a second where he loomed over me, his thick, roped arms stretched out and his jaw scruffier than ever, where he seemed to be staring at my mouth.

But then he ruined it by speaking.

"Listen, about last night—"

"You don't have to finish that sentence," I said.

"—obviously, it happened and—"

"Really, you don't need to do this," I said.

"—I don't want there to be anything awkward between us. Anything more awkward—"

"Oh my god," I muttered.

"—but I need you to know I'm not looking for anything. Anything serious. Anything at all, actually. I'm not interested in repeating—"

"Wow. *Wow*."

"—and I hope you can understand."

I blinked up at him, shocked but also a bit impressed by his ability to cram that much destruction into a couple of minutes. It was remarkable in its messiness. I almost admired it, as someone who was also known to engage in tragic messiness—*not* as the woman with whom he was making the mess.

"Okay. About that." I wiggled a hand in his direction. "I just need *you* to know that I have neither the desire nor the expectation of ever"—I dropped a repulsed glance at his scrub pants to guarantee no misunderstanding—"enduring that again."

"*Enduring*? I'm pretty sure you did better than endure it."

"Whatever gets you through the night," I replied. "If it were up to me, we'd never cross paths again, let alone —*ahem*." Another below-the-waist glance. "As far as I'm concerned, it's already forgotten. Hell, it wouldn't have crossed my mind once today if you hadn't brought it up, but since you did, we can agree it's best left in the past. Okay? All right. I'm on my way out so I'd love it if you could scoot aside."

He shifted to lean back against the stairwell wall. "You— what?" he called.

"Yeah, I'm heading out."

"Where?" he growled.

The balls on this guy. The epic, arrogant, presumptuous balls. He wasn't looking for anything serious—as if any guy who pinched pussies in a hallway was teed up for serious— yet here he was, badgering me about going for a walk.

Yeah, like I needed serious with that maniac.

His scowl faltered and with it went the cornerstone of my confidence. I could play this game so long as we stayed in the roles we'd assigned each other. I couldn't do it if he wasn't going to hold up his end of the bargain. I *couldn't*. If I let go for even a minute, I'd have to reckon with the reality that I'd had wild, filthy, *satisfying* sex with a man I despised on an exhaustive, thorough level.

With my neighbor.

With my colleague.

With my cellmate for the next six weeks of conflict resolution counseling.

And it had been so good, I couldn't really think about it

because it made me angry to know I'd wasted decades of my life on trash sex. I'd convinced myself that I couldn't get out of my head enough to find sex pleasurable and that it was a *me* problem, not a partner problem.

Yet all along, Sebastian with the good dick was living upstairs and working down the hall and busy being the moodiest, most antagonistic asshole in the world.

No, I couldn't think about any of this, and there was no way he could stop playing the game. If he did, I'd have to acknowledge that he'd touched every last inch of me, even the places I'd just stopped hating and didn't know how to love yet—and I didn't have time for that kind of work today. Probably not tomorrow either.

I motioned for him to say something, to give me a single reason to explain myself to him. He stared at me for a long, crackling moment before blinking away with a shrug. "Fine. Go. Whatever."

"Good talk," I called to him. "It definitely didn't sound rehearsed. Well done, Stremmel."

From two flights above, I heard him laugh. Then, "Shut up, Shap."

CHAPTER 9

SEBASTIAN

DESPITE ALL QUIRKS TO THE CONTRARY, I DID NOT HAVE A death wish.

I wasn't depressed either, though I'd been evaluated more times than I could count, especially during my emo-goth phase in high school. On more than one occasion, my mother had dragged me into the pediatrician's office, waved at my skintight, safety-pin-studded black jeans, my dress-code-violating black eyeliner, and the hair I insisted on wearing long and in front of my eyes, and begged the doctor to explain how any of that was okay. Each time, the doctor told my mother I was all right. She also explained that "all right" could be a lot weird.

By the time I left for college, I'd been evaluated for *every-thing*. I could ramble off the depression and mood disorder screening questions by heart. For a minute, I contemplated going into psychiatry because it seemed like I already knew the drill.

That said, I did spend the entirety of my twenties and a good portion of my thirties unpacking a storage unit full of deadbeat dad drama in therapy.

I wasn't depressed. Not anxious. I just lived with a simmering cauldron of rage and contempt for the assholes and idiots of the world, and that took up a lot of my time.

Despite my comments in our first conflict resolution session, I did have feelings. A whole fucking lot of them. So many that I had to be selective about the ones I'd let in on any given day. If I wasn't careful, I'd find myself consumed by feeling everything, all the damn time.

I wouldn't be as generous as to say I'd made peace with the fact my father fucked off when my sister Vivi and I were toddlers, or how he left my mother without child support or any means of providing for us. I'd never forgive him for the years of my life that I spent watching my mother panic-sweat her way from paycheck to paycheck, working two and three jobs to keep a roof over our heads and crying over registration forms for soccer leagues and summer camps because there was no way in hell she could afford that.

More than leaving us penniless, he discarded us like a bunch of dented cans of soup.

Except for when my mother remarried a guy with deep, real estate investor pockets and my dad *had* to take her to court for joint custody. Not that he'd bothered to seek us out at any point between the ages of three and seventeen. Not that he ever showed up for his legally guaranteed weekends with us. Not that he showed up at all, not until more than another decade had passed.

He showed up when Vivi was promoted to head of media relations at the University of Florida and he needed tickets to the Gators' home games.

And the time when I graduated from medical school and he had an investment opportunity to pitch to my friends.

It was funny how those "opportunities" came up every

few years. There'd never been an opportunity to acknowl-edge my birthday, never an opportunity to show up when we were kids, but now that we had access to SEC football tickets and friends with money to blow, the opportunities were endless.

Vivi was the strong one of us. She blocked his number after he called her a spoiled bitch for refusing to cough up a block of tickets, and when he showed up at the stadium demanding them anyway, she had a restraining order filed against him. Vivi didn't take any shit and she'd make it rain fire if you tried her.

He didn't hit me up too often, but I took the call if I was in the mood to be an antagonistic prick. So, most of the time. Whenever he wanted money, I sang a song of poor doctors crushed under their student loans. That hadn't applied to me in years, but he didn't have to know that.

Those simmering cauldrons. We all had them. The only difference between me and Vivi or anyone else was I wore mine on my face and I didn't give a fuck if anyone had a problem with it.

I didn't know whether the cauldron had come first or my fuck shortage. That didn't really matter to me. It was this dented soup can situation that woke me up before my alarm and haunted me like a ghost too curious for its own good, always swirling around my shoulders and asking whether I kept that cauldron on my face to distract everyone from the dents I hadn't been able to emo-goth or therapy or work or growl away.

CHAPTER 10

SARA

"We'll be on the floor today," Milana announced when I stepped into her office. She gestured to the coffee table and the space she'd cleared around it. "You know how I feel about play."

"Can't forget," Sebastian muttered from his usual post at the bookshelves.

He was too busy paging through a book to acknowledge me.

It was a game in which we'd become elite players over the last week. There was no avoiding our apartment or the surgical wing but we could turn five hundred percent of our attention to reading a fire exit map, checking a pager and then marching in the opposite direction, tying a shoelace, frowning *aggressively* at phones, even staring at the sky when all else failed.

For a game predicated on actively ignoring each other, it came with the consequence of extreme awareness of that person's presence. I didn't have to see him to sense him, and I wasn't sure how I felt about that. Was it a skill? Some kind of defense mechanism honed from weeks of stress and bad choices? Or was my blood thrumming with an unquenched desire to win, even when winning led to only a moment of smug satisfaction and the start of another go-round of this game?

I sat cross-legged in front of the table and opened the zip pouch of trail mix I'd brought along. My white coat took some unfortunate hits this morning and it was off to the laundry, leaving me to rely on the saddlebag pockets of my scrub pants. This was not preferrable for many reasons but it would have to do in this pinch. A girl needed her snacks.

"Sebastian, if you'd join us," Milana said. She sat on an orange footstool, her arms folded on her knees and an expectant smile on her face as she watched him.

Not that I noticed. I didn't care. All I knew was I had no intention of forfeiting this round.

I dug into my trail mix while Sebastian took his sweet, scowly time crossing the room. His legs came into view first, clad in the same bruised blue scrubs as always. He eased himself down to the floor, sighing and huffing the whole way. He didn't even apologize when his huge knobby knee jostled the table.

"I have a puzzle for you today," Milana said, pointing her clasped hands at the table. "It's a special one, as you'll see, that I save for special friends."

"There's nothing on these pieces," Sebastian said. "It's a blank puzzle? That's the trick?"

"They are not blank," she said, flipping one piece over to reveal shades of green and yellow. "But we aren't relying on the colors today. We're using more subtle cues. We're using nuances."

"Fantastic," Sebastian murmured.

Since I was deeply committed to winning this round, I

wasted no time in organizing the pieces closest to me. If we were smart—recent events really challenged that premise—we'd divide this puzzle up and not breathe a word to each other because we'd sooner flip this table than engage in the activity harmoniously.

Whether Sebastian had the same idea or he was content following my lead, I did not know, but I accepted the quiet that enveloped us just the same. It was the first time I'd downshifted from high-alert defensive mode inside this office. Maybe Milana was right. Maybe we were making progress all this time.

If she was right, how was I supposed to explain everything that'd happened outside this office?

Sebastian pinched a puzzle piece away from me. "The perimeter is the priority."

"There can be multiple, simultaneous priorities." Without meeting his gaze, I snatched the piece back.

Still winning. I had to win. After the stairwell, I needed this win. I'd strangle him before I let him take this round.

...*said the nearly forty-year-old woman who'd once possessed interests and hobbies separate from hating a man purely because he bothered her.*

"It would be more efficient to focus on the perimeter and then work our way in," he countered.

He sounded more exasperated than usual. I had to fight off a grin. His exasperation was like candy. It was terrible for me but that in no way minimized the fun of it.

I didn't respond, instead trying to make progress with a small group of pieces and steadily feeding myself nuts and dried fruit.

From the corner of my eye, I noticed Milana shift on her stool every few minutes. Clasping and unclasping her hands. She didn't know what to do with us when we weren't trying to kill each other with soft toys.

"It would be faster if you cooperated with me," he said.

I shrugged. "It would be faster if you stopped interrupting to tell me how to go faster."

He dropped the piece he'd been walking between his thumb and index finger. I couldn't be sure since I was still doing the averted eyes thing but it felt like he was staring at me. He could stare all he wanted. I had plenty of nondescript gray pieces to occupy me, their ins and outs blurring into an unending monologue of "Do you fit? What about you? Does this work? Does anything fit? Do you even belong in the same box or is that the gag here—that nothing goes together?"

I could do this all day. If I dissociated from the setting and the large, growly man across from me, the one who'd abandoned all pretense of working on the puzzle since I wouldn't follow his rules, I could find some zen in the repetitive motion of putting it all together. It was like those adult coloring books I'd hoarded a few years ago in the hopes of chasing away the constant squabbling in my head. My perfectionism had really struggled with getting the coloring *just right* and I'd realized I didn't like coloring but, for a brief time, the act was enough to draw me away from my stress and my worries.

A growl sounded from the other side of the table. "Could you—"

"Probably not, no."

"If you'd just listen to—"

"But I'm not going to," I replied. "Accept that I am doing it this way, even if your way is better, quicker, more nutrient dense, peer reviewed, and morally righteous. I've made my choice."

I joined several pieces together and tapped the gray surface to congratulate myself on making progress under these conditions. But then I noticed Sebastian had most of the perimeter complete.

Because I couldn't help myself, I gestured to the shell he'd constructed. "What's the point of harassing me into helping you when you don't need any help? Is it about compliance for you? You're hell-bent on getting me to obey?"

Sebastian sucked in a breath and I countered that with a petulant shrug-head-shake combo that I never would've risked as a teenager. He resumed his silent staring and I continued hunting for pieces to fit somewhere on the segment I'd started.

I figured we were running out the clock on this session—which was perfectly acceptable—but then he crossed his arms over his chest. In such close quarters, I couldn't help but hear the rustle of crisp fabric against warm skin and it threw me back to that night. To him stretched over me. To clothes and sheets everywhere. To his beard on my skin, his mouth all over me. To his sounds. His words.

I blinked down at my pieces. My pulse was hammering and I could feel heat rising in my cheeks. My earlobes were hot. All I could do was dive into my snack bag and cram three almonds into my mouth. It would take me an age to chew them up into the tiny, tiny pieces necessary for me to digest them without disaster and that process would be more than enough to sap me of all sexy thoughts. Nothing was less sexy than the threat of triggering an irritable bowel.

I would've gotten away with my memories and the

hammering of my heart if he hadn't been watching me, waiting for me to trip up and forget the game.

"Shap," he said knowingly, "what the hell are you eating?"

Since I was very consumed with my almonds, I held up the bag by way of explanation. He snatched it away, his scowl all plucked and offended by my unconventional trail mix.

"What…what the *hell*, Shap? Nuts, *cereal*, what are these things? What is this? Dried pineapple?" He helped himself to a chunk of crystallized ginger and, if the disgust on his face was any indicator, immediately regretted it. "Fuckin' ginger, my god, why?" He reached for the bottle of water I'd abandoned on the sofa and chugged half the contents. "Oh, that's fucking awful." He peered into the bag again. "M&Ms, dried cranberries of all the god-awful things, raisins—"

"Help yourself to the raisins," I said, a hand over my mouth as I chewed the last bits of almond. "I don't do raisins."

Only when Sebastian leveled me with a steady gaze did I realize I'd forgotten the game. It had only required some perverse amusement over his reaction to the ginger and— poof. A round surrendered.

"Then why is this full of raisins?" He shook the bag.

"Because that's how the trail mix comes from the store and I don't have the patience to separate them out."

I'd bought the biggest bag available and then dumped it all into a storage container. Store packaging and nutrition labels made me twitchy, and I always wanted to add extra bits like cereal and ginger, or pretzels when I needed to keep it on the bland side.

Shaking the bag again, he said, "This isn't trail mix. It's the discard pile from the bulk bins at a health food store."

I grabbed for the bag but he held it out of reach. "Thanks for weighing in but your opinion is irrelevant."

He pushed to his feet and paced away from the table. "Are any of my opinions relevant to you? Ever?"

He stood facing the wall of bookshelves, his back to me. With his head cocked to the side, it seemed like he was reading the spines but I couldn't be sure. I couldn't pry any meaning from the depth and grooves of his scowl either.

"When it comes to what I eat? No." I glanced at Milana, urging her with my eyeballs to do something. Make him sit down. Make him finish the puzzle. Make him stay on topic and out of my personal life.

Her brows arched up and she held out *this is the process, trust the process* hands.

"You don't see me registering my opinions on your choices," I continued. "I don't care if you want to put the edges together first and I don't care if you hate dried cranberries. I happen to love them but I only eat, like, five every few days and I savor those five cranberries. I save them for last and I am not interested in hearing any noise about it. Is that all right with you, Dr. Stremmel?"

He rounded the coffee table and sat on the edge of the sofa. He held out the bag. "You have the weirdest snacks in the world. It's disturbing."

I looked into the bag. Four crinkly little cranberries sat on one side, the nuts and other bits on the other. The raisins were gone.

I jerked my head up, over to the bookshelves, searching and searching for some explanation. Then I noticed the wastebasket beside the shelves. He'd sorted out the raisins for me.

"Why?" It was just a whisper.

Sebastian gave a single shake of his head. His elbows were on his thighs, his gaze on the puzzle.

"Why?" I repeated.

His shoulders lifted in a great heave. "I was tired of watching you paw at that bag. Not the first time I've saved you from yourself. Not the first time you've instructed me to fuck off while doing it."

Did that make this the last time? Or just one in a series of next times?

"We are just about at the end of our time for today." Milana gently clapped her hands together and lavished a warm grin on the partially excavated puzzle. "For your homework this week—"

"Not unless we can agree on reducing the total number of sessions," Sebastian interrupted.

She shook her head, that warm grin unfazed. "I haven't made a decision on that yet." She passed each of us a half sheet of paper. "I'd like you to arrive at this location at seven on Sunday morning."

"Way to choose violence, Milana," he murmured. He sounded jocular, almost friendly. Like he teased people every day and he could do it without being a dickhead. "Will you be joining us on Sunday morning? It would be good of you to come along, don't you think? Or should I call you to let you know we've arrived at the location? At seven? On Sunday morning?"

"I trust you to handle this on your own, Sebastian."

She crossed to the door, holding it open in a clear signal for us to get the fuck out.

Sebastian was closest and exited without further discussion. He was halfway down the hall and moving at a pace that said he had places to be. The door to the stairwell banged behind him and I had to *fly* down the first set of stairs to catch up.

"Would you just slow down for a second?" My voice echoed off the cinderblock walls.

I reached for his elbow as he made the turn at the landing. Instead of stopping, he backed me against the wall, his fingers splayed over my hip, his thumb an inch or two away from locations deemed not safe for work.

He stared at me, his eyes dark and his scowl forcing his lips into a pout that was a dash too aggressive to be attractive and digging rivers and tributaries into his brow.

"Something you need, Shap?"

That thumb drew circles over my scrubs, around and around as we stared at each other. I'd followed him for a reason but I couldn't find it now. I couldn't find anything but the firm press of his fingers and the way my skin just melted in response. That was it—I *melted*. I was hot and soft and everything inside me felt pliable, like he could shape me any way he wanted and nothing about it could ever be wrong.

"Speak words, screech owl," he rumbled.

All I could come up with was a jerky shake of my head. Sebastian watched me through those ridiculous lashes, his scowl softening in microscopic increments as he studied me.

"Shap," he warned, bringing his other hand to the back of my neck. He stroked his fingers along my windpipe.

I sucked in a breath, ready to tell him this was the worst place to strangle me and also, what happened back there with the raisins and why was a single thumb destroying my ability to function in the most basic sense?

I would've said this. I really would have, but a snarl sounded in his throat and something was decided, something irrevocable, because he brushed his lips over mine and it was like unplugging a radio. The noise stopped, leaving only his irritable, hungry growls and our mingled breaths and the clomp of my heart.

I locked my arms around his neck and climbed him like a flood was about to carry me away. There was no way of knowing whether that was my best or worst moment to date. It could've gone either way but now I knew how that pout tasted.

That counted for something, even if this was a slow-falling tragedy in action. He kissed his way along my jaw and down my throat to tuck a finger under the neck of my t-shirt. "This shirt," he growled, "is fucking perfect."

I had to force my eyes open and blink down at my chest. I didn't know which shirt I was wearing any more than I knew what the hell was happening between us or why I found it necessary to wrap my legs around his trim waist.

"'Heal with cold steel,'" he read, tracing a finger over the pair of scalpels crossed under a skull. "Love it." He dropped a kiss to my sternal notch. "Where do you get these shirts?"

As if there was any confusion about which shirts he was referring to, he ran a hand over my breasts, bunching the cotton in his fist as he kissed me again.

"Why do you want to know?"

"So I can stop thinking about it."

He sighed against my lips though I knew immediately it wasn't one of his usual sighs of aggravation. No, this sigh was laced with misery, with pain.

I was a second away from attending to all that misery before a door slammed a few flights above. We jolted apart as if we'd been stunned, scattering to opposite corners of the landing. I swallowed up a heavy blink of Sebastian adjusting himself before I whirled around to face the wall.

I managed two shuddering gasps before his hands landed on my shoulders. "I'm sorry," he said softly.

"For what?" I tried to straighten my shirt but my hands didn't work anymore.

He breathed a sigh as shaky as I felt. "Fuck if I know but—"

"Just stop. Okay? That's what I want. I want this to stop and"—I rubbed my temples against the sudden onslaught of competing thoughts—"this isn't happening. It's *not*."

His hands fell from my shoulders. The second he was gone, I wanted him back. "Message received."

I heard him back up and then jog down to the next level. His hands connected with the door, the hinges squealing. I pressed my fingertips to my lips. My body was shaking from the inside out. I hadn't felt this torn and out of control in a decade. Maybe longer. I didn't know how to fix it but I knew I had to.

We couldn't keep doing this.

CHAPTER 11

SEBASTIAN

Fuck my life.

No, seriously, just fuck my whole life.

I couldn't go another round with Sara. Not tonight, not this weekend, not ever. I was not capable of managing all the things she stirred up inside me while also being a semifunctional adult. I could do Sara or I could do life, but definitely not both.

Most of the time, I wanted to wrap my hands around her throat. That I wanted to do this while fucking her didn't improve the situation.

Since I couldn't cope with another hallway encounter right now, I ducked out of the hospital early and avoided the apartment building altogether. After a subway ride into Cambridge and a short walk from the station, I was standing on Nick's doorstep.

I'd texted him on the way so this wasn't a completely unannounced demand for food and shelter but I accepted his barely tolerant stare with a shrug.

"If you don't want people coming over, you shouldn't be so welcoming," I said.

He shut the door behind me, saying, "Somehow I doubt that's the issue."

I followed him into the kitchen where his wife Erin was seated at the long farmhouse table with her laptop and a pile of folders. She patted the empty spot beside her. "Who's bothering you today, Sebastian?"

I dropped down into the chair and rested my head on my upturned palm. "Everyone."

It was the only answer I had available. I couldn't tell her about my very blonde, very bratty catastrophe. Not unless I wanted to see Nick blow his top, which he would, because this was the stupid kind of catastrophe I should've known better than to run straight into with open arms.

She nodded. "That tracks."

I gestured to her screen. "What's new in geological climate science?"

"Old rocks, new data. Same shit, different day, you know?" She closed her laptop. "You look tired."

"Thanks. You're a good friend to insult me to my face." I glanced at Nick. He was busy moving around the kitchen, a dish towel draped over his shoulder and a bottle of beer within arm's reach. "Group therapy is exhausting."

"Probably because you're not allowed to get away with all your bullshit," Nick said. "And believe me, I'm fuckin' thrilled it's Shap calling you on it."

"Why?"

"Because she's this sweet little thing—"

"There is *nothing* sweet about her," I said.

"—and you hulk around like fuckin' Dracula—"

"Okay now that's just ridiculous. I have a great tan." I shoved up my sleeves and presented my arms as evidence.

"See? I blink at the sun and I look like this for the year. Nothing pale. Nothing shimmery. Not a vampire."

Acevedo gave me a flat stare.

"You do have a tendency to hulk around, though it reads more as Edgar Allan Poe and his raven to me than vampire," Erin said. "I think we're focusing more on vibe than skin tone, you know?"

"If you say so," I replied.

Erin had a way of staring at people and seeing into the stitching of their souls. She could flip through a mind like it was a book written in a language only she spoke and she did it in a manner that left you thanking her profusely for the intrusion.

"I know it's not the therapy aspect that bothers you," she mused, giving me a narrowed study through her tortoise-rimmed glasses.

She was right about that. I'd been through plenty of therapy. One of the many things Erin and I had in common. Another thing—we were both fucked-up kids living in adult bodies and pretending we had any clue what we were doing.

"Although it's therapy with a person you don't know very well but have had difficult interactions with so I guess that could be tough," she went on. "What's happening in your sessions?"

"We had to put a jigsaw puzzle together using only the cardboard side of the pieces." I ran a hand through my hair. "Last week, we had to juggle."

"Juggle? Like"—she bounced her hands in front of her —"juggling juggle?"

I blew out a miserable sigh. "We had to talk while we tossed things back and forth. It got a little out of hand."

Erin nodded slowly. "That seems to be happening a lot these days. How's Sara doing?"

"How the hell should I know?" I asked with way, *way* too much firepower.

"Remember who you're talking to," Nick warned. "If you're a dickhead to my wife, I'm sending you home without dinner."

Erin shot an amused grin in her husband's direction. "You know I can handle this, right?"

I didn't even care that I was an object in need of handling. Didn't have a single fuck to give, because my whole life was fucked. Sara was everywhere. At work, in my building, with my friends, inside my head, everywhere. And now I knew what she felt like. How she tasted. How she fell apart for me.

The only answer was avoidance yet I was expected to see her this weekend and—what? Not kill her the second she opened her mouth? Not kiss her simply to shut her up? Not touch her just to prove to myself she wasn't as good as the memories?

"Speaking of Sara," Erin said, "I need you to do something for me."

I rubbed my eyes because that could not be right. I was hallucinating—and I was cool with that. Far better than my present helping of reality.

"Anything," I murmured from behind my hands.

"We are having a little get-together in a few weeks," she started with a glance toward Nick.

"I have some new residents," he explained.

"This is what I'm saying. You're too welcoming. You two need to knock this shit off before you're overrun with strays and charity cases."

"Such as yourself?" he asked.

"No! I'm a friend of the family," I replied.

"That's such a funny way of saying you've hit on half of my sisters-in-law and selected my wife as your emotional support geologist."

I was an asshole. We knew this.

"I haven't hit on anyone *recently*," I argued.

"Facts are facts, Stremmel," he called.

"Back to the dinner party," Erin said with a laugh. "We have the new residents and a friend of mine from Oxford is coming into town as well. He's taking a visiting professor post at Harvard."

"Sounds great," I said. "Are we having barbecue or tacos?"

"We," Nick repeated. "This fuckin' guy. When did we adopt you?"

"Tacos," Erin said.

"Excellent," I replied. Acevedo was a boss when it came to Tex-Mex. "So, what do you need from me?"

Erin grinned. "Get Sara to come."

The restraint that it took me to keep from saying *I already have—twice*—almost gave me a hernia. I pressed my fist to my mouth because I didn't trust myself *at all* right now.

Erin continued on, seemingly oblivious to the alarms blasting in my head. "She's only been here a few times and it's always been with a big group, like when we said goodbye to the intern class and Alex's birthday, and she's never been available for any of our smaller dinners. Nick says she's shy and—"

"That is inaccurate," I said from behind my fist. I stood, stalked to the fridge in search of something to occupy my mouth. "The last thing Shapiro could ever be is shy. You're reading that one all wrong, Acevedo."

"Please," he said, holding his arms out. "Simply because she's not afraid of you doesn't mean she's not also shy."

I peered at him as I popped the top off a beer bottle. "Everything you just said is wrong."

Nick rubbed a hand down his face. "For someone who spends so much time thinking about himself, your self-awareness could use work." He pointed at a dish on the stove. "Make yourself useful, would you? Stir this."

"Promise me you'll ask her," Erin said. "Alex is working on it too. I hope that doesn't overwhelm her too much."

I took a long pull from my beer to keep from commenting on that. The Sara I knew was physically immune to any form of overwhelm. If anything, she lived in a continually under-whelmed state. There was a good chance I could rail her straight through a wall and she'd find a way to be unimpressed.

"Please?" Erin prompted.

I blinked at her. "What?"

"Ask Sara to come and do it nicely," Erin said.

"If anyone's doing the asking, it's her," I murmured. "And I'm not going to be nice about getting her there."

Nick glanced at me with alarm as he poured Erin a glass of wine. "What the hell did you just say?"

"Nothing. Nothing." I went back to stirring in earnest. "You should know she doesn't respond to nice."

"Listen," Nick said with a sigh. "You're the one spending all this time with her, albeit employer-mandated time. We'd like to see more of her outside work—"

I chugged my beer to keep my thoughts away from how much I'd seen of her.

"—and for reasons only my wife understands, we're asking you to convince our likely shy, definitely introverted colleague to attend our next gathering."

I swung a glance between them. "This feels like a punishment. Should I have brought some beer with me? Wine? I'll bring both next time."

"It's not a punishment," Erin said. "I really want her to meet Malakai."

"You—*what*?"

"Malakai Ford," she said. "He's the friend from Oxford. He's taking a visiting professorship and I think they could really hit it off."

"They could—" I turned to face Nick while violently waving in Erin's direction. "What the hell?"

He gave a weary shake of his head. "I don't know, man. Erin thinks they might like each other."

"Aren't we a little old to be fixing people up?" I asked.

Erin rested her chin in her laced fingers, a pleased grin on her face. "Maybe you are but I'm not."

"Walked right into that one," Acevedo muttered.

"You're the cradle robber," I said to him. "But listen. We can't be serious about setting Shap up with this guy. Schemes like this, they always backfire."

That sounded legit. It sounded like something a well-adjusted adult would say. Yeah, I was getting away with talking them out of this. They'd see reason. These two, they were smart. They wouldn't go through with this.

"They never work out for *you*," Erin said. "Mostly because you set your sights on people who are off-limits, like my sister Shannon. Like my sister-in-law Andy. Like my other sister-in-law Alex."

"Yes, I'm an asshole of great renown," I said. "Anyway. I don't want you setting up Shap. It's not going to end well."

"Who are you concerned about here?" Nick asked.

"I—I am simply stating," I said, more or less hiccuping out these words, "that your residents don't need to see Shap bag and tag a professor who is undoubtedly too delicate for the likes of a surgeon who *chose* to work on burns and wounds."

"We're not arranging any marriages here, Sebastian. I just want her to come to the party and meet a friend. What happens after that is out of my hands." When I didn't respond, she added, "If you really don't want to, it's fine. I'll just—"

"I'll do it," I grumbled. "Okay? I'll get her here."

Fuck my whole life.

CHAPTER 12

SEBASTIAN

EVEN THOUGH I WAS DUE AT THE HOSPITAL EARLY TOMORROW, I hung out with the Acevedos past my bedtime. There was no limit to the surgery stories Nick and I could share, especially when Erin set out a plate of tiny Portuguese custard pies from the bakery near her office. I also lingered longer than necessary because I couldn't chance another run-in with Sara.

By the time I emerged from the subway station, I was dead on my feet. I never stayed out this late anymore, definitely not without a midday nap for fortification, and it showed as I dragged my ass up Charles Street. And this weather sucked. My god. Late October was the worst. It was cold and windy all the time and everyone got excited about the fucking leaves. As if that would compensate for the scant bit of sunlight we saw each day.

This early winter bullshit was just as bad as real winter. The snow and ice were total misery but—

I jerked to a stop five feet from my building, my shoes frozen to the sidewalk as I found Sara staring at me with wide eyes. I could hear my pulse thrumming in my eardrums as we regarded each other for a long, tense moment. A gust of wind howled through the narrow alleyways between the buildings and sliced through every layer of my clothing. I squinted against the frigid air, saying, "Out a little late for a school night, don't you think?"

Her face twisted into a disgusted sneer. "Yeah, like I'm going to justify myself to you. Sure thing."

She reached into her pocket, taking out her hospital access card and lanyard with her keys. She was coming home from work. She'd been avoiding me as much as I'd been avoiding her.

There was a pleasant edge to that realization but it wore off fast, leaving me more annoyed than I'd been earlier.

I jogged up the short stone steps, saying, "Not everything is a battle, Shap. Learn to recognize that."

"Right," she called from behind me. "Let me grab my notebook so I can take life lessons from the guy who doesn't think he can learn anything from anyone."

I unlocked the outer door and then the door into the vestibule, not bothering to hold either for Sara because she didn't need my help with a damn thing.

"It's funny how you're hung up on me being inflexible when it sounds like you could learn a few things yourself. Lesson one: you don't have to scream at people all the time," I said.

The doors banged shut behind her, leaving us once again trapped in this reckless space where the walls seemed to curl inward and the dim light collapsed over us.

"I bet I should smile more. Right? That would help, wouldn't it? Smiling and nodding and letting the men tell me how irrelevant my specialty is to their work."

I whirled around to face her even though I should've

sprinted up the stairs and barricaded myself in my apartment. Stepped closer. "You know for a fucking fact that isn't true."

She held out a hand, but instead of using it to stop me, she curled it around the lapel of my coat. "And you know for a fucking fact you're guilty of exactly that so explain to me—"

Once again, I did not think.

I just shoved a hand into her hair and brought her mouth to mine. It took all of a second for her to grab the front of my coat and jerk me closer. If I hadn't been busy getting drunk off the taste of her, I would've laughed because she could not stand to lose the upper hand for a second. Not unless I drove her all the way out of her mind and obliterated any question as to who was in control.

And I hated that I knew this about her. I didn't want to walk around knowing how to push the right buttons so she could be *here* and not running in the eighty-five different directions in her mind. I didn't need to know anything about her buttons or her mind or—oh, fuck, I just wanted her out of these clothes. That was it. That was all I cared about.

I pushed her bag off her shoulder, pulled open her coat, pressed her spine to the panel of her door. "You're not so terrible when you shut up for a second," I said into her neck.

"If you're expecting some kind of reciprocal concession, you've come to the wrong place."

I ran a hand down the plump length of her thigh until I reached her knee, and hitched her leg high on my hip. I rocked against her center, my shaft ready to tear through my trousers.

Here we go for another round with my favorite mistake.

To her strangled moan, I said, "I think I'm in the right place."

She dropped her chin to her chest as another breath rushed out of her. "Your arrogance is suffocating."

I closed my hand over hers, prying the keys from her fingers. "Am I opening this door, Shap? Or am I taking my smugness"—I ground against her for some cruel emphasis —"home?"

"I prefer to be alone." She bowed toward me every time I rocked against her, as I stole and sucked and bit her lips.

I dragged the key ring over the tight bud of her nip, back and forth in a lazy rhythm. "I'm sure you do. It must be damn hard to find anyone who can even scrape the bottom of your exacting standards. But I think you like being alone with me."

"I can't decide if you're an idiot or a jackass," she mused.

I caught that nipple between my fingers and gave it a rough twist. "Why not both?"

"You're not that self-destructive."

I dipped my head to meet her gaze. "What the fuck does this look like to you?"

She blinked away but tugged hard on my coat, keeping me close. "We can't keep doing this."

I stole her lips again, kissing her hard and a little mean. She was right but I didn't want to stop. Not yet.

"Just this once," she whispered. "This is the last time."

"Good. I can't wait to get rid of you."

She slid her hand down my chest, over my torso, and past my belt to grip my cock through my trousers. "I despise you."

"All I want is to get you out of my system once and for all, tiny tornado."

Finally, she lifted her gaze to mine, her eyes narrowed. She went on stroking me while I teased her nipple and I knew we could do this all night. We could torture each other until time ran out—which wasn't even the most perverse part of this. It was that I craved this fucked-up hall foreplay and everything that followed it as much as I resented it.

She gave me a deep, firm squeeze that brought stars to my eyes and crushed the last of my good sense. "Open the door, Stremmel."

I knew where I was going this time. One less thing to worry about while I licked her neck and died at the feel of her under my hands. We stumbled into her dark bedroom and didn't bother with the lights as we lost our coats and shoes. As soon as I had her naked, I pushed her down to the bed. I shrugged out of my clothes, stopping only to point to my shirt. "I'm not letting you rip this one."

"Why are you still talking?"

Sara scooted back on her elbows, pressed her knees together as if we were polite people who had gentle, timid sex and spoke loving words to each other in the process. It was funny. "What the fuck are you doing?" I reached for her leg, gave it a rough squeeze. "What do you think there is to hide from me?"

"You really need to stop talking. It's much less effective than you imagine it is."

She glared up at the ceiling while I opened the drawer for a condom. In addition to the assortment of bottles and hair junk, I found a hot pink vibrator. "We are going to have fun with this." I tossed it to the bed and—though it made zero sense—she jumped halfway out of her skin in response. "What the fuck. Get back here."

"I do not have to share my toys with you," she replied in

the most prim, crisp tone ever. If she wasn't naked, she'd be smoothing a skirt.

I reached for her ankle, towed her to this side of the bed. She flailed and yelped. It was adorable in a very *get back in the cave, woman* way. "Didn't anyone tell you? It's more fun when you share."

"Then get up here and share that cock with me," she demanded. "Maybe then I'll let you play with my toys."

"Oh my fucking god, woman." I climbed over her and kissed my way from her forehead to her belly button. My cock was hot on her thigh when I reached for her hand and curled it around me. "Do your part," I ordered. "It works out well for you, remember?"

"Sorry, no, I've scrubbed it from memory." She said this with a sadistic grin that cranked my engine all the way up. I didn't want to like it. Hell, I honestly and truly disliked her. But that grin and the magical way she twisted her fist around the head of my cock, it brought to light an uncomfortable closeness between good and evil.

"This is for me," I said, my fingers finding the wet between her thighs.

"No, it's for *me*," she fired back. "That you happen to be involved is coincidental."

I pushed my fingers inside her. "You're addicted to my coincidences."

"You're such an asshole," she groaned as she tightened her hold on me. "It's a real tragedy that this fine piece of machinery came attached to you."

"Tragedies all around." I tossed the condom to her belly. "Take care of that."

She tossed it back. "It's your dick. Do it yourself."

"Oh my god," I muttered to myself, throwing it back and

hitting her square on the forehead. "I'm so tired of talking to you."

"Yeah, same. When are you going to shut up?"

I settled on my belly, my shaft drilling into the mattress, and shoved her legs apart. "Right now."

She cried out when my tongue hit her clit and I appreciated the enthusiasm. It made a difference in my technique and I didn't mind admitting that. Also positive—she dropped both knees to the mattress and shuddered when I got that pearl between my lips and sucked.

"Oh, fuck," she gasped.

"See? It's not that hard to be nice. You should try it more often. Good things will happen to you, you little demon."

I grabbed the vibrator and switched it on. She tensed before I ran it down her seam, the muscles in her legs and abdomen shaking just enough to make me doubt this decision, but then she went there. She stumbled into that place where she didn't have to be a screech owl anymore and she could hate me while loving the things I did to her. And all of that gave me the freedom to give her all the things I knew we both required from this fucked-up game.

Not even a minute passed before she yanked a pillow over her face and screamed into it. The whole-body tremble followed and the sweetest rush of wet I'd ever tasted, and I mentally added a point to the scoreboard.

Not that I was counting.

Fuck that, I was totally counting. *Always* counting.

"Where's the condom?" she asked. "Give me the condom and get your dick up here now because I am not in the mood to wait and—"

"Yes, yes, you'll get what you want." I crawled up her body, careful to drag my beard over her belly, her breasts.

She writhed beneath me as I teased her, even *giggled* at one point. This woman giggled. Who would've guessed? "Why are you always in such an epic rush? Let yourself enjoy something for five minutes, would you?"

"Because it doesn't last so you have to hurry up," she said, patting the mattress for the condom.

I handed her the packet. "I'll make it last."

"It's extremely bold of you to assume you can outmaneuver my body but I've known it longer than you have."

I watched her frantic hands roll the condom down my shaft. "Yeah, that makes sense. I don't really know what I was talking about. I definitely didn't outmaneuver you into getting me suited up, did I?"

"Not the same," she huffed as I brought her ankle to my shoulder.

"Not even close." I gave her a crazy grin, the kind that said I couldn't be trusted with anything. It was the truth. I could not be trusted. I pushed inside her but then my brain shorted out and I had to press my mouth to her calf to keep from blurting out a whole slew of things that had no business between us here. "Why is your pussy as hot as the actual sun?"

I was in big trouble. Big fucking trouble. I'd constructed a belief system around the incident last week, effectively convincing myself it hadn't been as good as I remembered. It couldn't be. Nothing could be as good as those oppressive memories of her skin and her heat and her sounds. *Nothing.*

But that belief system was bullshit and I was in trouble because I couldn't stand this woman, though I'd fall apart right now if I couldn't have her again.

"I don't know but what the fuck are you doing to me?" She thrashed her head on the pillow, her hair flying around her in a wild cloud. I hooked her other leg around my waist, leaned down to swipe my tongue over a nipple in need of attention. "Your cock is going to rip me in half."

I snatched up the hand she had fisted over her mouth, set it on the back of my neck. "Would it kill you to put your hands on me? Goddamn, woman, get in the game."

"If I start touching you, I don't think I'm ever going to stop." She curled her fingers around my hair as I rocked into her, harder and harder with every tightening twist. "That's why."

"Not a good enough reason." I glanced away because I couldn't look at her right now. Not when she was giving me eyes that said *it's the truth and I don't know what to do about it.* I didn't have a solution but I did have a vibrator and that was pretty much the same thing. "You better hold on, you little hellcat. I don't have a lot of patience for you right now."

"When do you ever?" She pulled her leg from my shoulder and shifted, locking her ankles around my waist. With that hand in my hair, she forced me down, brought my mouth to hers. "Not yet," she whispered, batting the vibrator away. "Don't use it yet. I'm not ready for this to end."

"And you think I am?" Pressure gathered at the base of my spine like a hot, blazing star, throbbing before it burned all the way out. "Just trust me for a fucking second, okay?"

She blinked up at me, nodded. Her lips said "Okay" but there was no sound. She hooked an arm under one of mine, wrapping her hand over my shoulder like she did trust me but she needed something to keep her steady while she did it.

I almost stopped and told her this was a mistake. She shouldn't trust me and I shouldn't have asked for that from her. I couldn't do any of the things she needed, not beyond this singular moment of sex and sparring.

I held my tongue. I didn't know why.

I pulled out just enough to position the vibrator where I wanted it and then thrust back inside as the first pulses rattled a groan from both of us. Anyone who passed on toys with a partner was missing the hell out. This was next-level fucking. I didn't have to tweak my wrist trying to give her clit the attention it needed, and all the while those rumbles did outstanding things for me too.

She kept herself locked around my shoulder, her nails cutting into my skin every time I bottomed out. The pillows were gone, once again, and the blankets a fucking disaster. Her heels were digging mean, bony bruises into the small of my back and I couldn't wait to groan about it in the morning. I had no depth perception to speak of right now but it seemed like we'd fucked the bed at least a foot away from its original position against the wall. She breathed her soft gasps against my ear while she raked her fingers over my scalp, drawing scrapes and swirls that made my eyelids heavy and my face tingle. I closed my eyes to drown in those sensations and I kept them shut because she'd see a million different things if she met my gaze and I couldn't risk a single one of them.

A tremor snaked down my legs as she clenched hard around me. The kind of clench that said she was close and all I had to do was get her there and then I could start resenting her for making me work so hard at proving her own rules wrong.

"*Fuck.* What are you doing to me?" I hadn't intended to say that. I'd heard the words in my head before I realized I was saying them out loud.

"I don't know," she whispered, her voice hoarse. "What are you doing to *me*?"

"Just get there, Shap," I growled. It was good to be back on solidly hostile ground.

"Who the fuck do you think you are? *Get there, Shap*," she mimicked. "Give me a reason to get there."

"You are demonic, how about that? Your hellcat demon body is torturing me right now and if you don't fucking *get there*, I reserve the right to put you on your knees and make you choke on this dick like the brat you are. How about that for a reason?"

"Okay, fuck yes, that works," she panted.

I would've known it worked even if she hadn't said so. Her pussy was molten lava, she wouldn't stop squirming, and her hands were everywhere. My hair, my shoulder, my neck—everywhere, all at once. "There's my good girl."

"Oh, no, no, don't you dare with that again," she yelled into my shoulder. "Not unless you're committed to it. Don't tease me like that."

"I can commit. You know I can." I blinked down at her. "Now give me what I asked for, you little brat."

"I hate you," she ground out as she exploded around me.

"It's all right, honey, you can hate me all you want."

She batted the vibrator away and proceeded to suck on my neck as she came in the most gorgeous chorus of quiet hums and wails.

It was like meditation but instead of getting in control of her thoughts, her cunt was controlling my entire life.

I lasted all of a second after the spasms rolled through her channel. That was it. A single second between adding another point to the scoreboard and my balls saying, *Yeah, that's enough. We're good.*

With the condom full and my chest heaving, I dropped my head between her breasts. They really were great. She was warm and sweaty and delicious there, and I saw no problem with affixing my mouth to the closest nipple.

"Well." She huffed. "Now, that's over with."

I bobbed my head against her chest. "Yeah. So. That's the end of that."

She grazed her lips over my forehead. "I guess you can leave now."

"Can you calm the fuck down? Really. I don't want to be here any more than you want me here and I'm over-fucking-joyed to get you out of my system. I'll be on my way just as soon as I can feel my limbs again. All right?"

She looped her arms around my shoulders. "Do you do anything other than complain?"

I tilted my head back to glance at her. "I think you know I do much more than complain."

She shrugged, dragged a finger down my jaw. "Doesn't sound like it."

I grabbed a handful of plush ass and squeezed hard. "I hope you know what you're asking for."

Another shrug while she traced the tendons in my neck. "I thought you were leaving."

"I am," I said, dragging my fingertips around the curve of her ass to where she was swollen and drenched and still stuffed full of me. "In a minute."

"Okay." She pouted as she nodded and that was the equivalent of issuing yet another challenge. It was like she was daring me to prove that I could get her aroused twice in a night. Make her come twice more. Like I could do anything for her, if she'd let me. "Leave, then. In a minute."

I bit the side of her breast. "You really are a demon."

"Maybe you're a demon too." She ran a hand down my back and then up again. I couldn't help but sigh in pleasure at the trail of sparks she left on my skin. "Have you ever thought about that?"

I shook my head. "I will when I leave. In a minute."

CHAPTER 13

SEBASTIAN

I DIDN'T LEAVE A MINUTE LATER.

I didn't get her out of my system either.

This wasn't the end. Not by a mile.

And I didn't know what the fuck to do about that.

CHAPTER 14

SARA

"THIS CAN'T BE IT," I MURMURED.

"Looks like it is," Stremmel replied.

"It can't be," I said, more heated this time. "There's just no way we're supposed to row ourselves down the river." I shook my head at the collection of small boats lined up along the dock in front of us at the Massachusetts Institute of Technology Sailing Pavilion. "We don't even know what we're doing."

"I can agree with that," he said under his breath.

"We'll just tell Milana this was a bridge too far."

Beside me, Sebastian snorted. When I turned a glare in his direction, he said, "It's funny. There are bridges on either side of us. I'm as shocked as anyone that you said something passably humorous." When I went on glaring at him, he continued, "We're here. It's the first thing in the fucking morning and it's bright as hell but we're here so let's get it over with. Why not? We only have to get from here to there." He gestured down the Charles River toward the Longfellow Bridge and the docks located immediately before it. "See?

Here are the instructions Milana left. 'Cross the river to get to the other side.' Easy. It will take half an hour, tops."

I blinked at him, completely unconvinced. "Do you even know how to swim or do you rely on that ego for buoyancy?"

"Do I know how to swim?" he muttered. "I'm from Florida. Of course I know how to swim."

I eyed him with a touch of wary amusement. "Being from Florida can mean many things, Stremmel. No guarantees in that."

"Well then, Miss Quippy Questions, do *you* know how to swim?" He started down the dock, not waiting for my reply.

"Yes," I called. "I'm from Southern California."

"That explains a few things," he tossed over his shoulder.

"Why are you so excited to get in a little boat on freezing water with me?" I said to his back. "You're uncharacteristically eager to do this."

"Because it will be quick, and if we don't do it, we'll piss away another weekend morning with a different activity."

"But that activity won't involve a canoe—or kayak—or whatever the hell this thing is," I said with a gesture toward the two-seated boat at the end of the dock.

"But I am already out of bed," he growled back. I had to swallow hard to keep from feeling that growl inside me. "And I don't want to give up another weekend morning. I cherish my bedtime."

The image of a sleepy Sebastian swaddled in blankets and morning sunlight was not one I needed at the moment. Still, it was the one I got.

"Here." Sebastian shoved a life vest in my direction. "Put this on."

"Since when are you in charge of this exercise?"

"I'm not getting into another endless debate with you," he said. "Put on the vest. Get in the boat. Shut the hell up."

"You can wait a damn minute," I said, digging in my bag. "Give me your phone."

"If I wanted to chuck it in the river, I'd do it myself, thanks."

"Give me your phone," I repeated. "If we flip this boat like I think we will, I'd rather not lose my phone in the process. See?" I held up a reusable silicone pouch. "They'll float and stay dry."

He glared at the pouch as he handed over his device. "You had croutons in there the other day."

"You're going to have to choose, Stremmel. Crouton crumbs or river water. Can't make that choice for you."

He sighed as he cast a scowl over the water. "I'm too old for this shit."

"You're not wrong about that," I said as I secured the items in my bag.

"You think I'm old?"

"I think you crave attention and often get it through self-deprecating means." I zipped my fleece jacket all the way up to my chin. "Aren't you supposed to be in the boat? What are you waiting for?"

He turned that dark-eyed scowl on me, the one that should've tripped all my frantic people-pleasing alarms but only hit me with the buzz of a challenge. I didn't have to rescue anyone from those scowls, least of all me, not when I could stand toe to toe against them. He could yell and growl and complain all he wanted. It didn't scare me. It didn't even bother me—and that made hardly any sense at all.

Sharp words and a scowl of that magnitude should've sent cold panic through my veins yet all I could feel was the absolute certainty that I had nothing to fear. That scowl was the least threatening thing in the world. Not only that but I was firmly in control here.

"All right, Shap," he grumbled. "Get that fucking vest on, would you?"

————

IT DIDN'T TAKE thirty minutes to get across the river. It took us thirty minutes to push off from the dock and point the boat in the right direction.

On most days, I took pleasure in Sebastian being wrong. This was not one of those days.

"We need to row more to the left," I said, lifting the left oar for emphasis.

"Could you just stop? Seriously, do less. You're going one way, I'm going the other. You're fucking us all up."

I hooked a glance over my shoulder at him. "If anyone's the problem here, it's you."

"If you'd let me do the rowing, we wouldn't have this problem," he fired back.

"I'm not going to sit here while you row us to the boathouse," I said, slapping my oar against the surface. The oar connected with the water harder than I'd intended, sending a spray back at Sebastian.

"Shap," he growled. "There will be no splashing this morning."

"It was an accident!"

"You cause a lot of accidents," he muttered. "Something to consider."

We got our oars into position and started rowing in a slow, sloppy rhythm. We weren't going anywhere quickly but we weren't veering off in a circle this time. At this pace, we had at least another hour of rowing ahead of us.

"You know...this is bullshit," Sebastian grumbled from behind me.

"What are you complaining about now?"

"All these exercises where we have to work together to get to the end—they're bullshit."

"Did you just now discover the point of all this?" I asked. "And if so, can I ask where you went to med school because I have questions."

"UCLA, and no, I didn't discover it now. I'm just annoyed about it now."

I glanced back at him. "UCLA? I went to USC undergrad."

"What did I tell you about the splashing!" he yelled as he ran a hand down his face and shook water droplets from his fingers. "You want to talk about LA, you do it without turning around or wiggling in your seat. The next time I get wet, you get wet."

I knew what he meant.

I understood the context clearly.

The only trouble was, he was right behind me. *Right there.* And those words were so rough and impatient and deep that the primordial portion of my brain heard something different than a threat about rogue waves in rowing. My brain heard growls and groans, and skin moving together. My brain heard all the unthinkably good things that happened when we argued while naked. My brain *loved* those sounds.

And I hated that I went there. I hated that he could awaken those thoughts in me without trying. I hated that I wanted it, regardless of whether it was very, very bad for me.

"At what point do we go ahead and beat each other with the oars?" I asked. "I'm wondering because I'd like to get in as much splashing as possible before that time."

"You're a sociopath," he murmured.

"Are we diagnosing each other now? Because that will be fun."

He made a noise, something like a laugh that'd taken an unexpected turn into a groan. "Maybe later."

"The oar beating? Or the diagnosing?"

He didn't respond to that verbally but the sigh he released could've filled our sails...if we had any sails.

We found the rhythm again and made decent progress though it never seemed like the boathouse got any closer. My arms were somewhere between the fire and noodle stages.

Eventually, Sebastian said, "Did you stay in California after USC?"

"No." I shook my head. I'd needed room to breathe then. Needed to be far enough away from home that I could establish boundaries, even if the only boundary was distance. "Hopkins med. Columbia residency. Stayed in New York for fellowship."

There was a pause. Then, "*Really.*"

I shifted to glance at him. "Wait. Did you just realize I'm competent?"

"Did you just turn around and splash me again?" he asked, shaking the water off his sleeve. "Jesus Christ, Shap. I hope you're prepared for me to turn hypothermic back here."

I wagged a finger at him. "You just decided I'm not some

random plastics airhead who only knows Botox and breast implants, didn't you?"

He crossed his (soaked) arms over his (soaked) chest and glanced at Storrow Drive to the right. "I've never suggested you aren't qualified."

I laughed. "You've suggested you're *more* qualified. Now, I don't have any med school ranking lists on me at the moment but I'm pretty sure the Hopkins surgical program has bested UCLA a few times. Columbia too. Does that sound right to you? What do you think, Stremmel? I'd really love your professional input. A real peer-to-peer moment if you could manage it for me."

And that was when I got wet.

With frigid river water.

"Shut up and row," he said.

"You're not going to toss out your residency stats? Not even trying to get back in the game, are you?"

Another bracing splash of water hit the side of my face and arm. It was awful and I was cold in my bones but I laughed as I shook it off because it was so much fun to harass this man.

"Unless you'd like to see how long it takes us to sink this boat, I'd like you to shut up," he said. "And I'd like you to do it now."

———

IT TOOK us more than three hours but eventually we made it to the boathouse, and we did it without getting completely soaked. Mostly but not completely.

"Never again," Sebastian said as he reached his oar to the dock.

"That group over there, the foursome, they left at the same time we did but they went in the opposite direction," I said, waving toward the other rowers on the water. "They're all the way down at the Longfellow Bridge now. I don't know much about this rowing stuff but I don't think we're very good. We might be bad at this."

Sebastian pushed out of the boat and stepped onto the dock. He reached back to help me but I waved him off. "We're tragic," he said, his hands perched on his hips as he scanned the water. "But those people"—he jerked his chin in the direction of the foursome—"they're professionals."

"You think?"

"Or collegiate athletes. These are not ordinary people who do this for fun or exercise, or, you know, sado-masochism. These are—oh, shit, that's Stanton from nephrology, isn't it?"

A displeased sound echoed in his throat, something resembling a bored snarl.

I brushed my hands together as their boat blew past on one perfectly coordinated stroke. Despite being terrible at rowing and weary from putting up with Sebastian's complaining, I was bouncing on my heels from all the endorphins. It'd been an intense exercise, physically demanding but also emotionally demanding. Rowing was complicated and moderately dangerous for people who didn't know what they were doing, and it required a ton of communication. We did this—together—and we didn't kill each other. That was a really big deal. We could've made quite the horror show of this.

My blood was humming, I felt like I could do any crazy team-building task, and I wanted to burn all this fizzy energy *immediately*.

"So, that was"— I gestured toward our boat.

"Yeah." He nodded, his hands still on his waist. "It really was."

"I think I deserve some kind of commendation for not cracking your skull with an oar."

He rolled his eyes, saying, "Then I deserve the same commendation and let's not forget about the hypothermia. You're lucky it's a warm day."

I pulled his phone from my bag, making a point to brush off any crumbs it might've collected. "Listen, I know you come by that thin blood honestly, being from Florida and all, but it's not *that* cold here. Buck up, buttercup."

He accepted his device from me, his gaze fixed on mine. "It's fucking freezing here most of the year."

I shrugged. "Then go back to Los Angeles."

He matched my shrug. "Can't."

"Why not?"

"Because I hate the cold and the forty-two different seasons this city experiences and the leaves"—it had to be noted that he said *leaves* with jazz hands, and I couldn't tell if those were ironic jazz hands or not—"and then cobblestones, which must've been invented by an orthopedic surgeon, and everything is old as fuck and that's supposed to be special, and the roads"—he cringed with his entire body—"the fucking roads look like a child with no object permanence drew them. They make no sense, none at all, and don't get me started on the sports. These people and their sports. *My god.* Do you know about the turkeys? There are *turkeys* here, Shap, they're all over the place, they don't appreciate that we're sharing their habitat, and they'll chase the fuck out of you if you're not careful. And then there's the coffee, which used to be the only part of my day that didn't piss me off but now I can't just order coffee, I have to also join a cult. And you can't park. You just can't park in this town. Don't try. Not worth it, but it means you have to walk on the danger rocks and you better believe they'll be slippery as hell because all the leaves came down between hot wind season and cold hurricane season so you'll roll an ankle just to dodge the turkeys and order a regular coffee which you must drink with cream and sugar by order of the cult but it's going to be free because one of the sports teams finally won a game—and thank fuck for that because they're not out driving drunk or beating on each other for one blessed night." He gave a brisk shake of his head. "That's why I can't leave."

I had to bite my lip to keep from laughing. "Because you hate everything?"

"Yeah. I hate it all so thoroughly that I'm sure I'd never find anywhere else to hate with such completeness. Without all of this resentment, I'd be empty inside."

"Oh, so that's what it is." I reached out, ran my hand from his chest to his waist. *Blame the endorphins for this.* "Resentment."

"Also avocado." He glanced at me, half a smile on his lips and a question in his brows. Fair, seeing as I'd just rubbed his belly. "When I can find a decent one."

I studied him, still trying to suppress that laugh. "And the rumors I've heard about you being the next Chief of Emergency Surgery? That has nothing to do with your insistence on staying here with the terrible avocados and the cold hurricanes?"

Sebastian started up the dock toward the Esplanade, the footpath that ran the length of the Charles on the Boston side of the river. We were a block away from the hospital and another block from our apartment building though he wasn't heading in that direction.

"I don't know about that." He slipped his hands into his jean pockets. "Nothing has been finalized. Especially not while I'm stuck in treatment with you for apparent anger issues." He shot me a knowing glance. "How do you like Boston? Coming from New York and Southern California and all."

I looked around. "It's nice. I never imagined myself living in a small town but I like it here. It's quaint."

He barked out a laugh. "You are brutal."

"You've mentioned that before." I grinned at him. "Boston was a good change for me." Especially after my dad's college roommate was appointed Chief of Surgery at my last hospital. "I liked New York a lot but it was never my town."

"And now you get to enjoy the leaves." The jazz hands made another appearance and now I was fully smiling. *Damn endorphins.* "Look. I'm starving and I require a gallon of coffee. You can interrogate me about this when I'm caffeinated."

"I have little desire to interrogate you," I said, turning down the path, away from Sebastian. "Enjoy that coffee."

"Wait. *Wait*," he called. "Come on. We'll get breakfast."

Hot tea sounded good. Maybe toast. But— "I've endured one meal with you. I don't need a repeat."

"Why are you like this?" He fell in step with me and took hold of my elbow, turning me back in his original direction. "I actually need an answer."

"You'll have to explain what you mean as I'm certain I don't know."

I knew—of course I knew. I was messy and aloof. That raging bitch of mine poked holes in a lot of my relationships but I needed the boundaries those holes created. The good girl could befriend anyone and people-please her way to some super-destructive behaviors. I knew all of these things —I just wanted to hear him articulate a few of them and see how long it took for him to describe me as bitchy to my face.

He was silent for a considerable time, long enough to make me wonder whether he'd respond or ditch the question altogether. Then, as we approached the Fielder Footbridge, he said, "I mean, you're a five-foot-whatever plastic surgeon with all this hair"—he gave my ponytail a sharp tug —"and you take zero percent of my shit, whereas most people take a minimum of fifty percent, often upward of seventy percent. Why the fuck are you like this?"

I glanced at him as we crossed the bridge. He hadn't…he hadn't said anything I'd expected. That I'd prepared myself to hear. "I don't drink coffee."

"Of course. Tornadoes don't require caffeine for propulsion. Just oxygen."

With a laugh, I said, "I could go for some tea. Maybe toast or, I don't know, a muffin. No blueberries though."

"Did you—wait." He stopped walking but I continued on as he said, "Did you agree with me? What the hell? I've always heard people talking about the effects of sea air but I've never seen it firsthand. This is amazing."

"I don't believe we're close enough to the sea for any such effects," I called.

He jogged to catch up with me. "There's a little brunch place up ahead. They have bakery stuff. Bread. You know, for toast."

I didn't respond to that because I couldn't decide whether I was making a colossal miscalculation by going along with this or simply having an ordinary, healthy interaction. Could I have a normal, healthy interaction with a man when our entire relationship was extraordinary and profoundly unhealthy? Was that possible? What about *this* man? Could I do it with him?

But I felt good and energized, and I didn't want to strangle him right now, not entirely. Maybe this wasn't a miscalculation. Maybe it was just tea and coffee, and enjoying our success in not drowning one another this morning. It didn't have to mean anything.

We cut through several side streets toward the café on the corner of Mt. Vernon Street. "Up ahead," he said, turning his face to the sun. The rays shone bright against his dark hair. "It's warm. How does this happen? There was frost yesterday morning and we're in the strangely hot and also spooky part of October now. As if that's normal."

"You can complain about the cold but not the heat," I said, stripping off my fleece jacket. I rolled my shoulders as the strain from the rowing throbbed in response. "Oh, shit. This is not good."

"I said *one thing* about the erratic autumn weather," he replied. "Nothing else to say—on that topic."

"I meant my shoulders," I said. "I didn't think I'd feel it so much. I have three skin grafts back-to-back tomorrow and I really don't need my hands shaking because I'm remarkably bad at rowing."

We stopped outside the café. I stepped toward the windows to read the menu posted there while kneading my overworked muscles. I needed to make sure there was something I'd actually eat—not just hate and pick at for half an hour while pretending everything was fine—before going inside. I couldn't sit there with a cup of tea and answer questions about what I did or didn't eat as I'd prefer falling into a bog to any such discussion.

"Enough of that," Sebastian growled, batting my hands away.

I expected a lecture about me working the wrong spot or a bit of him reveling in my discomfort. I didn't expect him to bring his hands to my shoulders and work his fingers into the knots gathered at the base of my neck.

"I—uh," I said, my eyes drifting shut as he pressed into the tender spots. "You're not even going to take the shot and agree that I'm bad at rowing?"

He worked his way down the ridge of my shoulders to my upper arms and I really didn't understand this. We weren't in the apartment foyer and no one was yelling and when did sidewalk massages before brunch become something we did? *Together?* How did it become part of our power struggle, and where was I when that transformation occurred?

"Nope, not going to do that." He was so close. If I leaned back a tiny bit, I'd connect with his chest. "Though I'm not in the OR tomorrow and I did offer to handle the rowing so this is entirely your fault."

"Oh, great," I said. "I'm glad we're back to assigning fault. That's fun. When should we start on the psychiatric diagnoses?"

"Why haven't I seen you at any of Acevedo's dinner parties?" he asked.

I stifled a groan. There was no way to go into a dinner party as both an introvert and a criminally picky eater and come out alive. Even the strongest, most fully recovered parts of me struggled with this because it was simply rude to go to someone's home and not eat the food they prepared. It wasn't people-pleasing this time. It was manners—and bad manners were one big people-pleasing fire drill.

"I've been there several times." My tone was way too defensive to be believable. I tried again. "Nick is amazing and his wife is really sweet. I've always had a good time when I've been to their house. It just doesn't work out all the time. That's all."

"Acevedo lived in the third-floor apartment before me," Sebastian said. "Emmerling has been on the second floor for as long as I've known her and—"

"And Cal Hartshorn lived in my apartment before me. I know. I'm familiar with the recent history of the doctor dorm."

He murmured something as he worked back up to my shoulders and neck. "I'm just saying, it's a good group."

"Yes and that's not intimidating at all," I sang.

"Excuse me but did you just suggest you find anyone intimidating? Because I'm pretty sure you could boil water with nothing more than your side-eye as a heat source."

"Has anyone ever told you that you exaggerate profusely?"

"No. Never. That is completely new information." He brushed the loose strands from my neck and twisted my ponytail around his fist. "The Acevedos are having a small party in a few weeks. You should come."

I tried to shake my head but he stroked a thumb down the line of my neck and I melted a little more. "I will have to think about that," I managed.

"What's there to think about? Acevedo's making tacos. End of deliberation."

"Maybe I have other plans," I said.

"Maybe you should cancel them."

"Maybe I don't like parties," I replied.

"Neither do I," he said. "I don't like people. They're exhausting." When I didn't respond, he continued. "You should come anyway."

"Why?"

If there was one thing I always wanted—regardless of whether it was healthy or safe—it was approval. Choose me, include me, praise me, validate me. I wanted it when it was unavailable—hello, mother; hello, father—and I wanted it when it didn't make sense. Like right now. I wanted Sebastian to tell me that he wanted me at this party. No damn sense—and also, what the fuck was wrong with me?

We were white-knuckling it through conflict resolution counseling, not coupling up for dinner parties with the friend group.

"You're thinking too hard, Shap. It's tacos and Acevedo's new residents. Hartshorn will show up at least an hour late, Emmerling's husband will do something crazy like climbing on the roof to check the shingles, and O'Rourke will tell stories about Minnesota."

"And what about you? Which role do you play?"

"I find a comfortable spot to sit and not speak to anyone. But listen, you should come along. All anyone talks about is surgery, the food is amazing, and the people are chill. You'd like it."

"That sounds…" Honestly, it sounded fun. But also overwhelming and impossible to slip away unnoticed when I was maxed out. "It sounds great but I really need some time to check my schedule."

He stopped rubbing my shoulders and peered at me. "What's the real issue?"

I pivoted to face him. "Why does it matter?"

"Because there are people falling over themselves to spend time with you but you can't be bothered, and I just want to know why."

"I am not required to explain myself to you," I said. "You're entitled to exactly nothing from me."

"Oh, trust me, honey, I'm aware." He crossed his arms over his chest. I did the same. "For the life of me, I can't understand their thinking on this but Nick and Erin have someone they want you to meet."

"What…does that mean?"

"It means Erin has a friend, some professor guy, and she thinks you two could hit it off." He scowled at this, saying, "Can't really see why they'd want to torture the guy but whatever. I'm just the asshole tasked with getting you there. Not my problem after that point."

I stared at him for a long moment, remembering in a horrible rush why that approval kink of mine was so dangerous. Every time I allowed myself to believe I'd get the inclusion and recognition I wanted, shame was waiting there to slap me back for thinking I deserved anything of the sort.

Sebastian didn't want me at the party, and I was stupid for thinking otherwise. But I wasn't going to shrink in front of this man.

"So, you drew the short straw?" I asked.

"Don't I always?" He rolled his eyes toward the sky before saying, "Since I get to spend so much quality time with you, I'm supposed to close the deal." He frowned as he looked me up and down. "Is it working?"

I reached into my bag, pulled out my phone. "Oh, yeah. It's working." I opened a text message to Acevedo. "Consider your mission accomplished. I'm telling Nick that I'll be there." I sent the message and shot Sebastian a satisfied grin.

"I can't wait to meet this professor. I have a good feeling about this."

I didn't think it was possible for Sebastian's scowl to deepen but it did, turning his entire face into a dark, scruffy storm cloud.

I glanced to the café behind me. "I'm not in the mood for tea anymore."

He replied with a slow blink that seemed to indicate he wanted his hands on my neck again though not to work out my knots.

"Enjoy the coffee," I said, backing down the street. "And hating everything. Good luck with all that."

I left him staring after me and that gave me a quick jolt of pleasure but it didn't last. Before I even reached the next block, the pleasure was gone and in its place was a cold, crumbling dread.

Every time we clawed out an inch of progress, we fell back a foot. Since neither of us were willing to budge, the cycle went on repeating. I didn't know how much longer I could do this before it really started to hurt.

CHAPTER 15

SARA

Sara: Hey! I hear there's a thing at Nick and Erin's place in a few weeks? What's that about?

Alex: Yeah, I remember Nick mentioning that the other day, but I wasn't listening because my resident was being a fool.

Sara: Okay.

Alex: Are you thinking about coming along?

Sara: Sigh…

Sara: Stremmel and I got into an argument about the party. I texted Nick on the spot to say I'd be there.

Sara: Didn't think that one all the way through.

Alex: Ha. You and Stremmel, getting into another fight. Imagine that.

Sara: I know, I know.

Alex: You know what's funny to me? For the most part, you're cheerful and energetic, and even when you're tough, you're kind and positive about it. You are widely admired and appropriately feared. It's a great balance. I'm still working on reaching that level and will do anything to know your secrets. But the second you see Stremmel, the war paint goes on, the gloves come off, and you throw the fuck down.

Stremmel breathes and you're like "I'm gonna kill that motherfucker for all his motherfucking!"

Sara: You're feared. Don't worry.

Alex: Feared, sometimes. Admired, rarely.

Sara: You're being too hard on yourself.

Alex: And you're being too hard on Stremmel. I say the same thing to Riley all the time. He lets Stremmel push his buttons and that's what's happening here.

Sara: I'm not sure if it's exactly the same…

Alex: Have you ever stopped to examine which buttons he's pushing on you?

Sara: I am very familiar with that button. I know it well.

Alex: Then maybe don't let him keep pressing it.

Sara: Yeah…I'll think about that.

Alex: Please do.

Sara: There are lots of nerve endings involved with that particular button. It's a sensitive one.

Alex: Believe me, I understand, but you can't let it run your life.

Sara: Yeah. I'll think about that.

CHAPTER 16

SEBASTIAN

"WELL, IF THIS ISN'T THE MURDERERS ROW," O'ROURKE CALLED as he approached the picnic table in the park where we'd congregated for lunch. "If I have Emmerling, Acevedo, Hartshorn, and Stremmel all in one spot, is anyone cutting right now?"

Hartshorn leaned into my side, asking, "Is he going to be a pain in the ass?"

I lifted a shoulder. It was bitterly cold, not that anyone else noticed, and I was in a wretched mood. The last thing I had time for was decoding my fellow's mercurial behavior. "He was incredible yesterday. This morning too. Who knows what we'll get now."

"Neither of you are required to be assholes. You do it for free," Alex said under her breath.

"Blame me," Acevedo murmured. "I invited him." Ever the includer, Acevedo waved O'Rourke over. "I have a grilled cheese with your name on it."

"Thanks, man."

O'Rourke dropped onto the bench beside Emmerling,

who sent him a measured glance. He didn't notice. "Grilled cheese?" she asked. "Really."

"It's one of the things I picked up from Minnesota," he replied. "A deep and abiding love for cheese."

"You got that…from Minnesota," she said.

O'Rourke unwrapped his sandwich, saying, "It's very close to Wisconsin and all their cheese. And it's not like good dairy farming stops at the state lines. Nah, that shit permeates."

Hartshorn bobbed his head. "I can see how that would be the case."

I leveled a stare at my fellow. "Please tell me you've cleared all your pages and consults."

"No one needs me, no one wants me," he replied around a mouthful of bread and cheese.

Nick passed a hand over his face to hide a grin. "That is one way to put it."

"Are we talking about Stremmel's problems?" O'Rourke asked. He pulled a small spiral-bound notebook from his pocket and thumbed through the pages. "Because I have thoughts I'd like to contribute."

"I'm not sure if there's ever a time when we're not talking about Stremmel's problems," Alex mused. "It's that and Hartshorn trying to get his wife pregnant again. That's all we have to entertain ourselves. Stremmel and sperm counts."

Cal glared at her. "We have never once talked about my *sperm count*."

Alex held up both hands, shrugged. "Not directly, no, but if Stella isn't pregnant next month, we'll be elbow deep into count, morphology, and motility."

Cal turned his glare on Nick. "Do something about this, would you?"

"I hear good things about eating walnuts though I can't say I've read the research," Nick replied. "Otherwise, stick to the basics. Avoid hot tubs and switch to boxers."

"I *have* read the research on the walnuts and the outcomes were positive," O'Rourke said, "for men under thirty-five."

Cal Hartshorn was in his late forties, a former army Ranger capable of killing everyone at this table with a teaspoon, our future boss as soon as the current Chief of Surgery retired, and presently grinding his molars at my fellow.

"So then, Stremmel's problems," Nick said. "What do you got for us?"

O'Rourke tapped a greasy finger to a page in his note-book. "He was an absolute monster on Monday and that wouldn't be especially strange but it's the second Monday in a row he's been a monster."

"That's just"—Alex waved a hand at me—"that's neither new nor concerning."

"No, you're right," O'Rourke conceded, tapping the page again, "but Dr. Shapiro's residents have observed the same pattern from her and they've indicated it's a new develop-ment. Of course, her worst is nowhere near Stremmel's—"

"Stand in the eye of that storm and then try saying that to me," I muttered.

O'Rourke hit me with a knowing grin. If this little fucker was going where I thought he was going, I'd borrow that murder spoon from Hartshorn and kill him here in broad daylight.

"Shapiro's residents describe her worst days as her being even more high-octane than usual—which sounds fun, it really does—but the Monday pattern is what's new here." O'Rourke pointed his triangle-cut sandwich at me. "Have to wonder what's happening to make these Mondays so monstrous all of a sudden, huh?"

Nick, Alex, and Cal stared at me. "What?" I cried. "I have no idea what her problem is."

"Then what's your problem?" Nick asked.

"I have no problems." When the group shot me unconvinced eyebrows, I added, "Nothing new. Nothing beyond my usual stable of problems."

"Where is Shapiro?" Cal asked. "Why doesn't she ever come to lunch with us?"

"She doesn't like peopling," Alex replied. "You gotta respect her boundaries."

I snorted because her boundaries were my private ropes course. Then I shoved food in my mouth and waved off all the so-called friends gaping at me.

"We're friends, we're not people," Cal argued.

"Friends are people," Nick told him.

"But she's very outgoing whenever I see her," Cal said. "Doesn't strike me as someone who needs a lot of alone time."

"Your observation doesn't make it true. Lots of people can be really strong in work settings and then require twelve hours of uninterrupted silence in order to get up the next day and do it all again," Alex said. "And you know I love you, but I don't think you guys are aware of how socially demanding you can be."

"We haven't been demanding," Cal said, looking around the table for support. "Did Shapiro say we're demanding?"

"No," Alex said firmly. "But I am telling you that you can be a lot to handle. Not everyone is prepared to be initiated into a crew that"—she held up her hand, started ticking off on her fingers—"goes jogging together, eats lunch together, hangs out after work together, has a ton of dinner parties together, even goes on vacations together." She pointed at Nick and Cal. "Believe it or not, some people leave work and elect to live their lives without the involvement of their colleagues."

"Right, so," Nick started with a gesture toward me, "what's wrong with you now?"

"Nothing is wrong with me," I replied.

"You were bellyaching to my wife on Thursday night about these conflict sessions with Shapiro," he went on. "It stands to reason you'd be pissed straight through to Monday. Am I wrong?"

"Fuck, yes, you're wrong," I replied. This was great. I didn't even have to lie, seeing as I'd pissed myself off with how I handled things with Sara after rowing. "What I do on my weekends and why it makes me miserable has nothing to do with those Thursday afternoon sessions."

Alex folded her arms on the table, leaned closer to O'Rourke. She was hooked. Entranced. "What are Friday mornings like?"

"Well," he started, "I actually learned shit these past two Fridays. That's an anomaly. Dr. Shapiro's residents indicated she was very relaxed last Friday. One of them used the word 'mellow.'"

Hell yeah, she was. I had to steal Acevedo's apple to hide my grin over that.

Cal snatched up the butcher paper from his sandwich and mine, saying, "Is there a point to any of this? We're sitting here reading the tea leaves of this bastard's behavior as if there's ever any rhyme or reason to his moods. And Shapiro, well, I don't know what to say about that. For all we know it's her residents, the ones selling stories about her down the hall, who are ticking her off. What's there to be done about any of this? Nothing." He pushed to his feet. "I gotta go find some walnuts."

"I don't have a point," O'Rourke said after Cal stalked off. "Just a few things I've noticed."

"That's great because I don't need a point," Alex said. "Though I am wondering if my residents spend this much time talking about me behind my back."

"They don't," Nick said.

At the same moment, I replied, "Of course they do."

"How are those sessions going?" Alex asked. "Any progress?"

There was no way to answer that so I didn't. "Define progress."

O'Rourke flipped a page in his notebook. "Another thing I've noticed—"

I reached for the notebook but he pinned it under his elbow. "Oh, for fuck's sake, that's enough noticing from you."

"No, I need to hear this," Alex said. "What else?"

"Everyone has noticed that they take great effort to avoid each other," O'Rourke said. "Especially on Thursdays."

"If you have this much time on your hands, I'm not giving you enough to do," I said. "Believe me, I'll fix that today."

"Right, right," O'Rourke murmured. "Because I'm so good at following directions and meeting expectations."

Nick clapped me on the shoulder. "Best of luck. That's all I've got for you. Best of luck."

I was going to need it.

CHAPTER 17

SARA

Alex: Do my residents talk about me behind my back?

Sara: Constantly but you have to ignore it.

Alex: Whyyyyyyyy though?

Sara: Because they're residents. They need something to gossip about and we're one of the easiest targets.

Alex: How can you be so chill about this?

Sara: I'm not. I've just compartmentalized it enough to be able to say that it's normal and it's not about me. I can disconnect myself from it.

Sara: Unless there's something you've heard that you think I should know.

Alex: It's not something you NEED to know. I'd tell you if it was. It's just chatter.

Sara: Now I have to ask. What's the chatter?

Alex: The trauma fellow appears to have befriended some of your residents.

Sara: Has to be the trauma fellow, doesn't it?

Alex: He's noticed that you and Stremmel seem to avoid each other on Thursdays.

Sara: Hmm. That's an interesting observation. Can't say I avoid him more on Thursdays than I do any other day of the week.

Alex: Like I said, chatter.

Alex: Anyway, Riley and I are going to a new restaurant tonight. Will you come with us?

Sara: I am not a great third wheel but thank you so much for thinking of me.

Alex: One of these times, I'll get you!

Sara: Just be honest…you're really looking for a third in your threesome, aren't you?

Alex: It's a damn good thing you didn't say that around my husband because he'd never be able to unhear it, babe.

CHAPTER 18

SARA

IN THIS WEEK'S SESSION, WE HAD TO COMPLETE A MAZE GAME using vague clues Milana read from a set of cards she kept in a janky old Ziploc bag. We had to navigate taped-off squares on the floor using these clues. Any time we misinterpreted the clues, we were sent back to the beginning. We went back to the beginning eleven times before Sebastian insisted that requirement be suspended.

He'd demanded my bag of trail mix upon arrival. It was mostly pretzels on account of an overly ambitious run-in with baby carrots the previous day, and he sorted out the raisins as I watched.

That evening, he'd bent me over the back of my sofa. When we were finished and I was a hoarse, boneless wreck, he left me on that sofa, a blanket tucked up to my chin and a glass of water within reach.

———

THE FOLLOWING WEEK, we roleplayed difficult conversations from a binder with *Demanding Dialogues in Healthcare* splashed across the front. Sebastian rolled his eyes into next month at my croutons and then helped himself to the rye, which were my least favorite.

We yelled and stumbled over several of the conversations until Sebastian plucked a pen from the pocket of my white coat and started rewriting the prompts on account of them lacking any connection to reality. He told Milana he was doing her a favor.

After the session, Sebastian followed me around while I visited a few patients. The scowl I received upon informing those patients that Dr. Stremmel was observing me for his skill development was worth the torture he inflicted upon me later.

It was good torture, the likes of which I'd only heard about from clickbait headlines and the noises coming from Alex and Riley's apartment. It was *really good* torture.

We didn't talk about it. We didn't even talk when it was over. He tore me to shreds and then put me to bed with a glass of water and a growly warning to lock the door, and that was our routine. He didn't stay and I didn't offer. There was no cuddling, no kisses good night, no promises to text later, not even a shuddering laugh and some *wow, I didn't know my body could do that.*

We never ventured into the waters of *what the fuck are we doing* or *why can't we stop?*

That was safer, which only spoke to the unbelievable danger of the situation we'd chosen for ourselves. It was bound to blow up on us at any moment and it was going to hurt like hell when it did. It was going to leave marks.

My perfectionist desperately, urgently needed me to stop doing things that made my career, my reputation, my entire life messier. I didn't pay attention to her often, but when I did, she was *this close* to losing it. I was really testing her.

My bitch stood stoic against the chaos and kept insisting I was allowed to feel good and I didn't need to build a fire-wall of distance and denial to protect myself from that. I sure as shit didn't need to apologize for it. Most of all, I didn't have to run away from it.

I wanted to believe her.

————

THE NEXT SESSION was an especially spicy one where we were tasked with building a bridge using marshmallows and pipe cleaners. We'd spent the majority of the time arguing about engineering and the last few minutes actually building the thing while Sebastian treated us to a chorus of, "This is a waste of marshmallows. It's a damn waste."

Once we were dismissed, he'd tucked his fingers into my waistband and steered me out of the hospital, up the street, into our building. The press of his knuckles against my flank did wild things to me. It made me forget myself, forget everything. He'd fucked me slow that evening, so slow, like we had all the time in the world. Like there wasn't a cliff coming for us, an end whether we accepted the inevitability or not.

Much like the perfectionist and the bitch who shared a hostile existence in my head, my feelings for Sebastian Stremmel were contradictory, one never more than a minute away from declaring war on the other. Part of me despised him in the stickiest, most unbearable way. The other part of me…that part did not despise him.

And as these days and weeks passed, it was becoming

clear that those parts were unequal. Unbalanced. One side was much, much greater than the other, even if they did exist on the brink of total annihilation. There were moments when I struggled to believe that the other side existed at all. I had to search for it, press it like the echo of a bruise to dredge up the last twinges of pain.

I knew his scowls now. I could decode them with a single glance. I knew when he was tired, stressed, annoyed. I knew when he was irritable about his cases rather than irritable over the waning November sunlight.

I also knew that the scowl was his drawbridge, the mechanism he'd perfected for keeping everyone at an arm's length. In most cases, he'd succeeded in doing that. I'd been one of those success stories. I'd written him off, filed him away as arrogant and unpleasant and too self-involved to bother acknowledging me in the halls.

I knew I was wrong. I knew that his wordless nods and chin jerks *were* his greetings and that he was dreadful at small talk. I knew I did not despise him as much as I wanted to believe.

He stared down at me before he left that night, his scowl fresh and unguarded, and there was a second where it seemed like he wanted to say something more. Instead, he pointed a meaningful glance at the water he'd poured for me and reminded me to lock the door behind him.

I wasn't even sure I *wanted* to despise him anymore.

————

THE SUN WAS bright in a blinding way that only seemed to occur on cool mornings in November. These days made me feel electric and alive, like I could juice the sun straight into my veins.

I liked these kinds of days—except when I found myself conscripted into yet another weekend homework assignment.

Perhaps it wasn't the sun blinding me this morning so much as Sebastian's neon orange bubble suit. I could *hear* him scowling clear across the outdoor jousting ring as the instructor secured him into the suit which resembled a massive ball of bubble wrap.

I had to turn away because he looked like some kind of citrus-themed mascot, a tangerine stuck with arms, legs, and murder in mind.

"Shut up, Shap," he called.

"I didn't say anything," I yelled back.

"You are doubled over laughing," he said flatly. "As soon as you're suited up, you're dead."

"Well, now, folks," the instructor said. "We like to think of bubble suit jousting as an opportunity for friendly competition, not—"

"You're going down, Florida," I called to Sebastian. "And you're not getting back up."

"Big words from a little bit," he shouted.

The instructor helped me into a cobalt blue suit as Sebastian paced the perimeter of the sparring ring. "Being closer to the ground is an advantage," I said.

He shook his head as he muttered to himself. It was unacceptably funny to see such a tall, powerful man trapped inside an orange bubble, his arms skewered straight and his steps unsteady. Even the helmet was hilarious, and for no specific reason other than he looked so unlike his usual self. "We'll test that theory," he shot back.

Once I was buttoned up, the instructor, a twentysome-thing guy with long, curly hair trailing down from under a beanie, who'd introduced himself as Paxton, set a pair of oversized foam jousting lances in the center of the square ring. "Okay, folks. Let's review the rules."

"Fuck the rules," I said.

"No rules," Sebastian agreed.

"I know this is exciting," Paxton said, a warning hand raised, "but we do have safety protocols and—"

"If I kill him, I'll clean up after myself," I said.

"There will be damages," Sebastian said. "Charge me whatever is necessary."

Paxton glanced between us, his jaw slack. "Well, let's wait a second. We don't want anyone getting hurt—"

Sebastian grabbed the lance. "Even if I could hurt her with this, I know how to put her back together."

Despite Paxton's increasing concern, I shuffled up to my lance and took it in hand. "He won't admit it but I know how to put him back together too." I wagged the lance at Sebastian. "Surgeons. Mass General. We can't hurt each other any more here than we hurt each other without the sticks."

Though this didn't appease Paxton, it was all the invitation Sebastian needed to wail me in the bubble belly and send me floundering backward. It was not a great moment as far as my battle strategy went but I was laughing like I'd never laughed before.

From the other side of the ropes, Paxton called, "You folks signed all the waivers, right?"

Getting up meant rolling to my side and climbing to my knees. Sebastian was there waiting for me, his lance poised to crack over my head. But there was power in being close to the ground and I used all of that leverage to topple him with one shove to the bottom curve of his suit, leaving him sprawled and flailing. An overturned turtle with the temperament of a bull.

While I scrambled for my lance, Sebastian managed to heave himself onto his side and gain his feet. He wasted no time in whacking me again but I was prepared for it, my legs braced and my grip on the lance firm.

"Accept that I am going to win," I yelled as he pounded my side. "There will be no victory for you."

"I don't need victory," he shouted over my laughter. "I just need to kick your ass. You can thrash me when I'm done."

"Hey now, folks," Paxton called, his hands raised as if he could stop us by will alone. "The objective isn't—"

"The objective is to make her beg for mercy," Sebastian replied. "I'll accept nothing short of complete and total submission."

I knocked him upside the head. "You'll die unfulfilled."

"Trust me, I'm planning on it."

"Folks," Paxton cried.

"We've got this," Sebastian said to him. He sent me rolling end over end and then grabbed my hand and yanked me to my feet. "We do worse things to each other at least once a week."

"And we don't wear helmets when we're doing it," I added.

Abandoning the lance, I plowed straight into Sebastian and knocked him over like a bowling pin.

"Get back here, you evil little blueberry!"

Bubble suits weren't designed with running in mind but I was able to pull off an effective scurry. Score one for short girls.

Sebastian did not have the same success. He stumbled and bumbled. He chased me from one corner of the ring to another while I cackled and hiccuped. I bounced off the ropes. He somersaulted, then rolled once more. We took up the lances again and bludgeoned each other while we shouted and swore and laughed ourselves to tears. We didn't stop when Paxton blew the air horn that signaled the end of our time in the ring. It was only when I lost my hold on the lance and, instead of knocking Sebastian off his feet, I took us both down and into the ropes like a pair of skewered cherry tomatoes that we stopped.

Everything inside me was blown wide open in the most vital way and I wanted to bottle this fun, this silly joy, and press it into the palms of people who couldn't get out of their heads for a minute. I wanted them to know that all the terrible things they'd endured, all the things they'd inflicted upon themselves, could feel like the tiniest pinprick of a memory. I wanted them to know what it was like to go flying backward, ass over ankles in a bubble suit, and laugh so hard their ribs ached. I wanted them to know it got better.

Paxton stepped between us then. "You two are mean," he muttered as he freed me from the suit. "I'm a little concerned about it."

"Not the first time we've heard that," Sebastian said. He watched me flop down to the mat from his overturned turtle position.

I was drenched in sweat and breathing hard. My hair was a wreck from the helmet but also because it was always wrecked. My leggings were up my ass yet also falling down. One boob was achieving above and beyond the bra cup. I smiled up at the sky. Everything felt amazing.

"Nothing to worry about with us," I told Paxton. "We're

as right as holes in the ozone."

Paxton yanked the bubble suit off Sebastian and gave us a weary shake of his head. "Have you tried therapy?"

"Yeah," Sebastian said, joining me in collapsing on the mat. "Therapist sent us here."

"Well, shit." Paxton hooked an arm through each suit and trudged off, the air horn hanging out of the back pocket of his jeans.

Sebastian reached over, his palm landing in my hair, his fingers splayed over my forehead. "You're a tiny tornado," he panted. "You leveled me."

"Told you I would."

"Consistent," he said hoarsely. "You're so fucking consistent."

"If you're trying to compliment me, you should try harder."

He rolled, caged me with his hands on either side of my shoulders, a knee between my legs. "How hard do you want me to try?"

I lifted a hand to shield my eyes from the sun. The long-sleeved black t-shirt fit him in a manner I could only describe as inappropriate. Even if I didn't know what I'd find under the stretchy cotton, this shirt left no mysteries. No imagination required.

It was too bright out here. Too warm.

"Depends on what you're expecting to get," I replied.

He shifted to sit on his heels, my leg still trapped between both of his. Reaching back, he grabbed my free ankle. "The last thing I ever do is expect."

"What does that mean?"

He shook his head as he bent my leg, my knee to my torso, before he propped my sneaker on his belly. It was the prime position to knock him on his ass but we both knew I wasn't going to do that.

"It means there's no point in expecting anything." He pressed his thumbs to the back of my calf, rubbed his way to my ankle. "Expectations just fuck you up."

"Anything can fuck you up. Believe me, I could write a book on all the little things that can fuck you up."

"And you could probably distill that book down to a single word. Expectations. Either you expected more or you expected less, and whichever way it went, it fucked you up."

I watched him as he hiked my foot to his shoulder, the sun circling him in a halo of blazing heat that seemed to bounce off the black-clad mountain range of his shoulders and the dark cloud of his hair.

"I don't like that," I said.

He shrugged, dragged his lips to my ankle.

"You should expect things," I continued.

He stared down at me, his lips still fixed to my skin. "Why?"

"Because—" I slapped my hands to the mat. "You should."

He narrowed his eyes. "What would you have me expect?" I didn't have an answer for that. When my only response came in the form of some fast, frustrated blinking, he went on. "What would you like me to expect from you?"

He pressed his teeth to my ankle. His beard tickled enough to send a twitch down my leg. He tightened his hold and everything, *everything* inside me pulsed with need.

"I don't know."

A ripple passed through his brows, something grumpy to hide his disappointment. Yet there was no hiding that he was disappointed. I'd said the wrong thing though the right thing was a mystery baked into this twisted mess of mutual resentment and hate sex.

Muscle memory instructed me to smooth this over, to ease the disappointment. "You're hugging my leg."

He ran his hand from my ankle to the hinge of my hip, squeezing the thick of my thigh on his way back down. "It's a nice leg."

"Nice?"

"Don't go fishing, Shap. It's not a good look." He scraped his beard along the flash of skin exposed between my leggings and sneakers. "Maybe this guy Erin has lined up for you won't mind such obvious requests for flattery but I do."

I pressed my heel to his chest. "Why do you have to do that?"

"What? I just assumed you were looking forward to meeting him tonight." His brows climbed again. "Erin Acevedo knows her shit. I bet this guy is a perfect match for you, god help him. By my estimation, he's partially to fully deaf to handle all your screeching, has a sky-high tolerance for ambiguity on account of all the natural disasters you create, a very solid sense of self to balance out you needing to be right all the fucking time, thick skin because you insult people without any regard for their feelings, and the palate of a very boring child."

I glared at him. I hadn't thought about that party all week, mostly as a means of keeping myself from obsessing over it. As was my tradition, the obsession was localized to how I'd navigate the food and beverage situation. I'd ignored all parts of this alleged fix-up. "Mmhmm. Sure. That checks out."

"Don't pretend you don't have it all gamed out."

I pushed against his chest. "*Gamed out?*"

"Yeah, I mean, I know you, Shap. You have a plan of attack lined up. You're going to show him your non-sociopathic, non-feral side. Pretend you don't rip off heads just to remind everyone you can. Before you know it, you'll have him lulled into some nice, hollow complacency. The story writes itself. You'll have matching gold bands and a pair of semi-sociopathic children. Then you can tear his guts right out of his belly and he won't even see it coming. Horror ever after. Just what you've always wanted."

I stomped my foot against his sternum and sent him sprawling backward. "You don't know me," I said, scrambling to my feet. "Whatever the fuck you think you know— you're wrong. You're really fucking wrong."

He rocked to his knees. "What just happened?"

I backed up, crossed my arms over my torso. His expression was flat, almost confused. That made no sense considering he'd obviously spent some time thinking about those comments. "Oh, I don't know. How about you telling me how I intend to trap some guy and how that's my grand plan or something? Where do you get off saying these things to me? Really, Stremmel, where the fuck did you get the right?"

"Tell me I'm wrong," he said, still on his knees. "Tell me you're not hunting for a husband and some kids you'll hand off to a nanny because you'd sooner die than cut your on-call hours."

I took another step and felt the ropes at my back. "I've given you more than enough. I'm finished."

I climbed over the ropes and walked away as Sebastian called, "Would you just calm the hell down? Get back here, Shap."

I was wrong. The torture wasn't worth it.

And I still despised him. Quite thoroughly.

CHAPTER 19

SEBASTIAN

MALAKAI FORD WAS THE KIND OF GUY WHO WORE JEANS AND A button-down shirt with a pinstriped suit vest *and tie* to a Saturday night taco party and that was all you needed to know about him. A tie to a taco party. For shame.

Everyone else wanted to know about his work in forensic climatology and how long he'd be visiting from England and whether he was enjoying it here in Boston but I did not give a single fuck about any of that. I didn't want to hear about his research or his endless struggle to find a decent cup of tea in this town. His observations about the public transit system could go fuck his mother for all I cared.

For the fortieth time this evening, I shot Erin a side-eye glare. In response, she pried the half-empty beer bottle from my cross-armed clutch and replaced it with a fresh one. "Lighten up," she ordered under her breath.

"I couldn't if I tried," I said. "You know that."

"Some day," she started as she buzzed around me, "you will explain this behavior to me. Until then, I will pray you don't actually sever any heads with that glare. This crew would have a lot of fun trying to reattach that head but I draw the line at sutures in my kitchen. Full-on surgery is a hill too far, you know?"

In spite of myself, I snorted out a laugh. Erin was right—this group of surgeons would makeshift the shit out of this kitchen. I glanced at Alex and Nick. They were debating the merits of a new robotic surgical tool as she expertly opened and pitted one avocado after another and he mashed them. O'Rourke was telling two of Nick's neuro residents about a case he saw last week involving an off-road vehicle crash. You could take the surgeons out of the operating room but you couldn't take the OR talk out of the surgeons.

Except Sara, apparently.

She stood on the opposite end of the kitchen between Alex's husband Riley Walsh—who happened to be Erin's brother—and that fool in the vest. I'd missed the introductions because I was late in getting here—and I'd been running late because I didn't want to come—but it was obvious Sara was putting some effort into getting to know this guy.

My life could go fuck itself right to hell.

Not for the first time, I was responsible for my own tragedies. I'd lost my fucking mind with Sara this morning. I couldn't explain it. All I knew was I'd opened a door and invited her to walk through it. Instead of doing that, she slammed it in my face. Seeing as I was my own worst enemy, I'd opened another door and then another—and instead of her traveling from here to there with me, she bolted them shut.

I'd responded to that in the only reasonable fashion and acted like a fucking tool. I'd crossed at least eighty stupid lines and then pretty much demanded she stab me with my own scalpels. I'd deserved to be kicked in the chest. It was fine. It was cool. I survived all the other shit I inflicted upon myself so I'd survive this too.

That left me to do the only thing I knew how to do: park myself in a corner and glare at the asshole running his A game on Sara from across the room. That I had a beer in my hand was an added benefit. And the food Erin kept leaving in my vicinity helped too but there was nothing shaking me from this spot until I could figure out how to kill this guy without inciting an international incident.

"Hey, I'm wondering something," O'Rourke called, his beer bottle held aloft. "This kept me up last night and I need it settled tonight so I can sleep."

"You were on call last night," I said. "*That* kept you up."

"Was I on call? Yes. Was I amusing myself with stupid ideas instead of answering pages the first and second times? Also yes," he said. "Back to the topic at hand. Very serious. I need the best minds in the room on this so you two"—he pointed his bottle at the neuro residents—"just sit down and be quiet. I'm sorry but you won't be ready for this conversation until after your third years. You're not there yet. It's you, it's not me. Anyway." He held his arms out wide. "Which surgical specialty could you take in a fight to the death?"

Nick barked out a laugh. "Why is this a question, O'Rourke?"

"Just like neuro to answer a question with another question," he said. "We all know you're using this time to source your strategy."

"Why are we fighting anyone to the death?" Alex asked. "Why not just fight them until they're down for the count? I don't need to kill anyone but I would like to dominate them."

"That's right," Riley murmured to her. "That's exactly right, honeybee."

"You're doing it wrong," O'Rourke said. "You're all doing it wrong. You're supposed to think about the other specialties and then explain why you'd be able to kick anesthesia's ass any day of the week."

"No, no, no," Nick said. "Anesthesia keeps paralytics in their pocket. All they need to do is throw one syringe and it's lights out."

"I could take cardio," Alex said. "But don't tell Hartshorn I said that. It'll hurt his feelings."

"It would hurt his feelings but he'd agree with you," I said. "Then he'd say he could take nephrology with both hands tied behind his back."

"He'd say that and he'd start a holy war," Alex replied, busy taking a paring knife to at least a million small limes.

"I figure I could throw down with ortho," O'Rourke added.

"Dude, they have saws. They break bones," Nick said, moving on from the avocados to squeeze the limes into a pitcher.

"And they drill so deep into their own specialty that an ankle guy would have one trick in his bag and would be helpless when I threw an elbow," O'Rourke replied. "They're only specifically intimidating, not broadly."

"What you're saying is you could take on every specialty?" Sara asked him. "Is that a feature among trauma surgeons or a defect?"

Before I could stop myself, I said, "A defect, for sure."

I met her gaze from the other side of the room and held it while the conversation continued around us. I tightened my grip on the beer bottle and silently dared her to look away first. She would. She'd blink down at her drink or the man she was politely ignoring or over at the infantry of limes or to O'Rourke and the mask of apathy he wore so flamboyantly. She'd end it like she always did.

"Pretty sure plastics would be an easy hit," I said.

And that did it. She rolled her eyes, muttered "Asshole" under her breath, and shifted just enough to pivot her attention toward O'Rourke.

"Yeah, that's obvious," O'Rourke agreed. "Plastics, uro, neuro—"

"Wait a fucking second," Nick snapped. "You are not seeding neuro with urology. Not while you're drinking my beer."

O'Rourke glanced at the bottle in his hand. "Did I say neuro? I meant nephrology. Totally nephrology. Did I mention I was on call last night? And I haven't slept since I was twenty-three?" He glanced at the residents. "This is why you can't play the game. You need to reach and exceed this level of deprivation. You need to be broken. Then and only then will you be ready to play the game of surgical specialty fireball."

"Fireball?" Alex repeated. "Where did the fire come from?"

"And the balls," Riley added.

"Sounded cool," O'Rourke said with a shrug. "I'll workshop it some more this week."

"Ahhh. Dr. Hartshorn, right on time as usual," Nick called as the cardiothoracic surgeon stepped through the back door with his wife Stella in tow. "What can I get you two to drink?"

Hartshorn was good enough to give a bashful smile as he and Stella joined the group in the kitchen.

Stella gestured to the pitcher Nick was mixing. "I see a bottle of tequila and a whole bunch of limes. Whatever that's about, it looks good."

"That looks like I'll be on the floor tomorrow morning," Hartshorn replied, shooting a grin at Erin. "I'll have whatever the very tolerant and very kind Dr. Acevedo is having."

Erin, the volcanologist with a pair of doctorates to her name, lifted her beer bottle, saying, "Coming right up—but it's Walsh when I'm Doctor."

"How did I not know that?" Hartshorn asked.

"Because you're always late to the party," Nick muttered.

"Walsh earned the doctorates," she replied, handing him the beer. "I'm Acevedo on evenings and weekends."

"Unless she's on a volcano that weekend," Nick added as he squeezed another lime into the pitcher. "All bets are off when she's on a volcano."

"Now that's an actual fireball," O'Rourke muttered.

"I'm with you on the maiden name," Stella said to Erin. "Stella Allesandro built a reputation in sports publicity and communications. Stella Hartshorn is someone else entirely."

"Oh, for sure," added Alex. "Dr. Emmerling survived a brutal, soul-crushing residency and then a beast-mode fellowship. I won't care if my kids' teachers or friends call me Mrs. Walsh but I sure as hell won't erase Dr. Emmerling because he put a ring on it."

"But I didn't put a ring on it," Riley murmured. "You didn't want a ring. Do you want a ring? I'll get you a ring."

"That's not the point of this convo, babe," she replied.

For no rational reason whatsoever, my gaze drifted to Sara. She glanced between Erin and Stella as they groaned over the obstacles they'd face if they ever changed their names professionally. Her features were stiff and fixed, like she was working very hard at presenting her best idea of a neutral expression.

Worst of all, she looked hot enough to start fires with her fingertips. Her jeans functioned as a vicious reminder of exactly how thick and perfect her thighs were, and the pale gray sweater she wore only furthered the torment. I wanted to run my palm over the wool-covered contours of her body, and I wanted to be a little cruel about it. I wanted to curl a finger through one of those belt loops and drag her to me. Wanted to pinch and twist those nipples until her eyes watered. Wanted her hair wrapped around my fist and the helpless cry that always came when she knew I had her.

I always had her, at least for those rare, secret minutes we shared before one of us fucked it up.

With a stifled groan, I rolled my eyes at myself. I was such a fucking moron to stand here thinking about this woman. It didn't matter what happened when we were alone because it never lasted. It was one mistake after another. The visiting professor could pull her hair and twist her nips for all I cared. He could be my fucking guest. Hope he liked croutons and ceaseless shrieking.

I set my beer down on the countertop and headed for the doors leading to the backyard. Beckoning to O'Rourke, I said, "Come on. There's a basketball hoop out back."

"Does this mean you've decided to teach me today?" he asked.

This kid was such a douche. I liked it too much. "If you're lucky."

———

HARTSHORN WANTED to talk blood clot protocols while we ate and that was a fine introduction to the man and his mind. On the upside of this, I was too busy arguing with him over the reality of treating critical care cases as opposed to his fantasies of trauma surgery to adequately glare at the visiting professor.

He was seated diagonally across from Sara but it was far too loud at this table for them to carry on an intimate conversation with that much distance between them. Still, I wanted to throw a fork at the guy every time he gave her another *aw shucks* laugh-shrug. Did he not realize she would eat his soul? Didn't he see that evil in those big hazel eyes or the hell-branded fury in that sweet little mouth? She'd verbally castrate him in four seconds flat and she'd make him thank her for it. He was blind if he didn't see this. The woman was lethal and he did not have the stones to roll with her.

I nodded to Hartshorn—who was still on about clots— and gnawed a chunk of ice as I shot a glance down the table at the professor. This poor bastard didn't know what was good for him. As for Sara, well, she had to know this was a disaster in the making. This guy was not on her level. Maybe she'd have fun brutalizing him for a bit but he'd serve as nothing more than a snack to her. She had to know he'd never satisfy her. He'd never know her or what she needed.

"So, you can see why this is a priority to me," Hartshorn said, nudging my arm with his elbow. "And it would be great if you could—"

"Where the hell did Shap go?"

Hartshorn scanned the table with a frown. "I don't know. Is she on call this weekend?"

"No." I glared at the professor again. A snarl rattled in my throat. This was his fault. I didn't know what *this* was but it was his fault. "She's not."

"Bathroom, maybe," Hartshorn said. "Anyway. I could really use your support on this protocol—"

"Hold that thought," I said, reaching for the vibrating phone in my pocket. "We'll catch up on this later. Okay?"

A weird splash of surprise hit me when I realized it was a hospital number and not Sara calling me. But that was dumb. Why would she call me? She wouldn't. That wasn't something she did, and she definitely wouldn't do it from somewhere in Acevedo's house. She didn't want— No. I wasn't going to entertain any of that bullshit. We weren't going to—well, we only did that on Thursday nights.

Since I was surrounded by surgeons—I was ignoring the existence of the visiting professor on principle—and their significant others, no one needed an explanation when I pushed away from the table with a finger pointed to my phone in explanation. I wandered down the hallway to the front of the house, tapping my screen to accept the call as soon as the group's noise was behind me.

"This is Dr. Stremmel," I said automatically.

The typical rapid-fire jumble of patient data came across the line in a manner exclusive to interns. I was more surprised when they knew how to report correctly at this point in their rotations. I nodded to myself while mentally reorganizing but my focus—not that I'd admit it to anyone—was finding Sara. This place was three floors of old-as-hell house and I knew there were loads of strange little rooms and hidden closets. She could be anywhere.

But she wasn't. She had a shoulder leaned against the wall in a shadowed corner of the front entryway, her back to me and her head bowed. It seemed like she was reading something on her phone. I stared at her for a moment, willing her to turn around or acknowledge that she knew I was *right here*.

When she didn't move, I made my way into the living room as the intern said, "Okay. That's everything, I think."

He was breathless and his report was a fucking mess—wasn't even sure I could find the primary complaint—and I would've made a teachable moment of this if I wasn't stupidly preoccupied with pacing past the door to glance at Sara again. I wanted her attention for a minute, just one minute, so I could complain about the visiting professor and annoy her until she wanted to both scratch my skin off and get fucked up against a wall.

Just one minute.

"That's plenty." I completed another circuit of the living room in time to watch Sara's shoulders rise and then fall, like she was blowing out a deep breath. "Dr. Tavares will appreciate this level of detail when you page her, seeing as she's your on-call resident tonight and should be in the building somewhere."

I heard something that resembled a hand slapping a forehead followed by "*Shiiiiiit.*"

"It happens." I glanced around the room to keep from stomping back out into the hall. There were books everywhere, photos too, and lots of little things that seemed appropriate in the home of a geologist and a neurosurgeon, like several dog-eared copies of *Science* on the sofa and a crystal dish filled with ugly rocks. It was all I could do to keep from putting myself in front of Sara just to bother her. I really loved bothering her. Couldn't stand the idea of anyone else being on the receiving end of her withering glares. Definitely not that fucking professor.

"Thank you, Dr. Stremmel," the intern said. "So sorry to bother you. Have a good night."

"Hold up." Once again, I caught Sara blowing out another breath. What the fuck was this all about? I stopped near the door, close enough to watch her yet far enough to make it seem like I wasn't. "Get your report prioritized before you page Tavares. Communicate the primary complaint, then get into comorbidities and history if relevant."

I heard notebook pages flipping and another "*Shiiiiiit*" before he said, "Right, right. Thanks again, Dr. Stremmel."

With that issue resolved, I slipped my phone into my back pocket and headed for the hallway. Sara was exactly where I'd left her, that one shoulder pressed to the wall like she was holding up the house, phone in hand, and her back to me. It was classic *leave me the hell alone*.

"If you're playing a round of hide-and-seek with the professor, the fact you're still waiting here doesn't bode well for your G-spot."

"For fuck's sake, Stremmel," she said. "Would you shut up? And go away while you're at it."

"Don't tell me you'd rather have the professor," I said as I approached. "Come on, Shap. Let's not pretend you want another minute with that guy."

"Seriously. Shut up."

As I came to a stop in front of her, I realized she wasn't on her phone. Her hand was flat on her abdomen and her eyes closed. There was a fine mist of sweat on her brow and her face was pale. Something wasn't right. "What's going on here? What's this all about?"

"It's nothing," she said with a slight shake of her head.

She was breathing a little too quick for me to believe that.

I plucked her hand from her belly, finding her pulse with my fingertip. "Why don't you have a smartwatch like the rest of us? You think I like taking vitals the analog way? Fuck no. Give me a heart rate reading for every minute of the day and an ECG while we're at it. You gotta get in the game here, Shap."

"Those things make me twitchy," she said under her breath.

I nodded as I loosened the strap on my watch. "Then we'll only keep it on for a minute."

"Don't doctor me, Stremmel."

"Then do a better job of disappearing the next time you want to be alone. You're stuck with me now." I held her wrist in one hand, now sporting my watch, and moved two fingers to the arterial pulse in her neck. It wasn't actually necessary—none of this was necessary—but I wasn't walking away. I'd come here to bother her after all and I intended to do that. I shifted my palm to her jaw and ran my thumb across her cool cheek. "Look at this," I said, holding her wrist up to view. "What is this all about? This heart rate is far more elevated than I'd like to see from you when your clothes are on. Explain to me why you're in distress or expect me to use my own methods to figure it out."

She started to shake her head but whatever was happening behind her eyes was stronger than her desire to tell me to fuck off. "I'm out here because I'm trying to get it under control. If I go in there"—she motioned the bathroom around the corner—"the nausea will win. I don't want that to happen."

"What's causing the nausea? What am I working with here?" I prompted. I hadn't noticed what she'd eaten but I knew she'd skipped the margaritas because Nick had asked her three times if she'd wanted one. She'd looked ready to rip his ears off the second time he asked and I was just surprised he was still alive following the third.

She blew a breath through her mouth and I saw it the second she gave up the fight. "My body is very well trained. It doesn't even have to be asked to vomit after a meal anymore. After all these years, it knows what to do."

I blinked between Sara's creased brow and the readout on the watch face. I needed that minute to realign everything I knew about her.

"Snacks like croutons and trail mix are no problem, but long, social meals screw me every time," she continued. "Either I eat too much or I eat too fast. Or I allow myself to get too hungry and my stomach is already agitated when I do eat. Or none of those things happen and my body just taps into decades of muscle memory that remembers we never keep meals down."

She blinked up at me now, her eyes wide and defiant. Instead of being the pain in the ass she expected me to be, I gave her a quick nod, saying, "Focus on your breathing."

"What does it look like I'm doing?"

I shifted my hand away from her jaw and over her shoulder, down her arm. I traced my thumb along the well of her palm. "Do as you're told. Just this one time. Okay?"

There was a beat where it seemed like she was going to fight me because there was no other way with us—it was always a fight, even when it was fucking—but then she closed her eyes again. With her shoulders shoved back, she drew a breath through her nose while she tapped out a five count on my wrist. She blew it out, touching her fingertips to my wrist eight times.

"Good. Two more. Deeper this time. Get out of your shoulders and into your diaphragm."

"Don't mansplain breathing to me, Stremmel."

"Then do it correctly, Shap."

Her brows pitched up as she inhaled, and that was fine by me. She could be as annoyed as she wanted. I'd annoy her every day if it distracted her from stomach spasms.

I stroked her palm through another round of deep breathing. After two more, she said, "You don't have to stay here. I can usually talk myself through the worst of it. That's why I came out here."

"And what happens when you can't talk yourself through it?"

"I have meds." She lifted a shoulder. "You should get back in there. They're going to wonder where you went."

"Have you seen the empty tequila bottles? No one is wondering where anyone went." I glanced down at the watch face, pleased to find her heart working slightly less hard than it had been. "Who's taking care of you for this?"

"I told you not to doctor me."

I scowled at her as I loosened the watch from around her wrist. "Answer the damn question, Shap."

"I have an eating disorder recovery specialist in Baltimore. I've been working with her for about five years."

Only five years, my god. That wasn't enough. Not nearly enough.

"And your stomach? Who's looking after that? Emmerling knows all the best people in GI."

She huffed out an aggravated breath. "Thanks, but I'm not sharing my bulimia-induced gastroparesis and irritable bowel with any of my colleagues. Definitely not the ones I mingle with after-hours." She dropped her gaze to the floor. "Not sure why I shared it with you."

I stared at her as the same question bounced around my head. She pressed her lips together and that tiny gesture loosened something in the middle of my chest, and I couldn't stop myself from wrapping my arms around her and holding her tight to me.

For a second or two, Sara stayed frozen in place, her hands hanging at her sides. Then she softened against me, her arms linking loose around my waist and her forehead settling against my chest.

Of all the ways I'd ever touched her, I'd never touched her like this. Never without the intention of stripping her down, taking everything she offered. It was strange, this feeling. I couldn't explain it but I couldn't let her go either. I had to do this, I had to hold her—even if it was awkward and uncomfortable.

If I had to categorize it, I'd say this was what a pulmonary embolism felt like. I was reasonably confident I wasn't experiencing an embolism but there was something thick and deadly and new pulsing behind my sternum. There was a quick kick to my heart rate and my head felt fuzzy as my chest cinched again, and I couldn't decide whether I'd feel better if I let her go or held her closer.

"Let me see if I can find it. Give me just a minute to look —*ohhhh*." At once, we swiveled in the direction of the hall and found Erin blinking at us. "Sure. Yep. Okay."

"Noooo," Sara replied, jerking away from me. "Oh, no. Not okay. Nothing is okay. There is nothing, actually. This is not—it's *not*." She stared at me, her gaze sharp enough to saw bones. "Tell. Her."

I crossed my arms. Maybe I really did have an embolism

because it felt like all the air had been knocked out of me. My chest ached and every muscle clenched when I said, "It's nothing."

Erin swung an impatient frown between us. "You could've told me. I wouldn't have meddled myself into Malakai's business if I knew this was happening. And, oh my god"—she brought her fingers to her temples—"I don't want you to have to sneak around in my house. We have a very strict no-sneaking policy here. You know that, Sebastian."

Sara hit me with *fix this right now before I fix you into a body bag* eyes.

With a great, douchey snicker, I said, "Really, Walsh. There's nothing to tell. Nothing to see here." I waved a dismissive hand at Sara like I hadn't suffered a very confusing and very somatic embolism at her hands. "We were just talking."

"It was a professional conversation," Sara added.

Erin bent an eyebrow up. "You two are funny. This is funny."

"Walsh," I warned.

She glanced at me. "If you're insistent on lying, lie better. That's all the advice I have for you this evening."

I shoved my hands in my pockets and tipped my head up to study the ceiling. "Nothing to lie about." The old staircase curled and crooked above, and competing shafts of moonlight and street light shone in through the landing windows. I shifted to face Sara. My chest still ached. "Isn't that right, Shap?"

CHAPTER 20

SARA

I WAS USED TO THIS.

I knew how to simultaneously manage a hurgly-burgly belly and complex surgical procedures, so I could handle Sebastian and Erin, and everything else.

This was extremely manageable. If I had to list my skills in order of proficiency, holding it together and getting through stressful times without breaking a sweat outranked anything I could do surgically. Even during medical school and residency, when I was at my sickest and most broken, I looked like the most confident, controlled woman in the world. Maintaining complete self-assuredness while crumbling on the inside was my superpower.

"Yes, that's right. Nothing to lie about here. Just a quick discussion," I said, turning my attention to Erin because I couldn't stand to see Sebastian's reaction.

"And y'all concluded that discussion with a hug?" She pushed her glasses up her nose, her gaze trained on Sebastian. "You could've told me. The only things I know how to keep are secrets."

Sebastian stared at me for a long moment. Then, "You

don't know this but Shapiro is a compulsive hugger. Hugs everyone. All the time. For no good reason. Must be a plastics thing. Just wait, she'll probably hug all over you on her way out of here tonight. It's actually very unpleasant so prepare yourself." His lips turned down into a deep scowl which I didn't understand seeing as he just threw me under the effusive affection bus. He should've been smirking his ass off. Before I could mine that reaction any further, he plucked his phone from his back pocket, saying, "I gotta head out, Erin. I got called in on a case. Thanks for feeding me—again."

"You're not on call," she said as he backed away.

"Something came up," he said, pointing to his phone. "They need me for a thing."

"That doesn't happen," she said. "I'm serious about you lying better. You're terrible at this." She swung a glance toward me. "Both of you."

Sebastian's gaze met mine. He was still scowling and I couldn't dismiss the feeling that, once again, he was disappointed about something. He gave a brief shake of his head before disappearing down the hallway. Now I was sure of it —he was disappointed in me. And for what? Preventing our coworkers from finding out we were carrying on a toxic game of enemies with benefits? There was no way I did anything wrong here, and if his head was too far up his ass to realize it, that was his problem. Not mine.

I was still staring after Sebastian when Erin asked, "Have you ever heard of rift valleys?"

I blinked away from the empty hall. "What?"

"Rift valleys. They're a product of extensional tectonics. The plates pull apart over time, creating a linear lowland between highlands or mountain ranges."

I bobbed my head but I was *so* confused. "Right. Yes."

"Some of the world's deepest lakes are actually rift valleys. Lake Baikal in Siberia holds almost a quarter of all the freshwater on this planet." She laced her fingers together and then drew them apart until only her fingertips touched. "It's this spectacular place where the earth is cracking apart and it's been doing it for twenty-five, maybe thirty million years. It's the most ancient lake in the geological record and that's a wild ride all on its own."

"Oh, wow. Really?"

"But it's not the whole story. When I want to scare myself —and I mean *really* scare myself—I think about Lake Baikal, and I'm going to tell you why."

I motioned for her to continue. Was I supposed to understand any of this? "Please do."

"Baikal is the deepest lake in the world. It's more than twice as deep as Crater Lake, as Tahoe. It's more volume than all the Great Lakes combined." She brought her fingers together again and pulled them apart. "It's nearly a mile deep, but when you hit that mile mark, you haven't really reached the bottom. There's a thick layer of sediment"—she wiggled her barely joined fingertips at me—"adding another four *miles* of depth. This rift valley sits at least five miles beneath the surface."

"And that's, I mean, it's five miles. It's a lot. So, that is very scary," I said. "I can see that."

"No, you're not scared. Not yet." She dropped her hands. "There are bigger lakes out there. Much more prominent. All the ones that come to mind when someone talks about a good-sized lake. Even several of the Great Lakes, the ones I blew off a minute ago, are much, much bigger than this long, ragged, skinny crescent of broken earth in Siberia. Baikal doesn't look remarkable on the surface but then you keep going down and down and *down*, all the way to these dark, unimaginable depths. And when you get to the bottom, you find the great open wound that makes Baikal what it is."

What...why was she telling me this?

"That's what scares me. Thinking of a lake about half the size of Lake Michigan but six times as deep and *broken at the bottom*." She stared at me for a heavy moment, edged her glasses up again. "It's cold and lonely down there, you know?"

I gulped. This wasn't about lakes or valleys. "Yeah."

"I thought you should know that. I thought you might understand. I *hope* you do." Nodding to herself, Erin took a step backward. "I'll just say that lake is important to me. I'm protective of that lake. The last thing I want is someone coming in with heavy machinery or risky new drilling ideas. I know what that lake has seen and I don't want anyone putting it through anything more."

This wasn't about lakes at all.

"Now if you'll excuse me, I have to go find the meteorite I left somewhere around here," she said.

"Sure. Yeah. No problem."

This was fine.

———

I STAYED AT THE ACEVEDOS' party another hour though my stomach was still very unsettled and I couldn't stop thinking about that frown from Sebastian. Oh, and the lakes. Those damn lakes—and that warning. *Shit*. Who knew Erin was the secret mama bear of this social circle?

I splashed around in these thoughts while parking

myself next to Alex, my designated extrovert, while she kept the conversation going with Stella and Malakai. Alex's husband was busy peering up the chimney with a flashlight and I bounced between watching that ER visit waiting to happen and tuning into the chatter around me until Hartshorn sidled up and decided to talk my ear off about blood clots. He didn't require much more engagement than a few nods and murmurs of agreement, which was great because what the hell did Sebastian have to be disappointed about? What on earth could I have done wrong here?

Of course there was nothing. I did nothing wrong and Sebastian knew that. He just loved being impossibly moody, even at the expense of logic.

I wasn't missing something. I couldn't be. I understood the situation perfectly.

After breaking away from the clot conversation, I made a quick round to say goodbye to everyone and then headed home.

What could I have done wrong? What did Sebastian expect from me here? There was no fathomable reason for us to give Erin a true accounting of our toxic cycle of sex, violent team-building activities, and resentment. Definitely not. There was no explaining that to anyone.

I didn't dare begin to explain it to myself.

I stopped in the foyer when I arrived home, my keys clutched in my fist and my gaze traveling up the twist of the staircase to where it led up to Sebastian's apartment. After a minute, I started toward the stairs but I turned back before reaching the first step. An eternity passed where I paced the foyer, replayed every minute I'd spent with him earlier today and this evening, turning it all over and over until the only thing I could recall was the moment when he wrapped his arms around me, holding me with more possession than I'd ever received from him.

That was the one thing I didn't understand.

He'd never hugged me before, but more importantly, it hadn't been necessary. He'd made a choice to reach for me without sex being on the table. Obviously, we were both insane but not insane *enough* to get naked in the middle of Acevedo's house so that hug wasn't about sex, it wasn't about hating each other, it wasn't about any of the things that had previously brought us together.

One of these things was not like the other.

That jolted me out of my pacing. I ran up the stairs before I could think better of it.

I approached his door, not hesitating a second before bringing my knuckles down on the wood. The sound echoed in the stillness around me but I was positive I'd heard movement on the other side of the door. A creak of a floorboard, a bit of shuffling, something. I waited, convinced Sebastian was busy being an obstinate ass who got off on making me wait.

But then I realized I'd waited far too long. Even if he was inside, he wasn't going to let me in and I would not beg for his attention.

Oh, hell no.

I finally took myself downstairs and tried to settle in for the night but that was out of the question. There would be no settling. Not after…everything.

I couldn't keep doing this with Sebastian. I couldn't keep taking his bait. And I couldn't confide in him ever again. The only explanation I had for telling him about my recovery was nausea-induced delirium. I couldn't find any other reason. It wasn't as though I wanted him to know, that I wanted him to understand how difficult it was for me to participate in the simple ritual of eating with other people, that I wasn't the relentlessly hostile woman he took me for but someone who was just trying to keep it together while he turned my life upside down with his side-eyes and his penis and his scowls.

I didn't want any of those things, but most of all I didn't want anyone to use my private mental health and medical history against me. All doctors were held to an odd double standard—we weren't supposed to get sick or experience chronic illnesses—and female docs had an extra layer of that double standard. If we had to menstruate, get pregnant, or progress through menopause, we were expected to do it without anyone else becoming aware of those conditions.

But the truly exponential standard came in the form of mental illness. I knew people who'd been exited from internships, residencies, and fellowships as a result of their mental health concerns. That was never the official reason. It was always something like inadequate clinical skills or misfit in the specialty or failure to keep up with the coursework—and I'd nearly killed myself avoiding that fate.

I wasn't ashamed of myself, my disease, or my recovery, but I wasn't ready to let others into this side of my life.

Yet somehow I was certain Sebastian wouldn't divulge anything I'd said to him tonight to anyone else. He'd silently judge me for it but he wouldn't gossip.

At the same time, I was certain we were very, very bad together. We clashed and scraped and wounded each other, and we couldn't seem to stop. I couldn't keep doing that. I wasn't in the business of harming myself anymore and that meant I couldn't allow him to upturn my safe, healthy life. Yes, he'd listened and he'd helped me tonight—

Oh my god.

He'd held my hand the whole time.

There had been some doctoring but he'd held my hand.

While I'd been deep-breathing away the reflux and spasms.

He'd held my hand.

CHAPTER 21

SARA

I glared down at my paper. "You're giving me terrible directions."

"You're terrible at listening," Sebastian replied.

"I'm listening to you give me terrible directions," I said, nudging his flank with my elbow. "'It's round and sometimes wooden.' What the fuck is that?"

"It's the best description I can give you based on the rules," he said, elbowing me back. "Can you stop squirming? Jesus Christ, you're like a sack of angry cats."

"Why would anyone ever have a *sack* of *cats*? No wonder they're angry, they're in a sack being carried around by some maniac like you."

I capped the marker and shoved it in the cup on the coffee table. We were sitting back-to-back on the floor of Milana's office, Sebastian holding a card with an object on it while I attempted to draw that item based on his vague clues.

It wasn't going well.

We'd walked in here with a cloud of awkward hanging over us. Aside from the very weird way we left things over the weekend, we hadn't seen much of each other all week. It could've been a product of my schedule being chaotic or he could've been avoiding me. I didn't know which one it was, though the part of my brain that liked to believe everything was my fault *and* I could make everything better if I just tried hard enough was eager to dismiss all matter of my schedule. Even if it was especially chaotic on account of an upcoming event. I'd shared so much personal information—all the uncomfortable, unpleasant stuff too—and no one liked that. No one wanted my problems.

"The object was a fruit bowl," Milana said in that warm, *marveling at the whole damn world* way of hers. "A fruit bowl. Sara, you had the right idea going. Sebastian, you offered some good clues. It was a tricky challenge that tested your ability to hear each other and process that information through your own filters. Well done."

Without any warning at all, Sebastian pushed to his feet which had the pleasant effect of sending me sprawling back on the floor. "Thanks for nothing," I said.

He rolled his eyes at me and offered his hand, but I didn't need it. *Nope, all good here.* But then he barked out a laugh, a mile-deep belly laugh that filled me with heat like I'd been doused with actual fire. Pointing at my t-shirt, he said, "Wrong. Completely wrong."

I glanced down at my shirt. Inside an anatomically correct rib cage sat a hot pink cartoon heart. The text read *The way to my heart is through the fifth and sixth ribs.* On the back it said *And also food. Don't forget food.*

"Any idiot would aim for the ninth and tenth. Same result, half the mess." He shook his head at me like I'd insulted him to his core. "Really, Shap. I expected more from you."

"I thought you didn't make a habit of expecting anything at all."

He lifted his brows as though he hadn't hammered me over his thoughts on expectations in the jousting ring. "When it comes to you"—he dropped a glance to my shirt —"I guess I expect better than bad practice."

"Bad practice is what landed us here." I waved at Milana's office.

"We put that argument to bed weeks ago," he replied. "You should leave it there. *In bed*. Where it belongs."

I didn't know what the hell he was trying to accomplish with all those references to beds, but I ignored him as I rocked up to my knees.

Once I was settled on the sofa and busy with the croutons I'd brought with me today, Milana said, "It's my observation that you experience the most friction in the places where you're most similar."

Sebastian snorted and I was proud of myself for ignoring him. Very proud. Meeting his eyes and acknowledging inside this room that we were carrying on a sexual relationship wouldn't end well for me. For either of us.

Even if it was a train wreck in process, a disaster built of anger and resentment, and blankets tucked up to my chin and glasses of water, I wouldn't be able to hide the fact that I wanted it again tonight. I wanted it to end, but I didn't want that at all. I wanted to stop screaming at him all the time, I wanted to stop being angry about everything, but the crazy, disastrous thing we had seemed to require that catalyst. I couldn't get what I wanted without dropping all pretense of being perfect, being in control.

I couldn't control him any more than I could control the tides, and dammit I'd tried. All I ever did was try to exert some control over him and every single time he shot me down and he swore I didn't want that control, I didn't need it.

"The things you struggle to accept in yourself are the same things that activate you in response to each other," Milana continued.

"That's funny, seeing as I don't have much history of screeching at people or destroying exam rooms," Sebastian mused from his usual spot at the bookshelves.

"You are a trauma surgeon." I said this as if I was speaking to a small child. "All you do is yell. We've all seen it. We've all heard it. You yell in the halls, you yell in the elevators, you yell in the OR. I'm not sure which part of your training teaches the shouting, but it's high time you accept that you and your brethren are loud as hell. You're not an ortho bro. You're not calm like neuro and you're not cranky like cardio. You're trauma and you yell. It's how you tell us that what you're doing is really fucking urgent and everyone else has to get out of your way. Sometimes it is necessary to yell *at* you to get your attention. You are so accustomed to communicating that way that you don't listen unless someone meets you at that level."

There was a solid minute where it seemed like Sebastian heard and received those words, but then he said, "I've never once destroyed an exam room."

I turned to Milana, shaking my head. She gave me another one of those *trust the process* nods. "I won't be here next Thursday so—"

"Where are you going?" Sebastian asked.

"Does it matter?"

He rolled his eyes the way someone would wind an old

watch. I could almost hear him ticking. Then, "I asked, didn't I?"

"Asking doesn't entitle you to an answer," I replied.

"Sebastian, it is worth noting that you are scheduled for time off next week," Milana added. "At least that's the information that was provided to me. Your medical assistant told me you had travel plans."

He pushed a hand through his hair, nodded. He was completely unaware of these plans and something about that tickled me. "Oh. Right. Yeah."

I gestured to myself because I could be tickled and prove a point at the same time. "Look at this. It's me not badgering you for information about your plans. See how it works?"

Milana gave a soft clap of her hands and smiled at us like this conversation was a real breakthrough or something. "Seeing that you'll both be off-site and unavailable for our session, I'd like to give back an hour of your time in appreciation for the work you've done over these past few weeks. When you return, we'll engage in our last session." She nodded, adding, "No homework this week. Just promise me you'll both give yourselves the opportunity to rest and refill the well before returning. You deserve it."

We went in opposite directions when we left Milana's office. Sebastian took the stairwell of stolen kisses, I opted for the roundabout journey through several annexed buildings. There was no way we'd cross paths unless one of us veered off course and I really hoped Sebastian didn't do that. I had a few cases to check on before leaving for the day, but more than that, I needed a minute to straighten myself out before running into him in the foyer once again.

I'd changed out of scrubs (and the offensive t-shirt) and almost made it to the hospital exit without running into

Sebastian when I spotted him waiting beside the door, his arms crossed over his chest and his foot propped on the wall behind him.

I gave him a thorough study as I passed, the sort that said I *was* taking in the crisp gray trousers with which he'd replaced his bruised blue scrubs as well as the white button-down he wore open at the collar. He ran a hand over his jaw to hide a smile.

He caught up to me on the sidewalk, his hands shoved deep in his coat pockets. "Tell me where you're going."

"Home," I replied, tipping my chin in that general direction.

"Next week," he growled.

"Really, does it matter?"

"The fact I've asked multiple times should serve as proof that it does matter," he said.

I shot him an impatient frown. "And why is that?"

"Because I want to know." He said this as if I was the one being unreasonable here.

"I have a conference. Okay?"

"Why the fuck are you doing *that*? And where is this thing? Who are you going with? Please tell me it's not just you out there on your lonesome."

We stopped at the corner, waiting for traffic to clear the crosswalk. "You don't need any of that information. Not a single bit of it. You're being"—I looked him up and down again, but this time it had nothing to do with appreciating the way his clothes hugged his body—"unnecessary, okay? You're being very unnecessary."

He pressed a hand to my back as we started across the street. "Do you have any idea what people do at these conferences?"

"Listen, I know I look good for my age—blame it on the sunscreen—but my first plastic surgeons rodeo this is not."

"People lose their minds at conferences," he continued, completely ignoring my comments. "Get some free liquor in them and they lose their damn minds."

"I'm not sure if this is good news or bad news, but liquor and I don't get along, so I won't be losing my mind." We walked up the slight incline of Beacon Hill toward our building, his hand still low on my back. "It's barely even four days. In, out, over, and I am more than capable of traveling to a professional event and back without incident."

Sebastian climbed the steps to the building, his keys in hand while he shook his head. "Then I suppose you know all about the pharma sales bros and the gross doctor dudes who leave their wedding rings at home." He held the outer door open with his shoulder while he unlocked the foyer door. "The ones who make it their goal to cheat on their wives as many times as possible. Because those assholes talk, and even though you'd probably warn them off with your screeching and all, I just want you to be aware—"

"Wow. *Wow.*" I pressed my fingers to my temples. "How do you manage to dig a hole that deep and throw your entire body into it in less than thirty seconds? I want to know because it's so unbelievable. I want to squeeze the juice out of your brain just to study it."

"I am preparing you for your conference." He paced the foyer, his hands on his hips. "I just think you should know about the things that go on before you get there. That way you can decide, I mean, you need to decide what you're doing."

I cocked my head to the side. "What are you trying to say? That I'm going on some tropical dick-hunting mission?"

"I'm saying that you're"—he wagged both hands at my body—"*this* and they're assholes and—"

"You seem to know quite a bit about the behavior of men at medical conferences."

He waved that off with a dismissive hand. "Don't start with that."

"And why not? You're standing here telling me about all the guys I'm going to sleep with next week and—"

"Seriously, Shap." He stopped pacing to rub a grimace from his brows. "Take it back. *Please*."

"Are you…jealous?"

He shot me a scowl that could've burned this building to the ground. "Of what?"

"I don't know," I admitted. "Pharma bros? Doctor dudes with obvious wedding ring tan lines? I'm not sure." That topic hit *way* too close to home for me. "Why don't you explain this outburst to me?"

"Why don't you just tell me you don't plan on doing any dick hunting?"

"Regardless of what I do while I'm away, it's none of your business." I pulled my keys from my bag and turned toward my door. I couldn't watch while those words settled over him. It was bad enough feeling them twist through my belly. "I'd also like to mention that I have no problem with you taking a vacation and doing whatever the hell you want."

He crossed the foyer, set his hands on either side of my door. "You're gonna need to work a little harder if you want to convince me of that, you little liar."

CHAPTER 22

SEBASTIAN

THERE WERE DAYS WHEN I LEFT THE HOSPITAL AND I DIDN'T have any words left in me. It was like I had a specific allotment, a number that varied daily and was never shared with me until I'd surpassed it. When I was out, I was *out*. The only option was passing out on the sofa after some cheerleaders and avocado, and praying I woke up with the ability to speak.

Obviously, I'd survived medical school and residency where thirty-six-hour shifts were not unheard of so I knew how to power through, though it was never with much grace. Not that I usually had much grace, but I came off like a complete ass when I was overextended.

I was out of words right now. There was no good reason for it, but I was drained and I didn't know how or where, but I found the energy to trap Sara against her front door and say, "You're gonna need to work a little harder if you want to convince me of that, you little liar."

I gripped the doorframe as hard as I could. I wasn't going to touch her until she stopped with this bullshit.

"What do you want me to say?" she asked.

"Say you're not going to a conference to get laid." I leaned in, pressed my lips to her hair. She had it tied up in another one of those buns, but she didn't seem to accept that her hair would not be restrained in that way. Add it to the list of very obvious things Sara Shapiro chose to ignore on a daily fucking basis.

With an exaggerated sigh, she dropped her forehead to the door, saying, "I'm not going to this conference to get laid. I don't like people, especially people at conferences, and I can spot cheating husbands a mile away. Not that it's *any* of your business, but I attend for the professional content and spend the rest of the time in my hotel room. If I didn't have to go, I wouldn't."

I wrapped my arms around her torso and kissed the side of her neck. "Poor, antisocial screech owl."

"I'm not antisocial," she said. "I just can't do high doses of people in those kinds of settings."

"I know." I turned her around, leaned down to kiss her once. "There must be men tripping over themselves for your attention."

"The disgusting doctor dudes?" I nodded as I ran my lips over her cheek, her jaw. "I wouldn't even know what that looked like."

"You're not as cute when you fish for compliments, Shap. We've covered this."

"I'm not fishing for anything—"

I didn't have the words, but that didn't stop me from kissing the fight out of her. I could do that. I could take us into the pastel cloud of her apartment and bang the bed away from the wall all night long. I could do that for her. I could—

A loud creak sounded behind us. "*Fuuuuck.* Why does this always happen to me?"

Sara ducked her head to my chest and I tucked her in close as I glanced over my shoulder to find Riley Walsh descending the stairs. "Can I help you with something?"

He shook his head, straightened his gaze toward the doors. For the first time in his entire life, he didn't douse me in death glares. "Nope. Just wondering why the gods punish me this way. Carry on." When he reached the door, he called, "Good seeing you, Sara."

She groaned into my shirt. "I have no more than three minutes before Alex blows up my text messages."

"Give me your phone," I said, patting her pockets to find the device. Found it on the first try and set it to silent. "You're not dealing with anything other than what I want you to deal with tonight. I promise I'll give it back when I leave."

Some combination of those words was wrong. There was no other explanation for the way Sara tensed in my arms. A beat passed before she took a small step back, putting enough space between us to make it clear that something had changed. Then, "We have to stop doing this."

I really didn't have the words right now. I didn't and it killed me. "Inside," I said, returning to her pocket for the keys. "Let's go."

"We don't like each other," she said when we had the door closed behind us. "We are so, so unhealthy when we're together. Have you noticed that?" She brought both hands to her chest, her fingertips leaving little dots of color behind every time she tapped her clavicle. "I am not like this around anyone else. I am aloof, yes, but I don't get into fights over every little thing and contemplate pummeling people with an oar all the time. Don't you see it? We are a *disaster*. We're toxic. It's what we do to each other and—"

"Oh my god, shut up." Wincing, I held up a hand. Those words, they fucking *stung*. "Just stop before you actually drown in your own drama."

"I am not drowning in drama." She responded with an exaggerated frown when I slipped off my coat and dropped it to the back of her sofa. "I'm saying a week or two apart is probably a good thing." She shrugged, hugged her arms across her torso. "Maybe we'll break this little cycle of ours."

"That's what you want?" I stepped closer to her, traced a finger down the line of her arm. Her sweater was impossibly soft, like a baby's blanket repurposed for the likes of women who always hated the things they wanted.

"Maybe we'll leave town and realize we've gotten it out of our systems."

"You didn't answer me."

She forced a smile that would've annoyed the shit out of me a month ago, but only made me sad now. "We only have one more session with Milana. I'm sure it won't be an issue."

I hooked my fingers around the waistband of her pants, pulled her closer. "You still haven't answered me."

She pursed her lips together in a way that seemed like the precursor to her kicking me to the curb, but then she dropped her hands on my chest. "I've been looking at apartments. I mean, I've been looking for months. I do it every night to help me fall asleep." She glanced up at me. She didn't need any help falling asleep when she was with me. "Well, almost every night. But I was thinking it's time to make that move. I'm not cut out for doors that don't work when it's wet."

I nodded because there was no point to stopping her

now. She was head and shoulders into this one-sided conversation and there was no arguing with her. Not that I even had the words to argue. I'd fumble it in the worst ways and I couldn't let that be how this went down.

Also, I couldn't let this go down. This wasn't a toxic cycle. There was no getting her out of my system, not when the only thing I required in this life was to know what Sara looked like when she woke up and what she felt like curled around me in the middle of the night, and what she liked to do when she wasn't busy screeching and whether I could keep her with me for the rest of my time on this earth.

Did I have the language to articulate any of this? Not at all.

Did I assume I had a bit more time before I had to learn that language? Fuck, yeah.

Did I have any hope of getting through this night with my vital organs intact? It was anyone's guess.

With that tragedy in mind, I yanked her by the waistband into her bedroom and relieved her of her clothes while she rambled about apartments.

"And I wouldn't mind something a little farther away from the hospital," she said as I planted a hand between her breasts and shoved her to the bed. "This location was perfect when I first moved here, but now I know all the other neighborhoods and I understand how to get around so I'm open to Cambridge. Maybe the Back Bay. I'm not sure. I have to look around some more and—*oh*."

"I know you'd like to dissociate, but I'd prefer you enjoy some part of this." I flipped her on her belly because I didn't trust myself to be close enough to see the gold in her eyes and keep myself in order. One look and I'd say something wrong, something dangerous, and I'd ruin it. I mean, fuck, she wanted to break the cycle while I was busy mentally scrambling to cancel that vacation of mine because this cycle was the only thing in the world I wanted.

"I'm not dissociating." I could hear her pouting.

"Don't be a brat." I delivered a light slap between her legs. "I've had enough of that from you tonight."

She glanced back at me. "Why haven't you taken your clothes off?"

I opened her top drawer and spent a solid minute reorganizing her hair ties. My only explanation for this mess was that she sleep-shuffled through this drawer every night. "I will when you're ready for that."

"What are you actually saying with those words?"

I grabbed one of her vibrators—she'd handed over the full collection weeks ago—and clicked it on, then off. I shook my head. "If you don't shut that little screech owl mouth, I'll find another use for it."

That did the trick.

I teased her with the vibrator for a bit, careful to keep my hand between her shoulder blades and her face on the mattress because I was pretty sure I was staring at her with murder eyes, but I couldn't help it. She was talking about two-bedroom condos to have a room for yoga, and throwing the happy, non-toxic life she intended to live without me over her shoulder, so, yeah, I couldn't see straight.

She came once on the vibrator, another time on my tongue and fingers. It wasn't a struggle to get her there several times in one night now that she'd given up on the impossibility of it. It'd be great if she applied that logic to other situations.

I was still giving her the murder eyes when I stepped out of my trousers and rolled down the condom. Her body was warm and humid with sweat and her bun had morphed into a crazy halo of wisps and curls, and I could've tortured her for another hour or two, but this didn't feel good for me anymore. It felt like I was drawing her a map, but instead of allowing it to function as a map and tell her where to go, she saw nothing more than a pretty picture.

I couldn't keep drawing the map. It hurt to create something and have no one notice.

I clasped her wrists at the small of her back and pushed inside her slowly. I had to go slow this time. I had to remember how she felt around me and why I loved the first few seconds of overwhelming heat and pressure the most. I had to remember and then I had to say goodbye.

I wanted to taste her neck and stow that memory away with the rest of them, but I didn't trust myself to lean in, press my chest to her back. I needed a bit of distance to keep me from getting too honest.

She was always quiet when she came, but this one surprised me. Her lips parted on a silent cry, but her body went wild, jerking and pulsing against me like she was trying to break loose. The erratic rock of her thick thighs kept it going longer than I'd expected and that was when I lost myself imprinting those memories into the most sacred corner of my mind. That was when my control slipped for a minute and this came to an end I wasn't prepared to accept.

The orgasm ripped me apart. It reverberated into my chest and shoulders, and left me sore, as if I'd twisted every muscle the wrong way. I stared down at her, stunned and aching while my cock went on spurting like my body meant to drain every ounce of me into the condom. That it left me empty and unsatisfied seemed to be the point.

Sara twisted her hands from my grip and rotated her

wrists several times. That shook me from this stupor. "What's wrong?" I pulled out with a miserable groan, truly rather surprised her pussy hadn't succeeded in biting my dick off this time. "Was that too tight? Are you okay?"

She rolled to the side and dropped her gaze to the fringe of a small pillow. "I'm okay."

"Let me see your wrists."

"No," she said. "I'm fine. I don't need any doctoring." Finally, she glanced up at me. That I had to be ripped apart after coming with my entire soul while she stared at me seemed unfair. This was all really fucking unfair. "I think we need to see what happens when we don't have sessions and homework assignments all the time. I think we need to figure out what that's like."

I snatched a tissue from the bureau to clean up the condom. "Seems like you've already figured it out."

"Don't be an asshole."

"It's what I do best." I stepped into my boxers and trousers, dropped my focus to latching my belt. I grabbed my shirt off the floor and shrugged it on as I marched out of her bedroom. I couldn't stay there any longer. I almost left, but I couldn't make it to the door without passing her kitchen and that shelf of colored glasses.

I stared at those glasses, just fucking hating their existence and all the big and small things they represented. I did not want to walk back into her room, the one with pillows all over the floor, the bed a wreck, the scents of me and her and *us* in the air, and the drowsy naked girl who owned me inside and out, but refused to see it. I didn't want to do it.

"Fucking water," I muttered, grabbing a glass off the shelf and flipping on the faucet. "She doesn't need me to do this.

Doesn't need me for anything. Nope, nope, nope. Fuck the water." I dumped it out only to fill it again. "Just...*fuck*."

I did this three times and seriously considered throwing the fucking cup at the wall, but then she'd probably cut herself on the broken glass and I'd have to patch her up, which would kill me all over again. For all I knew, she didn't even notice the times I'd straightened her blankets or brought her water after fucking the fight out of her. She probably didn't care, so I didn't care.

But I cared very, very much and it was incredibly inconvenient. I knew if I didn't bring her that water, I'd as much as forfeit my right to ever bring her anything ever again.

And since that wasn't something I could live with, I walked back into her room. The pillows were all over the place and the bed was nowhere near the wall and the air was thick enough for me to taste her on my tongue. As for the drowsy naked girl, she was staring at me with an annoying little smile that drew me out of my misery long enough to roll my eyes.

I set the glass on the bureau and leaned down to brush a kiss over her lips. I should've walked away then, should've dragged my ass upstairs and cried into some avocado, but I couldn't stop myself this time.

"I'll see you in two weeks, you little liar. Maybe then you'll be able to admit what you want."

CHAPTER 23

SARA

Alex: My husband just told me something that can't be true.

Alex: I'm going to ask you this and I'm going to need you to not lose your shit when I do it because it's super invasive.

Alex: I want to preface it by saying my husband has been known to pop some weed gummies during the day if he's trying to get creative or whatever so it's possible he's imagining things.

Alex: Architects, man. Who knew there was a job where getting high at work could be a good thing?

Alex: Honestly, I wish he'd just lock himself in his office when he does it because otherwise I get a hundred texts about the birds in Copley Square or something and when I finally get a chance to respond, he's busy jerking off over rooflines.

Alex: I don't mean that literally. I'm sorry for putting that visual into your head. I just meant that he gets really, really excited about things I don't understand.

Alex: Back to my original question: How is it going with you and Stremmel?

Alex: Are these sessions helping? Are you getting a little closer as friends? Or something?

Alex: Okay I can't do this. I'm not subtle. I can't pretend to be subtle. Are you sleeping with Stremmel?

Alex: It's fine if you are, obviously, I'm just shaken to my core and questioning everything I know to be true in the world.

Alex: Either you're ignoring me or…wow, okay, or you're sleeping with Stremmel right now.

Alex: I immediately regret this entire conversation. Pretend I never asked.

———

Alex: It's been a few hours so even if you did that thing I never asked about, you can't still be doing it. Now, you're probably ignoring me.

Alex: And that's fair because I came at you with a whole lot of crazy today.

Alex: I'm sorry for being intrusive. This was all very intrusive.

Alex: I really am sorry.

Sara: Hey. My phone was off. I'm just catching up now.

Alex: Are we okay?

Sara: Yeah, no worries at all.

Alex: That's what people say when they have many, many worries.

Sara: Really, it's all good.

Alex: That's what people say when they're not even close to good.

Sara: I promise you, everything is all right, and please don't try to translate that. I'm fine. We're fine. Everything is fine.

Alex: And Stremmel?

Sara: Can't speak for him.

Alex: Are you okay? I can come downstairs if you want.

Sara: You are too kind. Thank you, but no, I really need to decompress. It's just been a long day.

Alex: You're sure? I feel like I've screwed things up.

Sara: Not at all! No, please don't think that. I swear, I'd tell you if there was an issue.

Alex: Would you though?

Sara: Yeah, of course. Sorry, I really need to get some sleep.

————

CONTROL WAS TRICKY FOR ME.

The less I had, the more I needed and that *more* often required borrowing from the most high-interest sources. The cost never mattered in the moment. The only thing that mattered was getting my hands around the neck of *one thing* —just one, that was all I needed—and squeezing it hard enough to make the stress and upheaval in my life feel manageable.

It had always worked for me. It didn't matter if my homelife was going off the rails once again or med school was insane or residency kicked my ass. It didn't matter if I traded greater and greater pieces of myself every time I went in search of that control and it definitely didn't matter that I'd made myself brittle and broken in all the places I was meant to be soft and pliable. All I had to do was get from here to there, so what was the trouble with killing myself for the journey?

Unlearning those rules had been difficult. The desire to be quiet and obedient and worthy of external validation never quite disappeared, but I could grab ahold of the threads of it now. I could twist them around, turn *obedient* into the practice of caring for myself without exception, turn *quiet* into a sensation I kept inside my body rather than a lock on my voice, my needs—and that was the plain core of it. Good little girls who grew up into people-pleasing women didn't get that way through any innate altruism or feminine urge to keep the peace. We got there because we learned, at some point, that our needs were a problem best kept to ourselves. We were most worthy when our existence didn't bother anyone.

There were days when I was great at bothering people. I'd bothered Sebastian into a paralyzing game of bickering, insults, and sex. Other days, I couldn't accept the simply offered aid of a friend without viewing it as the byproduct of being pitifully and disgustingly needy. I couldn't impose. I physically could not allow that to happen—because control was tricky for me. It didn't pack itself up and move on to another host. It changed. It shape-shifted. It turned into an obsessive need to heal, a cycle of interrogating my thoughts until I'd bled out the most invasive of them, an endless battle between the perfectionist and the savage inside me.

I couldn't pry my fingers loose from the stranglehold I had on those last few fringes. I wasn't strip-mining my body and spirit for control any longer, but the mission was unchanged. Find peace from the chaos, no price too high.

CHAPTER 24

SARA

THE FIRST HALF OF THE WEEK SEEMED TO PASS IN DASHES AND dots, some hours flying by while others dragged on until I was certain I could feel the weight of every passing second gathering on my skin. I couldn't stop myself from looking for Sebastian down every hall and in every stairwell. I knew he wasn't there. I mean, I'd peeked out from behind my curtains to watch him climb into a cab early Saturday morning, a black ball cap pulled low over his eyes and his scowl loud enough to stop traffic. I knew he wasn't here but I couldn't stop myself from looking.

On several occasions, I seriously considered bailing on this conference. I never wanted to attend these things but this one in particular was ripe for any reason to beg off. The topics being presented were only obliquely related to my daily work and I'd already met everyone worth networking with, and worst of all, my father was attending.

And that was why I *had* to be there.

The thing about hardcore narcissists like my father was that attention was their oxygen. If they didn't get enough, they suffocated. By that logic, I could cut off contact with my father—which I'd done at various points since moving out on my own—and live a happy, narcissist-free life. Except that logic held no water, not when I worked in his field and he had the personal cell numbers of all the people who made decisions that directly impacted my career.

Unless I wanted my father to turn blue and prove which one of us really knew how to throw tantrums, I had to show up at this boondoggle and play along. If you asked him, he'd say we were as close as any father-daughter plastic surgeon pair could be and he'd weave a very convincing tale about handing over his practice in Orange County to me whenever I was ready to return home.

The list of things I'd do before I'd ever move home and take over a practice focused almost exclusively on cosmetic surgery was miles and miles long. Aside from that, my father would sooner burst into flames than hand over a damn thing. His practice was the only thing in the world he loved in a real, true sense. He admired many people and had fondness for many others, but he *loved* the empire he'd built. If, for some unimaginable reason, I returned to California, he'd micromanage and second-guess me into a complete and total breakdown and that didn't begin to cover the ways he'd erode my mental health. The only things that had ever saved me were distance and independence, and I had to do whatever it took to preserve both of those.

It got ugly when I didn't.

That was the thought living rent-free in my head through takeoff and landing, while waiting for my luggage, and the dark cab ride to the resort. That ugliness was the reason my hair was freshly cut and colored, my nails professionally manicured, the creases in my forehead paralyzed with the most precise, careful injections of Botox in the land. It was the reason for the inexcusably expensive sandals and dresses I'd ordered as well as the refills on all of my gastrointestinal meds and the multitude of plain crackers I'd packed.

It was late when I arrived at the resort, too late to get any feel for the surroundings. Not that I wanted to go exploring. I hadn't slept well since the last evening I'd spent with Sebastian. I couldn't keep replaying the conversation and trying to parse out why he'd been so upset with me. I still didn't know, but now I was tired enough from traveling that I'd probably manage a few hours of deep sleep before I had to gird myself for these next few days.

I waved off the help of the resort staff because I couldn't manage small talking when I just wanted to be alone, instead accepting a map with lots of scribbled highlighter as a guide and steering my suitcase in the vague direction of my bungalow. That was how this resort rolled—bungalows. Nothing so dreadful as a building with rooms lined up, one beside another, on top of another. No, this place was all about bungalows, beach huts, villas. If I had to suffer through this event, at least I could stay in a beachfront bungalow with a fully stocked fridge and an outdoor rain shower. Seemed only fair.

"Sara."

I whirled around, searching the lobby for the too-familiar voice. When I found the source of that voice, it felt like I'd ripped a giant bag of jelly beans clear open and now they were spilling out of my hands, pinging off the stone floor at my feet, rolling and scattering and shooting across the room. I'd never be able to gather them all up and I'd never be able to put them back in the bag because the bag was a tattered scrap of plastic that could never exist the way it had before I'd torn it open. All it could be now was a blown-open wreck, something that'd once contained every single one of these jelly beans. I couldn't go back to the before, to anything other than a reality where Sebastian Stremmel was no more than ten feet away from me in shorts and a t-shirt.

But it was completely real, right down to the blindsided expression on his freshly sun-kissed face.

And…and he'd called me Sara.

Not Shap, not Shapiro. Not tiny tornado. *Sara*.

I didn't want that to mean something—I didn't want it to mean *anything*—because we weren't doing this anymore. We couldn't. I couldn't continue hurting myself this way.

So, I did the only sensible thing and bolted in the direction of my bungalow. Or I hoped it was the right direction. It was dark and I hadn't paid enough attention to that map and then my nemesis-lover appeared like a willpower mirage so there was a solid possibility I was lost in more ways than one.

"Sara," he called, a snap of impatience in his voice. "What the hell do you think you're doing?"

"Walking away," I replied, hanging a decisive left at a fork in the path.

"Well, honey, you're walking in a circle."

He grabbed my elbow and jerked me to face him. I avoided his gaze, instead glancing at the buildings nearby. The asshole was right—I'd traveled in a damn circle, making it all the way back to the lobby and accomplishing nothing.

"Is there something you want?" I asked.

"You could start by telling me what you're doing here." He released my elbow, slid his hand down to my wrist. "End with explaining why you took off like that."

"What am *I* doing here?" I shook my wrist free from his grip. "What are *you* doing here?"

"I'm on a fucking vacation," he thundered. "And you're supposed to be at a fucking plastics conference."

I stared at him for a second before blinking away. "I am. I *am* at a conference, it's just not here," I said, suddenly hit with all the exhaustion of this week. "The conference is at another resort. On the other side of the island."

"How the hell did this happen?" He stared at me, clearly struggling to accept that we ended up on the same Caribbean island without trying. I was paddling the same boat. "How did I not know your conference was in Jamaica?"

"We don't have much experience with asking each other questions. We don't talk, okay? We fight about nothing and have angry sex and say mean things instead of doing anything normal or healthy or professional."

He opened his mouth, an argument at the ready, but stopped himself before saying anything. Then, "Why?"

"Why, what?"

He glanced to the side, taking a minute to stare at the tropical plants lining the path. "Why don't we talk?"

"Because we hate each other," I said.

"Is that what this is?" When I didn't respond, he said, "So, you're here."

I bobbed my head. "Yes."

"For the week."

I waved at my luggage. "Just a few days."

He shoved his hands into the pockets of his shorts and stared at me like he was searching for something. Like he'd lost something and if he just looked hard enough, he'd find it. Eventually, he growled, "Sara…"

"Why are you calling me that?" I snapped, my exhaustion quickly replaced with a crackling frustration that was primed to explode. "Why am I Sara here, but back home I'm Shap, I'm Shapiro, I'm the evil silicone wench."

"I have never called you an evil silicone wench," he said, slicing both hands through the air. "Never."

"Maybe not to my face." I scowled at him. A good, snarly scowl. See how he liked it. "You've thought it."

He snatched the hotel paperwork from my hand and leafed through it as he shook his head. "You're going the wrong way. Come on."

I stared after Sebastian—when had he become Sebastian to me? How had that happened?—as he took off in the opposite direction. I looked around, noticing for the first time the beach just beyond the path. It was completely empty and awash in moonlight, and I wanted to plop down there and be blissfully alone. I didn't want to fight with him every day and I didn't want to live with this kind of constant upheaval. It felt too much like the drama I'd grown up with, like my parents and their chaos. I wanted Sebastian to go back to his room and his vacation and his whole damn life. I wanted him to leave me alone.

I wanted those things. I *truly* did and I believed it as devoutly as I believed in gravity and karma and antibiotics.

Yet I followed Sebastian to my bungalow.

I allowed him to open the door and show himself inside, glance back at me with a frown like *are you waiting for a fucking invitation, get in here*, and then return outside to snatch the suitcase away from me. I let him press his hand to the small of my back where I was sweat damp and so very painfully imperfect, and I let him guide me into the bungalow. I watched while he carried my luggage into the bedroom—why use the wheels when you had arms like that?—and I nodded in agreement when he announced he was taking the bag from my shoulder too.

I didn't stop him because I didn't want him to stop, and more than that, I didn't want him to leave. That was so much worse than my baseline frustrations with this man. I hated him for bringing all these contradictory emotions to my life and I hated myself for letting those emotions make room for themselves and *stay*.

"Why are you doing this to me?" I suddenly snapped into action, marching toward the kitchen. For no apparent reason, I needed to open every drawer and cabinet, peer into the refrigerator, turn the tap on and off, touch every dish towel, and examine every random object I encountered. All while shouting, "Why? Just tell me why."

Instead of answering me, Sebastian trailed behind me at a leisurely pace, shutting the drawers all the way, refolding the towels, straightening all those random objects. "What am I doing to you?"

"This," I cried, stopping in the center of the living room, my arms thrown out wide. "You're doing *this* and it's driving me crazy. Do you understand that?"

He stood behind a creamy white sofa, his hands curled around the back. "What have I done to you? Explain it to me. I'd really like to hear that."

"Don't do that," I warned. "Don't pretend that I'm the one who can't handle this when you're the one doing it to me. My entire life is out of control when you're around. It's like the only thing in the world I can do is yell at you or rip your clothes off, and I want it to stop. I need it to stop. Every week, I promise myself it's not going to happen again, I'm not going to do this with you anymore, but then"—I dropped my arms, shook my head—"it's like I'm someone else. Because this isn't me! I don't go around screaming at people and having sex every week and—"

"It's the frequency? That's the real problem? You should've said something sooner."

I grabbed a pillow from the sofa and lobbed it at his head. "Shut up when I'm talking to you!"

He fetched the pillow from where it landed and returned it to the sofa before pacing toward me. "If you're trying to make the case that you're not a psychotic little screech owl, you're going to need to stop saying illogical shit like that."

"This isn't me," I whispered, heat gathering behind my eyes and emotion tightening my throat. I wasn't going to cry. Not happening. Not here, not now. Not in front of him. "I can't be this person anymore. I feel like I am coming apart at the seams, like I'm crumbling, and I can't do it anymore."

I stepped toward him, my hands raised with the intention of showing him to the door. Tears streamed down my face in another promise to myself broken.

"I know." He took my hands in his, pressed them to his shirt. "I know."

I mashed my face against his chest, blotting tears and madness on his t-shirt. "You don't know anything. You think I'm awful."

He brought his chin to the top of my head, let out a sigh that would've sounded like contentment coming from anyone else. "I don't think you're awful at all."

"You just said I'm a psychotic screech owl," I said with a sniffle.

"You know I say that with love."

"Shut up. The only thing you love is getting me angry enough to want to have sex with you."

For a long moment, the only sounds between us came from my sniffles and shuddering breaths. It seemed like we could've stayed there for hours, laced and locked together while the world went on without us. I hated that it was so easy. All I had to do was rub my cheek against his hard chest and suck in a lungful of his clean scent, and I forgot all the reasons I needed him to leave. I forgot *everything* I'd sworn I'd remember. Everything that made this so damn messy for me.

"I want a cease-fire," Sebastian said, his lips pressed to the crown of my head. "From now until you leave, no fighting."

"I don't think we can do that."

He shrugged. "There's only one way to find out."

I hid a smile against his chest even though I wanted to lunge for him. Wrap my hands around his neck and watch those obscenely long lashes fall shut while his scowl shifted into a smile. He *would* smile. He'd grin while I pressed my thumb in the exact spot to cut off his air supply, and that said something about the toxicity we created when we were together. If it also said something about trust, I didn't have the proper ears to hear it.

"Stop falling apart for a minute and see what it's like when we don't fight," he said. "Show me who you are without all the screeching. Who knows? I might like her better."

"If you want a cease-fire, you're going to have to put your fighting words away."

"Tell me you want a cease-fire and I will," he replied, giving our joined hands a squeeze. "Be as strong as you always are for me and say you need a couple of days where it's just us and none of the bullshit we left at home, and I will give you everything you want." He ran his lips over my forehead, my temple. "You know I will."

Another rush of tears burned my eyes as I nodded. "I want it."

The scary part was that I meant it and I couldn't even blame it on losing my mind as we tumbled into bed because there wasn't a single sexy thing about this moment. I was sweaty and snotty and sobbing into his shirt for reasons that had nothing to do with the miracles his penis worked.

He freed his hand, skimmed a thumb across my cheeks. "Don't cry, tiny tornado."

"Believe me, crying in front of you is the last thing I want to do."

His scowl twisted tight across his lips as he gave me a quick nod. "Right. Yeah. How about a shower?"

I dropped my forehead to his chest again, heaved out a breath. "I'm gross. I know. There's no pretty way to travel from winter weather to tropical weather."

"No, honey, you're *clothed*," he said. "That's the problem I'm attempting to address."

"It's because I threw a pillow at you," I said. "And yelled about my life being out of control. That's what turns you on."

"It's really not." He ran his knuckles down my back, silent a long moment before letting that hand travel over my backside. He gave me a rough squeeze, jerked me closer to him. "I haven't stopped thinking about you once. I thought I was hallucinating when I first saw you. That I was so out of my mind with wondering what your t-shirt said today that you materialized out of thin air."

"'Let the Beat Drop,'" I said. "With a drawing of a QRS complex on an EKG."

"Oh my god." He growled against my neck, a deep,

rumbly sound that seemed to go on forever. "Yeah, I need to get you out of these clothes. You're a nerdy little nutcracker, you know that?"

Not waiting for a response, he shoved his hand in my back pocket and steered me toward the bedroom, pulling off my shirt and thumbing open my button fly as we went.

"Did you bring any toys?"

"Like, sex toys? No. I don't need awkward airport situations, thank you."

"What does that mean? Never mind. What is this thing? Is it a sports bra?" he asked, running a finger under the band.

"It's a bralette," I replied. "It's comfortable and I'm not interested in your opinion of it."

"All I want to know is how to get it off." He reached for the band again, but I batted him away.

"I'll get it," I said, elbowing my way out of it.

In my brief glimpse of the bedroom, I caught sight of a huge bed with gorgeous white linens and a dreamy canopy. I almost asked him to take me to bed, but then he flipped on the lights in the bathroom and I knew this was the way to go. The shower itself was the size of the kitchen in my apartment. All my appliances and all of my counter space could fit in there, and there was still room for me, Sebastian, and all seventy or eighty of the showerheads.

"Whoa."

Sebastian reached behind me to switch on the water and suddenly it sounded as though I was standing behind a waterfall.

"*Whoa*," I repeated.

"Yes, indoor plumbing, very nice," he said, pushing my jeans down my legs. He gave my panties an impatient glare. "Less talking, more naked and wet, please."

I stepped out of my jeans and underwear, kicked them aside. I motioned to him, saying, "Practice what you preach."

He yanked his shirt over his head. "Your hair," he said, confusion creasing the corners of his eyes. "It's different."

I reached for his waist, unlatched his belt. Sent his shorts falling to the floor. "Yeah, I had the color done. A little lighter, the roots touched up." When he went on studying me, still confused, I added, "This isn't my natural color. It's medium brown. I would've thought you'd figured that out by now with…you know, everything."

"I would've thought you'd realized I am stupid and helpless and single-minded when I get your clothes off," he replied, tucking a few wisps of hair over my ear. He looped an arm around my back. "The only thing I ever want to figure out is how to keep you naked."

"I don't think that's true." When he didn't respond to that, I asked, "How does this work? This cease-fire thing? Aside from not insulting each other, what are we supposed to do?"

He stared at my mouth for a second, shook his head, and then pressed his lips to mine. Steam rose around us and that damp heat licked at my skin while everything inside me turned soft. That was it, I was soft when he kissed me—but also needy and starved and mindless. There was nothing else in the world when we collided like this, and while I was here, with his hand in my hair, his shaft hard against my belly, and everything inside me lighting up in response, I didn't want anything else.

Sebastian backed me into the shower, a gentle mist raining over us while we kissed and climbed and pawed at each other. "I didn't come here with the intention of having sex," he said, his lips on my jaw.

"Consider this a happy accident."

"I mean," he started, rocking against me, "I don't have condoms with me because I didn't come here with the intention of having sex."

I blinked water out of my eyes. "Neither did I."

He dropped his forehead to my shoulder and gave a groan that echoed around us. "I'm both very happy to hear that and a little devastated."

I brushed a hand down his back, curled my fingers around his shaft. Gave him a firm stroke that had him groaning again. "I have an IUD."

I felt his teeth on my neck, my shoulder, the hinge of my jaw. "And you're comfortable with—"

"Has there been anyone else? Since the start?"

He sucked in a breath as he thrust into my hand. "I went in fully expecting your pussy to bite my dick off. It's just you, honey."

I hooked my knee around his hip, leaned back against the cool tile. "Then I'm comfortable."

"You don't have to be." He took hold of my knee, notched it higher. Dragged his fingers up my inner thigh, over my folds. "Don't say yes because you think it's what I want to hear."

I grabbed for the back of his neck, my fingers sliding through his hair and forcing his mouth to mine. "I can't figure out why," I mumbled between kisses and bites, "but I don't know how to do anything just because I think it's what you want. *Ever*. It's like I don't even know how to people-please around you. It's freaking me out."

"That's right," he growled, spearing his fingers inside me. "Give me more of that. Give me that strong badass who takes no shit from anyone and then comes for me like such a good girl."

"Don't say that. You know it does crazy things to me." I tipped my head back against the tile and stared at the water pouring out from the heads stationed along the ceiling. "Really crazy things."

"That's why I say it." He swiped his tongue over a nipple, but quickly pulled back. "Sara. You're bleeding. Is that okay?"

"What? Oh, shit." I twisted out of his grip, scrambled to the other side of the shower. Of all the times for my cycle to remind me it was irregular as hell. "Sorry. I thought my period ended yesterday. Now *this* is freaking me out."

He shoved both hands through his hair while his erection jutted out, proud and ruddy. "Are you okay?"

I glanced around for soap or a washcloth—anything to occupy my hands. "Yeah. I didn't mean for you—well, it's fine. I'm fine."

"Do you want to stop?"

Even though I'd never done this before, I shook my head. "Not really."

"Then why the fuck are you all the way over there?" he asked, crossing the kitchen-sized shower in two strides. "What kind of child do you think I am? If you're okay, I'm okay. For fuck's sake, we are in a *shower*, Sara. And after we're done here, I'll put a towel down if you're worried about the sheets."

I reached out, flattened my hand over his heart. "I'm okay."

"That's a real fucking relief since I'm about a minute away from painting the wall because you're here and wet and naked, and all of those things are my *favorite* things. Can you end the freak-outs and let me fuck you? Please?"

A hysterical laugh burst from my lips and I shifted that

hand down his torso, over that gorgeous line of dark fuzz, to grip his cock. "Come here."

"*Thank you*," he groaned, backing me up against another chilly wall of tile.

Water poured over one shoulder, slicking us up as we moved together to find the right fit. He reached for my knee again, brushed a thumb over my clit, ground his shaft between my legs. He murmured in my ear about my skin, my body, how much he wanted me, how hard he was for me, but the exact words always got trapped in a box that seemed to hold them a minute before sharing them with me. As if a delay was required to keep me from spontaneously combusting.

He pushed inside me with a slow rock and that was all it took to remind me why we did this. Why we couldn't stop. Why getting it out of our systems was a funny little lie we told ourselves to make it seem like we weren't flat-out addicted.

We fit together in a way that made me question everything in the world. Every choice I'd ever made. If it didn't lead to this man and my ankles over his shoulders, what was I even doing with my life? Nothing, that was the simple answer. Anything that existed outside us didn't matter. Jobs, families, counseling sessions. None of it mattered. This mattered—it was special and rare and terrifying.

"Talk to me," he said, his arm hooked under my knee as he pounded me into the wall. "I know what you're thinking, but I need to hear it."

I slipped a hand up his neck, into his hair. "What am I thinking?"

"You're thinking that it can't be this good, but it is and it only gets better," he panted. "And that's insane."

"It's insane." I pressed the pad of my thumb to his lips. He sucked at me, bit down. That bite sent a strange, glorious throb to my clit. "What are you doing to me?"

"I think you're doing it to me," he said. "Now, be a good girl and come on this cock. I'm going to pinch your clit until you do."

"I'm not ready," I whined, my fingers twisting and pulling at his hair.

"Yes, you are," he yelled. "Stop fighting. Let me give you what you want."

He was so thick and made me feel so full, so over-whelmed with sensation. All I could do was tug his hair and watch while he stared down at me, his gaze filled with certainty and his jaw tight. I couldn't even move. I was pinned to this wall, spread as wide open as I could be, and clinging to the edge with every last toe and fingernail because I wasn't ready to fall over.

"I can't," I insisted.

"Do you feel that? Do you feel your clit throbbing? I do. Maybe I should make you pinch it. Then you'll see how ready you are."

"I'm *not*."

"You know you've earned it. You know you deserve it. Stop fighting, sweetheart. Give it to me."

I didn't want to fall over that edge. I really didn't. But those words worked on me too well. They hit right where I needed them.

"That's a good girl," he drawled, an arm drawn tight around me as I shook and cried. "That's my good girl. There you are." He released his hold on my clit and that sudden rush of blood set off another wave inside me, one that hurt in a confusingly nice way. "Is that how you're playing tonight? You're giving me the demon pussy magic right now?"

"I'm not doing anything to you," I said, my words as loose and shuddering as the spasms between my legs.

He touched his forehead to mine, moaned out a breath. His hips punched up and his eyelids drifted shut, and he pressed a roar into my shoulder. He jerked against me, his fingers flexing and digging into my skin as the orgasm moved through him. "You sucked the soul out of me, sweetheart. I hope you put it to good use."

"I will." The smile that stretched across my face wouldn't quit. It was the brightest, most thoroughly pleased I'd felt in forever. I did this. I gave him that pleasure, that joy. It came from me and the things we found when we came together, and I could probably do it again. There was something pure and perfect about getting out of my mind and using my body to tear someone to shreds.

Sebastian was good at that—getting me out of my mind. Better than I wanted to admit. He teased and tortured and chased every last inhibition out of me with barely more than a sharply bent eyebrow. For the first time in fuck if I knew, I felt free in my body. I felt as though I could ask him for anything and not only would he give it, he'd devour me because he wanted it too. He lost himself in my body like I was a treasure rather than a messy perfectionist with a savage heart and an irritable gut.

Like I was someone worth keeping.

CHAPTER 25

SARA

SEBASTIAN STREMMEL WAS ONE HELL OF A CUDDLER. HE WAS straight up snuggly, his body tucked tight around mine. His scruffy chin rasped against my shoulder, his breath warm on my skin. He was thick and rigid where he pressed into my backside, and his hand rested low on my belly.

It was a whole lot of wonderful to wake up this way except I didn't enjoy anyone touching me there. I loved that my body did its damnedest to carry me through this life and keep me going, though I didn't know how to love the soft and the squish of that spot. Especially when someone else touched it. I didn't mind him seeing it and knowing it existed, but touching lived in a different class of awareness.

"Whatever you are thinking about, stop," Sebastian grumbled.

I moved his hand to my thigh. I hadn't made peace there either, but my legs were very strong and I admired that. It was like that strength had earned me the right to accept my legs, and I knew that was kind of fucked-up, but I also knew that perfection wasn't the goal of a safe relationship with my body. I could hold difficult, complex, even uncomfortable feelings. I could move his hand from one spot while still wanting it everywhere else. I could be messy. I could do all of that and love myself at the same time.

"How do you know I'm thinking about something?"

"I could bounce quarters off the tension in your shoulders. What was a cozy pillow a few minutes ago is now a hard bag of bones."

He shifted his hand back to my belly. I batted it away.

"What?" he snapped. "You're warm and your vagina is made out of devastating magic. Let me hold you."

"You can hold me, just not there."

"But I'm obsessed with that spot," he argued.

"But I can't be comfortable when you're grabbing my fat."

"No, Sara. *No*. We're not doing that. I fucking mean it. Soft bellies are the sexiest thing in the world."

"Please don't. It's nice and well-intentioned, but—"

"Nothing about me is well-intentioned. Or nice for that matter," he said as he shifted my hair off my shoulder. "I'm telling you I find this overwhelmingly, distractingly sexy. These thick thighs too. I'm saying this is beautiful to me. I fucking love it."

"But—*why* do you love it?"

He rolled me to my back, scowled down at me like I'd really offended him. "Why do I need a reason? Why can't I just love it?"

"Because no one loves a belly roll," I said. "Anyone who says they do is lying."

"I'm not lying," he grumbled. "If I didn't think you'd throttle me, I'd put my head in your lap every time we're on the couch in Milana's office."

"What the hell are you talking about? You won't even sit next to me!"

"Because I want to put my head in your lap, you screechy little owl. Seriously, woman. You're killing me here. Just once it would be nice if you'd listen to what I actually say to you."

None of that seemed like a good idea. Not happening, thank you very much. "But look at you! I mean, *you* don't have a pudgy belly!"

"Am I supposed to be attracted to myself? I really don't think that's the way it goes. Bad logic, Shap." He dragged his lips from the ball of my shoulder up to my neck. "I am attracted to you. So attracted to you that I can't think when I see you. Can't even speak. All I can do is stare while you walk by with those nerdy t-shirts and thighs like a fucking wet dream and that chaos bun."

"You called it a chaos bun," I said to myself, laughing. "And you're not wrong. Dammit, you are *not* wrong."

"How do you fit all this hair into a scrub cap? I have been dying to know."

"I order them from a creator on Etsy," I replied, hiding my grin in his bicep. "I get them custom made. The chaos bun special order."

He passed his fingers over my lower abdomen. "I love this, Sara. I fuckin' love it." He shifted to trace the line of my leg from my hip to my knee. "But I don't have to if it's going to stress you out."

I lay there, my head swimming with rebuttals because this could not be true. It could not be. No one would ever choose to love this.

"What time do you have to leave for the conference?"

With my fingertip, I drew circles on his arm. "The presentations start after a keynote lunch, but…" I glanced up at him though I couldn't catch his eye since he was still busy with my belly. "I don't have to go today. Tomorrow is essential, but I can get out of today without issue."

"But you're a grade A geek. Why would you skip it?"

"The content doesn't line up with my interests," I said. That was the most mild, generous way I could say it.

"Then...what are you doing here? Did you actually orchestrate this? Did you get my itinerary from Acevedo's wife? Did Erin tell you where to find me?"

"Erin had no part in this, and listen, I can barely mastermind my way through a day. Forget about international travel," I said with a laugh. "It's a plastics conference, but it's geared more toward cosmetic surgery than anything I do."

"Let me ask you one more time: What are you doing here?"

"It's a whole long story that I don't want to deal with right now. I can promise you I didn't orchestrate this. If anyone orchestrated anything, it was probably you."

"Me? Hardly. A couple months back, Erin wouldn't leave me alone about taking time off. She made me hand over a credit card when I was at their place for dinner one night and booked this whole thing. She and Nick came here with Hartshorn and his wife last winter. I didn't even know where I was going until two hours before I left for the airport." He kissed the side of my neck, drew a small shiver from me. "You're going to ditch your conference and hang out with me today?"

"Unless that screws up your vacation vibes."

"My vacation vibes consist of sitting on the beach, rereading a book I don't like, and debating if it's too early to order a beer. You would be a substantial improvement to those vibes."

"What are we going to do?"

"We'll figure it out," he said. "Can I ask you something weird?"

"This is going to be exciting," I said flatly.

He dragged his teeth over his bottom lip, his brows drawn together. "Do you ever use leeches?"

A laugh hooted out of me as I rolled away from him.

He crawled over me, flattened me on my back with his knees tight against my hips and his hands planted beside my shoulders. "Is this what I get for asking about your practice? You laughing your ass off? It can't be that strange a question."

"Strange, no. But you've spent two months side-eyeing my work and now you want to talk about my methods of addressing microvascular congestion. No, that makes perfect sense."

He bent down, nipped at my jaw. "Will you tell me the next time you use them? I've never seen it."

"Never? How is that possible?"

He tucked himself into the space between my ear and shoulder. "They don't let me out much. I've spent the past fifteen years parked in emergency and trauma." He sucked at my skin, growling deep and low like it was the best thing he'd ever tasted. Then, "How do you feel about breakfast?"

"I am the pickiest eater you've ever met and eating with me will make you miserable. You'll never want to go anywhere with me again."

"Seeing as I'm miserable as a baseline, let's go up to the restaurant. They have a huge breakfast buffet. I ate enough for five people yesterday. You'll find something you like. Then I'll decide where I want to go with you."

"I'll probably find a piece of toast and some tea, and you have to swear to me you won't comment about me only eating toast when there's every breakfast item in the known world available to me. It makes me very twitchy when people invite themselves to talk about what I do or do not eat, and eating while anxious fucks up everything for me. I'd rather eat nothing than end up with reflux all day."

He kissed the corner of my mouth. "I won't say a thing. I swear."

"Okay. We can get breakfast, then." I ran a hand down his flank. "As soon as you get off me."

He growled into my neck. "Yeah, you must've missed the part where I get you before I get breakfast."

"You've mentioned nothing of the sort."

"Didn't think it needed to be said." He shifted, rocking his shaft against me. "What do you think about that rain shower outside?"

I glanced to the double doors leading out to the patio. "I don't know. Is it private?"

He jerked a shoulder up. "Let's find out."

And that was how we ended up outside, giggling and naked under the shower enclosed with vines, hedges, and weathered, old fencing. "I've never done anything like this," I admitted, my hands on his chest as water sluiced over us.

He was hard against my belly, but there was no rush. We'd rushed last evening—and several times in the night. We didn't have to do that today.

"Can't say I have either," he said, a wide, true smile on his face.

That was what did it for me. The smile. It was such a rare sight from him that I couldn't help but drop to my knees. A full breath passed before he understood my meaning and then he reached for me, his hands curling around my upper arms and a growl in his throat.

"No, no, no," he said. "Sara. No. Get back up here."

"Are you saying you don't want this?" I asked, wrapping my hand around his length. Whether he intended to or not, his hips jerked forward and his crown tapped my bottom lip.

"I won't have you gagging," he said.

"I know my limits." I brushed my lips over him, barely a touch, and received another sharp jerk in response. He wanted this. The agonized groan that followed was proof. "Trust me to take care of myself while I take care of you."

He shoved his fingers into my hair. "Promise me you won't try to swallow."

I took him into my mouth, the luxurious weight of him heavy on my tongue and the unbelievable stiffness stretching my lips wide, leaving me to hum in agreement. I stroked his base hard as I worked the head, the water pouring over us making everything superbly slippery. The hold he had on my hair was not gentle, not at all kind, and the feral groans moving through him matched that.

I slipped a hand between his legs as he mumbled a string of obscenities that made no sense though the way he spoke it, like a series of rough, unapologetic slaps to the ass, was exactly right. I gave his balls a minute of my attention before skimming my knuckles along his crease.

A breath shuddered out of him and his cock surged into my hand. I tasted warm salt on my tongue. "*Fuuuuuck.* Since when do I like that?" he gasped.

He reached down, cupped my jaw. With his thumb, he traced the stretched line of my lips. I peered up at him, met his dark, hooded gaze, and traveled over that pleated entrance again.

"I think it's you I like," he wheezed as he took half a step back. "*Fuck,* Sara. I'm—oh, fuck, *yes*. Now."

As he thrust into my fist, I stroked him hard with both hands, one twisting over his head and the other tight around his base. He covered that hand with his, angled himself away from my mouth. For a man who was about to come all over my tits, he was too thoughtful. Too damn considerate. He wasn't even selfish when he was getting a blowjob and that sent tears to my eyes.

This would be so much safer for me if he was truly an asshole.

His eyes widened when the first spurt hit my chest. He swallowed thickly, his gaze skating between my hand, the puddle between my breasts, and my face. At the second spasm, he groaned out a glorious "*Fuuuuuuck*" and reached for my arm, but he didn't have the coordination to get me off my knees. If I wasn't busy hiding my tears in the spray of the shower, I would've laughed at that. After the final series of spurts hit, he managed to get a hold of my arm and yanked me to my feet. He crushed me into a hug and held me to his chest, his fingers doing wicked things to my clit while he murmured into my ear about how I was so good, so *very* good.

If I could live in this rain shower—in this perfect little minute where nothing was wrong and everything was as it should be—I would. I'd give up everything for this moment to be my life rather than one accidentally happy morning.

———

SEBASTIAN GRABBED a plate from the stack at the start of the buffet and extended in my direction, but snatched it back at the last second. "I know I said I wouldn't say anything but I have one question."

I groaned, crossing my arms and slouching into a sulk. "You swore."

"Yeah, I know I did." He motioned to the mile-long buffet snaking around the room. "Can you tell me your thought process as you go?"

I eyed him skeptically. "You want to know why I choose something or skip it?"

He nodded, held out the plate. "Yeah."

"Why?"

He grabbed a plate for himself. "Because you've already brought me into the croutons and candied ginger crazy. Why stop there?"

"All right," I muttered. "But I don't want your opinions."

"We'll see how I do with that," he replied, shuffling toward the first table. "I'm assuming you're a pain in the ass about eggs."

"And you'd be right." I grimaced at the trays in front of us. "Eggs Benedict is a fast nope. The sauce is too rich for my stomach and I don't do ham. Hard-boiled eggs are obnoxious."

"Obnoxious? That's bold."

"They're just not an option. Soft-boiled can be okay, but hard are a nightmare. Scrambled eggs, sometimes, but I have to see them. I can't order them off a menu. I have to confirm they're not too runny, too cheesy, too herby. Any of that would be a bad idea." I reached for the serving spoon. "I can give these a try."

When I was finished, Sebastian took the spoon from me and heaped scrambled eggs on his plate. It was an actual heap. At least three eggs could be accounted for in that heap. "You could be more of a pain in the ass. I expected a lot more from you."

"Just you wait." I laughed as we moved to the next table. "Breakfast potatoes break my damn heart. Every time. I want them to work for me, but they are almost always sautéed with onions and garlic, which is the quickest way to put the *irritable* in irritable bowel."

"Ew." The server stationed behind the table cringed with her entire body.

"Sorry," I said to her. "We have no filter when it comes to these things."

"With some things, we do," Sebastian said, staring at my legs. "Not with inflammatory gastric diseases."

"This is why we can't go places," I said to him.

"We can't go places because you're picky. Don't change the game while we're playing it." He hooked his hand in the crook of my elbow. "So, no potatoes for you," he said, depositing some on his plate. "Bet we're skipping the sausage and bacon too."

"I can't even think about sausage," I said, moving ahead to the breads and pastries. "That kind of grease is terrible for me, but the idea of sausage—no." My shoulders pitched up as my stomach twisted. I had to press a hand to my mouth. "I can't even think about it."

"Do not cause your own problems, Shap," he called. "We are not doing that today."

"All of this is a problem I've caused," I said. "It's not lost on me that the reward for twenty years of disordered eating is a lifetime of disordered eating, but now it's mandatory, and instead of counting carbs I count dried cranberries so I don't overdo it on acid, all because of what I did to myself in those twenty years."

"I'm all for wallowing in misery, but you gotta knock that

shit off," he said. "We all fuck ourselves up in a million different ways. That we live to tell about it is the reward."

"Are you always this moral in the morning?"

He dragged his gaze from my sandals to my shorts and up to my loose top. "Not always," he said.

Since I didn't know what to do with that heavy stare, I gave the pastries a thorough study, using a pair of tongs to peer at items I didn't immediately recognize. "None of this," I said, wagging the tongs. "If I'm not reasonably certain of the ingredients, there's no way I'm touching it. That's how I get fucked over by sneaky citrus."

Sebastian stared at the small helping of scrambled egg on my plate. "One more question. No, no, it's not going to give you anxiety," he said when I glared at him. "Calm down. I just want to know what you usually eat in the morning if this is the only thing you've chosen so far."

"Two, please." I gestured to the basket of white bread and the server dropped the slices into the toaster. "You know when you're young and you get stupid drunk on something like Jäger or some silly kind of schnapps? And you puke up your skeleton the next day? And forever after that, you can't go near that alcohol because if you even smell it, you'll remember the trauma of vomiting up your entire rib cage? That's how it is for me with, well, shit, everything. The list of foods that do not have traumatic memories attached—self-inflicted or otherwise—is short. That leaves me with oatmeal, porridge, yogurt, poached eggs. Maybe some stewed apples. Raw apples require a ton of energy to digest. There's a lot of toast."

He reached for an almond croissant, bit into it while I went on inspecting the baked goods.

I pointed at a basket of grainy bread. "Too much going on

here. I love it, actually, but all those seeds would make my belly gurgle for at least two days. Do you have any idea what it's like having a gurgly belly for the entirety of a ten-hour surgery? It's an experiment in seeing how many times I can say, 'It's fine. Don't worry. Really, it's fine. No, I don't need anything. Just ignore it.'"

"You're not picky. You're specific. There's a difference."

"Picky is a simpler word for it," I said as we moved toward the French toast and Belgian waffles. He chose one of each.

"Okay, what about fruit? Ruin my day and tell me what you hate about all of these."

"I love raspberries, but the seeds are a disaster. I can't even look at blueberries without getting reflux. Melon and pineapple are good in small quantities. Same with mango and papaya. Guava and I don't get along. Bananas are supposed to be safe but are not, and grapes fuck me up." I added a few strawberries to my plate along with some cantaloupe. "Plain yogurt with honey is my better-day breakfast. It always does me right after a bad day."

He inspected the carton of yogurt I selected. "Okay. I get it."

I trailed my fingertip over the array of tiny jars of honey. I pointed across the room, to the open-air deck far away from the mingled scents of roasted meats and frying egg. "Let's sit out there."

After we settled at the table, Sebastian glanced at me from under those thick lashes. "Was that okay? Did it make you anxious?"

"Not too much." I opened the jar of honey, gave it a sniff. The smell of honey always made me happy. "I know it looks crazy and it probably sounds crazy, but I don't *feel* crazy when I'm in control of my options. I can come back here tomorrow because I know I can have toast and there's yogurt along with some of the fruits I like. Even if these eggs don't work out, other items will, and then I know I don't have to obsess over how to get through something as basic as breakfast."

When a server swung by the table, Sebastian ordered juice and coffee for himself and hot tea for me.

When she stepped away, I added, "It helped that you weren't a giant asshole about it. I was prepared for that."

Pouring syrup over his French toast, he asked, "Were you prepared because you expect me to be an asshole to you or because you have experience with people being an asshole when you try to tell them what you need?"

I speared a tiny amount of eggs onto my fork. "Little bit of both."

He watched while I sampled the eggs, gave me a questioning nod. I wiggled my shoulders in response. They were all right. Not my favorite, but not bad. Then, he said, "I'm sorry."

"Don't be sorry," I said, and I meant it. I didn't know what it was about this cease-fire, but I no longer felt like he was doing something *to* me. Rather, we were doing this to each other. And I didn't feel as though I had to protect myself from everything. "I mean, you can be whatever you want, but you don't have to apologize for that. For any amount of asshole you've given me, I've given you raging bitch right back."

He jabbed his fork in my direction. "Don't say that."

"No, it's okay. That word is complicated, but it's not complicated for me. I know what it means to me and for me," I insisted, tapping a hand to my chest. "It's probably time I explain to you that I have the heart of a savage bitch and I'm quite proud of her. She tells the perfectionist in my head when to sit down and shut up, and she makes me stand up to trauma surgeons who think the only appropriate method of closure is a staple."

He stared at me with a slight smile, his chin resting on his palm. "Is that who I have to thank?"

I rubbed a hand to my sternum. A warm pressure seemed to build there. It heated my cheeks too. "Yes."

"You should know I like her. A lot," he added. "I like it when you show me how strong you are. I think you like it too. You just don't think you should."

I'd always known there was something odd inherent in talking about these parts of myself as if they were disembodied people whose voices I happened to hear, but it helped me isolate the origins of all my conflicted emotions. It helped me to see the perfectionist as a kid who desperately needed something in her life to be safe and the savage as an angsty, rage-filled teenager who refused to be misunderstood. It helped to cleave all those feelings into two parts and hear them separately.

For all the years I'd lived with that knowledge, I'd never once felt the singular glow of someone choosing the messiest, most volatile part of me as the one worth treasuring. The good girl got all the attention. She asked for nothing and did everything, making her so damn easy to love. But that love was shallow. It was ankle-deep love, the kind that drifted in and out with the tides. It took from me more than it gave. It didn't matter and it didn't last.

Not that this was love. This was…a cease-fire. A reprieve. A moment where we didn't capitalize on every opportunity to torment each other.

This was *not* about love. Not even close.

"You're right. I don't think I should let my savage bitch out that often," I replied, dipping my spoon into the yogurt. "I can't live every day like it's bubble suit jousting day."

"We should do that again," he mused. "Maybe I'll win the next time around."

"Don't get your hopes up."

He dragged his gaze over me, slow and scowly. "Too bad. Already have."

————

IT WAS THE COMFORTABLE, pleasant kind of humid here on the island, the sun was high and bright without being too intense. The ocean was close enough to provide a light, hammock-nap kind of soundtrack and soft, pale sand was only a few steps away from the patio outside my bungalow.

For once, Sebastian had not a single complaint about the weather.

That did not mean he was free of all complaints.

I pushed my sunglasses to the top of my head and glanced over at him. He had the end of a highlighter between his teeth as he frowned at an article in the *Journal of Emergency Medicine*. It was the type of frown that could mean he disagreed vehemently or he was head over heels for the content. Anyone's guess.

"I'm getting a drink," I said as I crossed the patio into the bungalow. "Do you want anything?"

With a parting grimace for the journal, he asked, "What does that mean in your world? The only thing I've ever seen you drink is weak tea and water."

"I can drink mellow white wines and beers that aren't too

sour or hoppy, but I usually pass unless I'm feeling really good." I leaned against the door. "I asked the resort to stock the fridge, so I'm sure there's something for you in there."

"I never would've thought to ask for that," he murmured.

"Yeah, if there's one thing I've learned from my mother, it's how to travel comfortably." I hooked a thumb toward the bungalow. "Can I grab something for you?"

"Unless it's croutons and crystalized ginger, I'm good with whatever you're having."

Inside, I poured myself a glass of water and selected a beer from the assortment in the fridge. I was about to return to the patio when I spotted a paperback book on the table near the entrance. It didn't look like any of the other books tucked into the shelves around the bungalow and it was just sitting there on the edge of the table as if someone had forgotten about it.

With the book tucked under my arm, I walked out to the patio. "Is this yours?" I asked, holding it up.

Sebastian accepted the beer bottle, saying, "Oh. Yeah."

I glanced at the cover. "You're reading *The Chronicles of Narnia*? The allegorical fantasy series written for small children?"

He held up a hand. "I can explain."

"I cannot wait to hear this." I settled into the lounge chair beside him. "Please. Don't leave me in suspense."

He ran a hand through his hair, sighing like a highly inconvenienced teenager. "I found a copy of *The Lion, the Witch and the Wardrobe* in the ER one night. It was during the time when every day was hell and it just didn't get better. When I didn't leave the hospital for days. The world was terrifying and it wasn't like I could sleep, so I read a book."

"And you're *still* reading it?"

"No. I mean, obviously, yes, but I don't like it. I have so many problems with this story. I don't even know where to start with my problems."

I murmured in agreement. "Yeah, that does seem to be a theme with you."

"You're lucky you're so cute," he said with a sidelong grin. "I read the first book and I had to see how it turned out, so I read the other six."

"That is a serious commitment for a story you don't like."

"There's a lot I don't like, but there was a thread running through all the books that just—I don't know. There's something that stuck with me."

"I want to hear about the sticky part."

He flipped through the pages for a minute. "It's about these kids who walked through the back of a closet into a new world. They had no idea what was waiting for them on the other side. Nothing could've prepared them. They're thrown into it. They have to take sides and fight wars—and then they have to go home. They climb out of the closet and go back to their old lives as if nothing had happened. As if they'd been playing in the backyard all that time. They couldn't tell anyone where they'd been or what they'd seen. They couldn't talk about the losses they'd experienced or the ways the war changed everything about them. They had to stare out at the world through eyes that had witnessed all these things and—and act like they were the same kids who'd gone into that closet."

I wrapped both hands around my glass. That hit close to home. "Whoa."

He bobbed his head. "Like I said, there was a lot of material I didn't enjoy, but there was an artery of truth in there. The subtle part about living through a war and coming out of it changed, yet not having anywhere to put all of that change, hooked me hard. I started going back to the books just to press that artery again. I guess that's the choice, right? Cut the oxygen to my brain or keep wondering if I'm crazy."

I didn't have the words to make any of this right. Instead of trying to do that, I set my glass aside, plucked the book and the abandoned journal from him, and tucked myself in beside him on the lounge chair.

"You get it," he murmured, his hand on the back of my head.

I nodded against his chest. "I do."

He was quiet for a minute, then he brushed his lips over my hair. "Thanks."

CHAPTER 26

SEBASTIAN

FROM THE BED THAT I WAS STILL HOPING SHE'D RETURN TO, I watched as Sara buzzed around the bungalow. She wore a fluffy white bathrobe that brushed the floor because she was a little teapot and she had her hair twisted up in a hot pink microfiber towel that she'd brought with her from home.

It was a luxury to watch her prepare for the day. I would've forked over every cent to my name just for the privilege of watching her apply moisturizer to her entire body one more time.

When she switched on the hair dryer, I resigned myself to the fact she wasn't coming back to bed. I wandered around the bungalow in my boxers and read the headlines on my phone while I made myself some coffee and heated water for her tea.

But then an eruption of noise sounded from the bathroom—a crash, a slam, a snarl—and the hot pink towel flew out the door as I approached. I found her with her hands braced on the edge of the long marble vanity, the hair dryer on the floor and a load of makeup spread out before her.

"What's happening in here? Are we having a tiny tornado

moment? Please don't break the windows. I don't want to get thrown out of here today."

"Don't be an asshole to me right now. I can't do that with you this morning."

She shoved her shoulders back, held a hand close to the hair straightener to check the temperature. I knew that because my sister had the same one. Vivi also had a series of small burns on her forehead from it. The majority of our video call conversations involved that straightener in some capacity. I did not trust that straightener.

"Then we're throwing towels and small appliances just because it's fun? I'm cool with that, by the way. Just loop me in. I can throw towels too. Watch." I yanked a bath towel from the shelf, tossed it over my shoulder. "Did you see that?"

"Now you're just being a dickhead."

"See, I don't think that's accurate," I argued. "I think dickhead is a little too strong for the situation, no? Dickhead implies some degree of malice. I just want to throw shit with you. I don't want to be left out. No malice there."

"Is this what a nervous breakdown feels like? I've always wondered."

I paced toward her, set my hands on her waist, met her eyes in the mirror. "You are not having a nervous breakdown. Tell me what's happening."

"I am freaking out. Okay? That's what's happening." She edged me away so she could continue with her hair. "A nervous breakdown for breakfast, a plastics conference for lunch, and a fresh new disaster for dinner. Perfect. Best day ever."

"Can you tell me *why* you're freaking out? Because I don't get it."

She rolled her free hand, saying, "My father's going to be at this conference."

"And…you don't wish to see him?"

"Actually, no, but that's not the problem," she said with a bitter laugh. "Everyone else wants to see him and they are going to swarm and trample me in the process."

"Sara. What the *fuck*?"

"Yeah, it's always a nightmare."

"Okay, so, I'm going with you," I said, stepping into yesterday's shorts.

"No, you're not. That's not necessary. I can deal with it. I just hate it. You know I hate being around a lot of random people, and when you add the fact they're using me for access to my father, it's even more unpleasant."

"Hold up. What are we talking about? I'm gonna need a lot more information. Explain it to me like I'm a child. Simple terms."

She set the straightener down and blinked at me. "You don't know."

"No, honey, I don't. What's going on?"

"My father, he's Ross Shapiro. He owns University Image Clinic. The plastic surgery center with forty-eight outpatient locations up and down California. My brother just opened a new location in Scottsdale last summer. My mother's busy working on Maui. That's the official reason she's been there for the past year and a half. The unofficial reason is probably twenty-five and a fitness influencer who hopes she's going to invest in his personal training business. She probably will, just as my father will keep all his twenty-two-year-old side pieces with more than enough cash in their pockets."

"Holy shit." I pressed a hand to my mouth because yeah, I'd heard of the plastic surgery mogul, but I'd never connected that dot to Sara. All the times I'd heard loose references to her father, I assumed it was something in the legacy admissions and family money veins. Never had I made the jump from Sara, the surgeon in the first floor apartment, to the man who dominated West Coast cosmetic surgery. And, well, never in a million years would I have guessed the rest. *"Holy shit."*

"That's a fair assessment." She went back to running her hair through the straightener. "I assumed you knew. Everyone knows. It's the thing that walks into a room ahead of me."

"I didn't. I don't really pay attention to the things people say."

"Then you know what they say," she said.

"Not really," I admitted. "The only people I really talk to are Acevedo, Emmerling, and Hartshorn. Acevedo was fucking thrilled when we snagged you from New York."

"Snagged me," she repeated. "That's funny. I left New York because my dad's college roommate was appointed Chief of Surgery. His first act of business was telling me that my father wanted me to move back to California and work with him within the year, and he wanted to help my father with that in any way he could."

"What a dick." I leaned against the doorframe. "You never planned on going into the family business, I take it."

She laughed, but there was no humor to it. "Plastics wasn't my first choice."

"What was?"

"Anything else," she said. "I grew up in a world built on body dysmorphia. I didn't want to keep doing that. I didn't want to fix people who didn't *need* fixing. I didn't even think I wanted to go into surgery."

"Then…what changed?"

Another harsh laugh. "My father refused to pay for med school unless I committed to plastic surgery. I called that bluff one semester and had to ask my grandmother for help, but she'd already been warned off. It didn't occur to me back then that I could take out loans like everyone else and just tell him to fuck off." She brushed out a section of hair, started on another. "Eventually, I did. I went after a reconstructive surgery fellowship. The way he tells it, he got me into that fellowship. The truth is, he threatened to have me removed from the fellowship and reassigned to something more quote-unquote suitable. The dean of that program was a friend from his residency. My father swore it was only a matter of making a call and I swore I wouldn't speak to him ever again if he did that. The dean pulled me into his office, said he had a spot for me in a different program. That was the last time I took a penny from my family and we've barely spoken since then."

"But you came here," I said. "To a conference that doesn't interest you."

She stared at her reflection in the mirror. "I came to keep the peace. I know how fucked-up it sounds, but doing this one uncomfortable thing will buy me a couple years of distance."

"I'll go with you," I said.

She tossed a damp washcloth at my head. "There's no reason to do that and you'll be annoyed the minute you walk in because no one is talking about collapsed lungs. I just need the chance to freak out beforehand and get it out of my system. I'll be fine."

I aimed the washcloth at her hip. "I'd like you to be better than fine."

She sucked her bottom lip between her teeth, glancing between me and her reflection for a moment. Then, "The conference isn't that bad. It's a lot of social interaction for me, but once I'm there and in the groove of smiling and nodding, it passes quickly. If you really want to do something, you could come to dinner with us tonight."

I watched as she brushed out the last section of her hair. She looked like an entirely different woman without the wild hair I'd always expected from her. This was a transformation, but not for any of the reasons I'd assumed. She was putting on her game face. Her hair was smooth and golden, the lines in her forehead were frozen, and there were enough products to make her face flawless. It worked exactly the way armor was intended. Except she didn't need any of this. Did she have no idea how strong she was on her own? Didn't she see it?

If she didn't, I'd have to see it for her. "I'll be there."

———

I DIDN'T KNOW what to do with myself without Sara.

I ate breakfast, read two newspapers, and swam in the ocean, all before noon. At that point, I was bored as fuck and half convinced I needed to get myself to this conference. It wasn't like I could sit on the beach the rest of the day. What was the point? I didn't want to sit there alone. I didn't want to *be* here alone. Not after knowing what it was like to be here with her. I didn't even enjoy breakfast without her running commentary on the offenses of blueberries.

After lunch, I read a few more chapters of *Narnia*. Those fucking kids. When reading didn't distract me anymore, I went for a walk. I called it a walk. In my head, it was a walk.

Some might say I paced in front of the resort entrance for two hours because I wanted to see Sara the minute she arrived and confirm for myself that she was all right, but it was a walk.

When she emerged from the taxi, she looked me over with a laugh. "What is this about?"

"I'm taking a walk," I said, folding her into my arms. "You just happened to pull up." I pressed a kiss to her neck. "How'd it go?"

"Ugh. Fine. Whatever." She dropped her head to my chest, let her shoulders sag. "I need to change. I can't wear this to the restaurant."

Sara was quiet as we returned to the bungalow. She stripped down to her bra and panties, and pinned her hair away from her face to freshen her makeup. Since I was physically incapable of leaving her side, I leaned against the vanity and watched.

"Here's what's going to happen tonight," she said, makeup brush in hand. "This is what will go down. He'll be the most warm, charming person in the world if he's in the mood for it. If not, he'll just make sure everyone knows he's very, *very* busy and very, *very* important. The cell phone never leaves his hand."

"You don't have to prep me," I said. "I'll manage just fine."

"He knows everyone, everywhere," she continued, "and the inconvenient fact of the matter is that many of those people will throw themselves in front of traffic if it gets them a few minutes with him. He really does know everyone, so he can shoot a text and get someone an interview. He can connect you with someone who wants to develop a new tool or procedure or he can hook you up with someone who already has the newest tool so you can learn how to use it.

He has a ton of money and he knows people with tons of their own money, and he adores the attention that comes with that power."

I nodded. "I know the type."

"And everything will be great and fantastic until he makes a comment about how the restaurant scene in Boston must be outstanding because I'm looking so well-fed," she said. "Or that the hospital must be working me too hard because I seem tired. Or I must be struggling to find exciting cases since he hasn't heard anything through all his channels and networks. It's always something backhanded like that, something that shows up as concern, but it's actually bullshit at the center."

I folded my arms over my chest. Nodded. I wasn't letting that happen.

"So, I'll sit there while he pleasantly informs me that my work is a waste of time and my hospital is garbage and my choices are dumb, and I won't even be able to look at him. I'll stare at my plate for two hours because even at thirty-nine *fucking* years old, I know I'll crack in half if I have to watch him tell me that I'm all wrong. I'll nod along like I'm agreeing with him because arguing is so much worse, though it's not like I'm ever able to argue in the moment. Even when I prepare myself for these situations, I don't have the right responses at the ready. They disappear. It's like I'm helpless. Like a child who can't stop and say, 'Who the fuck do you think you're talking to?'"

"Then I'll respond. I'll handle it."

She popped a tablet in her mouth, washed it down with water. "You don't have to do that."

"I'm a great buffer," I said. "I don't get to be the buffer too often these days, but I'm very good at it. I can tell you're not in any condition to hear a story about my mother and sister or about my chief resident and every other resident in the building, but suffice it to say, I can soak up all the toxicity around me and spit it out with only a dash of passive-aggression."

"You breathe passive-aggression." She pushed another tablet out of a blister pack. "But you can be my buffer."

I gestured to the pills. "Are you all right?"

"I'm trying to be but my gut doesn't deal well with this kind of stress." She uncapped a bottle, shook another tablet into her palm. "We'll see how well it works."

"Just for my reference, who am I to you?" I asked. "Tonight."

And always?

"He's not going to ask," she replied. "He only cares about proximity to power."

"Right." I slipped my hands into my pockets. "It's good we cleared that up."

We took a taxi to the restaurant on the other side of the island. It was close to the hotel where the conference was taking place, and as the minutes ticked by, I could see the tension building inside her. She kept her gaze fixed on her lap while she ran the pad of her thumb over her nails. I didn't think I could remember ever seeing her nails polished before. I would've remembered.

When we stepped out of the taxi, I brought my hands to her shoulders and steered her away from the entrance.

"Where are we going?" she yelped.

"Over here," I said. "Just for a minute."

"We're going to be late."

"It's just a minute." Once we were tucked away behind a tree, I turned her to face me and lifted my hands to her jaw.

"I need you to listen to me now. *Listen*. Be strong for me like I know you can, and when you can't be strong anymore, you'll let me do it for you."

She gave a quick, unconvincing nod. Then, "Don't mess up my face."

"I *will* mess up your face," I replied. "What do you think we're doing when we're done here?" I took her hand, squeezed it to remind her that she didn't have to let anyone make her small. "I've been thinking about bending you over that bed all day. I found a foot stool so you can reach, little bit. I plan on testing it out later. Just keep that in mind."

She rolled her eyes. "Yeah. That's exactly what I need to think about right now."

"It's better than anything else you're thinking." I rested my hand on her lower back. "Come on. Let's do this."

We made our way through the restaurant and found Dr. Shapiro seated, his attention fixed on his phone.

"Dad," she said, standing beside the table like she wasn't convinced she should sit.

I *hated* that hesitance. Hated the way she twisted her fingers together, hated how she shrank in the face of his indifference. Where was the woman who ripped a fucking curtain from the ceiling because I dared to dismiss her criticism? Where was she? And who the fuck was this guy to chase her away with nothing more than the chill of his presence?

I didn't fucking know, but I was ready to scoop her up and get the hell out of here if it continued. I could be the asshole in this situation. I had no problem with that.

The man finished typing before looking up at his daughter, and that was all I needed to know about him. That was fucking it.

"Sara," he boomed, pushing to his feet. "I was beginning to think you'd forgotten." He folded her into a hug while catching my eye over her shoulder. "She's always been such a scatterbrain."

What a fucking asshole.

"Dad, this is Sebastian Stremmel. I told you about him earlier. He's the top trauma surgeon at Massachusetts and the next Chief of Emergency Surgery."

I accepted his outstretched hand. "The part about emergency surgery is true. The part about Sara being a scatterbrain is not. Can't say I've ever seen her less than completely composed."

"Then you aren't looking very hard, Dr. Stremmel," he said, the words cracking into a chuckle.

Sara gave me *I warned you* eyes. I shrugged, giving her my *this doesn't scare me* scowl.

As she'd promised, the older man asked nothing of our relationship or even why I was here in Jamaica. Instead, he launched into a long story about bumping into another surgeon, someone who'd once been something of a rival and now wanted Dr. Shapiro's assistance.

"That's always how it goes. They always come back around," he said, motioning to the server with his empty tumbler. "Another bourbon on the rocks, splash of soda, and something for the kids." He ran a tight, impatient grin over Sara. "You look like you could use a drink. What do I always tell you? You need to lighten up!" He leaned toward me, his elbow on the table, his fist under his chin, a conspiratorial glint in his eyes like I was the kind of dickhead who'd join him in slamming his daughter. "Always serious, this one. You'd think the world's ending every day. Can't even scare a smile out of her."

What a *fucking* asshole.

I pulled my most confused expression. "You think so? Huh." I grated my knuckles down my jaw. Sara passed a hand over her lips to hide a grin. "I don't see that at all."

Since that wasn't what he'd expected, he forced a smirk and went back to his phone while Sara and I ordered a bottle of wine apiece. Bottles because this place was too classy to bother with wine by the glass, but also because ordering a fine bottle was as big a power move as anything with rich guys like this. Even bourbon drinkers who could probably buy the entire island of Jamaica.

When the server stepped away, Dr. Shapiro edged toward me again, renewed interest in his eyes because I'd obviously leveled up with that wine order. "My golf buddy likes that vintage," he said. "Morty Speeback. Hands it out to his staff around the holidays. They don't understand what they're getting, don't respect the quality, but you can't talk him out of it. I'm sure you've heard of Dr. Speeback, Dr. Stremmel. One of the best heart surgeons in Orange County."

"If you know cardio guys, you must know Cal Hartshorn." I glanced at Sara, expecting her to chime in, but she gave a slight shake of her head. "He's one of the best in the country."

Dr. Shapiro picked up his phone, read a notification at the top of the screen. "Can't say that I have."

After the server corked and poured, I reached for the glass of wine in front of me. "He worked on that pro football coach a few years back. Lots of press coverage for that one. I couldn't go a day without seeing Hartshorn's face all over ESPN." I tapped my glass to Sara's. "He's a big fan of Sara's."

"As he should be," Dr. Shapiro replied. "She's also one of the best. Massachusetts is lucky to have her."

In any other conversation, his comments would've landed with pride and admiration. In this shitshow, they resembled both inadequacy—being the best was the bare minimum—and an accusation—our hospital had something they didn't deserve. It was remarkable the way he packed so much toxic waste into a few words.

"I know for a fact the Chief is very interested in Sara," I said. She turned her head, staring out at the water as a slight laugh rolled through her shoulders.

Dr. Shapiro picked up his menu with a pointed glance at his daughter. "Have you looked at this? They have some interesting salads. I can't imagine you get much fresh produce in Boston. Everything must come trucked in from the west or shipped up from South America. What a shame. It's never very good unless it's truly fresh. You'll like one of these salads."

Before I could get my hands around that oblique comment, a man waved from a few tables over and Dr. Shapiro immediately stepped away to speak with him, saying to us, "I'll need a minute for this."

When he was out of earshot, Sara said, "Are you amusing yourself?"

I reached for my wineglass. "Somewhat."

"You can't impress him. It's not possible. He's the only one allowed to do the impressing. It doesn't matter who you know, where you've been, what you've done. He's cornered this market. It's his. You and Hartshorn could be conjoined twins and my father would not care because he didn't discover you. He decides whether you're worth telling everyone about. He does the impressing."

"You might doubt me when I say this, but I know that already. I know my way around this game. Just let me play, okay?"

"Don't start any fires," she warned.

"As long as you don't break any windows," I replied.

"It was *one time*," she whisper-cried. "One window."

"And don't think I'll ever let you forget it." I laughed and a wide grin pulled at her lips.

See that smile? You're wrong about this one. You're all wrong.

Dr. Shapiro returned to the table, saying, "Always running into someone who wants to talk. That was Dr. Kim. He's in from Dallas. He's taken on ten new partners this year. He was smart to listen to me." He glanced between me and Sara with a self-important grin. "How's business in Boston these days? Enough to keep busy? It would be a real shame for you to lose your skills."

Sara shrugged, and though it read as a casual gesture, all the levity we'd just shared was gone. In its place, tension that burned like a fire that crept along the walls, low and hot and destructive enough to take down the whole damn house. "My skills get more than adequate use."

"And they should," he replied, again occupied with his phone. "I didn't get you into that fellowship to sit on your hands all day."

This motherfucker.

Sara blinked at him, not that he noticed. I dropped my hand to her knee. She shook her head, telling me she didn't need the support, but I gave her a light squeeze anyway. She rolled her eyes as if I was overreacting and that would've been believable if she hadn't shifted in her seat and pressed that knee into my palm.

The similarities between my father and Dr. Shapiro

weren't hard to find once the artifice of medicine was stripped away. They both loved the sound of their voices and believed the people closest to them were the least relevant, the least precious.

We placed our orders and Dr. Shapiro went on grabbing his phone every twenty seconds, motioning to someone he knew on the other side of the restaurant, and simultaneously registering his opinions on the topics presented at the conference. He was capable of carrying on a conversation without the involvement of anyone else, and that didn't bother me one bit. I was content to sip wine and stroke Sara's knee and let this guy be a fool drunk off his own Kool-Aid.

From the sounds of her occasional murmurs and "Oh, that's interesting," Sara had the same idea.

When the meal arrived, Dr. Shapiro was two tables away, his hands braced on the backs of the chairs of a couple seated there. I stared at him for a moment, waiting for him to catch my eye. I wasn't in the business of making his daughter wait and I was very good at glaring holes through skulls.

He knew I was watching him. I could tell from the way he cut his gaze to the side and shifted to avoid accidentally meeting my eyes. He wasn't budging.

I glanced over at Sara only to find her frowning at her plate. "Excuse me," I said to the server as she filled our wine, "this is not what the lady ordered. She asked for grilled, not pan-seared, and none of the mango salsa." I picked up the plate, handed it to the server. "Thank you."

"I'll take care of that right away," she said.

Sara lifted her glass to her lips, took a tiny sip. "You didn't have to do that."

"You weren't going to say anything, and as I believe

you've stated on more than a few occasions, I like being an asshole."

"You aren't being an asshole."

"No? A dickhead, then?"

"Not that either." She laughed. "You're using these powers of yours for good."

I glared over at Dr. Shapiro again. The couple he was talking to noticed, making some playful shooing gestures, though he responded to that by fully turning his back to me.

Another thing he and my father had in common was that you couldn't tell them anything. You couldn't argue with them, couldn't reason. That was the trap of the narcissist. Trying to have a conversation with them was like playing one of those finger trap games, as it was never a conversation. It was stupid chess. None of it mattered, but they'd weaponize everything in reach and change the rules while they played, all to keep up the pretense of winning.

They were never, ever wrong—which meant everyone else was *always* wrong. Even if I rattled off the twenty most offensive things he'd said tonight and called on him to account for that shit, Dr. Shapiro would spin that into me being a lunatic, Sara being an idiot for bringing me along, and he being the victim for having to endure it.

I couldn't tear into the guy. As much as I wanted to, I couldn't. It would follow Sara forever, much like the single scatterbrained moment that probably wasn't scattered at all yet still trailed her like a ghost. More than that, it wouldn't help. No one ever told off a narcissist and lived to tell tales of victory.

No, I wasn't going to yell at this guy on Sara's behalf.

I could do better than that.

It wasn't the reactions that gained ground. It was pivots. Maneuvers.

In record time, Sara had a new plate of grilled red snapper sans salsa, and Dr. Shapiro showed himself back to the table. He motioned toward her with his rocks glass. "Good choice. That looks light."

And that was it. That was fucking *it* for me. "You know, I'm surprised to see a smart guy like you drinking bourbon," I said to him. "But I guess we all choose the ways we kill ourselves."

Sara brought her napkin to her lips, smothering a laugh.

"Bourbon? No. No worse than anything else." He turned his attention to the plate in front of him, his face twisted in a smirking pout. "No worse than wine. I've done my research."

I reached for my glass. "I bet Morty Speeback knocks back no more than two glasses of red a day and tells everyone he meets to do the same. That's why he hands it out by the case."

"Actually, yes, he does do that," Sara said. I could hear the fight in her voice and I loved it. "He's been saying that for ages. Isn't he eighty-seven? Eighty-eight?"

"And still practicing?" I asked.

"Apparently," she replied. "I might have another twenty surgical years in me, but not a day more."

"Then it's about time you stop trying to save the world," Dr. Shapiro said. He set his fork down, visibly perturbed. "I don't know what the point of working in Boston is, but you can do all the reconstruction you want at home. You know my facilities are better than anything you're going to find anywhere else. What more do you need?"

I held up a hand. "You're trying to *poach* her? From one of the largest and most widely respected teaching hospitals in the world? The one with access to an unimaginably vast research system? The one with the nearly unlimited alumni network? And the *facility* is your selling point? That must be one fuck of a facility."

He brushed that off with a curt shake of his head. "Teaching is a waste of time. Sara shouldn't be spending her days with interns and residents nipping at her heels."

I turned to her. She was picking at her fish. "I've never once seen a resident or intern anywhere near your heels."

"That's because I know how to work them and not let them work me."

I motioned to the goddess beside me. "That's how we do it in Boston."

Later, I'd milk her for advice on handling O'Rourke because I obviously needed it.

Ignoring me, Dr. Shapiro said to Sara, "You don't want to waste your time at a big, bloated facility like that. Your OR getting bumped for emergent cases, different techs and nurses every day, no control over your schedule. The hours alone are reason to walk away. You don't want those kinds of conditions."

"I've always believed it's better not to tell people what they want, but that doesn't seem to be the standard here so I'll say with comfort that Mass will fight you to the bourbon-hastened death for Sara."

He was polite enough to force an appeasing grin before saying to her, "I just want what's best for you." He held her gaze for a second before beaming at someone over her shoulder and calling, "Did they let Ron Gilletti in here?"

Dr. Shapiro pushed away from the table, his cloth napkin falling to the floor as he moved to greet the man.

"That was fun," Sara murmured.

"I know you're being sarcastic, but I have to say it *is* fun to run through an offensive line like that. I'm not positive, but it feels like I worked through some issues tonight. It sucked, yet it was strangely productive."

"I'm happy you feel that way," she said, managing a small laugh. She rubbed her knuckles across her chest several times, winced. "I might require your services again in the future. Not sure I'll ever be able to endure another one of these evenings without you running interference."

"Sign me up. I'll be there." I gave her leg a squeeze. She didn't look great. "Are you okay? You demolished that snapper."

"It's what I do," she said. "Shove food in my mouth to avoid being mentally present for the backhanded flogging." I followed her gaze to her father, the man he'd called Ron, and a pair of women who seemed much too young for either of them. Much too familiar with them as well. The body language spoke in bold shouts. "Gross."

I reached for my wallet. "Are we done here? Or do we have to play a few more rounds of being less important than everyone else on the island?"

She set her napkin on the table. Flattened a hand to her belly. "You're not paying for this."

"Oh yes, I am." I flagged down the server, handed over a card. "Just you wait."

Sara continued sneaking glances at the women speaking to her father while I signed for the check. "They could be my children."

"Tell those thoughts to shut up." I wrapped my hand around her elbow. "Let's say goodbye."

"Awesome," she mumbled as we crossed the restaurant to join two men in their late sixties and a pair of women who couldn't be a minute over twenty-one. Yeah, they could be my children too. My knees ached thinking about that reality.

Dr. Shapiro pivoted when he spotted us, clapping the other man on the back and saying, "Dr. Ron Gilletti, this is my daughter Sara and Dr. Stremmel. They're in from Boston. Still working on convincing them to quit the winters and come to California for the good life."

Ron shook our hands and offered some boilerplate reasons to flee New England. He insisted Vegas was wonderful and the summers not nearly as bad as we might assume. I nodded that away, saying, "Nice to meet you both. We have to head out. Ross, dinner's on me."

I didn't know what was going through Dr. Shapiro's head, but his face looked very much like I'd thrown a bowl of hot soup in his lap and informed him his wealth manager was missing. Didn't even know which insult to address first. Within a few blinks, he recovered, saying, "It's my treat. I insist."

"Already done," I replied, stepping away. "Safe travels back to California." I pointed at Ron. "And Vegas."

Sara took hold of my hand and led the way through the restaurant. She moved quickly, and when we exited, she shook me off. "I need—"

She ran toward the bushes and it took me a second to process what was happening. I went to her, gathered up her hair as she gagged, smoothed a hand down her back. To the valet attendants watching from the curb, I called, "Could I get some water? Tissues? Thanks."

She tried to elbow me away but that wasn't happening. I should've kept an eye on her. Should've slowed her down instead of goading her father. Should've kept it low-key. I waited while the spasms moved through her. The tissues and water arrived, along with a very concerned restaurant manager who was quick to summon a taxi to take us back to the resort. No one wanted a woman tossing her cookies in front of their restaurant.

When Sara was ready, I ushered her into the back seat of the taxi and tucked her close beside me. "What do you need?" I asked.

She shook her head against my bicep, kept the wad of tissues pressed to her lips. Tears streaked her makeup. I kissed her forehead. She was clammy there. I didn't care.

As the taxi pulled onto the road, I said, "My dad left us when I was three. It was two weeks before Christmas. Right before I turned four. It's wild that I remember it, but I do. Every bit of it. There was an investment that had paid off. He said things were changing for him and we had to change too. I thought that meant we were moving into a bigger house. Nah. He was getting the fuck out. He was done. We were holding him back. He left that night. My mother said he'd return and she believed that too. She put me to bed, saying he was going through a phase. That he was out sowing some wild oats and he'd return as soon as he was done with that." I thumbed a tear from her cheek. "My sister was two at the time. She has no memory of this, but she likes to say I told her oats were very, very bad and must be avoided."

A soundless laugh shook her shoulders. I kissed her forehead again.

"It was years before my mother stopped believing he'd come back for us. I was probably eight or nine by the time she gave it up. Took off the wedding band. The part I'll never forget is how he made her think she wasn't up to his standards. None of us were, but I was barely four. I didn't have a lot to show for myself. My accomplishments were limited. My mother, on the other hand, had been with him for years before I came along. Before my sister came along. And he just blew her the fuck off because he got some cash in his pocket and decided he deserved better than her."

Sara drew in a deep breath, counted it out with light taps to my wrist. I waited until she did it twice more.

"We didn't see or hear from him again until I was finishing high school and even that was little more than a fly-by. He didn't want anything to do with us. He wanted attention and he wanted to make noise, but he never wanted us. Not until my sister came to control tickets for a Division I football team and I got an MD. My sister—bless her and her big, brass balls—doesn't participate in that shit, though I take some of his calls. I take the self-aggrandizing speeches and the circuitous asks for so-called investment capital. The asks to present some of his wealth-building opportunities to my colleagues because they're the valuable ones in this equation."

I ran a hand down her back, over the silky dress that hung beautifully from her body, but had no business in the closet of the Sara I knew. The Sara of yellow sneakers. The Sara of sweaters I wanted to pet. The quippy t-shirts. The jeans that blew my fucking mind. The pastel cups and the velvet furniture. The Sara I knew. The Sara I loved.

"I always tell him to fuck off because I'd wanted to do that from the very first moment I learned the expression. I never get tired of it." I dropped a kiss on her temple, tucked her hair over her ear. "I will always run that interference for you."

When we arrived at the resort, we strolled to her bungalow. Mine was all but forgotten. She wanted to shower alone and she did. That I leaned against the bathroom vanity, my arms crossed and my jaw locked as I watched did not change that fact.

I wrapped her up in another long, fluffy bathrobe and tucked her into bed with a bowl of crackers and a large carafe of water. She twisted her wet hair up into a bun and sent me to find the heating pad in her suitcase. I cued up a new movie on my laptop and settled in beside her.

"This isn't what you had in mind for tonight," she said.

I nabbed one of her crackers. They were not terrible. "Yeah, it is."

"Don't do that," she said. "Don't pretend this is the same as whatever crazy, wild sex plan you had for me."

"I like how you think I have crazy, wild sex plans. Like, I'm sitting at home and writing out naked itineraries."

"You're not?"

"If I'm sitting at home, I'm probably trying to ignore the noises coming from Alex and Riley's apartment downstairs."

She dropped her head to my shoulder. "Are they that loud or are the walls that thin?"

"I think it's both," I replied. "The honeymoon never ended for them."

"Must be nice," she murmured. "I'm sorry about, you know, everything."

"I am still in bed with you," I said. "This is exactly what I wanted."

CHAPTER 27

SARA

Sᴇʙᴀsᴛɪᴀɴ ᴘᴏɪɴᴛᴇᴅ ʜɪs ʙᴇᴇʀ ʙᴏᴛᴛʟᴇ ᴅᴏᴡɴ ᴛʜᴇ ʙᴇᴀᴄʜ ᴛᴏ where white chairs and an orchid-draped arbor stood. Hotel staff were busy lining the perimeter with flower petals. "Are we going to a wedding today, Shap?"

I groaned from the comfort of my beach chair, pushed my toes deeper into the sand. "As long as I don't have to fly to Nashville for the bachelorette or spend five hundred dollars on a dress that won't be worn again, regardless of what the bride says, sure. Sign me up."

He turned toward me with a chuckle. "Always the bridesmaid?"

"Between my sorority sisters, the four girls I lived with during med school, and my friends from back home, I think I've been in a dozen weddings and attended a dozen more."

He peered at me, a small smile twisting across his lips. "Wouldn't have guessed sorority girl, but now that you say it"—he dragged a knowing gaze over my body and back up—"yeah, I see it."

"Don't look at me like that. You would've demolished the twenty-year-old version of me."

He barked out a laugh. "Probably not. Let's just say I didn't know what to do with pretty sorority girls when I was in college."

"Really? You didn't hit the ladies with your scowl-and-growl routine?"

He ran his knuckles along his scruffy jaw. "It didn't work as well before the beard."

"Shocking," I murmured. "I wouldn't want to have the whole traditional wedding thing on a beach."

"Why not?"

"If I'm getting married on a beach, it has to be simple. No huge dresses, no rose petals, no perfect little white folding chairs."

"Then you want to get married?" he asked.

"Maybe. I think so. If it works out." I peered at the ceremony site as it took shape. "What about you? You'd really spice up the Acevedo-Hartshorn double date circuit."

He shook his head. "I don't think so. My parents didn't sell me on the institution if you know what I mean."

"Neither did mine," I replied. "They're probably the worst possible models for a healthy marriage. They are textbook examples of people who should get divorced."

"And here you are, planning your non-traditional island wedding."

"I am not planning my wedding. I just know I wouldn't want it like that." I gestured toward the arbor. "I hate being the center of attention, so I'd never want a big wedding with walking down the aisle and a first dance. Cutting the cake? I'd disappear. I'm not kidding. I couldn't handle that."

He tapped his beer bottle against my water. "Call me if you ever need a getaway."

"Yeah, Stremmel, I'll do that," I said with a laugh. "I

love all my friends and I've loved being part of their weddings, but there have been a few occasions where I've seriously wondered whether they were getting married because they wanted to be together forever or because they wanted to have a really big party. And I feel terrible saying that, but a few of those marriages have already ended and a few others are headed that direction. There was one that didn't last a year and I just felt like 'Why are we doing this?'"

"Because they need something to do after finishing school and getting a job," he said. "People look at life like it's a series of checkboxes. Graduate, go to work, get married, get a house, have a kid, get a dog, have another kid, go to Disney World, send the kids off to school, retire, spoil the grandkids. There's always something to do next. Always another checkbox. It keeps you busy, keeps you from looking around and wondering 'What's the point of all this?'"

I glanced at him. "No checkboxes for you?"

He shook his head. "I don't know. I could see myself having a kid someday."

"You'd have kids, but not get married?"

"Maybe? I don't know what I'm talking about," he said. "But I don't think the two have to go hand in hand. People can create a family without getting married, without having kids. A family is a bunch of people who love and care for each other unconditionally, people who show up for each other unconditionally. It doesn't have to be legal. Doesn't have to be blood. But it does have to be unconditional. Family can't blow each other off. Does that make sense?"

"It makes a lot of sense," I said. "I don't think kids are for me. My body works too hard taking care of me. It really doesn't want to grow someone else. Sure, there's always adoption, fostering, surrogacy. But I don't think I'm right for that. Like you said that day at bubble suit jousting—"

"Don't," he groaned. "I was a douche that day because I was jealous about the professor."

"I'm not willing to cut my on-call hours," I continued, "so I'd be looking at full-time help for these fictional children of mine because there is no work-life balance to be found in this career. I know right now I'd shame and guilt myself over it every day, even if plenty of other people do it. I know I'd try to be the most perfect wife-mother-surgeon-everything until I ran myself into the ground. I'd rather not do that again."

"I was a douche that day," he repeated.

"I heard you the first time," I said.

"I'm sorry I said it."

I shrugged. "It was true."

"Doesn't mean I should've said it."

I nodded, silent a long moment as we continued watching the staff hang bouquets from every chair along the aisle. Eventually, I asked, "Do you go home to Florida for the holidays? Are you heading back there next month?"

"I usually cover the ER on Christmas Eve and Christmas Day," he said. "I didn't do it last year because I was fucking exhausted, but Hartshorn started me picking up shifts on holidays. It gives other docs a chance to be with their people, and aside from the fact I get a lot of long weekends out of those returned favors, it's not a bad day to be there. Everyone brings in food, the cases aren't too bad, and Acevedo insists I stop by afterward so he's not drinking whiskey by the fire alone. No complaints from me."

"You don't go home?"

"Home isn't *home*. Acevedo's house is more home to me

than the place where my mother lives now. My sister Vivi is there in Gainesville and she's amazing, but the holidays are her busiest time with bowl games. Besides, my mother and her husband like to travel a lot. I think they have a condo in Aruba. They go there for the holidays if they're not on a cruise or off somewhere else."

"Your mother's husband. So, your stepfather?"

"Mother's husband is fine," he murmured.

"Right."

"What about you? Where do you go, who do you see?"

I belted out a dry laugh. "You have to ask that after last night? I don't go anywhere. I hate holiday season travel. It stresses me out. Everyone is so frantic and hostile. I'd rather wait until January or February and take two weeks off to do this." I gestured to the beach around us. "I might do this again in the new year."

"I like that idea. I might be the one to surprise the hell out of you."

"I'd like to see you try," I teased. "I'm not nearly as good as you, seeing as I don't cover any services over holidays, but I usually get picked up by some extrovert to join their holiday events. Last year, Emmerling brought me along to Thanksgiving at her husband's family's place. That was wild. She also convinced me to join them for a multi-holiday thing at her sister-in-law's penthouse in the North End."

"I've been to that party," he said. "I hit on that sister-in-law. In front of her fiancé too."

"Of course you did," I said, this laugh far less salty than the last.

"You have siblings, right? What about them? You said one of them is in Arizona."

"Caleb is in Arizona. He's the middle child and my

father's clone. He opened the Scottsdale clinic, he golfs all day Thursdays and Sundays, and he has a ten thousand square foot house on Camelback Mountain for him, his wife, and two Pomeranians. He's too busy augmenting breasts and being the favorite child to care what my brother Eli or I do. If he's noticed that I haven't been home in years, he doesn't mention it. Hell, he hasn't been home in years either. He's riding the expansion tide pretty hard and it's worked nicely for him." I paused for a sip of water. "Eli is the baby and the rebel. If I have a savage heart, he has a savage existence. He was in the military just long enough to properly horrify my parents. Now he's based out of Louisiana and works in regional disaster response as a medic. He's deployed for natural disasters and crisis events, that sort of thing. We text a lot. He takes issue with me doing things like coming to conferences because my father demands it. He thinks I'm letting this shit into my life rather than enforcing boundaries."

"Family is complex," he said softly. "Not a lot of right answers."

"Nope." I glanced over at him. "You were telling me about college. How you didn't have any game with the girls. I'm burned out on family problems. Finish that story."

"I didn't have any game. That's all there was to it. I was preoccupied with hating everything about college, but since it was such an improvement over high school, I didn't complain," he said.

"Somehow I doubt that," I said. "That you didn't complain. I'm certain you hated everything and complained constantly."

"I didn't complain as often," he said. "I went to this private Southern Baptist school from pre-kindergarten through high school because my mom worked at the school. She was the headmaster's secretary. That granted free tuition to my sister and me. She took the job for that reason alone. It was good because it meant she didn't have to scramble for childcare. We'd just go to school with her every day and wait in the library until she was done." He paused, took a sip of his beer. "But we're not Southern Baptist so it was a fourteen-year experiment in what the actual fuck. My mother raised us Catholic-ish. She did her best, but that shit is time-inten-sive and we were getting all this other noise at school, so we were over-the-top hostile toward it on the weekends. We basically broke my mother of her Catholicism by the time I was ten. Vivi was barely eight, but she was like, *fuck this shit*. It was a relief to get to college and not have to bite my tongue to keep from arguing with a minister every day at school."

"Same. I can't believe I'm saying it, but *same*." I closed my hand over his forearm. "I grew up Jewish. Very Reform, mostly culturally since my parents don't have a spiritual bone between them. They sent me and my siblings to a private Episcopalian school, but they didn't have any good reason like free tuition. No, it was just the poshest private school in Orange County and all the families they socialized with sent their kids there. Fortunately—I guess?—there were kids from all different backgrounds there and it was actually a very diverse learning environment and I came to under-stand a ton about other cultures, but we still had weekly church services and required Bible study courses. I remember my parents explaining to me at a really young age that I'd hear these things in school and I'd just have to go along with it, even if it was different from what I'd learned in Hebrew school. Somehow, as a child, I was able to negotiate that dissonance without completely melting down. What the actual fuck is right."

He peered at me for a moment, his brow wrinkled as he thought. He skimmed a glance over my body. "Was there a plaid skirt involved?"

"Are you being a pervert right now?"

"That depends on how you define pervert," he said, still studying my legs.

"Are you thinking about me in a starched school uniform? As a child?"

"I'm thinking about you as you are today," he said, a lazy gesture at my breasts, "in a starched school uniform."

"You're still being a pervert," I said but I couldn't hide my smile.

"Was there a blouse involved?" He motioned to his chest and I nodded. "Blazer or sweater? Tell me it was a sweater. Lie to me if you have to because you're a fucking snack in sweaters and I need to complete this visual."

"You like my sweaters?"

His brows lifted as he continued dragging his gaze over my body. "It's the best part of living in an icebox."

"You love that icebox."

"I have grown to tolerate it as an inevitable part of my existence," he replied.

"You're never leaving."

He nodded. "That's probably true."

Though I didn't have a reason to, I said, "I might leave."

He turned his attention back to the ocean. "Why?"

I gave a single shake of my head because I really didn't know why I'd brought this up, but I couldn't take it back now. "I don't get the sense this is a particularly good fit for me."

"Why not?"

I should not have brought this up. I'd never verbalized it before, only batted it around in my head and invented unproductive stories that boiled down to imposter syndrome and my father's unending influence on my career. "My outcomes are great. My residents are great. Everything's great. But I get the sense no one really knows what to do with me. Like there should be something more to me, some extra sparkle I can't seem to conjure." The sparkle was my father. Everyone wanted access to him, and even though I looked like I could provide that access, nothing could be further from the truth. "And since the accident in the ER, well, that hasn't helped."

"You don't care what I think, but none of that is true," he said.

"It's true to me." *And I do care what you think, I just don't know how to bring those words to my lips.*

"It makes sense that you lie to yourself frequently," he said. "You're the one eating croutons straight up and pretending it's normal."

"I eat croutons now because I didn't let myself have them. Before," I added.

With a sigh that sank his shoulders, he said, "Sara. I wish you'd told me that sooner."

"How could I?" I ran my palms over the edges of my armrests. "We were very busy hating each other. Couldn't possibly peel back my bulletproof vest to show you my weak spots. Would've been poor strategy on my behalf."

"I still wish I'd known."

I shot a glance in his direction, but he was glaring at the waves and didn't notice. "Why? Would you have trashed my croutons any less?"

"No, of course not. I just—I just wish I'd known."

I wasn't content with that. "Why? What would've changed? Would you have been measured and cordial that day in the ER? Would you have sat next to me on the sofa in Milana's office? Would you have stomped up to your apartment instead of slamming me up against my door?"

After a moment of consideration where it seemed his scowl couldn't get any deeper without his entire head caving in, he said, "All I can say is I want you to trust me enough to let me hold these pieces of you. I like looking after you."

Reflexively, I said, "I don't need looking after."

He rolled his head against the back of his chair to stare at me, his eyes as dark as night and his pout infinitely kissable. "Yes, you do."

There were no fewer than a million things I wanted to say about that, but Sebastian was already moving on, giving me impatient gestures and *let's get on with it* eyes.

"And where would you go? If you left Boston?" he asked.

I lifted a shoulder. "I don't know."

"Then you're not entertaining offers," he said. "You're just entertaining the idea of another hospital fawning over you, making sure you know you're their prize gem. And you say I'm the arrogant one here."

"I have offers." None that interested me, but that was beside the point. "And it's not about fawning."

"Hartshorn and Acevedo adore you. They'll fawn. Just drop a hint and they'll fawn." He said this with a splash of accusation, like I'd really crossed a line in garnering the respect of my colleagues. What an insufferable bitch, right? "They'll blame me until the end of time if you leave. They'll whip me, both literally and figuratively, until the actual end of time."

"Oh, no. That sounds so awful for you," I deadpanned.

"I'm just saying, you have fans. And you know Hartshorn is teed up to take over as the next Chief of Surgery," he continued.

"And you're teed up to take over emergency surgery."

"Hah. Not until I prove I'm not a liability," he said, but there was no heat behind those words. "I know you think that day in the ER fucked things up for you, but it's going to be okay. It's gonna blow over. It was an accident, and everyone knows that."

I knew he believed that. It didn't make it true for me. I had to see it to believe it.

He reached for his drink, saying, "I don't want to talk about work anymore. We're not there. It's not our problem right now. What were you like in high school?"

"You go first," I said.

"I was a moody little emo-goth asshole," he said. "I was very concerned with moody music and goth books that weren't actually interesting, but made me feel superior for being able to quote them conversationally. If the school uniform would've permitted earrings and eyebrow rings, I would've had a dozen. I would've tattooed my eyelids. Just for the joy of being contrarian. But I was also an expert at all matters related to school offices. I could fix every printer and copier. I was a genius with the laminator and the giant paper cutter of death. I knew the phone system better than anyone."

"That is adorable," I said. "I don't have nearly as much amusing material to share with you. I was a cheerleader, but—"

"Oh my god what?" he sputtered, a drop of beer rolling down his chin. "What was that?"

"Oh. It's nothing. I just—I wasn't very good at ballet or any of the dance classes my mother put me into because I was a chunky little chicken nugget of a kid, which she hated, but I did well with gymnastics. I mean, I'm short. It's not a shock. When I reached high school, I tried out for cheer. Since I could tumble, I was chosen for varsity my first year."

My cheeks heated as he continued staring at me. He was going to say something awful about cheerleaders and how there was probably a cheer-to-plastics pipeline, either surgeon or patient, and I should be proud for leaning all the way in to that stereotype. Then, "I *love* that. Sara. I can't even handle it. There's like a painful hiccup stuck in my chest right now because I love that so much. Is this a heart attack? I don't know. Don't care. Tell me more."

"Okay, but why do you love it?" I asked, laughing.

"Because I am obsessed with small, strong as fuck women who can flip around and shit. *Obsessed*. Just fuckin' obsessed. I watch college cheer competitions on ESPN all the time." He looked me up and down again. "Can you still do that stuff? No, wait, forget I asked. That was stupid. The mental picture is all I need. But hold on, do you have a yearbook anywhere? No, never mind. Don't answer that. What are you doing?"

I pushed to my feet, tugged off the sarong, smoothed my hands down the sides of my thighs. "We'll start small. I think I can still do a back handspring. It used to be my intro story. You know, 'let's go around the table and say one interesting thing about ourselves.' I did a back handspring. I was Back Handspring Girl. It followed me to med school. I've tumbled in a lot of empty surgical hallways."

"Sara, no. I am telling you no. *Don't*. I can't bring you home with a broken wrist. Or ankle. Or anything."

I waved that off. "Just go back to pretending I'm a teenager and you're a pervert. It's fine. I've got this."

I glanced over my shoulders, blew out a breath, and threw my first back handspring in years. My form was sloppy and the landing could only be described as *drunk girl in uncomfortable heels*, and I laughed as though I did something truly miraculous. I kind of felt miraculous too. Like I was inside a miracle right now.

"I think I can probably land a roundoff back handspring too. Just give me a second to—"

"We need to go back to the bungalow," Sebastian said, jumping out of his chair, haphazardly draping the sarong over my shoulders, and marching me up the beach.

"Why? What's wrong?" I asked, giggling as I struggled to match his pace.

He leaned into my hip, his shaft hard and hot through his shorts. "I have something I need you to handle."

"And I'm guessing you'd like me to be aggressive with it. B-E aggressive," I said in my chirpiest cheerleader cadence.

"Oh my god," he groaned. "Not another word until we're inside, you perky little demon."

"Then you don't want any go-fight-win?" I asked, clapping out the words.

"*Oh my god*. Sara. If you don't shut up right now, I—" He stopped, threw me over his shoulder, and stomped into the bungalow. "You're trying to kill me. I know it."

"I'm not," I cried.

He brought his lips to my thigh, pressed a small bite into my skin. "When I put you down, you take this suit off immediately. Understand?"

I tried to push my hair out of my eyes, but hanging upside down made that difficult. "Maybe."

He delivered a light slap between my legs before lowering me to the living room rug. "You'll take it off."

I gathered up my hair as best I could while Sebastian sat on the sofa, his legs wide and a hand curled loose over his crotch. "I think I can still do a few of the jumps. Let me try."

"*Noooo*. Get over here."

Ignoring him, I backed up to stand in the open space of the living room. I mimed the motions of a toe-touch jump before deciding I could pull this off. I counted out the beats as I threw my arms into a T, popped off the floor, came back down. "I can't believe I can still do that! Thank you, yoga. Did you see that?"

"*Get over here*." He crooked a finger and arched a brow, and my center throbbed. That was all it took. "And lose the suit unless you'd like me to rip it off you."

"That seems unnecessary," I said, running a finger along the shoulder strap.

"Then don't make it my only option."

I wiggled out of the high-waisted two piece and stood between his knees. He drew a hand up my leg, pushed my thighs apart. He leaned forward, brought his mouth to my mound. Licked over my folds, circled my clit. It was the kind of attention that registered as exactly what I needed, but not nearly enough of it. Still, I wobbled under his teasing, had to steady myself with a hand on his shoulder. The ache inside me was unlike any other. It curled and squeezed, and the tension moved out from my center like spilled ink. I felt that need in my belly, my thighs, my ass. It was everywhere, clenching and pulsing, and I didn't think I'd survive if I didn't feel him inside me.

He glanced at me, his big hands digging into the soft of my legs. "Take your hair down."

"No, it's crazy from being in the water earlier."

"I love it crazy." Despite it being a tangled mess, I shook out my hair and tossed the scrunchie aside. He leaned back against the cushions, patted his upper thigh. "Right here. Right now."

Since I didn't have to be asked twice, I climbed into his lap, my knees on either side of him and my breasts in his face. I didn't drop down, didn't connect with the thick shaft trapped under his shorts. Not yet. "Like this?"

He nodded, his forehead between my breasts and his hands on my waist. "Exactly like this."

"Are you thinking about the teenage cheerleader version of me?" I laced my hands behind his head, sifted my fingers through his hair. "Or the private school version of me? Or is it a blend of both?"

He shifted his head, bared his teeth against my breast. "I'm thinking about the woman who yanked off her skirt, did a back flip in front of me, and filled my fantasy bank for the rest of eternity. That's who I'm thinking about. Now, give me those perfect little tits."

He bit a mark into the side of my breast before yanking my face down to his and kissing me hard enough to steal my breath. Whatever inhibitions I had left, that kiss shook them free. I was burning from it, from the absolute heat of him all around me. Though the thought had never once crossed my mind before, I knew this was what it felt like to be branded. To be claimed. To be such a fucking mess and still surrender myself to him for safe keeping because I knew he would do exactly that.

It was a good thing my body was too busy rocking against his erection and clenching around nothing right now because that thought was enough to make me want to run the hell away. Just get up and go—go anywhere, anywhere else, anywhere but here, where I could be stuck and trapped and powerless because that was what happened when someone else was in control.

"Whatever you're thinking," he started, "don't doubt that I'll fuck it right out of you."

I reached for the waistband of his shorts with unsteady hands, edged them down just enough to allow his shaft to pop free. "I might need you to do that."

He ran his hand over my hip, around to my ass. Drove his fingers into the soft tissue, shaking as if he wanted to see how hard he could grip me. He sucked a nipple into his mouth, sighing and growling as he went on squeezing me. I didn't think I could endure much more teasing when he dragged that nipple between his teeth, the barest of bites, and I fisted his cock between us.

We watched as I lowered myself, as he disappeared inside me. He pushed all the air out of me. All the sense too. The only thing I could do was gasp down at us, at the thickness between my legs that led to the searing heat inside me. My thighs shook from the strain of this position, but I wanted it this way. I wanted my hands on those broad shoulders, my perfect little tits in his face. And I wanted to be in charge this time. I wanted to feel it this way.

Sebastian flexed his fingers on my backside, saying, "If you don't move in the next six seconds, I am going to do it for you."

I shifted forward, my knees closer to his hips now and his fingertips drilling bruises into my ass. I felt him everywhere. Even the predatory way he stared at me, his jaw tense. I felt that—and I felt like I'd belonged to him for a lifetime, like everything that was mine had always been his, and I realized I wanted it that way. I wanted to be possessed in every filthy and beautiful and painfully real way I could be, and I wanted him to be the one possessing me. And the secret I wasn't prepared to share with him—barely with myself—was that I wanted to possess him too. I wanted to own him with all of my savagery, collect him and gather him up with all of my frantic perfectionism. I wanted him so much that I could barely breathe around my desperation to escape from these truths.

Every inch of me was hot and sensitive, and my nipples needed so much attention, they hurt. "I know what I'm doing," I whispered. "Just watch."

I couldn't tear my eyes off him as he stared down at where I was spread around him, as a gulp moved through his throat. "I think I'm watching you kill me with your cunt."

I moved my hips, found a slow, rolling motion that sent his head falling back against the cushions. His lips parted, the hand on my ass tightened. "Is that what I'm doing?"

"If you kill me here, you'll have a lot of explaining to do. Just remember that."

He brought his free hand to my breast, swiped a thumb over my aching nipple. That swipe went directly to my center, a deep, glorious throb that set off a small wave of shivers that radiated out, out, *out*, until I was trembling.

Looking me over with that same, old arrogant grin, he said, "That was quick."

"It's your own fault," I said, arching my back and sinking down on him once again.

"I'm aware of that. I'm damn pleased about it, if you don't mind me being honest."

His hold on my ass was brutal. It was like he wanted to tear that piece of me off, keep it for himself. Or maybe he just wanted me to remember him tomorrow when— No. I wasn't thinking about that. Wasn't going there. We had eighteen hours left before the real world came calling. Eighteen hours before we slipped back into our old world, our old cycle, the old patterns. The way it was before we found ourselves on the same island. I wasn't thinking about that. I *couldn't*.

"I'll get you there again," he promised, going for my nipples. He drew one between his lips as I found a fast, bouncing rhythm over him. "If we had that little clit sucker toy, you'd already be there."

I edged my thighs wider, trying to get him deeper. I needed all of him, every last inch. I needed it now because I didn't know what came next. "Why do you like my toys so much?"

He switched to the other nipple, gripped my ass harder still. "Because *you* like them."

I felt the first twinge of fabric burn on my knees. I didn't care. "That's not why."

"All right, yeah, that's not why," he said, sliding an arm across my back and anchoring me with a hand on my shoulder. He jammed me down hard, almost as hard as the cock shuttling over my swollen skin, and we cried out together. "I love it when you're strong. When you're just fucking *strong*, Sara. And I love it when you fall the fuck apart for me, but all I have is a dick and some fingers and a tongue, so I'll take all the help I can get because you don't fall apart the first time. You need me to make your blood pump so fucking hard that you can't hear any of the noise in your head. You need me to break you down, piece by piece, until all you can do is blink up at me with those big eyes and ask for more.

You need me to do that for you, and Sara, sweetheart, I need it just as much."

My knees burned. Heat bloomed across my face, my chest. Sweat slicked my back. My hair was everywhere, a thick cloud scented with saltwater and sunscreen. Everything between us was wet and slippery. It was desperate too, like we were out to prove something.

Maybe that was just me. Maybe I was the only one who needed to prove this was perfect in a way I'd never believed perfect could exist. This was it, wasn't it? This was the perfect I'd chased, the rightness, the worthiness. All the validation I could ever want was between my legs, hard and swearing into my skin and bruising me with the promise that this was right and this was real.

"Sara," he groaned, his lips on my sternum. "Come on, honey. Come for me. Put me out of this misery."

The pressure building inside me resembled that groan. It was a roar, a snarl waiting to break free. It was the kind of scream that rippled with primal possession. The kind of scream I'd never dared to voice because I wasn't loud, I wasn't demanding, I wasn't the center of attention—I wasn't anything.

But now I screamed. I screamed into Sebastian's skin, into his mouth. Screamed as the orgasm unfurled from behind my clit and wrapped my center in a brutal throb. As he speared up into me again, again. As he shook with me. As he held me.

CHAPTER 28

SARA

"WE'VE BEEN HERE A COUPLE OF DAYS," SEBASTIAN SAID WITH A gesture toward the ocean, "and you haven't tried to drown me once. If you're going to do it, you better get a move on. This is your last chance."

I spared him a glance before returning my gaze to the water. Waves lapped at our ankles as the sun climbed out of the horizon. I had less than three hours before I had to leave for the airport. I didn't remember why I'd been so adamant about flying home immediately after the conference. I regretted it now. This felt like the last seconds of a video game where the music sped up and the lights started flashing and everything was about to end whether I was ready or not.

"We've been here a couple of days and you haven't tried to be a condescending asshole. It's your last chance."

Sebastian shifted a bit, dipped his hands into the pockets of his shorts. I really enjoyed these shorts, but it was the breezy linen shirts rolled halfway up his forearms that did it for me. That I hadn't ripped every single one clear off his chest was worth recognition. I wanted the medal for that. *Restraint, beachy linen with bared forearms* category.

"You are such a brat," he said, softly enough that it seemed largely for his benefit rather than mine.

There was no suitable response for this comment. I wiggled my toes in the sand and pretended these weren't the final minutes of our perfect little island bubble. Life was a lot better without the real world. Even if the real world did insist on meeting me for dinner and being as self-absorbed as always.

"It's not because you're spoiled," he added out of nowhere. "Although you are. You're a brat because you push the limits."

Savage bitch heart, your order is ready.

"For, well, forever, basically," he continued, "I assumed that was because you liked getting your way. You do, there's no doubt about that, but now I think you push because you haven't gotten your way enough."

I stared down at the water, at my toes half hidden in the sand. I didn't say anything. Somewhere in the past few hours, I lost the glowy haze of this cease-fire. I felt none of that glow and tons of scrappy, agitated tension that seemed to tighten in my chest. I wanted to run away, push him away, do anything at all to get away from the pressure growing inside me.

After a moment, he went on. "I like when you push. I like pushing you back."

"Yeah, and that's a lot of fun, but sometimes you push the wrong way and much more than necessary."

He ran a hand down my back. "Is that what you think, you snarky little goblin?"

"It's what I know," I shot back. "You should give it a try

when we get home. Just cut the pompous commentary in half."

"That's what you want? That's the only change you'd like to see?"

I rubbed a toe over a smooth pebble. "That would be enough."

A growl sounded in his throat though I decided to commit myself fully to the examination of this pebble. It wouldn't do to get carried away with his growls when I still had to pack.

Then, "Does that mean you have no desire to take this"— he wrapped an arm around my waist and shoved his fingers through my hair, forcing me to acknowledge him—"home with us?"

"What of 'this' are you referring to?"

He bent a single eyebrow and that was *just about* enough for me to lead him back into the bungalow and forget this conversation. To forget my desire to run. But then he said, "I'd rather not have to play pointless team-building games before feeling you up, and waking up next to you is worth all your brattiness."

"You're not going to have to play pointless team-building games with me much longer."

He laughed into my hair. "You're good at this."

"At what?"

"Evading. Dodging. Hiding. I don't know why you think you need to hide from me at this point, but you are *very* good at it."

"I am not—"

"We don't have time for you to be impossible about this. You have to leave and I have to know. Tell me how you want it to be when we're back home."

I stared at his shirt, fixating on the fine weave of the linen. "I don't know yet. I need some time to think about that."

Those words seemed to hit him like a solid blow. We were silent for a moment, but Sebastian shook his head slowly, as if he was carrying on a debate to which I hadn't been invited. "What is there to think about?"

"Oh, I don't know, how about the fact that barely more than a week ago we agreed this was toxic and we needed a break from each other?"

"*I* didn't agree to that."

I pressed my hands to his chest. "That doesn't make it any less true."

"I know you think your version is the correct one and I know you think you're doing the right thing by hiding, but you have to consider for a single fucking second that you might be wrong this time."

"And what if you're wrong?"

"Is it that bad?" he asked. "Am *I* that bad?"

I dropped my forehead to his sternum. I needed to shake off the oppressive weight of this moment. It was swelling inside me, choking me. "I am enough of a mess on my own. I can't add another ounce to it."

"Don't do that," he rumbled. "Tell me I'm a condescending asshole, tell me I'm nothing more than the guy you hate-fuck on Thursdays. Hell, just tell me I'm an ugly son of a bitch. But don't you dare tell me I'm going to screw up your life, Sara."

I lifted my shoulders as I glanced around. "I have one question for you."

He sifted his hands through my hair. "You know you can ask me anything. No need to dick around about it."

"When everything happened in the ER, and the two of us were hustled out of there and upstairs to the Chief's office while we were covered in glass and blood, he called you in first. What did you say? How did you explain what'd happened?"

He stared at me, the corners of his eyes crinkled and his scowl soft enough to touch. "I said it was an accident. I said we'd had a strongly worded discussion about a case and the rest of it was a million-in-one shot."

I bobbed my head because I'd figured that much. He wouldn't have complied with the group therapy if he'd blamed me for the entirety of the incident. "What was the *outcome* of that conversation?"

"Same as you," he said with a heaving eye roll. "Eight weeks of counseling and an emphatic request to not create more problems."

"Except it wasn't the same," I said. "There's a formal reprimand in my personnel file and I got a lecture from the Chief that included the word 'tantrum' and a detailed reference to my father and all of *his* professionalism. Apparently there was some expectation of apples and their short fall from the tree."

"That's bullshit," he said. "But you know it's institutional bullshit, not bullshit I've caused. You know the difference and I'm not going to let you pretend otherwise."

"These two months have been difficult for me. This has been stressful, Sebastian. I told you before, you have all the power. I have a formal reprimand and a reminder to play nice. So, when you ask me if it's been that bad? Yes. This has been bad for me. Have I discovered that, under all your growls and scowls, under your arrogance and contempt for the entire world, you are not the miserable asshole you want everyone to believe you are? Also yes. Yeah," I added when he looked out at the ocean, "you're not the only one who knows how to hide."

A moment passed when it seemed the only next step would be wrestling each other into the water, but then Sebastian let out an aggrieved sigh, saying, "I don't want to go home to screaming at each other outside your door and—"

"Be real. You love screaming at me outside my door. That has a pretty high rate of positive return for you."

The stare he gave me said he didn't appreciate my attempt at humor. "I don't want to go back to fucking and fighting only to go home alone afterward. Fuck, I *really* don't want to go back to watching a visiting professor hit on you and—"

"If you think I am going to another one of those dinner parties, you're insane," I muttered.

"—and not have the right to make it clear to everyone that you're my screech owl."

I shook my head. "Is that supposed to be a term of endearment?"

"I don't want to walk down the hall and have to pretend I don't know you in a way no one else does. Do you hear me right now? Because I'm not promising I'll never fight with you again—god, that's out of the question—but I'm saying it doesn't have to be the way it was. We can start over—or start where we are right now. We can start wherever you want, but I need you to want it too."

I was so certain that I knew myself. That I knew my mess, my perfectionism, my savagery. I knew what I wanted, what I needed, and what I believed.

I was *so* certain.

Until this man with his dark eyes and dark moods showed up and sent my perfect little stack of index cards flying. Every last one of them, flying. It didn't matter to him whether they were color-coded and alphabetized, whether some were creased and dog-eared while others were taped together. He'd scooped them back up and he'd taken good care of those cards, but his handling meant they'd never be quite the same.

And I was so very certain that there was something dangerous and destabilizing about his card-throwing entrance into my life that I'd never considered the possibility that I'd choose to keep him around.

All those times we'd hurled insults at each other and fought over little scraps of nothing, I'd coded that as toxic. Filed it into my deck of cards as very bad for me, must avoid.

The sex—which I'd participated in willingly, which had crushed my preexisting notions about pleasure and how I experienced it—had been very good, but also very bad. It existed in the risky borderland where hate wasn't hate and enemies could fight on the same side so long as they both got what they wanted. Very bad. Must avoid.

And all those moments when it wasn't sex or anger or any of the other things we did to each other, those were just the in-betweens. The timeouts. The cease-fires. If we could've been gentle and generous with each other, we would've done that from the start.

Those moments when we'd stopped being awful, they were the exceptions. This was the exception. Nothing we'd found here this week was the rule.

That was how I'd organized these index cards, all without considering whether I had any of it right. Whether I was so busy being a mess, a perfectionist, a savage-hearted bitch that I didn't pick up on Sebastian playing an entirely different game. Whether I was allowed to forfeit my game and choose his instead, I still had to figure out.

"I need to think about that," I said. "I—I just need some time."

He gathered my hair up in his hands, let it fall. Then he did it again. "Time," he repeated.

"I'm sorry, I—" I stopped myself. I didn't have to breathe life into those ancient aches today.

He gathered up my hair again, twisted it around his hand. "What have these days been if not time?"

"This has been a break. An escape from our regularly scheduled mutual hate and loathing."

"I've never hated you," he said.

"Sure, you just do a fantastic job of pretending otherwise."

"I've *never* hated you, you crotchety little witch. Even when I wanted to wring your neck. *Especially* when I wanted to wring your neck. And you know that." He dropped my hair and stepped back, a deep sigh rattling out of him. "What the hell are we doing, Sara? What do you want us to do? Answer me this time."

Eventually, I admitted, "I don't know."

He watched as I shifted, stared out at the ocean. "Would you tell me why it's so difficult to envision a world where the time we spend together isn't employer-mandated? I want to understand why that looks so terrible to you, because it can't be all about institutional bullshit and me picking on plastic surgeons. You're tougher than that."

"Has it ever occurred to you that requiring me to be tough is half the problem here?"

He stepped in front of me, blocking my view of the water. "It's *not* half the problem. You're the toughest little cookie I've ever met and I know a lot of tough cookies. You just haven't realized that you don't have to be tough with me."

"You pick fights with me all the time," I yelled.

"Because it's fun," he yelled back.

"All this time, I've been battling you and you've—you've been having *fun*?"

"And you weren't?"

"No!" I cried.

"The time you pummeled me with stuffed animals? That wasn't a tiny bit fun for you?"

"It was—you know what that was," I said impatiently.

"And the time you paid a hostess to ask me if I was the most arrogant surgeon in the city? You weren't having any fun then?"

"I didn't have to pay her," I replied with a sniff. "She did it for free."

"And what about the time you tried to drown me in the Charles River? There wasn't a single drop of fun in that for you?"

"You have to stop saying I tried to *drown* you. Your sleeve was damp. There's a significant difference between a few splashes and holding your overinflated head under the water for a prolonged period of time."

"And this?" he asked. "This isn't fun for you? Not even a little?" When I didn't respond, he went on, "Because I think it is, Sara. You just don't want to recognize it. You're so much fun to fight with. You get all worked up and you're so damn gorgeous when you're furious for no reason, and because you like it too. Admit it, for once, that you love battling me.

That you can push and push and push, and the only thing I'm ever going to do is pull your hair and fuck you harder."

"Even if a fraction of that is correct—and I'm not saying it is—don't you think I get tired of that?" I asked, still louder than anyone should be speaking on a beach in Jamaica at sunrise. "Don't you think I want some nice, simple interactions that don't involve screaming or beating the shit out of each other at jousting?"

He brought his hands to my shoulders, up my neck. "*No.* I think you want to be loud. I think you want to be as wild and prickly and sweet as you know you truly are, and I think you want someone who sees that mess and wants more of it. Who wants all of it."

I needed a minute to think. That was it, just a minute to think. And breathe. And also get the hell out of this conversation and into a place where this man wasn't crawling inside my head, scooping up my thoughts, and forcing me to look them in the eye. "I haven't packed," I said. "I should do that. Now. Soon. I mean, I have to go soon and I should pack now."

"Sara." My name was a sigh.

"If you want to continue talking to me, you can do it while I pack," I said, storming up the beach.

It took me all of a minute to reach the bungalow and another minute to drag my bags from the closet and start shoving my things inside. If I knew anything about folding clothes or organizing garments, it didn't show. No, this was fully slapdash and that was the goal. I was doing exactly what I intended and no one was going to tell me otherwise. I knew myself and I was certain, *so fucking certain*, of all the things. I had it all right here in my contradictory little pocket. I wasn't trying to reorient my entire world while also gathering my things for international travel.

It took several more minutes for Sebastian to appear in the doorway, his hair tousled like he'd run his fingers through it a million times. He tipped his head to the side, silent a moment as he watched me fill the suitcase.

"No one," he started, then thought better about it and pressed his fist to his mouth.

"I just need some time to think. That's all," I said. He stared at me in a way that confirmed he knew my words were little more than bandages over bullet wounds. He *saw* me and he *wanted* me, and I couldn't even begin to consider that until I processed the possibility that we weren't a toxic mistake. Of course we were a toxic mistake! But what if we weren't? What if... No, I couldn't go there. Not yet. "You have to know I'm not good at this. At being with people. That has to be obvious to you and—"

"No one will ever love you the way I do," he said.

I dropped the things I was holding. My hairbrush slid off the bed, onto the floor. One sandal landed in the suitcase. I wasn't sure where the other one ended up. "What?"

"You own every valve and chamber of my heart yet you could leave here tonight and meet someone who will give you everything you need, everything you've ever wanted. And I'd be happy for you too. Do *you* get *that*?" He sounded irritable, like I was intentionally missing the point. "I'd be happy for you, even if you weren't with me. You could walk away from me now and take"—he slapped a hand to his chest—"everything I have to give and keep it with you as proof that you are deserving of all the love I have to offer. But you need to understand something, Sara. That person who will love every weird and stubborn side of you? They won't know the first thing about fighting with you all the way down the Charles River while you do your damnedest to drown them, and they won't know how ruthless and relentless you are when it comes to winning at team-building exercises. They won't know the absolute pleasure of dying by your hand in bubble suit jousting and knowing that is the best and only way to leave this world. They won't know anything about arguing with you while trying to get under your clothes in a foyer and they won't know when to remind you of the right way to breathe and they won't know that no one will ever love *me* the way *you* do. Before you start screeching at me about—"

"I do *not* screech."

"—how you've never said that you love me, let me tell you that I don't give a fuck about the words. I don't need them, Sara. I don't. You've spent these past few days with me and given me everything of yours to hold safe. You let me block and tackle your father. Even before this week, you let me doctor you at Acevedo's house and tuck you in before I left your sweet little demonic face in bed. I don't need the words. I already know what I need to know. I just need you to choose me."

I wasn't sure when I started crying, but there were tears streaming down my face and they weren't stopping. "Sebastian…"

"Don't say anything. Okay? Just don't say anything right now. Go home and think about—about all of this. You want time? Take all the time you need. You know where to find me. But don't find me until you've realized you *are* ready to choose."

For a second, neither of us moved. We didn't even blink.

Then Sebastian crossed the room and came to my side,

his arms wrapping around me at once. He pressed his lips to my temple. "I don't want to be alone with anyone but you. Understand?"

I gave a watery sniff and nodded. "Yeah."

He gave me a bone-crunching squeeze and another kiss before stepping back. I pressed my palms to my eyes because this was not what I wanted from our last day together.

When I blinked at the room, I was alone.

CHAPTER 29

SEBASTIAN

I SPENT THE REST OF THE WEEK SITTING ON THE BEACH, WISHING Sara was with me. I wasn't sure if it was an exact match but this seemed a lot like going on a honeymoon alone. Hollow, empty, questioning every one of my life choices. It was close enough.

I reread the entire *Chronicles of Narnia* series because what the fuck else was I going to do? I parked my ass on that beach, read books I didn't actually like, and kept up an argument with myself as to whether I'd made a colossal error in dumping all that information on Sara while she was already freaking out.

If I was smart—and we all knew I wasn't—I would've said nothing. Not a goddamn word. What I could've done was accept that she wasn't ready for me to jump in and take possession of the next fifty years of her life. It wasn't like I had to tell her I loved her and no one else would ever be able to give her what I would. I could've shut my fucking mouth. I could've done that. I could've continued being her enemy with benefits, the guy she fucked whenever she was in the mood to stop holding everything in. I could've been that guy for her. The one who gave her the space to be free and knew how to watch while friends fixed her up with the right guys.

I was never the one friends fixed up and I knew better than to expect it. I was never the right guy. I was the wrong guy, the douche waffle guy, the egotistical guy, the guy who glared at everyone, the guy who growled instead of speaking. I was the fucking worst. I was the guy who flirted with unavailable women. I was the guy who hadn't cracked a smile in years. I was the guy who found everything annoying and loved hating things for no good reason. I was the *worst* guy and I got that. I understood the situation thoroughly.

With that rosy reality in mind, I seriously considered leaving the island early. I would've done that if I didn't think Sara would've interpreted that as an attack on the time I'd promised her. She needed to figure out what she wanted from me—if anything, but please, god, let it be something—and I needed to grant her that time without impatiently stomping around her. I needed her to take that time and realize she was as ready as she needed to be.

Not that I even understood the issue of *being ready*. Hell, she'd been ready since the day she ripped my shirt open. I'd bet anything she was still finding those buttons around her bedroom. That perfect little tyrant knew exactly what she wanted. She just had to climb out of her head long enough to let herself want it.

————

IT WAS cold and wet when I landed in Boston on Sunday.

I hated myself for it, but I couldn't suppress the twinge of disappointment that came from walking through the terminal and not finding Sara waiting there for me.

I hated myself a little more when I stomped up the stairs to my apartment and slammed the door as hard as I could, only to stare at that door for a solid ten minutes in hopes of her coming up to say hello.

I really hated myself the next morning when I glanced out the window and spotted her chaos bun crossing the street toward the hospital.

Coming to the airport was a reach and assuming she was awake when I got in last night was poor form, but she would've waited for me in the foyer this morning if she wanted to see me.

She didn't want to see me and there was nothing I could do about it. That was the problem inherent in sending her off with an ultimatum. I should've known better.

And I did. I knew better. I knew no one ever chose me.

CHAPTER 30

SEBASTIAN

I ALWAYS KNEW I WAS HEADED FOR SOME KIND OF WHOLE-LIFE implosion, but I never expected a screech owl plastic surgeon would press the detonator.

I knew it would be bad though I hadn't anticipated quite this much destruction. I didn't think I'd go to bed feeling like a pitted cherry and wake up with the exact same through-and-through wound the next day—and I didn't think it was possible to experience that for days on end.

The unfortunate truth was that I couldn't avoid Sara, not in any practical sense, and trying to avoid her only made this worse as I never stopped thinking about her. It was bad enough with wondering what her t-shirt said today and whether it was a crouton day or she was back on the trail mix, but now I had to watch from the third floor landing while she wrapped a scarf around her neck and buttoned her coat before leaving the building. I had to listen from around a corner while she rounded with her residents and I had to take my life into my hands every time I ventured into a stairwell.

I didn't like to devote a lot of time to flipping through the implosions of my past, but I knew this one was the worst of them.

We had the whole deadbeat dad thing and that had been pretty awful, though in all fairness to my mother, I wasn't the one who got fucked all the way over in that situation. She took the brunt of that bullshit, but it definitely left me with the knowledge that the people meant to love you couldn't be relied upon to do that. They'd leave, and life would be really shitty and you'd always wonder what you did wrong, even when you knew there was nothing valuable to be found by mining that cave.

We had some run-of-the-mill heartbreak in college, then again in med school, and once more as an intern, and those had seemed significant at the time, but now resembled obviously poor choices that ended in dramatic if not inevitable ways. Nonetheless, I'd devoted a load of energy to convincing myself that opening up to another person was a terrible idea, and those breakups stood as my incontrovertible proof. The risk outweighed the reward. It was a fool's errand to go looking for love. I'd *proven* it.

And then we had my time here in Boston where it was easier to be a wrecking ball who systematically flirted with an unavailable colleague—and literally everyone else who crossed my sight line—than acknowledge the fact I was lonely as hell, and making some uncomfortable eye contact with the possibility that this was it for me. That I was meant to be on my own. That things wouldn't magically work out and I wouldn't grow out of my bullshit. That college cheerleading, the quest for one good avocado, and tagging along with Hartshorn and Acevedo and their families was all I had. It was all I'd get.

I hated thinking it wasn't enough because it was a lot

more than most people had to their name, but it just felt so fucking wrong. Like I'd missed a turn somewhere and now I was barreling down a whole different turnpike and heading in the opposite direction, but there were no exits, no getting off. And even if I did manage to turn this shitshow around, where would I go? Sara didn't want me the way I wanted her. She didn't want me when I was an asshole and she didn't want me when I'd presented her with all the things I'd never dared to share with anyone else.

I was too old to pick myself up and try again. I didn't care if forty was the new whatever the fuck. I couldn't do this again. I couldn't wait around for another person to show me that I was right, the people meant to love me couldn't do that for more than a minute. I couldn't arrange my existence on a silver platter again only for someone to look it over and choose to walk away.

Like I said, I'd proven this point.

CHAPTER 31

SARA

ONE OF THE THINGS I'D LEARNED IN THE PAST FEW YEARS OF getting my shit on track and not allowing myself to self-destruct was that kids who grew up in chaotic homes were often highly sensitive to the smallest shifts in tone, behavior, energy. They learned how to protect themselves by picking up on subtle changes that often led to bad situations. They knew the pattern.

I'd known all of my parents' patterns. I knew when someone was going to start an argument, when someone was going to storm out of the house, when I'd need to close myself away in my bedroom and stay quiet. The piece I hadn't noticed—probably because I was busy patrolling two grown adults who were hooked on the drama of fighting with each other—was that I didn't have anywhere to put the adrenaline that came with all that vigilance. I didn't see that binging and then purging was an attempt to calm myself down after listening to another blowout from the people who were supposed to be in charge. I didn't recognize my ritualized food and activity tracking as one tiny, hollow attempt at dragging some order into my life. I didn't notice that my frantic, obsessive attention to schoolwork and college admissions was a desperate desire to find an area where I could earn a steady stream of validation and approval.

And I wasn't aware that it was worth identifying as a really bad situation until I was in my early thirties and my body was breaking down because I'd convinced myself I could outrun, outwork, outperfect a whole lot of family garbage. The kind of garbage that didn't stop when I moved out because that stuff knew no limits, no boundaries. The kind of garbage that shaped me—a double board-certified surgeon who was really fucking good at her job—into someone who lost her shit at the idea of meeting my father for a meal. Someone whose first instinct was to gallop in the other direction when a good man offered his love.

Another thing I hadn't understood was that paying attention to all these little cues for all those years turned me into a dysregulated wreck. I'd been working on straightening out my nervous system for years now. But I still hadn't sorted out the contradiction inherent in desperately, *desperately* wanting to be deemed worthy—my *pick me* problem—and refusing to believe that anyone could ever want me because I was an epic mess.

Want me, please, though you won't and you absolutely don't so leave me alone at once.

Big old messy mess.

That was the state in which I found myself stalking the halls of the surgical wing on Tuesday evening. I was finished with my cases for the day, but I didn't know where Sebastian was—and I needed to know.

The thing about us grown kids of chaotic homes was we never stopped noticing everything. Maybe we weren't living on the edge of that knife anymore, but there wasn't a time when we stopped tuning into tones and behaviors and energies.

I knew Sebastian wasn't thrilled with me right now, and that was why I needed to keep an eye on him. Not because I was concerned about running into him. Not for *me*. No, my concern was for him. I had to make sure he was all right. The way we'd parted in Jamaica was not the best, and even if I could've done better in those moments, that didn't change my need for time. Another thing I needed was to keep Sebastian in one piece while I worked through this. All I had to do was keep an eye on him. From a distance. Without him noticing.

Nothing messy about that.

I dropped my hands to my hips as I stalked back to the top of the hallway. There were tons of hiding spots in this hospital. I knew because I'd played this exact game with him before and it had taken me an eternity to find him camped out in that weird little exam room in the ER.

As I hooked a right down another hallway, I spotted a familiar face. I held out a hand to stop him. "Hey. Hi. You're the trauma fellow, right?"

The man grabbed the badge clipped to his waist, the one that announced his name was Bay O'Rourke and he was a surgeon, and he frowned at it for a moment. He appeared confused by the information he found there which wasn't a great sign. "Yeah. I guess so."

"Right, then, do you know where I can find Dr. Stremmel?"

His gaze sharpened as he stared at me. "I know where he is, yeah."

"And?" I crossed my arms over my chest. "Will you tell me where he is?"

He gave me an all-over study, the kind that said he didn't know me but he already knew he didn't like me. Then, "No, I don't think I will."

These freaking trauma surgeons. They were made of stubborn stuff. "Why not?"

"Let's just call it professional discretion," O'Rourke said. "Judgment call, you know?"

I pressed my fingertips under my glasses, to my eyelids. I was exhausted yet too wound up to get much sleep. I just needed to buy myself a little time and then everything would be fine. Everything would settle down. "*My* professional discretion suggests you should tell me where to find him."

"Is there a specific reason I should do that?"

I did not need any more power struggles in my life. I did *not*. "I need to check on your boss. If you don't tell me where he is, I will assume you don't know and have been wasting my time. I'd prefer to not waste my time."

"Why do you need to check on him?"

"I see you've conceded to wasting my time." I turned on a heel, my sneaker squealing against the tile. "Thanks."

I didn't make it two steps before O'Rourke called, "I sent him home."

I swung back to face him. "You sent Stremmel home? Are we talking about the same person? Because the Dr. Stremmel I know takes orders from just about no one."

O'Rourke laughed. "I wouldn't say he takes them, no, but he needed to go." He shoved his hands in his coat pockets. It was obvious he didn't want to elaborate. It was also obvious I wasn't leaving without more information. "He has a migraine. Depth perception"—he waved a hand in front of his face—"all fucked-up. I took his last case of the day and kicked him out. He needs to sleep it off."

He'd held my hand.

That was all I could think.

When I was sick and struggling, he'd held my hand and teased me enough to get my mind off my stomach. He'd stayed with me while I vomited in a bush and he'd gathered up my hair, kept it away from my face. I didn't know when it was that I'd convinced myself I didn't need that, but I did. I needed someone who would stay when I wasn't pretty or perfect, who didn't expect me to hold myself in or smooth down any of my savagery.

And if I needed that, Sebastian did too.

"Okay. Thank you." I went to leave, but quickly realized I needed a little more. "O'Rourke. Do you know where Dr. Emmerling is right now?"

He let out an irritable snicker. "Do I look like a switchboard? Wait. No, don't answer that. Forget it. No one from my generation should know what a switchboard looks like. Emmerling went into the OR the same time I did. Probably closing now, if she's not already done."

"Thanks," I called.

"He doesn't let me slack off when he's fucked up," O'Rourke said. "Don't fuck him up again, okay?"

"Can't promise that," I said to myself.

I caught Alex as she exited from her OR, her hair in two perfectly plaited French braids and a slight imprint on her forehead from wearing a headlamp and loupes for hours.

"I need your help," I blurted out.

"Can you walk with me to post-op?"

I grabbed her by the shoulders. "Send your residents to

post-op. You don't need to go with them. They don't need you to micromanage and you don't need to waste your time doing their work for them."

"Wow. We are having some real talk and you're telling me how to get my house in order tonight. Okay, then," she mused. Before I could apologize—my good girl was *dying* from all this—she gave orders to a pair of residents. When she was finished, she leaned back against the wall. "What's up, babe?" She ran the back of her hand over her mouth. Her stomach growled loudly. It sounded like a jungle cat. "Ignore that. I just need thirty or forty tacos. I'll be fine."

My stomach gave a matching cry, though this one was less *feed me tacos* and more *all the stress hormones you're dumping into your bloodstream are gonna mess up your gut for days.*

"I'll ignore yours, you ignore mine," I said. This was it. This was how a bitch leveled up to best friend status. Out with it in a surgical hallway while one person's stomach yelled for tacos and the other's threatened an irritable bowel war. "That thing you asked me about? With Stremmel? Yes. Okay? Yes. For the past two months."

With both hands, she mimed an explosion. Then, "That's awesome. I like both of you. Now I get to like you together."

"Really? Oh—I mean, thank you?" I waved that away. "You told me once that you had keys to my place and Stremmel's. That Hartshorn and Acevedo had given them to you back when they lived in the building, and if I ever needed someone to water plants or be there for a delivery—"

"Right, right. Yeah." She frowned. "You need my keys? Why? If the sounds I've heard coming from your place are any indication, I think he'll be happy to see you." The shock must've registered on my face because she pushed off from the wall and wrapped an arm around my shoulders. "What I meant to say was let's go down to the locker room and I'll get you that key. Also, good for you. I know you're super private and I have to remind myself to respect that—"

"It's difficult for me," I said. "Being open with people. Private is so much simpler, you know? I can keep on pretending that everything is fine, everything is just as perfect as it looks on the outside, and no one has to know about the mess on the inside." I ran a finger across my fore-head. "I'm an enormous mess, Alex. So much of me is a mess. It doesn't even make sense how much of a mess I am. How is anyone allowed to be my age and do this job and also be"—I waved a hand at my scrubs—"held together with nothing more than a stretched-out hair tie and five dozen wonky medical t-shirts?"

She gave my shoulders a squeeze. "I'd give my left tit for your t-shirt collection."

I blinked fast and sucked in a deep breath. I was not going to cry at work. I was *not* going to cry at work. "Well, you'd need to give that tit just to fit into my t-shirts. How did you get *all* the boob and I got none?"

She shrugged. "It's not like it does me any good."

"You make it seem like I don't live downstairs from you," I said. "I've heard what your husband has to say. I own three white noise machines and keep them running all the time for that exact reason."

"Ahhh. That's why it was all so muffled," she said. "It sounded like you were getting pounded in an aquarium. I was very confused. Not that I was listening closely or anything. I was aware of the events in an abstract sense. Abstract only. Although I was like, 'Good for her. Good for Shap. Get some, girl. You deserve it.'"

A loud, gangly laugh burst out of me. "I can't believe we're talking about this."

"Doesn't it feel good though?" She steered me down the hall, away from the operating rooms. "To actually say what you want instead of what you should? Don't waste that kind of energy on me, okay? Whether you like it or not, I need you. I need a girl surgeon friend, but more importantly, I need *you*—the very smart, very sophisticated mess who jumps in the middle of me micromanaging my residents and lets me make a fool of myself in text messages."

"Thank you for saying that," I said.

"I'm not just saying it. You should know I'm a mess too. Whatever you have, I have it in a double-D cup."

I was prepared to argue this point. To tell her there was no way she could have the same fucked-up souvenirs I had, but then I realized it didn't matter. It didn't have to matter. I didn't have to let the mess matter. "Thanks, Alex."

"No problem." When we reached the lounge, she marched toward her locker and fished her keys from her bag. "Are you staging a surprise attack on Stremmel?"

"We need a bit of time," I said, fluttering my hands because I didn't know what else to do with them. "Apart, that is. But I have to check on him."

"Do you actually need time apart or is it safer to put distance between yourself and big feelings, and call it time?"

I fetched my coat from my locker, scarf too. "In this instance, I really need to do something. I need to *prove* I can do something. And big feelings are completely terrifying."

She bobbed her head as she unthreaded the key from the ring. "Don't prove yourself out of a good thing. I say that with zero context on your situation and a lot of history with my own desire to prove points." She held out the key. "Make choices that scare you. They're the best ones."

———

IT DIDN'T OCCUR to me until reaching the landing outside Alex's second floor apartment that I had no plan to speak of for this visit, no idea how I was going to explain my presence. There was no way around it: I was breaking the rules Sebastian had established last week in Jamaica.

I knew he didn't understand why I needed this time and I couldn't justify that to him right now, but I could be that person who stayed with him while he needed it. I didn't know for sure though it seemed like that was better than justifying anything. Or, I hoped it was.

When I arrived on the third floor, I was shocked to find that I could see straight down to the foyer from here. The staircase wound its way up the building, a perfect oval of railings and overlooks, and I should've made this connection sooner though I'd missed it. I'd missed so much.

"Sebastian?" I knocked on the door and waited a minute.

A spike of doubt hit me when I pushed the key into the lock. This could be an enormous mistake. He could hate me for inviting myself into his space when he'd never once asked me up here. And maybe he wanted to be alone. It wasn't like I wanted anyone around to witness a truly terrible irritable bowel flare. There would be no handholding through that.

"If he wants to be alone, he'll tell me that," I murmured to myself as I turned the key.

The apartment was dark, the only light coming from the street-facing windows. I closed the door as soundlessly as I could manage and used the brightness from my phone's screen to orient myself. I found a bread crumb trail of outerwear and shoes leading into the kitchen, a deep, brick-walled galley blocked by a pair of legs in navy blue scrubs. He held his forehead in one hand, his elbow in the other.

I dropped to my knees beside him, ran a hand over his scruffy jaw. He kept his eyes closed. If he was surprised by my appearance tonight, he didn't show it. "What do you need?"

"Nothing."

"That can't be true," I whispered. "You're sitting on the floor and making like you intend to stay here for more than a minute. Tell me what you need right now or expect me to use my own methods to figure it out."

If he recognized those words, he didn't let on, giving a single shake of his head. Then, he leaned his cheek into my palm. We stayed there, silent with his skin warm against mine. After a minute, I took his wrist in hand, found his pulse.

"Don't doctor me," he rasped.

"Sorry, have to. I don't make the rules." I reached for the prescription bottles sitting open on the countertop, read the labels. "How long has it been since you took these?"

"Don't know. An hour, maybe? You don't have to—whatever. You don't have to stay."

Ignoring that, I put the lids on the bottles and gave him a quick study. "Do you usually need to sleep it off?"

"Yeah." He hooked an arm around my waist, caught the edge of my t-shirt between two fingers. His touch was light, like the way you embraced someone you barely knew and hadn't seen in ages. *Hello, you resemble someone I met in another life. Are you that same person? Will you be that person today?*

"Then we need to get you off the floor and out of those clothes." I knew he really didn't feel well because that last remark earned neither an arched eyebrow nor an amused scowl. "Can we do that?"

"Are you here right now?" he asked, those two fingers clinging to my shirt becoming a fist at the small of my back. "Is this actually happening?"

"No, I'm not here," I whispered, pushing his hair off his forehead. "Not yet."

"But, *Sara*—"

"Shh. Let me put you to bed. Okay? Let me do that. There's nothing else for you to worry about tonight."

There was a second where it seemed like he wanted to push back, wanted to push me away. I knew because I did the same thing. Then, he flattened his hand on my back, saying, "My right eye is a disco ball. I was going to stay put until it resolved."

I stood, held out my hands to him. "I'm not allowing you to go forward with that plan."

He gave me several solid moments of defiance before gaining his feet. With a heavy exhale and a blink that made it clear he had doubts about everything, he slipped his hand into mine.

We made our way toward his bedroom, slower and more unsteady than I'd expected. I helped him out of his clothes, even though he huffed about it, and pulled back the covers on his pristinely made bed.

He pressed a thumb to his temple as he asked, "Are you leaving now?"

I almost laughed at the way those words cracked out of

him in a whispered challenge. "Cold or heat?" I asked. "Do either help?"

With his boxers riding low and his hip cocked, an arm banded across his chest, and that thumb still grinding his head, he looked like an angry underwear model. Eventually, he said, "Ice, sometimes."

I pointed to the bed by way of command. "I'll be right back."

In the kitchen, I found a reusable cold packet and a dish towel, and filled a glass with ice water. Though it was dark, I could see enough of the space to realize Sebastian's apartment was ruthlessly clean. *Ruthlessly.* A place for everything and everything in its place. I could perform surgery here.

He probably hated my apartment. It looked like the inside of my head—a lot of contradictory things happening all at once—and I kind of loved it that way because it was comfortable and made me feel like I could follow whichever rules I wanted. But I liked this too. It was the exact opposite of my home yet there was something freeing about the complete absence of stuff. I could see the walls, the countertops, the floors. Night was too far set in to know for sure but I had to believe the windows would just gush with sunlight in the mornings. There was nowhere to hide here and—maybe this was why I liked it so much—no reason to hide.

I didn't have to be perfect. I didn't have to be good. I didn't have to be anything at all. Nothing more than me and all the mess that came with me.

The prescription bottles loitering in the middle of the countertop were the only sign that life wasn't without its bursts of disorder. I gathered them up and tucked them beside the sink. It was the least I could do.

When I returned to the bedroom, I found Sebastian

sprawled on his belly, the blankets pooled at his waist while he pinched his brow between his thumb and forefinger. I set the water down and crawled in beside him, my back against the gray upholstered headboard and my ankles crossed in front of me. I brought the towel-wrapped cold pack to the nape of his neck. "Tell me if this is too cold."

"It's okay," he murmured.

Holding the cold pack in place, I dragged my fingers through his hair and scraped my nails over his scalp. At first, it didn't seem like any of this was helping since the corners of his eyes were still creased, his lips were still pulled tight, and his breathing was quick. I was extremely ready to take my phone into the other room and call my friend Jill, a neurologist I'd lived with during med school. But then his shoulders sagged and a heavy breath shuddered out of him, and he shifted his head to my lap and tangled both arms around my waist.

"Will you keep doing that?" he asked.

"Of course."

I slept sitting up, his head in my lap and my hand numb from holding the cold pack. He didn't notice when I slipped out before dawn. It was better that way. I couldn't explain everything to him now, not yet.

But soon.

CHAPTER 32

SEBASTIAN

I DIDN'T KNOW WHAT DAY IT WAS. I MEAN, I COULD LOOK DOWN at my watch and see the date and time at any moment, but none of it mattered. It was just another day, another stumble through the daylight hours, another long stare into the night. Another round of waiting for Sara to invite herself into my apartment, into my bed, even if she disappeared before dawn the next morning. Another reminder that expectations were stupid and only kicked me in the ass.

I didn't have the luxury of taking a week off to swim around in my misery, seeing as I was fresh off a week away, and it wasn't like time spent suffering on my sofa while surrounded by rotting takeout containers would help matters. And the real upside of surgery was that it extinguished everything else from my mind. I wasn't hungry or tired or sore or broken the fuck apart when I was working a case, and I loved that. I needed that.

I'd thought I was doing a decent job of concealing my hollowed-out existence from anyone who might notice, but Nick Acevedo wanted me to know I was wrong about that. Without asking a single question, the man yanked me up by the scruff and ordered me into running shoes and enough layers that I wouldn't complain about the freezing November wind. Then he forced me to run for eight grueling miles and had the balls to chat about football the whole way. He was content with a one-sided conversation.

For my part, I leaned into the misery. It felt good to feel so awful. It almost came as a relief, as if I finally could pin my emotional aches to something real.

After cleaning ourselves up, Nick dragged me home with him to Cambridge. He didn't ask what happened or why I was giving everyone the most vile scowls in my long history of scowling, and that suited me well enough.

But then he deposited me on a stool at his kitchen island, gestured to his wife, and said, "This is a problem."

Erin looked me over with a concerned frown. "I can see that."

He gathered her up in a tight hug and whispered something to her I couldn't hear while he rubbed her back. I couldn't watch. I had to look away. I didn't get to hug anyone when I came home at night and I didn't get to glance down at a silky blouse like it was something marvelous and I didn't get to have secret conversations in the middle of the kitchen. All I had was a blanket on my sofa that was reasonably cozy and a sound system that would tell me how long to bake a potato and whether the Lakers were playing tonight.

To Erin, Nick said, "I'm going to get dinner started. All he's done is complain about the wind—"

"It's very cold," I cried. "It's dark at two in the afternoon and no one pays any attention to the wind chill."

"—but I have to believe you're right about everything. It has to be. I've never seen this level"—Nick gave me a quick study—"before. I'm gonna need you to dig deep into your toolbox to fix him."

I folded my arms on the countertop and pillowed my head there. "What are you right about this time, Walsh?"

"Something happened between you and Sara," she said. "Something that's hurting your heart right now."

I nodded. No reason to dance around the truth. "I fell in love with her. I asked her to make a choice. She's not ready. That's it. That's all it is."

"When did this happen, Sebastian?" Erin asked. "There was the time I saw you two together here, but when did it start?"

"About two months ago," I said, "and also two years ago. I just—I don't know. It's over, so the timeline doesn't matter."

"No, no. I mean, when did these issues come between you?" she asked as she opened the refrigerator. She gestured to a bottle of beer and I nodded. I hadn't tried drowning my problems yet. That could be a fine solution.

"It started last week in Jamaica and then it took a turn for the worse Monday morning," I said. "And here I am now, in top fighting shape."

"Shap went to Jamaica with you?" Nick asked. He popped the top on the beer and slid it across the island to me.

"Yeah, but also no. It's complicated. She was there for a conference," I said. "We stayed at the same resort. We had some really great days and I got to tell her dad he's a dick, but she isn't ready for this to be more than—" I blew out a long breath. "Whatever. My life basically imploded. It's cool."

Nick grinned at Erin. "I told you it was a bad idea to try setting her up with Malakai."

"Let it go, Nick," she said with a laugh.

"That one fuckin' hurt," I admitted. "Just do me a favor and don't set her up in front of me anymore, okay? I know she's going to be around and I gotta deal with that, but don't blindside me. Also, it would be great if we could keep this between the three of us. We cannot have anyone taking sides or bringing this up to her in any way. Not only would she reach down my throat and rip out my organs, she'd hate me for putting her in a situation where she has to talk to people."

"That's not a problem at all," Nick said. "Hartshorn isn't going to notice a damn thing. He's got his hands full these days. I know Shap's close with Emmerling, but Emmerling will throw down with anyone who crosses her. No one will make it awkward for Shap, I promise."

"If you want to invite her over here, you have to be chill about it. Okay? You can't call up the squad and get everyone in on the peer pressure. It stresses her the fuck out. She's not going to tell you that, but she blew up my chest cavity so I have no filter left in me." I pointed the beer bottle at Erin. "And if you want to hang out with her, ask her to go shopping or out for a walk or whatever women do together. Keep it small. Not just the big dinner parties."

Erin touched her fingers to my forearm. She was cold from holding the bottle of sparkling water she'd plucked from the fridge. "Slow down for a sec, okay? You're spinning out."

"If I don't tell you this now, when am I going to tell you? This is my chance, Erin. I'm falling the fuck apart, so might as well let it all go."

"*Slow down*. You are not falling apart. You are not caving in on yourself. " She held up a warning hand and leveled me with a stare over the rims of her glasses. "Let's put this in perspective. Let's think about it and pull all the way back, out of this single unpleasant moment, out of this day, out of this place and time."

I gulped the beer. "Are you going to tell me something ridiculous and obscure now? Will it kick my ass?"

She lifted her shoulders and let them fall. "You are as good as impossible."

"Yeah, I know. I get that frequently. Nick's said it to me a million times," I replied.

"No. That's not what I mean," she said. "You are nearly impossible." She brought her hands to her chest. "I am nearly impossible. All of us, nearly impossible. That we are alive right here, right now, is such a practical impossibility that it makes everything else seem insignificant. When I pull all the way back and I gather up the contents of this universe as we comprehend it, I see the existence of us—and our great struggles in that existence—as wild accidents. There are entire galaxies forming and dying beyond us, all while we are here in this moment, stumbling around in these fleshy, emotion-filled bodies. We are grains of sand, we are accidents, we are ridiculous miracles—and this is the one, outrageously impossible existence we get." She twisted the bottle of water open. "So, we're not going to let one hiccup get in our way. We're not going to let it end us. We're not going to stop stumbling around. We're not going to stop feeling everything. And we're not going to forget that we are impossible in the *best* way."

I stared at her for a minute as her words settled over me. "Yeah. Okay."

"That wasn't enough," she murmured.

I shrugged. I really liked this woman—in an *extremely* platonic way, it was worth noting—and I lived for her weird stories. But the fact I was a mathematical improbability wasn't getting me where I needed to go tonight. In truth, I needed to go to a pink glass and teal velvet apartment and wrap myself around a heartbeat that I wanted more than my own. "It was great."

"What about the Marie Antoinette story? The one with the croissants. I like that one," Nick said.

"History doesn't work on him," she said.

"It doesn't," I agreed. "Sorry."

"I can do better," she said, her fingers on her temples. "Give me a second."

"Really, you don't have to," I said.

"Yeah, Erin, he's right. You don't have to do that. It would also make me very happy if you'd just sit down," Nick said from the stove. "Don't worry about this guy. He needs a couple of beers, a good meal, and some sleep. He'll shake it off in the morning."

"Is that the remedy?" I asked him. "Why hadn't I thought of that?"

"Because you're busy lurking around corners," he replied. "You're freaking the surgical techs out, you know."

"I doubt that," I replied.

"Doubt it all you want, but my circulating nurse said you were being a pain in the ass."

"I'm a lot of things, but I'm only a general pain in the ass. I keep my bullshit high-level. I'm *never* a pain in the ass to nurses or techs," I said. "I learned my lesson in that arena a long time ago."

"I've got it." Erin grabbed my arm, turned my hand over and pointed at the inside of my wrist. "What is that? That blue line?"

"Are you seriously quizzing me on anatomy? Radial artery. For fuck's sake, Walsh."

"And what's that artery pumping?"

"Okay, so, this *is* a quiz," I muttered. "Wow. Did not expect that from you. Arteries pump oxygenated blood."

"And what's blood composed of?"

"Well, you've got your red and white blood cells, your plasma, your platelets." I stared at her. "Why? I do not have the strength to donate blood tonight if that's where you're going with this. There isn't enough juice. Not enough cookies."

"Because I want to talk to you about hemoglobin." She made it sound like the most obvious thing in the world. "It's a structure built on four iron subunits."

"Oh my god, Erin. Are you telling him the iron story?" Nick called. "You don't have to do that. Is it really that bad? I don't think so, honey. I don't think you need to dig *that* deep into the toolbox."

"I think the situation requires it." She gave a sage nod and now I knew I was in some shit. "This planet is home to loads of iron and that's a good thing because it's essential to sustaining life for humans, plants, and animals. But when I stop and think about iron though, I'm reminded of the violent death in its creation."

I curled the ends of my sleeves into my fists. "Wait, what?"

"Iron doesn't belong to us," she said. "It belongs to the heart of a dying star."

"Here we go," Nick muttered.

She tapped the blue lines running up her arm. "Once upon a very long time ago, a red giant star digested all its helium and turned it into oxygen and carbon, which eventually morphed into iron. All that iron turned the star into a supernova and then its heart burned out the last of its fuel. There was a massive explosion, the likes of which we can't even imagine because the power and brightness exceeds anything we know in this world. But that explosion—the star's death—sent iron atoms flying through space along with oxygen and carbon. Gravity got in on the game and rounded them up into the planets we know today. The core of *this* planet is believed to be mostly molten iron. It's inside us and all around us and life wouldn't continue without it."

I ran a hand over my mouth. "Shit."

"You are made of stars. They're inside you, and even on your worst day, they don't stop shining for you. Don't ever forget that."

I bobbed my head, gulped down a whole lot of emotion that seemed disproportionate to a story about hemoglobin and supernovas. *"Shit."*

"Yeah. Right? I mean, sometimes I think about the creation of the universe and how everything matters, but also nothing matters, and—"

"All right," Nick interrupted, dropping a hand to his wife's shoulder and pulling her to his side. "I'm calling this meeting of the sad and broody kids club to an end for the night. Y'all can wait until next week to dip into the existentialism and the nihilism, okay? Thank you." He shook his head at me. "I don't know why I bring you home with me sometimes, Stremmel, but you have the dying star story now. Everything's going to work out."

"Is that what happens after she tells the star story?" I asked.

"No," he admitted. "But things don't usually get worse."

CHAPTER 33

SEBASTIAN

MILANA GLANCED AT ME BEFORE CUTTING A SUBTLE GLIMPSE AT the wall clock over my head. Patience pulled at the corners of her lips, which was generous considering my expression hovered somewhere around twenty degrees below freezing. My head was still killing me so frozen was the best I could offer. This was my best.

"I'm sure Dr. Shapiro will be along any minute," Milana said. "It's not like her to be late. I'm sure she'd send word if something was keeping her."

I lifted my brow, giving her some *you have no idea what this woman is about* eyes. Hell, I didn't know what this woman was about and I'd dedicated a fuck-ton of my life to figuring her out. What did I have to show for it? Not a whole lot.

Milana gave a slightly less subtle glance at the clock before reaching for her phone. She tapped the screen and started scrolling. I stared at my hands. This was the last time Sara would be required to speak to me and fuck if that didn't scare the shit out of me. She could move out of the building, she could leave Boston altogether. She could go and I'd always be the fool who dropped way too much on her, way too fast.

"Yeah," I agreed. "She's probably on her way."

Then, in full-blooded form, Sara blew into the office, her hair pushing the limits of what could be considered a bun, her black glasses askew, a stethoscope *this* close to falling off her neck, and her cheeks flushed pink.

"Sorry," she wheezed. "Sorry. I was on the elevator. It went up to five, then down to one, then back to five. Wouldn't stop anywhere else. Super weird. Finally got off at one. Took the stairs. So many stairs."

"It's all right," Milana said. "We're just happy you're able to join us."

I watched Sara as she dropped down onto the sofa, her chest still heaving. The elevator issue had distracted her to the point that she seemed to forget I was close enough to see the outline of her bra under her t-shirt and the tiny, wispy curls that congregated at the back of her neck. It'd distracted her enough to forget everything. Somehow, that was something she could do.

I didn't have that particular superpower.

Milana glanced between us, some kind of interest written on her face, but nothing I could decode right now. I didn't care to decode it. I couldn't take my eyes off Sara. I never could.

"Oftentimes when I reach the end of a therapeutic relationship, I find it valuable to reflect on where we started. I hope that you are both able to see the changes and progress that I see. Let's start off by identifying some of that progress."

Sara blinked over at me, then quickly away. She reached into her coat pocket for her phone, clicked it over to silent.

Why that hurt so fucking much, I didn't know. Maybe it was the casual dismissal. Maybe it was the fact her hands were shaking and I wanted to take them in mine, even if it meant I'd have another regret to add to the pile later.

Since I had no restraint, I said to her, "You're going to lose that stethoscope if you're not careful."

"Yes, I'd most certainly lose it while sitting here. It would fall off, disappear into the recesses of this sofa without my notice, and I'd never see it again. Highly likely."

"Why do you even wear that thing? You are a surgeon. How often do you actually use it? And what the fuck do you have residents for if not borrowing a stethoscope from them as needed?"

She gave me another sidelong blink. "Is that what we've decided to harp on today? My audacious use of a stethoscope? Or would you rather delve into the matter of our differing philosophies on the training and function of residents?"

I folded my arms over my chest. "I'm just saying you don't *need* it."

"Then I suppose the proper way to conduct myself, in your esteemed opinion, is without any tools or resources whatsoever." She gestured to me, saying, "No white coat, no stethoscope, no notebook, no pens. Just a badge and a body."

I opened my mouth to respond yet stopped myself, all while Milana regarded me with a slight grin that seemed altogether too entertained for my taste. Eventually, I shifted fractionally toward Sara and asked, "What do you even have in there?"

She set the stethoscope on the sofa between us and then peered into her coat pocket. "Phone, pager, some pens."

As she held up each one, I plucked them from her fingers

and deposited them on the coffee table. It was a fun way to avoid making prolonged eye contact and we were nothing if not great at games. "Why do you need this many pens? Again, residents. *Interns*. Those are the people who need to have pens."

"That's—that's not how I want to go through life. That might work for you, but I like pens. I'm keeping my pens." She reached into her other pocket. "Two snacks, some sterile gloves, a pair of thumb forceps—"

"Oh my god," I muttered.

"Would you just shut up? I use them, okay?"

I set the forceps on the table with a meaningful frown. "And then you keep them in your pocket, apparently."

She patted the thigh pocket on her scrubs. "A few more pens and my notes for the day."

"Fuck me, you really do use index cards." I shook my head as I scanned her notes. Her handwriting was so cute and precise. "Well, this is adorable."

Milana made a noise, some kind of swallowed snort, but waved us off when we turned our attention toward her. "Pardon me. Allergies. Please continue."

"Regardless of whether your assessment is appropriate or not," Sara started, "this is my choice for how I manage my work. Could I show up tomorrow without any of these things and still do a good job? Probably, yeah, but I'd get tired of asking to borrow pens and I'd be irritable without snacks on hand. Obviously, it doesn't bother you to lift stethoscopes and pens and whatever else you use from your residents, but you're not going to convince me to work that way. I'd like you to notice that I'm not asking you to work my way."

"Understood." I went back to reading her notes. She was

so thoughtful and precise. Every case on a different colored card. "I'd like you to notice that you found this little thing we did here"—I gestured to the table where I'd organized the disemboweled contents of her pockets—"amusing. Some might even say fun."

She busied herself with unscrewing the cap on her water bottle. It was mint green, just like the glasses in her apartment. It didn't seem like she was going to answer, then, "Yeah, Stremmel. I noticed."

We sat there a moment, no one saying a damn word while it seemed like I could hear my blood vessels dilating in my head. Then, I settled back into my corner of the sofa and watched her as she fixated on that water bottle. "Can you just tell me what happened? It's stupid that I'm asking and I realize I shouldn't care, but I want to know. I want to understand."

She ran her index finger around the base of the metal bottle. "Nothing happened."

"*Everything* happened," I whispered. "You know it, Sara. You *know* it. I just need to know what I did wrong. I have to know."

"You didn't do anything wrong." She gave a single shake of her head. "You did nothing wrong."

"Then—why?"

Milana leaned in, clasped her hands between her knees. I'd kind of forgotten about her. Sara continued tracing the bottom of her bottle. Yeah, I could definitely hear my blood. Those vessels were going to fuck me over tonight. Not awesome.

"I just need some time," Sara said. "I know that's not what you want to hear but"—she waved a hand at the coffee table—"we work differently, Sebastian. You don't need anything

but yourself. I need all of these things and I am *still* a mess."
She twirled a finger toward her hair, her glasses, and the t-shirt with a set of checkboxes that read *Eat, Sleep, Operate, Repeat.* "Let me work the way I know how. Okay?"

I gave her a jerky nod. "Yeah. Fine."

After another unbearable silence, Milana said, "Our hour is up, my friends. I want to thank you for the time you've spent in this space with me, as well as the time you put in outside our weekly visits. I know neither of you chose to be here though I want to applaud the honesty with which you engaged week after week. I know this work is challenging. I know it climbs into our discomforts and shines a spotlight on them. And I know you've both developed new skills and perspectives as a result of those spotlights. I have no concern about signing off on the completion of your sessions and expressing my satisfaction with your progress. That said"—she glanced at the clock, gave us a wink—"the next time I see you two, I hope it's not on the sofa."

———

WITH THE PASSING of each of the seventeen hours since leaving Milana's office at the end of our last conflict resolution session—yes, I was counting—I grew an increasing appreciation for the fact Sara and I hadn't crossed paths. We'd walked out of that office, turned in opposite directions, and hadn't said a damn word to each other. Definitely hadn't let herself into my apartment and rubbed my head all night. But that appreciation grew alongside my dread because we would cross paths and I knew it was going to fuck me up.

I'd prepared myself to run into her in a stairwell or back in our building, but at the same time, I wasn't ready for that.

I was also dying from the inside out with wanting to set eyes (and hands) on her, but I wasn't ready. It was an unpleasant way to exist. More unpleasant than my usual.

It was midmorning when I found myself waiting for a team to turn over an OR. Nothing about this was unusual, not until the Chief of Surgery breezed out of that OR, Boston Red Sox scrub cap in hand, and did a double take when he noticed me. This *really* wasn't the day for anyone to notice me.

"Stremmel! Just the man I've been looking for," he boomed. "We need to get some time on the calendar to formalize your transition into the emergency surgery chief role next year."

"Because we're done with the conflict counseling?"

"The what? Oh, no, that's nothing. It's barely a formality," he said. "The hoops we have to jump through these days."

I made a pointed glance at my watch.

"While I have you here," he continued, oblivious to my glaring disinterest in this conversation, "I need your thoughts on Dr. Shapiro."

"My fucking *what*?"

He held his hands out, shrugged. If he found my reaction disproportionate, it didn't show. "I've heard through personal channels that she has a lucrative offer in California. She's here to stay as long as we can keep her, though I want your opinion of her work. You have to know of her father's reputation—"

"I'm going to stop you right there. He doesn't work here, and as far as I know, he's not interested in moving his practice here, so any conversation about him or his reputation relative to a surgeon on staff is a waste of my time."

"Is it a waste? I don't know. That's why I'm seeking your

opinion on Dr. Shapiro. On paper, she's great, but that doesn't mean I should send high-profile cases to her or prioritize her work for grants. What's your take, Stremmel? Is she any good?"

"It's pretty stupid to ask me that," I said. This was the currency that came with being the guy. "She's obviously talented. Anyone can see that. She knows her shit. Her work is clean and thorough. Her residents are some of the best trained of any specialty in the facility. Acevedo and Hartshorn attend her skills lab sessions on a regular basis and I know they're not the only attendings who do that. A few require it for their residents. How does *that* look on paper? She has no problem taking on loudmouths, bullies, and assholes when patient outcomes are on the line, and frankly, we need a lot more of that seeing as we can't stop populating our ranks with loudmouths, bullies, and assholes. Of course, this question is a load of bullshit because I don't know the first thing about the plastics practice, but I do know Dr. Shapiro is far too accomplished to work in a place where her father's reputation precedes any conversation of her qualifications. Don't let anyone hear you saying that shit again. The world doesn't work that way today and it hasn't in a long time. You're gonna age your ass right out of here if you keep that up." I glanced at my watch again. "Excuse me."

By my estimation, I had at least seven minutes until my OR was ready and that was plenty of time to run up and down the stairs until I lost the desire to punch a wall. It seemed like a great plan.

All I had to do was execute on it every day for the rest of my life.

CHAPTER 34

SARA

I DIDN'T HAVE AHA MOMENTS. NOT OFTEN.

I came around to ideas the way people waded into a chilly pool—just a toe, then a foot, a doubtful dip up to the knees, inching toward thighs though not really wanting to do that, then—*finally*—making the eventual concession to waist deep, all while standing stiffly with arms held above the surface, teeth gritted with the conviction that getting wet was just a terrible idea.

Some people probably cannonballed their way into those cold pools, and that was fantastic for them. So fantastic. Aha people represent.

I never wanted to get wet. I definitely held my arms above the water long past the point of acclimation. Even when I was in it, I needed extra time to adjust. There was nothing more vulnerable than throwing your entire self into a body of water, and vulnerability was fucking scary. Aha moments were fucking scary. They required trusting your mind enough to let it lead the way, and my mind—well, it was fair to say my mind didn't have a good track record of leading me toward the healthiest paths.

When it came to Sebastian, I required a lot of acclimation —and then one epic aha moment where I belly-flopped into the water, loud and painful and flailing, and gave up all semblance of shielding myself from the risk of vulnerability.

I had to let the aha happen, as much as I hated it, as much as I resisted it.

That was why I was sitting on the landing outside Sebastian's apartment, furiously texting all of our friends.

Sara: Can I ask you guys for help?

Alex: Always assume the answer to that is yes.

Nick: What Emmerling said.

O'Rourke: I'm not as useful as those two. I'd advise sticking with them.

Alex: Please don't make me regret being nice to you, O'Rourke.

Sara: Okay. Here goes. Stremmel should be leaving the hospital any minute now. I know Hartshorn is having everyone over tonight...and I need you to send Sebastian home. Don't let him go. Just send him straight home. I have to talk to him. It needs to be today and it needs to be away from work.

Alex: We could tell him there's going to be sleet. He hates sleet.

Nick: I want to help you, believe me, but I don't know how we're supposed to uninvite him from the pizza party at Cal and Stella's. They do this the weekend before Thanksgiving every year. It's a whole college football thing. He fucking loves it.

Alex: You just don't want to be the one to make Stremmel cry.

O'Rourke: Was I invited to this party?

Nick: Could you grab him at the hospital instead?

O'Rourke: I don't think I was invited to this party.

Sara: I don't want this to happen at the hospital. I know it probably seems ridiculous and I know I'm asking you three to jump in the middle of this for me, but I really need to separate everything from work.

Alex: It's cool, I can take responsibility for him crying. I actually don't mind that at all.

O'Rourke: Since I'm not invited, am I off the hook here?

Alex: Listen, O'Rourke. You're invited. Hartshorn is absent-minded as hell. He forgets the whole thing until a day or two before when his wife asks how many pizzas to order. Then he goes around inviting everyone he sees. It happens every year. His wife sends out a big text with the details but she doesn't know you and doesn't have your number. You're invited.

Nick: Wait a second, everyone. Shap, I love and trust you, but I don't want Eeyore wandering off on his own if things don't work out. Eeyore is okay only because the group keeps him on the radar. I need you to text me if this takes a turn. My wife will kill me if I lose track of Eeyore.

Alex: I don't know whether to cackle over you calling him Eeyore or try to figure out whether I'm Tigger in this setup.

Nick: Can't go there with you until I've had at least two beers, Emmerling.

Alex: Who is Winnie the Pooh? Is that Hartshorn? Oh my god, it's Hartshorn.

Alex: Are you Piglet? No. That doesn't work. Are you Christopher Robin?

Alex: Maybe Shap is Piglet.

Alex: No, that doesn't work either.

Nick: ALEX.

O'Rourke: I guess I'm not in this universe at all. Fun discovery for a Friday evening.

Alex: Sorry. I'll take one for the team and send Stremmel home to you, babe. If anyone asks, we are playing the ear infection card tonight. We'll say Hartshorn's kid can't stay over with the grandparents because she wants mama, and dad is also a psycho when it comes to typical pediatric conditions, and we're bumping the rivalry game debate for another night.

Sara: That's perfect. Thank you.

Nick: Text me, Shap.

Sara: I will. Thank you for your help. I know I'm asking a lot.

Alex: You're not. Acevedo just likes getting into it with Stremmel over football. Big feels on both sides.

Nick: Maybe you two could come over to Hartshorn's. After your conversation or whatever you need to do.

Alex: "whatever you need to do" is cute. Very cute. I'm ordering one of those white noise machines now.

Sara: Seriously, thank you for everything.

Alex: Stop thanking me! I love schemes. Let me go pull this one off.

THE AHA WASN'T that I was finally ready to talk to Sebastian. I'd been ready since landing in Boston last weekend, though I'd needed time to make that ready right. The aha came this morning, when I overheard the worst conversation I could've ever stumbled into. The Chief went ahead and undermined the fuck out of my skills, my performance, my outcomes. He did the thing I feared the most—he asked whether I was good enough. He asked as bold as could be, right there in the hall with anyone walking by, and he asked a surgeon who knew nothing of my practice.

Except that last part wasn't completely true.

Sebastian could've blown off the question. At first, I'd thought he was doing that. But then he'd leaned into it. He'd answered the shit out of that question. Once again, he'd stood up for me—and he did it while I was holding him at a cold, silent distance. He did it without knowing I was standing on the other side of that corner and he did it without doubt.

That was the aha. The wild-limbed belly flop that slapped so hard, I'd nearly missed my chance to duck into a supply room and panic in private. Although it wasn't real panic. It was the kind of panic where my heart was pounding in my throat and I was ready to run a mile while screaming at the top of my lungs, but I wasn't afraid of anything.

Maybe it hadn't been panic at all. Maybe that was how it felt to watch someone love you out loud.

An unmistakable stomp sounded three floors below, followed by a muttered, "What even the fuck?"

I shoved my phone in my bag and smoothed my hands over my jeans. I didn't have time to futz with my hair or fix my face or anything. All I could do was sit here, just as I was, and hope it was enough.

He spotted me several steps from the landing, his confusion evident in the blink, the pause. Then, "Please tell me you're ready. I've had the worst fucking day and now

Hartshorn's kid is sick so we can't have pizza and I *really* wanted pizza. And why are you sitting there? You let yourself in the other night and then let yourself the fuck out, but you're sitting on the floor like you're not a misguided little criminal? If you're not ready, Sara, I can't—"

"I heard what you said today. To the Chief, I heard."

He arched a brow. "From who?"

"From you. I was around the corner." I ran my hands down my legs again. "Thank you."

"Don't thank me. Not for that."

"That's a mean way to torture a people-pleaser," I said with a laugh.

"Recovering people-pleaser." He glanced down the staircase, then back at me. "If that's why you're here—"

"It's not," I said. "I had to break the cycle."

He dropped a hand to the banister. "You—what?"

"I had to break the cycle," I repeated. "The Thursday cycle. I had to stop it."

"What the fuck are you talking about?"

"We had a cycle, Sebastian. We'd avoid each other until Thursday. Until we got to go crazy on each other. But then it ended and we'd start it up all over again. Sometimes we'd get a weekend day, but mostly it was us bottling up everything we had and exploding on each other come Thursday."

He shoved a hand through his hair. "And…?"

"And I hated that cycle. But more than that, I didn't think we'd ever get out of it. I couldn't come back here and slip back into that cycle with you. I had to let the cycle burn itself out. I needed this time. I needed us to finish that last session without any shadow of a chance of us ending up in bed together after. I needed us to leave that entirely behind us. All of it. I wanted to talk to you afterward, but I knew it would feel like the same old Thursday thing and I need you to know that I have a bad history with unhealthy cycles. They're my most harmful coping mechanism. I can work a compulsion so hard, I don't even feel the pain I'm inflicting upon myself. Okay? They scare the shit out of me because I never realize I'm in them until it's too late. I needed to break this cycle, even if I had to hurt you for a few days."

"You could've told me that."

"I could have," I conceded. "But it took me some time to figure out what I needed. To be really terrifyingly honest with you, I didn't believe that you could actually want me if you didn't have all that anger toward me to burn off. I needed to prove that we weren't going to come back here and slip into the old patterns again, that the thing we had was real and not a product of the cycle. When Thursday came around, I thought that we'd carry that little debate about the junk I keep in my pockets with us and we'd have some angry, pocket-junk-fueled sex, and I'd never believe that what we have is different from that. That we're not addicted to the drama. Also, I knew you'd tell me not to worry about it."

He scratched the back of his neck. "You *didn't* need to worry about it."

"Maybe not, but I had to see that for myself."

Sebastian settled onto the landing across from me, his back against the wall. "And now that you've seen it? What have you decided?"

"I've realized that even though we are chaos, ours might be the right kind of chaos. It doesn't hurt me the way I thought it did. It doesn't hurt me at all."

He nodded to himself for a moment. "Why did you come here the other night?"

"Because O'Rourke told me he sent you home sick and I didn't want you to be alone."

"What about proving your points?"

I shrugged. "You've never let me be alone and I've never forgotten it. I came here, you know, that night. After everything at Acevedo's. I knew I'd done something wrong and I wanted to fix it. You didn't answer the door."

"I was very busy being mad at you that night."

"Are you busy being mad at me tonight?"

He shook his head. "No. I'm not mad. I'm relieved. This is my resting relieved face."

"I made Nick, Alex, and O'Rourke lie about the pizza party being canceled. It's not. Hartshorn's kid is fine. I had to get you alone and I had to do it away from work. And everyone else."

"You—hold up. You talked to people? Three people? *By choice*?"

I handed him my phone. "See for yourself."

He let out a massive sigh, one that shifted into an impatient growl, as he read the messages. "You sweet little liar. I need to get a vasectomy."

"*What*? How did we go from pizza to vasectomies?"

"Well, I mean, you don't want kids and I'm fucking old, so why not?" He banded one arm over his chest, gestured to me with the other. "I know I said I don't want to get married, but you do and that's enough reason for me to change my mind. I'm good with it."

"Did—did you just propose? To me? Right now?"

"No, I'm just telling you how it's going to be, Sara. And you have to know that if you want to leave Boston, I will find a way to part with the turkeys and the roads and the coffee cult and"—the jazz hands reemerged—"the leaves to go with you. You're going to have to deal with that."

"Okay." I was smiling in a way that I couldn't stop. It wasn't a choice. "You should know I special-order most of my groceries so that they arrive without nutrition labels because those things trigger disordered eating for me. That's why I can't have a smartwatch. Why I can't know how many steps I've walked or activity rings I've closed. It's already in my head, all of it, but I can't make it real unless I also want to make myself sick again, and I'll do anything in the world to avoid that. These things—these issues—they're not going to go away."

"Do you think you're scaring me? Come on, Shap. If you are, you need to try harder."

I really didn't want to laugh at that taunt, but I did. "I was serious when I said I wanted to move out of this building. It's very pretty and very convenient, but I am not a voyeur. I can't listen anymore and I can't deal with the idea of them listening to us."

"I'm going with you when you move," he said. "Plan accordingly."

I smiled down at my hands. "So then, you'll want a room for watching competitive cheerleading."

"Only if you're in there with me. I want the insider's take on things." Sebastian beckoned me. "Come here."

I closed the narrow distance between us with some graceless knee shuffling. When I settled on his lap, his arms loose around my waist, I continued, "I've never let anyone know me. Not all the way."

He gave a shake of his head. "Neither have I."

"It scares me to open up."

"It scares me to feel things. This week has been...not great."

I dropped my head to his shoulder. "I'm sorry."

"You got what you needed," he said, his hand skating up and down my back. "I can take a few days of misery if it means I get to wake up with you tomorrow morning."

"You get to do that." I pulled in a breath. "If you wanted," I started slowly, "we could head over to Hartshorn's. I'm told you have strongly positive feelings about college football."

"You don't want to go to that party," he said with a laugh.

"Actually, I do—sort of—want to stop by. For a bit." When Sebastian pressed his hand to my forehead and looked me over like I'd lost my senses, I added, "I can't do it all the time and food is always going to be rocky for me, but I kind of like these people. I don't hate it when I'm around them."

"You know I love you, right?"

"I do know that," I said. "I saw it today. I've seen it before, but I didn't recognize it until today. I had to belly-flop into it."

"Of course you did, you wicked little otter," he said.

"I love you too," I whispered against his neck.

"I know," he said. "I saw it the other night. And before that too. You've never hid it well."

"Shut up. I hide many things very well."

"Then you didn't *want* to hide it," he said, his hands slipping under my shirt. "As much as I enjoy arguing with you in stairwells, do you think we could move this to a bedroom? Perhaps a couch?"

"I have to text Acevedo. Should I tell him we're coming to this pizza party?"

"I can't even think about that until after I hug you for a whole fucking hour."

I brushed my fingers through his hair. "Will there be any pizza left at that point?"

"We'll order more and have it delivered," he said. "We need to make sure there's something for you."

I folded my lips together as I blinked down at my phone.

Sara: Sebastian is with me. I've got him.

EPILOGUE
SEBASTIAN

I{\scriptsize T WAS COLD AND RAINY, THE KIND OF WEATHER} I {\scriptsize HATED} though it wasn't snow and I considered that a blessing. After all these years in Boston, I still hadn't figured out how to coexist with snow.

We took a car service to Hartshorn's house on the suburban fringe of the city. Car service because I didn't see how I could stop touching Sara long enough to drive without wrecking. I had a car that I rarely drove, parked in a garage I thought about only when it was time to renew the lease. It was one of the stranger, more expensive aspects of living in this city.

Shrouded in the darkness of the back seat with Sara tucked into my side, life wasn't too miserable. Even with the cold rain, I couldn't be miserable after playing a little game I liked to call *we'll take a quick nap*.

There had been no napping. More like five minutes of *let me hold you* followed by *I'm going to write my name all over you inside and out* and then thirty minutes of drowsing and debating whether we wanted to get up, get dressed, get over to Hartshorn's.

"We don't have to stay long," I said to her.

She bobbed her head. "I know."

I wanted to show her off tonight. Stand in front of all of our friends, loop my arm around her waist, say, "Do you see? This one's mine." At the same time, I wanted to barricade us behind locked doors and under cozy blankets, press her hand to my chest, and say, "Do you see? This one's yours."

We pulled up to a large, brightly lit colonial house. Cars with MD plates lined the street. Sara glanced at the neighboring homes as she zipped her coat. "This is a nice area," she said.

I grabbed her hand as we hustled toward the front door, our heads ducked down to avoid the rain. We still got wet. It gave her a reason to brush the droplets from my hair and it gave me a reason to kiss the raindrops from her cheeks.

"I'm not great at being the center of attention," Sara said. "I just want to say that out loud before we go inside and people will make us the center of attention. For a few minutes, at least."

"I know," I murmured, her hand inside both of mine. "I have this covered."

She sawed her teeth over her lower lip. I could *feel* her thinking. "Okay."

"You're sure?"

After a pause where she nodded to herself, bit that bottom lip, and squeezed my hand, she said, "Yes."

We traded shy grins before pressing the doorbell. Stella, dressed in a Clemson jersey and jeans, opened the door almost immediately. "You made it! *Both* of you!" Not pausing long enough for us to say much of anything, Stella herded us inside, calling to her husband, "Cal! Stremmel's here and he brought Shapiro with him!"

I helped Sara out of her coat as the doorbell rang again. Stella shooed us toward the kitchen and family room as she returned to the door. I ran a hand down Sara's back, as much for her as it was for me. "This sweater," I said under my breath. "It pleases me."

That was enough to shake a laugh from her. That laugh was enough to make me drop a kiss high on her cheek. "When did you get so obsessed with my sweaters?"

"Around the time I started wondering whether you wear underwear with your scrubs."

"And when was that?"

"Less recently than you'd think." I glanced at her. "Do you?"

She gave me that hunter's grin, the one that promised she'd kill me quickly. "You'll have to find that out for yourself."

We stepped into the kitchen to find our friends milling around, a dozen decimated pizzas lining the long center island. It took a second for them to notice us and another second for them to notice the narrow distance between me and Sara.

Cal approached us, a beer bottle in hand and an Oregon jersey stretched across his chest. He glanced at us, half a smile pulling at his lips. "Okay. All right. This is new. It's interesting. Not my place to comment so I'll just tell you there isn't much pizza left," he said. "But we can order a couple more."

"Already did," I said. "Should be here any minute."

The doorbell rang again. I pointed over my shoulder.

"Cal?" Stella called. "Did you order more pizza?"

"Then allow me to get you a beer, sir," he said to me. To Sara, he added, "We have beer, wine, some crazy eggnog martini thing Emmerling's husband made, and all the soft stuff too. What's your pleasure, Dr. Shapiro?"

"Water," she said, her gaze shifting as our friends closed in around us. "Thank you."

Erin stepped up when Hartshorn left to fetch those drinks. She looked us over with a careful, appraising glance. "This is good," she said eventually. "It seems my stories have worked on both of you."

I peered at Sara when Erin moved to join Nick near the pizzas. "You got an Erin Walsh story?"

Her shoulders shook with a quiet laugh. "Oh, yeah. Confused the hell out of me."

"That's how it's supposed to be," I told her.

Nick pointed at Sara from the other side of the island. "Thank you for the text," he called. "Glad this worked out."

Sara attempted to respond but Alex bounded over and gathered her up in a hug. "I love scheming with you," Alex said.

"I'm never trusting another word out of your mouth," I said to Alex. "That story you told me about Hartshorn's kid? Insane." I glanced down at Sara. "You should've heard it. The level of detail—it was like a case study. It was like I was studying for practical exams again."

Sara shrugged. "Had to be done."

"Next, you'll help me with my schemes," Alex said. "I have so many ideas, Shap."

Riley plucked his wife away from Sara, saying, "Okay, drunk girl. Come along."

For once, he didn't shoot me any death glares. A subtle side-eye, yes, but no death glare.

O'Rourke came bearing beer and water, and distributed both to us. "Here you go. Good. Now I can tell you that neither of you know how to be low-key about a damn thing. The next time you want to pull a stunt like the one you've fumbled through for the past two months, please sedate me."

I stared at my fellow for a long moment. I did not understand this guy's brain but I admired the hell out of it. Then, I clapped him on the shoulder, saying, "I probably won't. You're too useful when you're not dodging pages."

"Figured as much," he grumbled. He glanced at the island, watching while Stella consolidated the remains of the original pizzas and spread out the second wave. "Since free food is my love language, I'm gonna need to introduce myself to those pies."

O'Rourke grabbed a slice with each hand and then plopped down on a large sectional sofa between Nick and Riley. He seemed immune to the curious stares they gave him.

"So, that's it," Sara said. "That's everyone."

I slipped a hand into her back pocket, steered her toward the island. "Let's get you fed. You'll want that for the next part."

"What's the next part?"

"It's a bloodthirsty debate of the Thanksgiving weekend college football rivalry games," I said, gesturing to the whiteboard propped up in front of the fireplace. "This started as a conversation over lunch a few years back. Which was the best rivalry game? Which teams looked strongest that year? It spiraled out of control. Now, we get together and yell about it over beer and pizza." I tucked some hair behind her ear. "The USC-UCLA rivalry is one of the most notorious."

"As it should be." She reached for a plate, a tart little grin on her face. "Seems we'll be at odds once again."

I spent a lot of time thinking about obscure things. Thinking about everything inside me and also everything outside me. In that endless volume of mental work, I'd never once put thought into what it meant to choose someone for myself. To pluck her out of the rush of people who buzzed past me every day and say, "I'd like to keep you."

And here I was, standing in Hartshorn's kitchen with an empty plate in my hand and that woman's smile calling up my own. I couldn't help it. I *couldn't.*

All I knew was that I loved her and I loved who I was when I was with her. It was a gift that I was allowed to choose her, to convince her to choose me, and one of these days, we'd cement that choice with some legal glue.

I didn't think I was languishing any more.

————

THANK YOU FOR READING! I hope you loved Sara and Sebastian! If you'd like to read a bonus epilogue, sign up here.

FOR MORE STEAMY stories from the doctor dorm, these titles are available now:

    Erin Walsh and Nick Acevedo in The Spire.

    Alex Emmerling and Riley Walsh in Preservation.

    Stella Alessandro and Cal Hartshorn in Before Girl.

Join Kate Canterbary's Office Memos mailing list for occasional news and updates, as well as new release alerts, exclusive extended epilogues and bonus scenes, and cake. There's always cake.

Visit Kate's private reader group to chat about books, get early peeks at new books, and hang out with over booklovers!

If newsletters aren't your jam, follow Kate on BookBub for preorder and new release alerts.

ALSO BY KATE CANTERBARY

Vital Signs

Before Girl — Cal and Stella

The Worst Guy — Sebastian Stremmel and Sara Shapiro

The Walsh Series

Underneath It All – Matt and Lauren

The Space Between – Patrick and Andy

Necessary Restorations – Sam and Tiel

The Cornerstone – Shannon and Will

Restored — Sam and Tiel

The Spire — Erin and Nick

Preservation — Riley and Alexandra

Thresholds — The Walsh Family

Foundations — Matt and Lauren

The Santillian Triplets

The Magnolia Chronicles — Magnolia

Boss in the Bedsheets — Ash and Zelda

The Belle and the Beard — Linden and Jasper-Anne

Talbott's Cove

Fresh Catch — Owen and Cole

Hard Pressed — Jackson and Annette

Far Cry — Brooke and JJ

Rough Sketch — Gus and Neera

Benchmarks Series

Professional Development — Drew and Tara

Orientation — Jory and Max

Brothers In Arms

Missing In Action — Wes and Tom

Coastal Elite — Jordan and April

Get exclusive sneak previews of upcoming releases through Kate's newsletter and private reader group, The Canterbary Tales, on Facebook.

ABOUT KATE

USA Today Bestseller Kate Canterbary writes smart, steamy contemporary romances loaded with heat, heart, and happy ever afters. Kate lives on the New England coast with her husband and daughter.

You can find Kate at www.katecanterbary.com

facebook.com/kcanterbary

twitter.com/kcanterbary

instagram.com/katecanterbary

amazon.com/Kate-Canterbary

bookbub.com/authors/kate-canterbary

goodreads.com/Kate_Canterbary

pinterest.com/katecanterbary

tiktok.com/@katecanterbary

ACKNOWLEDGMENTS

As with just about anything in the 2020s, this book was a challenge. I'd brazenly announced in December of 2019 that Sebastian Stremmel would get his happy ever after in 2020… and then 2020 happened and it was not possible for me to *think* about healthcare workers without a significant amount of real anxiety.

The year that was 2020 required me to learn how to write all over again. Writing had always been a solitary journey for me, but up until then, I'd taken that journey in bustling coffee shops and bakeries around the city. I wrote books with people around and noise in my head.

Until I couldn't do that anymore.

Sebastian has been in my head since 2017, when he first appeared in *Before Girl* and then *Preservation* and *Thresholds*. I often joked that he spent his days flopped on the floor in my office, grousing about the world. And that was true—his constant moodiness never left, even when I couldn't bring myself to think about writing life inside a hospital. With that in mind, I want to acknowledge (again, always) that while tons of research goes into getting the details right, some of those details do get smoothed down and shaved off along the way. The most technically correct book about surgeons and life in hospitals isn't always the most readable or enjoyable. To those of you who know the healthcare life intimately, I apologize for spots that stick out to you.

Sara, however, has been in my head much longer. She received only passing mention in *Before Girl* and the slightest of appearances in *The Magnolia Chronicles*, but her heart has been with me for ages. I waited a long time to understand her well enough to write her, and to that end, I want to acknowledge that hers is only one story. It is not the only story of recovering from disordered eating and/or an unstable upbringing. Not everyone who experiences bulimia will also experience lifelong gastric disorders and those who do experience gastric disorders might not experience them as Sara did.

Finally, I have to thank my husband and my dearest friends. They know what they've done.

Lightning Source UK Ltd.
Milton Keynes UK
UKHW010712251122
412773UK00002B/265

9 781946 352989